THIEF OF THE TON

Misfits of the Ton
Book Three

by

Emily Royal

ARE YOU SIGNED UP FOR DRAGONBLADE'S BLOG?

You'll get the latest news and information on exclusive giveaways, exclusive excerpts, coming releases, sales, free books, cover reveals and more.

Check out our complete list of authors, too!

No spam, no junk. That's a promise!

Sign Up Here

www.dragonbladepublishing.com

Dearest Reader;

Thank you for your support of a small press. At Dragonblade Publishing, we strive to bring you the highest quality Historical Romance from some of the best authors in the business. Without your support, there is no 'us', so we sincerely hope you adore these stories and find some new favorite authors along the way.

Happy Reading!

CEO, Dragonblade Publishing

Additional Dragonblade books by Author Emily Royal

Misfits of the Ton
Tomboy of the Ton (Book 1)
Ruined by the Ton (Book 2)
Thief of the Ton (Book 3)
The Taming of the Duke (Novella)

Headstrong Harts
What the Hart Wants (Book 1)
Queen of my Hart (Book 2)
Hidden Hart (Book 3)
The Prizefighter's Hart (Book 4)
All I Want for Christmas is My Hart (Novella)
Haunted Hart (Novella)

London Libertines
Henry's Bride (Book 1)
Hawthorne's Wife (Book 2)
Roderick's Widow (Book 3)
A Libertine's Christmas Miracle (Novella)

The Lyon's Den Series
A Lyon's Pride
Lyon of the Highlands
Lyon of the Ton

Dedication

For Frankie, who showed an exceptional degree of ingenuity when it came to plotting the execution of theft

CHAPTER ONE

Surrey, May 1814

THE MOONLIGHT REFLECTED off the windows, giving the building the appearance of a mythological beast with multiple eyes trained on Lavinia.

But it was just a building—Stanley House, the country seat of Lord and Lady Francis, where she'd had dinner with Aunt Edna last month, and been subjected to a cut of beef that would have been better suited to upholstering leather sofas. Her ladyship had not invited Lavinia to tonight's party, which suited her very well, for it meant she'd be above suspicion.

Lavinia approached the building, and her heart hammered in her chest. Excitement filled her bones—the anticipation of finding her quarry, and securing the first victory on her road to the restoration of her family glory.

What pretentious nonsense, little Guinevere…

Hell's teeth—why did his voice always enter her mind at moments like this?

She shook her head to dispel the memory. She'd not set eyes on him for fourteen years—and had forgotten what he looked like, even. But, during those years, his voice had given her comfort, when she'd felt alone and in need of a friend.

Where was he now? Did he remember her as vividly as she remembered him?

Did he also dream of her at night?

You fool!

It was a fantasy—a childish crush that had swelled over the years as she grew into a young woman.

And the last thing she needed right now was to be distracted by the memory of a man who, doubtless, had forgotten that she'd ever existed.

Keeping to the shadow of the box hedge, she skirted the perimeter of the front lawn and approached the building.

The moonlight picked out the features of the masonry—the edges of the stones and the ornate carvings surrounding each window. An ostentation where the obscenely wealthy paid a stonemason a pittance to carve ridiculous features into the stone.

But ostentation was her friend—it provided the handholds needed to achieve her objective.

Lavinia cast her gaze over the upper-floor windows. The day had been hot, and residual warmth still hummed in the air. With luck, an obliging footman would have left a window open.

Then she saw it—a sash window on the first story, open enough to enable someone to lean out.

Or climb through.

She crossed the driveway, wincing as the gravel crunched under her feet. But there was no sign that she'd been heard—no other sound except for her own heartbeat, and the far-off screech of an owl.

Another hunter, though with a different quarry. The owl would swoop on any living thing it caught moving on the ground. Whereas Lavinia's quarry was something very specific.

And, as she'd discovered during a little reconnaissance during last month's dinner party, it resided in Lady Francis's bedchamber.

She pulled a sketch from her pocket. The moonlight illuminated the page, which depicted a plan of the upper floor with her destination marked with an X, as if she were a pirate hunting for treasure. She glanced up at the open window—it was three windows along from her destination.

After stuffing the sketch in her pocket, Lavinia reached up and ran her hands along the stone wall. The ornate carvings would provide plenty of purchase. She lifted her foot and placed it on a protruding piece of stone, then curled her fingers around a feature, which felt like a lion's head, and pulled herself up. After a few more moves, she found herself level with the window. She reached out to the ledge and pulled herself through the gap in the window, holding her breath as she lowered herself into the chamber inside.

A long, drawn-out rattle echoed through the room, and she froze, holding her breath.

The sound came again, followed by a sigh, and the deep rumbling of a digestive tract in serious need of relief.

An odor thickened in the air, reminiscent of the stench in the kitchen when Mrs. Bates was boiling cabbages, and Lavinia covered her mouth with her hand to suppress a giggle.

Heavens! What, in the name of all things holy, had Lady Francis served at her dinner table that evening?

As her eyes adjusted to the light, she discerned the shape of a man on a huge four-poster bed. He let out another snore, followed by a grunt, and she nodded in recognition.

His Grace, the Duke of Dunton, renowned lecher, avid consumer of rich foods, and a man in pursuit of a richer wife.

It was almost enough to celebrate the fact that she had no fortune.

She tiptoed across the chamber and slipped out into the corridor, making her way toward her destination where, with luck, Lady Francis slept as soundly as Dunton.

She slipped inside the lady's bedchamber. The curtains had not been fully drawn, and a sliver of moonlight picked out the shape of a bed containing a sleeping form, a dressing table and its polished oval mirror, items of jewelry, and a table beside the window, on which stood a small, round urn.

A very familiar small, round urn…

That's it!

Short and squat, the urn looked unremarkable to the un-trained eye. But her mother had taken a fancy to it when she'd come upon it in a tiny shop in an obscure little street in London. Fashioned from white porcelain and decorated with the image of a dragon, its tail swirling round the belly of the urn, it would be overlooked by those who preferred bright, gaudy colors.

But it was priceless to Papa—a gift to be cherished.

And exactly as she remembered from her childhood.

She approached the table and picked up the urn. It was as smooth as she remembered and, though made from porcelain, it carried a softness, and a warmth, as if it were alive. She ran her fingertips over the surface, feeling every familiar lump and bump where the painters had fashioned the dragon, centuries ago.

"Hello again," she whispered.

She reached into the bag over her shoulder and pulled out a cloth. Then she wrapped the urn in the cloth, as delicately as if it were a bird's egg, and placed it in her bag. Finally, she pulled out a piece of paper from her pocket and placed it on the table where the urn had been.

A long sigh echoed through the bedchamber, followed by a female voice.

"Where are you?"

Sweet heaven, I'm caught!

Lavinia suppressed a cry.

Then a male voice spoke.

"I'm here, my mare."

Surely Lady Francis wasn't enjoying marital relations with her husband? Rumor had it that his lordship had been looking elsewhere for years, having compared his wife to a buck-teethed ass, and her ladyship's eye had wandered in the direction of the dandyish Mr. Heath Moss, heir to Sir William Moss.

Then the female voice spoke again, breathy and hoarse.

The bedsheet rustled, followed by the unmistakable sound of kissing—wet lips clashing, punctuated by low groans.

Ugh.

"Oh, yes—that's it…"

Lavinia took a step forward.

"What's that?" the female voice cried.

Lavinia froze.

"I think we both know what *that* is," the man replied. "You were delighted to indulge in its exquisite pleasures earlier."

Dear Lord! What woman was fool enough to fall for such nonsense?

"Oh, *Heath!*"

Clearly Lady Francis *was* such a woman.

"You like that, don't you?" the male voice said.

"Oh, yes—but not *there*. Could you move, just a little to the… *Oh!*"

"Just there?"

"Oh, *Heath!*"

The shape on the bed reared up, and Lavinia caught sight of a face illuminated in the moonlight—handsome enough, but its features bore the streak of cruelty often seen in rakes.

Lavinia fought the urge to flee. But she'd have to pass the bed, and she couldn't risk being seen, even if the couple in the bed were occupied with their own gratification.

"Turn over." The male voice, low and thick, came in hoarse rasps.

More rustling of bedsheets, and Lavinia caught sight of a female form, in a white night rail, her hair hanging loosely about her face.

"That's my mare—my beautiful mare."

"Oh!" Lady Francis let out a shrill cry, which sounded distinctly horselike. Then the male form moved again, and she let out a low wail.

Was she in pain?

The wailing increased, punctuated by low grunts, then Lady Francis let out another cry.

"That's it, my beast! Ride me like a stallion—an Arabian stallion!"

An Arabian stallion?

Lavinia's body convulsed as she fought the urge to laugh.

But the couple on the bed were too occupied with each other to notice. Their breaths came out in unison, guttural gasps that increased in pace and intensity, until the bed began to knock against the chamber walls.

Lavinia dashed toward the door. The danger was not in the rutting pair noticing her, but in their waking the entire household and bringing all manner of guests and servants into the chamber. She needed to get away—quickly.

She exited the chamber and retraced her footsteps toward the sound of Dunton's snoring, wrinkling her nose at the odor as she slipped inside his chamber.

"Your Grace, you really should see a doctor about your stomach," she whispered.

Then she padded across the carpet toward the window and slipped through it. Once outside, she eased herself down the wall and jumped onto the gravel path.

Her mission accomplished, she dashed across the lawn toward the driveway, where Samson waited patiently, tethered beside a tree.

The animal lifted its head in greeting as she approached. She untied the reins, then lifted her foot into the stirrup and mounted the horse.

Aunt Edna would have a fit of apoplexy if she caught Lavinia riding astride—but she would never find out.

Nobody would.

The identity of the Phoenix would be the mystery of the Season, but they'd all be looking for a *man*.

She had taken the first step on the road to restoring her father's peace of mind before he was no more.

I'm doing this for you, Papa. One down, four to go.

She curled her fingers around the reins and steered her mount down the drive. Once clear, she urged Samson into a canter.

She was free.

But the image of the couple in the bedchamber remained in her mind. Though she grimaced at the notion of Lady Francis and her affair with Heath Moss, she couldn't help the frisson of envy.

Her treacherous body had ignited with a wicked little pulse of longing.

What might it be like to make love? Would she moan with pleasure like Lady Francis?

Lady Betty said that to make love was the most wonderful experience in the world—that the act elicited such delicious sensations that a person believed, for a moment, they might die of ecstasy. But she had also warned Lavinia that for the woman to experience pleasure, she needed a skilled man—one who took as much joy in *her* pleasure as his.

She'd also warned Lavinia that, for a woman, the danger lay in giving a man her heart as well as her body. But there was no danger of Lavinia giving her heart to any man. Her heart had been lost years ago—to the boy who had once called her his little Guinevere.

But he was long gone, his face blurred over time, until all she could recall was the intense expression in those clear hazel eyes.

They were the eyes of the boy she'd idolized as a child, desired in her adolescent dreams…

…and, as a young woman, had fallen in love with.

But, in all likelihood, he'd forgotten that she ever existed.

CHAPTER TWO

Fourteen years earlier, Sussex, August 1800

"WHY MUST WE leave, Papa?"

Lavinia kicked out in an attempt to break free, but the footman held her firm and carried her toward the carriage.

"Lavinia, nothing will prevent us from leaving Fosterley Park today," Papa said. "It's no longer our home. Surely you must understand?"

"No, I don't! I want to go back!"

"Be quiet, or I'll thrash you!" Papa roared. "Put her inside the carriage, Brannigan, and make sure she stays there. You're at liberty to use force, if necessary."

A shiver of fear rippled through her. Despite her mischief-making, Papa had never before threatened to raise his hand to her.

She went limp while the footman bundled her into the carriage. Two more footmen marched across the gravel drive, carrying a trunk, which contained all she had left in the world. She hadn't even been able to say goodbye to Samson, her rocking horse, because Samson no longer belonged to them.

Not even Millie was there—Lavinia had woken that morning to be told that her nursemaid had been dismissed and she must learn to dress herself.

Why was Papa being so unkind, so *unfeeling?*

He stood beside the carriage, talking to his steward in hushed tones, but when Lavinia tried to lean out of the carriage to hear, the footman pushed her back.

"You're not to leave, miss. Remember what his lordship said."

She pushed her lower lip out—an action that had often melted Millie's heart. But the footman stared back, his expression impassive.

It was so *unfair*!

Eventually, Papa shook hands with the steward, then climbed into the carriage, and they set off.

As they rolled away from the building, Lavinia noticed a number of people—servants and tenants—stop and stare. Some of the men removed their caps and bowed their heads, as if they were in church.

Papa stared out of the window, his mouth set in a grim line. Then he glanced toward Lavinia, as if he'd only just noticed her presence.

She opened her mouth to speak, and Papa lifted his hand.

"Lavinia, don't."

"But Papa, I only wanted to ask—"

"That's enough," he said. "*Please.*"

Her stomach clenched at his plea, the quiet, weak tone unsettling her more than his words of anger.

He seemed to have aged overnight. Of course, being an adult, he was far too old to have any fun. But today, his skin seemed to sag around his face, like an old gundog, the usual ruddy tone replaced by a grayish hue.

Perhaps he was unwell, and they were taking a vacation. Aunt Edna often overwintered in Bath. For her health, she said, to "take a rest cure and drink the waters"—whatever *that* meant.

Perhaps they'd return home when Papa had taken *his* rest cure.

She moved to sit beside him, then took his hand and ran her fingertips over the papery-thin skin, through which the veins of the back of his hand protruded.

"Don't worry, Papa," she said. "*I'll* look after you."

He blinked, and a film of moisture covered his eyes.

She squeezed his hand. "You'll be better soon," she said. "Then we can go home."

He sighed. "Fosterley is no longer our home, Lavinia."

Before she could quiz him further, he met her gaze, and her heart broke at the expression in his eyes.

The strong, capable man who'd always been there for her, when she'd scraped her knee, had a bad dream, or fallen from a tree, was gone—replaced by a frail, broken creature.

A mortal man.

She leaned against him, and he placed an arm around her shoulders.

"All will be well, little Lavinia," he said. "They think they've taken everything from me, but they cannot take *you*."

Who were *they*?

But she daren't ask.

He clung to her, as if his life depended on it, and though her shoulder ached where he squeezed it, she didn't have the heart to move. At length, his grip relaxed, and the next time she glanced up at him, he'd fallen asleep.

"Don't be sad, little Guinevere. I'll keep you safe. I swear on my honor, according to the codes of chivalry."

She was in the Fosterley woods. Sunlight filtered through the trees, forming a dappled pattern on the ground, illuminating the fronds of bracken—bright green feathers that nodded in the soft breeze.

She looked up into soft hazel eyes filled with warmth and compassion.

Her King Arthur—the older boy who had seemed so grown up when she first saw him—astride his charger. He'd befriended her with a warm smile and a handshake, as if she were a lady, rather than a scatter-

brained child, and he'd indulged in her wish to play make-believe, conquering fearsome enemies and fierce dragons together—a warrior king and queen. Her secret wish had always been that, one day, she would conquer the real world with her king at her side.

"My Arthur..."

"Lavinia!"

A hand caught her shoulder, jerking her back into the present. The sunlit woods dissipated into the air, and she opened her eyes to see Papa staring at her.

"Wh-what is it?" she asked.

"We're here."

The carriage had stopped next to a small, two-story building made of smooth, whitewashed stone, with a russet-colored tiled roof. Paned windows stared out at them, the glass reflecting the sunlight, framed by wood that had been painted a pale green that was peeling at the edges. The front door, overhung by a russet-tiled canopy, matched the color of the windows, the paint peeling to reveal the wood beneath. Surrounding the door was a trailing rosebush, which spread across the front of the building, wandering between the upper and lower windows.

Behind the cottage, trees stretched toward the sky, towering over a garden filled with foliage and color. Though overgrown, the splashes of color indicated that the flowers had not been entirely conquered by the weeds. A vibrant blue shimmered in the sunlight—a cluster of flowers at one end of the garden, interspersed with accents of bright orange.

It was magical—a faerie world to explore and play make-believe in. Perhaps dragons lurked among the bushes, which she could fight and conquer, when King Arthur came to visit.

A footman opened the carriage door, and Lavinia climbed out. Papa followed.

"Dear God," Papa whispered. "It's worse than I thought."

The cottage door opened, and a couple appeared—a plump, gray-haired woman, and a ruddy-faced man with an unruly mop of brown hair.

The woman wiped her hands on her apron, then bobbed a curtsey. "Oh, your lordship, we didn't expect you so soon. Welcome to Springfield Cottage."

"Springfield?" Lavinia asked. "Isn't that where Cousin Charles lives?"

"He's been good enough to rent us a property on his estate," Papa replied. "To think! From Fosterley—to this!"

"I like it," Lavinia said. "It looks like a fairy tale."

"Foolish chit!" Papa replied. "This is no fairy tale. It'll be cramped and cold."

"We can light a fire."

"And suffer the smoke?"

"We can make it comfortable, Papa. It's like my den in the woods. It…"

She caught a blur of movement, then cried out as he clipped the side of her head.

"That's enough!" Papa roared. "Can't you see today's difficult enough without your prattling?"

The couple in the doorway exchanged a look, then the woman approached Lavinia.

"Shall I take the child inside, Lord de Grande?" she asked. "Get her settled?"

"Very well." Papa sighed, "Mrs.….?"

"Mrs. Bates, at your service, sir," the woman said. "This is my husband, Joe. He'll be tending to the grounds."

"Grounds!" Papa gave a snort of derision. "A hovel, surrounded by weeds. What do *you* do, Mrs. Bates?"

"Housekeeper and cook, your lordship. I've got a bit of stew going for supper."

"Housekeeper *and* cook—ye gods!" Papa cried. "I never thought I'd see the day."

Lavinia rubbed the side of her head, which still smarted. Papa glanced at her, then he sighed. "I suppose we must make do. Come along, child."

He took Lavinia's hand, then led her inside, with the couple following.

"Joe, get the fire going in the parlor!" Mrs. Bates said. The man scuttled through a side door, then the woman turned to Papa. "Shall I show you the bedchamber? We've got it all comfy, like—and there's a separate chamber for the lass. Or would you like to take tea in the parlor first? I've a fruitcake ready to welcome you into your new home."

"Very well, tea it is," Papa said. "And perhaps a drop of brandy to go with it. I'm in need of something stronger than tea before I face what awaits me upstairs."

Mrs. Bates's smile slipped a little, but she spoke brightly. "I'm sure you'll feel much better after a pot of tea and some fruitcake, sir. You must be tired after your journey."

The woman's voice reminded Lavinia of Millie, who'd always used an overly bright tone to coax her into doing something she didn't want to.

Mrs. Bates led them into a low-ceilinged room on the ground floor. A large, deep red sofa dominated the space. Beside the fireplace—where Mr. Bates poked at the fire, coaxing the flames to dance among the coals—was a large wing-backed armchair, furnished with the same fabric as the sofa. Lavinia entered the room, her boots clacking against the floorboards, and she wrinkled her nose at the unmistakable odor of wood polish, combined with a delicate floral aroma. Beside the sofa was a round table, bearing a vase filled with wild flowers and grasses, a burst of color that gave the room a welcoming air.

The windows were set into the thick stone walls, with deep red curtains accented by flecks of orange and brown, tied back with emerald-green sashes. The windowsills had been fashioned into window seats, with green cushions to match the sashes on the curtains. Lavinia ran toward the window and looked outside, just in time to see a second carriage roll to a halt outside the cottage.

A liveried footman climbed down and opened the carriage door. A woman climbed out, straightened her back, and glanced toward the cottage, shielding her eyes from the light of the setting sun.

She was clad in a ruffled dress of black silk and gripped a cane, curling her claw-like fingers around the top. She spoke to the footman, her sharp voice carrying through the air, then strode toward the cottage, her sprightly gait indicating that she had no need for the cane—at least not to assist her in walking. Lavinia knew, from experience, that the cane served a different purpose altogether.

"Papa!" she cried. "It's Aunt Edna."

"Damnation," Papa growled. "As if today couldn't get any worse, *she* comes to poke her nose in and crow over my misery."

Shortly after, Mr. Bates appeared at the doorway. Aunt Edna's black-clad form was standing beside him.

"Lady Yates to see you, sir."

"Come in, Edna," Papa said. "Make yourself comfortable—if that's possible."

With a rustle of silk, Aunt Edna glided toward the sofa and sat, wrinkling her nose. "I don't know why you won't come and live with us at the main house, Richard," she said. "You'd not be in our way."

"I told you, Edna, I don't take charity," Papa retorted, then he burst into a fit of coughing.

"Richard, this place doesn't suit you," Aunt Edna said. "The damp will do your gout no good."

"We'll survive," Papa said.

"And the child?"

Lavinia's stomach clenched as Aunt Edna turned her disapproving, steel-colored gaze toward her.

"She won't grow up to be a lady *here*, not without a governess. I'll have to see to her education."

"I can teach myself, Aunt," Lavinia said.

Aunt Edna rapped her cane on the floor, and Lavinia flinched. Had she been any closer, that cane would, most likely, have come down on her knuckles.

"Insolent child!" Aunt Edna cried. She turned to Papa. "Speaking out of turn—it's worse than I thought, Richard. It's as well you've come to Springfield. I can take charge of the child's moral education, which I can see has been sorely lacking. And, of course, we all know the reason why, don't we, Richard?"

"I don't know what you mean," Papa said.

Aunt Edna gave a huff, then muttered, "Cavorting with that whore."

Mrs. Bates entered with a tray, carrying a pot of tea and two cups. She bobbed a curtsey, then placed the tray on a table. "Will you be wanting tea, your ladyship? I can fetch you a cup."

"Good heavens, no," Aunt Edna said. "I have no intention of staying."

"That'll be all, Mrs. Bates," Papa said. "Lavinia—pour the tea."

Lavinia approached the tray and picked up the pot. "Aunt—what's a whore?"

Mrs. Bates drew in a sharp breath, and Aunt Edna stiffened.

"I beg your pardon, child?" she demanded.

"I said—" Lavinia began, but Papa interrupted her.

"That's enough, child. Go and see your bedchamber."

Lavinia glanced at her aunt, whose grip had tightened on the cane, her knuckles whitening.

"May I explore the garden?" she asked.

"Oh, very well," Papa said, his voice filled with weariness. "Take your shawl—it's cold outside. And don't disgrace yourself."

"I think it's too late for *that*," Aunt Edna said. "I can see I've a task on my hands with the brat."

Before Papa could reply, Lavinia dashed out of the parlor. Aunt Edna was a formidable woman who had survived, through sheer force of will, the outbreak of smallpox that had taken her husband. Papa said that the Grim Reaper himself was too afraid to confront her, and had therefore decided to let her remain among the living, to terrorize them instead.

"Would you like to see your bedchamber, Miss Lavinia?" Mrs.

Bates asked. "We've made it ever so pretty for you."

Lavinia didn't have the heart to refuse. She nodded and followed the woman up a narrow creaking staircase, to a tiny landing with three doors. Mrs. Bates opened one of the doors to reveal a low-ceilinged bedchamber with white walls furnished in soft pastel shades of blue. The bed, though half the size of Lavinia's at Fosterley, looked sturdy, and was covered with a blanket embroidered with small blue flowers, which matched the embroidered design on the fire screen.

"I know it's not much, Miss Lavinia, and it must be very different to what you're used to. But I'm sure, in time, you'll be comfortable here."

The woman stood in the doorway, her expression conveying pity and a desire for approval.

"I like it very much, Mrs. Bates," Lavinia said. "I've always wanted to live in a cottage. Thank you for making it so pretty."

The housekeeper's face broke into a smile.

"Lord bless you, child! That's so kind of you to say."

"Mary!" a voice cried out. "The stew's boiling over!"

Mrs. Bates rolled her eyes. "Mercy me!" she cried. "Men! They think they rule the world, but they can't cope with a boiling pot—they don't have the sense to take it off the heat. Would you excuse me, miss?"

"Mary!" the voice roared again.

"I'm coming, Joe—you lazy oaf!" Mrs. Bates cried. "Why you can't tend to the stew yourself defeats me."

"Women's work, that is," the voice replied.

"Lord save me," Mrs. Bates huffed. Then she disappeared, muttering to herself, her footsteps thudding on the stairs.

Lavinia followed Mrs. Bates down the stairs, then headed for the front door. Before she reached it, she heard Aunt Edna's voice from the parlor.

"It's that whore—I knew it!"

What *was* a whore?

Lavinia tiptoed toward the parlor door.

"Lady Betty's no harlot," Papa said.

Ah—Lady Betty. Papa's friend, who'd often visited Fosterley.

"Don't be such a lovesick fool, at your age!" Aunt Edna cried. "That woman is renowned for spreading her favors up and down the country, and for her expensive tastes."

"You don't know her, Edna—you never did."

"I should think not! I've no wish to count doxies among my acquaintance."

What in heaven's name was a *doxy*?

"Why else have you had to sell most of the family heirlooms?" Aunt Edna continued. "And now—you've been forced to quit Fosterley and let it out to—to *riff-raff*!" Her voice tightened, as if she were about to retch.

"Mr. Manford may be a commoner," Papa said, "but I count myself fortunate in securing a tenant at such short notice."

"I feel a megrim coming on," Aunt Edna said. "Mr. Manford, indeed! To think of that hobbledehoy lording it over Fosterley Hall—and that wife of his! Nothing more than a scullery maid."

"Doubtless you see your fastidiousness as a virtue, Edna," Papa said, "but it's not a quality that assists in the repayment of debts—"

"Debts which are due to your own wastrel life—and that hussy!"

"—or the restoration of Lavinia's dowry."

"Dear Lord!" Aunt Edna cried. "You mean the child's dowry is gone?"

"Only temporarily."

Lavinia heard the cane rap on the floorboards. A sign of irritation—not that Aunt Edna tended to show any other emotion.

"That settles it!" Aunt Edna cried. "The child must come to live at Springfield Park. Charles would have no objection, and he can furnish her with a dowry."

"What—lose my only child?" Papa said. "No, Edna—I won't allow it! She's all I have left."

His voice cracked, and Lavinia's heart tightened at the sorrow in his tone.

Oh, Papa, what have they done to you?

"This isn't the time for sentiment, Richard," Aunt continued. "You've been too indulgent with the child. She needs a firm hand to mold her into a lady."

"There's nothing wrong with Lavinia," Papa replied. "I'll not take charity."

"If I don't intervene, Lavinia will end up penniless in the gutter!" Aunt Edna said. "Or worse, she'll end up selling her favors like that whore."

"Edna, for heaven's sake!" Papa cried. "I—" He broke off in a fit of coughing.

Unable to bear it any longer, Lavinia pushed open the door and rushed into the parlor.

Papa was bent forward, coughing, his face a deep shade of puce. He glanced up and fended Lavinia off with his hand.

"Lavinia, how many times have I told you not to eavesdrop?"

"I won't leave!" Lavinia said. "I won't! And I like it here—I don't want to live with Aunt Edna!"

"How dare you!" Aunt Edna cried. "Richard, this is disgraceful behavior. If this continues, she'll ruin our family name."

"The de Grande family name is nothing to be proud of anymore," Papa said. "Not when it'll die out with me."

"I meant *my* family name!" Aunt Edna snapped. "It's due to Charles's good grace that you're not out on the streets. If you don't wish to sink further before your demise, you must leave the girl's education to me."

Papa slumped back in the chair, defeat in his eyes.

"You're right, Edna," he said, "and I'm in no position to refuse. But I must insist that the child lives here with me. She can visit you weekly at Springfield Park, where you can oversee her education."

"Daily."

"Very well."

Lavinia opened her mouth to protest, but Aunt Edna shot her

a look of fury.

"How old is she, Richard?"

"I'm seven," Lavinia replied. Then she jumped as Aunt Edna rapped her cane on the floorboards.

"Do *not* speak before your elders!" Aunt Edna cried. "You speak when you're spoken to." She tilted her head to one side, staring at Lavinia, as if performing a calculation in her head. "That gives me at least ten years, provided the child doesn't drive me into an early grave," she said. "I pray that it will be enough—though, from what I've seen, I'll have a hard task on my hands."

"*Ten* years?" Lavinia replied. "Won't we have returned to Fosterley by then?"

Aunt Edna rose to her feet, her fact twisted with fury. "Did I not just tell you, child, that—"

"No, Lavinia," Papa said. "I'm afraid we won't be returning to Fosterley for some time—if ever."

Lavinia's gut twisted with sorrow. "But—what about my friend?"

"What friend?"

Lavinia's cheeks warmed with embarrassment. "We used to play make-believe."

"What was her name?"

"King Arthur."

"I know of no Arthur," Papa said. "Unless you've been fraternizing with the tenants when I've expressly told you not to."

Aunt Edna let out an exaggerated cry of horror. "Ye gods!"

"He used to ride over to Fosterley with his papa," Lavinia said. "They visited just before Christmas last year, and he said—"

Papa's expression, at first showing confusion, morphed into one of anger. "That's enough!" he roared. "They're nothing to do with us anymore, and you'll never see them again, do you hear me?"

"But…"

Papa rose, then burst into a fit of coughing and collapsed back.

Aunt Edna sprang to her feet—a little too sprightly for a woman who supposedly needed a cane.

"Wicked child!" she cried. "Can't you see your behavior is distressing your papa?" She nodded to herself. "That's it—I'll brook no argument. The child will come to me every day for rectification."

"Aunt," Lavinia said, "may I—"

"No you may not," Aunt Edna said. "Make yourself useful and fetch Mrs. Bates. Your father is unwell and needs his rest—not to mention respite from *you*."

Lavinia backed out of the parlor, tears rolling down her cheeks.

Her life was over. They were penniless, like the street urchins she'd read about. And from now on, she had to spend every day under the tutelage of her overbearing aunt.

She could have borne all that if she could still have those make-believe moments with her King Arthur—the boy she'd worshipped. Her only friend.

But she would never see him again.

CHAPTER THREE

Sussex, October 1800

T HOUGH IT LACKED the familiarity of her former home, Lavinia found herself falling in love with the Springfield estate. The main house was a little too overwhelming with its air of discipline—even the trees in the garden were clipped in order to meet the standard of propriety and *niceness*, rather than to enhance their natural lines. However, the surrounding estate provided plenty of places to explore—a lake filled with wildlife, fishes that danced across the surface, sending ripples of light, and birds whose cries echoed across the water.

There was no better time of year than autumn to appreciate the sheer beauty of nature—when the fresh green of the landscape gave way to fiery reds and oranges that shimmered in the sunlight. When the leaves began to fall, she could run about the land, trying to catch as many as she could.

He had told her once that for every leaf she caught falling from a tree, she'd be granted a wish.

This year, her first wish was to see him again. King Arthur.

And her second wish was to never spend another day under Aunt Edna's discipline.

Aunt Edna seemed to relish doling out punishments whenever Lavinia "acted out of turn." Lavinia's left palm still smarted from when her aunt had rapped it with her cane yesterday for slurping her soup. Apparently, young ladies were supposed to consume soup with a complete absence of sound. The merest scrape of the spoon on the dish indicated a vulgarity of character that risked destroying all chance of a good match.

As for embroidery…

The skin on Lavinia's thumbs had grown so tender that she'd had to bathe them daily in Mrs. Bates's ointment. She couldn't fathom how young ladies were supposed to drive a needle through silk without pricking their fingers. But Aunt Edna, of course, expressed greater concern over the unsightly bloodstains on Lavinia's work than the pain she endured.

"Broken skin can mend, child, but damage to a lady's reputation is irreparable."

Lavinia's *reputation*—the intangible entity that Aunt Edna had yet to fully explain—was in constant danger of ruination. In fact, the chances of her reputation surviving were only slightly better than the likelihood of her aunt's company becoming enjoyable.

As for Charles—he might be Lavinia's cousin, but he was old enough to be her grandfather. With four grownup children who'd long since married and left, he had no interest in a child running about his house, but he seemed kind enough, if a little reclusive, and he'd promised to let Lavinia spend her first London Season—whatever *that* was—residing at his London townhouse. Or, rather, he'd succumbed to Aunt Edna's persuasion.

But London was years away, which meant that Lavinia had time to enjoy her surroundings. She had already made a den in the cottage garden. Not as majestic as the one at Fosterley Park, but it was still her own Camelot, where she could play make-believe that she was Guinevere, waiting for Arthur to return from his quest. And Mr. Bates had been kind enough to fashion a tree house for her out of a few spare pieces of wood. She could spend the evenings there in peaceful solitude, before the winter months plunged them into darkness.

She drew near Springfield Village and skipped along the main street. The aroma of damp leaves—which always foretold the onset of winter—was joined by the deep, smoky scent of log fires, eliciting images of families huddled over a fire, warm and snug, protected from the elements.

Mr. Bates had shown her how to lay a fire. Aunt Edna would have a fit of apoplexy if she knew.

But what her aunt didn't know couldn't hurt her.

"Good afternoon, little miss!" a voice cried.

A plump, ruddy-faced woman stood in the doorway to the bakery and raised her hand in greeting.

Lavinia waved in response.

"Good afternoon, Mrs. Jenkins!"

"I've some muffins doing nothing. Would ye like one?"

Lavinia skipped over, her stomach growling at the scent of freshly baked bread, and Mrs. Jenkins held out a packet.

"I've no money, Mrs. Jenkins," Lavinia said.

"Lord bless ye, I'll not want no payment—not for a stale old muffin!"

Lavinia held the packet to her nose and inhaled the warm aroma. "It smells fresh."

"Well, it's not," came the reply. "Tell your Pa, if he asks, that I'd have only given it to the pigs otherwise. I know he'll take no charity."

"Thank you, Mrs. Jenkins," Lavinia said, cradling the packet.

"Be off with you, then! Ye'll not want to keep yer pa waiting. Mary said he's got a guest for tea this afternoon."

Lavinia skipped through the village and, ten minutes later, turned into the gate leading to Springfield Cottage.

It looked less forlorn than when she'd first arrived with Papa. Mr. Bates had repainted the door and windows, then weeded the garden—with the exception of where her den was located. The chimneys had been swept, so the fire in the parlor no longer smoked.

Mrs. Bates had proven to be an exceptional cook, and she often let Lavinia help in the kitchen. It was through Mrs. Bates that Lavinia had come to know many of the villagers—Mrs.

Jenkins was Mrs. Bates's sister, and she always had a smile for Lavinia. The first time Lavinia had seen Mrs. Jenkins, she'd been given a whole basket of cakes to take home, but Papa objected and told her to return them. Thereafter, Mrs. Jenkins only gave Lavinia the occasional stale cake or biscuit—though they always tasted the same as the fresh ones.

Lavinia entered the cottage and caught sight of Mrs. Bates bustling about with a tea tray.

"Miss Lavinia—help me with the tea, would you? There's another in the kitchen needing fetching."

Lavinia dashed into the kitchen and placed the packet of muffins beside the sink. On the table that dominated the kitchen was a tray laden with neatly cut sandwiches and an enormous, brightly decorated cake.

Heavens! She'd never seen anything so luxurious. Fashioned into two tiers and decorated with sugar roses in myriad colors, it must have taken Mrs. Bates all day. She plucked a sugar rose off the top tier and popped it into her mouth.

It melted on her tongue, flooding her senses with sweetness, and she closed her eyes, relishing the taste. She couldn't recall the last time she'd eaten cake, let alone one that had been *iced*.

"Mercy me, Miss Lavinia! What are you dawdling about here for?" Mrs. Bates bustled into the kitchen. "Your papa's guest will be here soon." She set her empty tray aside and approached the table. "Miss Lavinia! Have you taken one of the roses?"

Lavinia nodded. She'd never possessed a talent for concealing her emotions. Even when she was not at fault, her cheeks always warmed in anticipation of transgressions, past and present, being discovered. Besides, she didn't have the heart to tell falsehoods to Mrs. Bates, whom she'd come to love a great deal more than Aunt Edna.

"Tiresome child!" Mrs. Bates cried, though her voice carried a note of affection. "Never mind—it's nothing I can't fix, but don't let your Papa find out, or he'll be right angry."

"Who's coming for tea?" Lavinia asked.

"It's not my place to ask," Mrs. Bates replied. "But it's a fine lady, I'll warrant. My Joe was up all night seeing to your father's cravats." She glanced at the wall clock. "Be off with you now, and change," she said. "I've set aside your best dress in your chamber."

Lavinia nodded and exited the kitchen. As she approached the foot of the staircase, she spotted Papa at the top, resplendent in a charcoal-gray jacket and cream breeches, with a satin embroidered waistcoat and matching cravat.

"Papa—you look wonderful!" she cried.

"Hurry up and put your dress on," he said. "You were due home half an hour ago."

"Who's coming for tea?"

"Lady Betty Grey."

Lavinia wrinkled her nose. Lady Betty had been a frequent visitor at Fosterley Park after Mama's passing. With her overly loud voice and brightly colored gowns, she could never replace Lavinia's gentle, softly spoken mother.

"Don't pull a face, child!" Papa snapped. "It's most unbecoming. I'm sure your aunt would have something to say about it."

"I daresay she would," Lavinia retorted. "Aunt's often warned me about the dangers of inviting whores to tea."

"Oh!"

Lavinia heard a shriek, followed by a rattle of crockery and splintering china. She turned to see Mrs. Bates struggling with the tea tray. The shattered remains of a teacup lay at her feet, and the cake…

The cake was balanced on the edge of the tray. Lavinia darted forward and grabbed the cake before it suffered the same fate as the teacup.

"Oh, I beg your pardon, sir!" Mrs. Bates cried.

"*You* weren't to blame," Papa said. He turned to Lavinia. "How dare you disrespect Lady Betty? I'll not have my daughter using the language of the gutter!"

He descended he stairs, his knuckles whitening as he tightened the grip on his cane. Were Lavinia not holding the cake, she was sure he'd have struck her with it.

Mrs. Bates composed herself. "You can hand the cake to me now, miss," she said. Lavinia did so, then darted out of Papa's reach.

"Not so fast, young lady," he warned. "Mrs. Bates, take the tray into the parlor."

The housekeeper curtseyed and disappeared into the parlor.

Papa's eyes blazed with anger. Were Lavinia not afraid at the fury in his gaze, she'd have welcomed the spark of life that had been absent in her father since they'd moved to Springfield.

"I should have you horsewhipped for using such language," he hissed.

"But Aunt says—"

"I don't care what your bloody aunt says!"

Lavinia flinched at the profanity.

"Your aunt doesn't understand," he said, sighing. "Lady Betty's a dear friend."

Is that why you're spending money on a lavish tea we can't afford?

Something prevented Lavinia from responding. Not the fear of punishment—she relished the danger of behaving contrary to what was expected of a young lady—but the expression in Papa's eyes. Rather than the bent, broken man he'd become these past weeks, he was, once more, Lord de Grande—a man who took pride in himself.

His expression softened. "Perhaps I'm being a little extravagant today, daughter, but Lady Betty is one of the few friends who've remained loyal since my troubles. Where others have stepped aside and relished my downfall—or even been the cause of it—only she has stood by me."

What did he mean—others being the cause of his downfall?

He took her hand. "Please understand," he said. "My view of the world has changed much these past weeks, and I've now learned the true nature of friendship."

"And what is that, Papa?"

He smiled. "Only when we're reduced to almost nothing do our true friends reveal themselves. They love us regardless of our circumstances, and we can lean on them when the world around us crumbles into dirt."

He blinked, and Lavinia could swear she glimpsed a tear on his cheek. But then he turned away and waved dismissively toward her.

"Run along and put your dress on, then join us in the parlor—quickly, now!"

Lavinia climbed the stairs to her chamber. Mrs. Bates had set out her gown on the bed—a simple day dress of lilac muslin. The hem had begun to fray, but Lavinia didn't love the dress any less for that, even though she wouldn't have been welcomed in Society dressed so shabbily.

Papa was right. A true friend was there at the worst of times, as well as the best.

Her friend—King Arthur—had not come to visit. He'd abandoned her in the same way that Papa's friends had abandoned him.

CHAPTER FOUR

As Lavinia descended the stairs, she glanced out of the window. A small, neat carriage stood by the front gate, the horses' harnesses glinting in the light of the setting sun.

She approached the parlor and pushed the door open.

"Ah, daughter!" Papa struggled to his feet. "You know of Lady Betty, of course, but I don't believe you've been properly introduced."

Their guest sat beside the window, silhouetted against the sunlight. She rose in a smooth, elegant motion.

She was tall, and dressed in a gown of deep purple silk, trimmed with black lace. Her hair was piled into fashionable curls atop her head, rendering her statuesque. She approached Lavinia, and the air filled with the scent of rose and lavender.

"Miss de Grande, a pleasure."

Her voice, rich and smooth, was a note deeper than that of most women. But it rendered her less shrewish than the ladies Lavinia had seen at Fosterley Park during Papa's house parties.

Lady Betty offered her hand, and Lavinia stared at it.

"Lavinia!" Papa said. "Be civil, please. Betty, forgive my daughter."

Betty? So familiar an address?

Aunt Edna had warned Lavinia of the dangers of women like Lady Betty, who were content to debauch themselves to secure a man's affections. What *debauch* meant, Lavinia knew not, but it must be something wicked, for her aunt reached for her smelling salts whenever she uttered the word.

Lavinia continued to stare. Had Lady Betty been the cause of Papa's downfall? Aunt Edna had said painted ladies were not averse to bleeding a man's coffers dry. She glanced pointedly at the cake, which looked even larger in the tiny parlor than it had on the kitchen table.

"How much did that cake cost, Papa?" she asked.

Lady Betty glanced toward the cake, and understanding shone in her chocolate-colored eyes.

"Lavinia Amelia de Grande!" Papa roared. Lavinia flinched at his tone, but Lady Betty placed a hand on his arm.

"No, Dickie darling," she said quietly. "Your daughter has every right to be aggrieved. I am, after all, the reason why you're here."

Papa shook his head. "Betty, I cannot let you—"

"Hush!" she said. Then she lowered her voice and spoke so quietly that Lavinia almost missed her words. "Remember what we agreed."

"Papa?" Lavinia asked. "What have you agreed with this woman?"

"Nothing, my dear," Lady Betty said. She frowned at Papa, as if in warning, then resumed her attention on Lavinia. "My dear," she said. "I came here to apologize for the trouble I caused your poor father. He's been kind enough to forgive me, but I must also earn *your* forgiveness."

"I don't understand," Lavinia said. Why did the woman speak in riddles?

"It's *my* fault you had to leave Fosterley Park," Lady Betty said. "I have extravagant tastes."

"Betty, I—" Papa started, but she raised a hand.

"Isn't that right, Dickie?"

Lavinia gestured toward the cake. "And is *that* to your taste?"

"Lavinia!" Papa cried, then he burst into a fit of coughing.

"Dickie, don't distress yourself." Lady Betty helped him back into his armchair. "Perhaps I should leave."

Papa lowered his voice to a whisper. "Betty, I cannot let you take the blame for my folly."

"Neither can you waste your funds on an extravagant cake just for me, you fool!" Lady Betty hissed. Then she turned to Lavinia. "Forgive me, Miss de Grande. I assure you that your father won't be wasting any more funds on me."

"I wasn't—" Papa began.

"Dickie darling…"

"Good God, woman!" Papa cried. "Why must you be such a damned martyr? I never asked it of you."

"But…"

"The sooner my daughter learns about the world, the sooner she can ready herself for it." Papa gestured toward Lavinia. "The world is populated by predators who lurk in the shadows of Society, ready to prey on the unsuspecting. Better she knows the truth. It was not the greed of a woman that reduced my circumstances—but the treachery of men." He gave Lady Betty a smile of affection. "You have been my one true friend. I would not have anyone think badly of you—particularly my beloved daughter."

Lavinia's heart almost broke at the pain in his voice.

"Dickie, please don't distress yourself," Lady Betty said. "Your daughter's too young to learn about the treachery of men."

"But treacherous men exist," Papa replied. "Do you think Lavinia will be protected from them merely because of her youth?"

"No, Dickie, she'll be protected because she has people who love her and want the best for her. Those men cannot touch her. *I'll* see to that."

Papa leaned back and sighed. "She's the image of my Lily."

"I know, darling, but that blackguard won't take any interest in her. He's living out his days on the Continent, counting his riches."

"Riches he stole from me. I—" Papa broke into another fit of coughing.

"Your fortune will be restored in no time, darling. Besides, wealth doesn't make a man. You'll still be a better man than most of my acquaintance."

"I'll wager you say that to every man who patronizes you, Betty."

She let out a laugh. "I don't, and well you know it. I might remark on their looks, or the cut of their jacket—but goodness is not a quality found among Society, and nor is it valued."

Their words made no sense.

"What's a blackguard?" Lavinia asked.

They turned toward her, their eyes widening as if they'd forgotten she was in the room.

"A—*what?*" Papa asked.

"A blackguard, Papa. You said it just now."

"Your father didn't mean anything in particular," Lady Betty said. "He—"

"Earl Walton," Papa said, his voice filled with venom.

The name was familiar, though Lavinia couldn't place it.

"*He's* responsible for my downfall," Papa continued, his face twisted with hatred. "I should have bloody shot him when I had the chance!"

"And where would that have got you?" Lady Betty asked.

"A damn sight more content than I am now, knowing that he and his friends stripped me of everything I valued."

"What do you mean, Papa?" Lavinia asked.

"Did you never wonder what happened to cause me to lose everything?" Papa asked.

"Dickie, I hardly think—"

"It's time she knew!" Papa cried. "Walton's always hated me, Lavinia, because he wanted your mother for himself. But Lily loved *me*, and Walton never forgave me. So he hatched a plot to ruin me. Poor, trusting fool that he was, I walked right into it." Papa shook his head. "But that wasn't the worst of it. When my heirlooms were auctioned off to pay my debts, Walton and his accomplices took possession of my most treasured items—gifts that your mother and I exchanged, tokens of our love. I don't know how they did it, but they conspired to ensure that each item was sold for a fraction of its value. Two shillings each." He bent forward and placed his head in his hands. "Two shillings! Was that all our love was worth?"

"Hush, Dickie—don't distress yourself," Lady Betty said.

"But—it's like they each have a piece of Lily's soul," Papa whispered. "I can't bear to think of them in their possession—to think of Walton's grubby hands on the gift my Lily gave me as a token of her love."

"I know, my darling, but you have what matters most—your daughter, and the knowledge that Lily loved you. Compared to those men, you're the richest man in the world."

"I cannot help how I feel," Papa said. "I hate Walton with every fiber of my being. He deserves to be punished for his sins."

"And he will be, Dickie. Trust Fate, and don't let your hatred consume you—or he'll have secured his victory."

Lavinia's heart ached at the despair in her father's eyes. In a little under an hour, the man she'd seen on the stairs in a dapper suit, looking like the Papa she'd once known, had transformed into the defeated creature before her.

And it had been her fault.

She took his hand. "Papa, I'm sorry."

"It's not *my* forgiveness you should beg for, daughter."

"Dickie, no," Lady Betty protested, but Lavinia offered her hand to the woman.

"Forgive me, Lady Betty," she said. "Papa said we had a good friend—the only one not to turn their back on us. I've no right to be uncivil, if *you* are that friend."

"Dear child!" Lady Betty cried. "You're so like your sweet mama."

"You knew Mama?"

"A little. Never had such a sweet woman walked upon the earth! My heart broke when she died, but I'm thankful that, at her end, she believed that we live in a good world. And, if you permit me, I'll do everything in my power to protect you as your mama would have done."

Papa drew out a handkerchief and dabbed his eyes. Then he turned his face away, as if ashamed of his outburst.

But it wasn't Papa who should be ashamed. It was Earl Walton, and his friends—whoever they were.

"Shall I pour the tea, Papa?" Lavinia asked. "Lady Betty— would you like some cake?"

Lady Betty accepted the olive branch. "That would be delightful, my dear," she said. "Just a small slice, and perhaps next time I visit—if you wish to invite me again—*I* can bring a cake. Or a pound of marzipan? I hear it has medicinal purposes, as well as tasting delicious."

She rattled on, extolling the virtues of marzipan, and a shop in Bath that she said simply *must* be visited, while Lavinia poured the tea and cut the cake. But though the conversation focused on frivolities, Lavinia understood it for what it was—an offer of friendship from someone who would never betray them.

Unlike Earl Walton.

As Lavinia sank her teeth into her slice of cake, she made a silent vow. One day, she would avenge Papa's losses. She would retrieve the treasures he grieved for, and she would not rest until she had wreaked revenge on Earl Walton.

CHAPTER FIVE

Fourteen years later, Sussex, June 1814

WHEN LAVINIA ENTERED the dining room, Papa was already at the breakfast table, with Mr. and Mrs. Bates tending to him.

"Morning, Miss Lavinia," Mrs. Bates said. "Ye look like you've had no sleep."

Lavinia exchanged a glance with Mr. Bates. "I took Samson for a ride before breakfast," she said. "I fear I tired him out."

"And yourself, I'll warrant," Mrs. Bates said, "though I don't recall hearing you go out this morning."

"I was up before dawn," Lavinia said. "The sunrise was glorious."

That, at least, was the truth.

"Before dawn?" Mrs. Bates cried. "A young lady shouldn't go about riding in the dark. There's brigands on the roads, and you hear such dreadful tales of coaches being set upon."

"Brigands?" Papa glanced up. "What's this about brigands?"

Lavinia rushed to his side. "Nothing, Papa," she said. "I went out for a morning ride, that's all."

Papa's eyes widened. "You ventured out alone—on Samson?" He shook his head. "Oh no—that simply *won't* do."

"I can handle myself," Lavinia said. "If you're concerned, I'll take your pistol."

"Sweet Lord—don't let your aunt hear you say such a thing! She despairs of you enough as it is. If she knows you're carrying on like a hoyden, she won't take you to London next month."

Good.

Lavinia resisted the urge to voice her opinion. Papa set such store on her having a successful London Season, and she didn't have the heart to disappoint him—not when he'd been looking increasingly frail of late.

The last thing she wanted was to distress him when he'd suffered so much at the hands of others. His spirit had been broken by his enemies, and, whatever it took, she would devote herself to restoring what she could before he departed the world in which he'd been treated so unjustly.

And I took the first step last night.

Papa waved a hand at Mrs. Bates, who exited the dining room, her husband in her wake. Lavinia placed her shoulder bag and its precious contents on the breakfast table, then sat beside him. His blanket slipped to the floor, and she retrieved it, then tucked it over his lap.

"Lavinia…" He nodded toward her bag. "Your aunt would have a fit if she saw that on the table," he said. "You'll need better table manners if you're to grace the dining rooms of London."

"I've something for you," she said, lowering her voice to a whisper. "Would you like to see?" She reached inside the bag, pulled out the object inside, and placed it on the table.

At first, Papa's expression showed confusion. Then recognition shimmered in his eyes and he leaned forward.

"Surely that's not…"

He glanced up and met her gaze.

She nodded, then picked up the little ginger jar. "Check the maker's mark on the bottom."

Papa leaned forward, hands outstretched, as if reaching for his lost love. Lavinia placed the jar in his hands, and he sighed, caressing the smooth surface, tracing the lines of the dragon painted on the belly of the jar.

Moisture glistened in his eyes. "I-I don't understand," he said. "Where did you…"

She averted her gaze before responding. "I've been corresponding with a merchant in London—with Lady Betty's help."

"B-but, how?" Papa's gaze remained fixed on the object as he turned it around in his hand. "How could you afford it?"

"I-it…" She hesitated. "It didn't cost much."

Papa let out a snort. "It's worth a small fortune."

Lavinia's heart jolted in her chest—did he suspect her? Even the dullest wit would be able to work out the truth…

Then he leaned back in his chair and sighed. "That bastard Francis paid a pittance for it. Though why he'd sell after all these years…"

Lavinia placed a hand on his arm. "Papa, the Lord Francis you knew died two years ago, and his heir, the present incumbent, wasn't the seller."

In that, she'd spoken the truth. Lord Francis hadn't *sold* it to her.

Papa arched an eyebrow. "I wonder when Francis sold it, if you didn't purchase it from *him*?"

"I wouldn't fret about it," she said, "but given his lordship's animosity toward you, and the value you place on the jar, I think you should keep it hidden. You wouldn't want him knowing it's back with its rightful owner."

Papa let out a bitter laugh. "None of my former acquaintances would deign to come *here*. Hardly anyone knows where we are—and even fewer *care*."

Lavinia took Papa's hand. Her heart ached at the pain in his tone. "Aunt Edna might suspect something if she saw it," she said. "You know how strict she is over our spending. She said Cousin Charles was complaining about the cost of that side of beef Mrs. Bates cooked for us last week."

He turned the urn over in his hands once more.

"You didn't…*purchase*…it from him," he whispered. Then he narrowed his eyes and met Lavinia's gaze. Her stomach tightened.

He knows.

"Papa, I don't want you worrying about where the urn came from. You must concentrate on your health, and getting better."

He nodded and patted her hand. "Then I'll rejoice in its redemption, and say no more."

"Shall I help you into the parlor?" Lavinia asked. "Or perhaps you'd like a walk in the garden."

Papa shook his head. "Lady Betty's visiting for tea. I want to be well rested."

"Then let me help you into the parlor before I leave for my lessons."

"Best be quick—your aunt doesn't like to be kept waiting."

Lavinia laughed. "It's not even eight, Papa. Aunt will still be in her bedchamber sleeping off last night's sherry."

She stood and held out her arm. He took it and stood, shaking, and they shuffled into the parlor, where she helped him into the chair beside the fire, which was already lit courtesy of Mr. Bates.

Then she climbed the stairs and entered her bedchamber. She pulled a sheaf of papers from the top drawer of her writing desk and ran her fingers over the lettering on the top sheet, tracing the words she'd read a hundred times over.

Griffin & Sons, Bond Street
Sale September 17th, 1800
Catalogue of lots

She leafed through the papers, reading the list, pausing at the items she'd marked with an X, her lips moving with the words:

Lot 47: Lady's necklace in gold, one central emerald, with six rubies in graduated sizes

Lot 120: Ginger jar, presumed 13th century Yuan Dynasty, ceramic, complete with lid, decorated in blue

Lot 206: Louis XVI late 18th century ormolu boulle mantel clock

Lot 254: Landscape oil painting entitled "The Snow Field" framed with gilded mahogany, signed J.R. 1765

Lot 329: Sword bearing a crest with filigree design at the hilt, circa 12th Century

Beside each lot, she had scribbled a name—*Houghton, Francis, Walton, Hythe, Caldicott.* Smiling, she picked up her quill and dipped it into the inkpot. Then she flicked back to the page showing Lot 120 and drew a line through the description, together with the name beside it—*Francis.*

One down, four to go.

CHAPTER SIX

London, June 1814

"T HEY CALL HIM the Phoenix."

Peregrine, Viscount Marlow, glanced up from his newspaper.

In the armchair opposite sat Mr. Houseman, a rather unsavory character who considered himself an accomplished sleuth after he'd apprehended a thief last year. Quite by chance—he'd stumbled across the fellow on returning home from a night at Mrs. DeBauche's Establishment for the Entertainment of Discerning Gentlemen.

Houseman had an inflated opinion of himself, and a rather *medieval* attitude to punishment for even the most inconsequential crimes. Nevertheless, he'd ingratiated himself with the authorities to such a degree that he held a senior position, and often called upon Peregrine when the need arose, given Peregrine's knowledge of art and antiquities.

"The…what?" Peregrine asked.

"The Phoenix," Houseman replied.

"Is this some new case you're investigating?"

Houseman nodded. "A slippery creature, he is. But he's getting a little too arrogant."

It takes one to know one.

"I'm sorry?" Houseman asked.

Bloody hell. Had Peregrine spoken aloud?

"How do you mean, arrogant?" he asked. "What's he doing?"

"Surely you've heard of the recent spate of robberies?"

Peregrine shook his head.

"A number of items have been taken from houses all over the country," Houseman said.

"Such as?"

"Oh, various items," Houseman replied. "An item of jewelry here, a miniature portrait there, a set of apostle spoons. The latest one's a vase."

"From the same house?" Peregrine asked.

"No, all different. One item from each house."

Peregrine snorted. "A single item? In my experience, when a man claims that a single item has gone missing, it's because he pawned it to pay a doxy, then spun a pretty tale to allay his wife's suspicions."

He picked up his newspaper. With luck, Houseman would take the hint and leave him alone.

"Ah, but the Phoenix leaves a clue."

Peregrine set his paper aside, then raised his empty glass and caught a footman's eye. Evidently Houseman wasn't going to leave him be. Best to imbibe in order to weather a conversation with the arrogant arse.

The footman trotted over, decanter in hand, and refilled the glass.

"I'll have one myself, good man, if you please," Houseman said, lifting his glass. "And please ensure that Lord Marlow's drink is placed on my account."

Houseman wanted something. Like Peregrine, most members of White's came to seek solace from the world. Men like Houseman, however, came to seek out those with whom he wished to ingratiate himself.

And today, Peregrine was the object of Houseman's attentions.

Houseman raised his glass. "To your health, Lord Marlow."

Peregrine reciprocated the gesture. "Very well," he said. "Tell me about the Phoenix."

Houseman leaned forward. "He strikes at random times, and random places," he said. "There's no pattern to his actions…"

"No *discernible* pattern," Peregrine said. "Something will always link the actions of an individual, particularly one engaged in theft. Just because it's not been identified yet, doesn't mean it does not exist."

Houseman's eyes glazed over with confusion. "Quite so."

"So, why is he called the Phoenix?" Peregrine asked. "Does he leave a pile of ashes in his wake?"

"He leaves a drawing in place of the item he's stolen. A small drawing of a bird rising from flames. I have one here." Houseman pulled a piece of paper from his pocket and handed it over.

It was an unremarkable scrap—the torn edge of a piece of parchment used for writing letters. On it was a rough sketch of a bird, wings outstretched, engulfed in flames. The bird's neck was stretched toward the sky, as if the creature were ready to launch itself into the heavens after having been reborn in the fire. With sharp talons and a large, curved beak, the bird had an air of strength. Yet there was a peculiar expression in its eye, one of victory—and mischief.

"The Phoenix," Peregrine whispered.

"Exactly," Houseman said. "Though I fail to understand why."

Peregrine sipped his brandy. "It's obvious."

"Is it?"

Peregrine smiled. "Of course," he said. "He's taunting us."

"For what purpose?"

"That remains to be seen. But the image must mean something to him, and therefore what he uses to taunt us with may eventually lead to his downfall."

"How so?"

Peregrine refrained from rolling his eyes. However much Houseman rated his abilities, the man lacked both the wit and subtlety needed to solve the more intriguing cases.

"Your thief must have a particular reason not only for leaving his calling card, but for using the image of a phoenix. Once we've identified the reason, we'll be closer to identifying the thief himself."

"So you'll take on the case?" Houseman asked. "There's a reward already being offered."

"A reward?"

"The regent himself has offered a hundred guineas."

"Whatever for?"

"It seems that the Royal Pavilion was one of the first establishments that the Phoenix visited."

Peregrine straightened his stance. "Seriously?"

Houseman lowered his voice to a conspiratorial whisper. "The apostle spoons were a gift from Lady Jersey. I cannot imagine many thieves would be capable of an act that's akin to treason."

Peregrine let out a snort. "Given the public outcry over the regent's treatment of his wife—not to mention Lady Jersey's treatment of the princess—the thief could be anyone with a sense of justice."

Houseman drew in a sharp breath, as if Peregrine had uttered something seditious.

"I'd take great pleasure in seeing the Phoenix swinging from a gibbet."

"For theft?" Peregrine asked.

"The regent's interest necessitates a more severe penalty," Houseman said. "He's understandably concerned about his treasures."

"He should be more concerned about the state of the country," Peregrine replied. "But you've piqued my interest. I'll be glad to investigate, if you'd hand over the evidence to me. Mayhap I'll see a pattern that's eluded you so far."

Houseman frowned. "There is no pattern," he said. "There's nothing to link the items stolen, or the victims—the regent, a baronet, and a viscount. The viscount, the latest victim, is not acquainted with either the regent or the baronet, and the Phoenix didn't leave a drawing when he stole Prinny's spoons."

"That tells us that the pattern is a complex one, not that it doesn't exist," Peregrine said. "A simple pattern will display its regularity more quickly, and can therefore be discerned with little effort. A more complex pattern must be observed over a longer period. Surely you understand that?"

Houseman drained his glass. "As long as you agree to take it on."

Peregrine nodded. "You have my word."

"Very good. I'll send my man over with my notes this afternoon." Houseman offered his hand, and Peregrine took it. Then he rose and left the clubroom, barking an order to a footman to fetch his greatcoat.

Peregrine took another sip of brandy, savoring the taste. Fools like Houseman could never appreciate a good brandy. Or anything, come to that. Houseman sought quick gratification in all things—in the liquor he drank, the cases he investigated, and, most likely, the women he bedded.

Whereas drink, conundrums, and women were best savored at leisure, to elicit maximum pleasure. Doubtless Houseman would congratulate himself on passing on a case that he believed impossible.

But Peregrine relished a challenge. He cast his gaze once more over the drawing and the intelligent expression in the bird's eye.

"Well, Mr. Phoenix," he said, a smile slowly curling his lips. "You may be a cunning fellow, but I shall relish the challenge of besting you."

And best him he would.

"May we join you?" a male voice asked.

Peregrine glanced up. Two figures stood before him—Giles, Earl Thorpe, and Montague Fitzroy, Duke of Whitcombe.

"Is it a coincidence that the two of you approached me as soon as I was alone?" Peregrine asked.

"Monty and I had no wish for you to wallow in solitude," Thorpe replied.

Whitcombe let out a snort. "You're too bloody diplomatic for your own good, Thorpe," he said. "The truth is, neither of us wished to spend a single moment in that primped-up coxcomb's company."

"Whoever do you mean?" Peregrine asked.

"Houseman, of course!" Whitcombe laughed, not caring that the man in question was barely out of the clubroom and doubtless still within earshot. He put little stock in others' opinions of him. He had little need to care, with every man, and most of the women, in the world so desperate to ingratiate themselves with him that they were prepared to put up with anything—incivility, downright rudeness, and, in the case of the women, abandonment after he'd rutted them into ruination.

Thorpe gestured toward the sketch in Peregrine's hand. "What do you have there?" he asked. "I know you're a connoisseur of art, but I can't see Sotheby's taking an interest in it."

Peregrine pocketed the sketch. "It's something to do with a case I'm investigating."

"So *that* explains why that arse Houseman was here," Whitcombe said. "Don't tell me, he's foisting a difficult case onto you because he's too much of an imbecile to solve it himself, and he's hoping to take the credit for your efforts."

For a supposed rake and profligate, Whitcombe possessed an extraordinary level of insight. But that explained his attraction to the opposite sex. Whitcombe was able to ascertain, at a single glance, an individual's deepest needs—and he was able to convey, with a single touch, his ability to satisfy them.

"You should leave that sort of thing to paid subordinates," Whitcombe said. "There's better pleasures to be had in life."

"There's more to life than making love to a woman," Peregrine said.

Whitcombe barked with laughter. "Making love is for fools. I don't make love—I fuck."

A volley of tutting rippled through the air, accompanied by the rustling of newspapers as the other occupants of the clubroom voiced their disapproval in the only way an English gentleman knew how.

"I say, old boy, keep it down," Thorpe said in a low voice.

"A real man wouldn't shake his head and wave his copy of the *London Times* to express his disapproval." Whitcombe laughed. "He'd either call me out, or place a shiner on my face."

As if anyone would call Whitcombe out! With a body that vibrated pure, primal masculinity, no man would dare challenge him.

The trouble was, Whitcombe knew it.

"I take it you're using the language of the rutting boar because you've indulged in yet another session at Mrs. DeBauche's Establishment for the Entertainment of Discerning Gentlemen," Peregrine said.

Thorpe spluttered on his brandy "The *Entertainment of Discerning Gentlemen?*" He shook his head. "Why does the term *discerning*—presumably meant to convey a particularly educated sense of taste—give rise to the most sordid images when being used to describe a gentleman? Why not call it what it is—a bawdy house?"

"Doubtless because Mrs. DeBauche can charge an extra shilling," Whitcombe said. "And no—I've never patronized her establishment. I prefer a hunting ground of a finer caliber."

"Such as Lady Foxwell's ball next week?" Thorpe asked. "I hear Lady Irma Fairchild is attending. I suspect she's hoping you'll ask her to dance, Monty."

"Ugh." Whitcombe wrinkled his nose. "I suspect it's so cold between her thighs that one session with her would freeze a chap's manhood. Lord help the poor man who saddles himself with her."

"As for that friend of hers..." Thorpe said.

"What friend?" Peregrine asked.

"Miss Juliette Howard. Beautiful to look at, but she'd nag a man into the grave." Thorpe leaned closer. "Her older sister's rumored to be a little—*soft in the head*."

"Who told you that?" Whitcombe asked.

"Lady Irma," Thorpe said. "Or, perhaps, she said *eccentric*."

"*Eccentric's* a term men use when a woman has refused their attentions," Peregrine said. "Perhaps you should look to Miss Juliette's sister, Monty. She'd pose more of a challenge than the likes of Lady Irma."

"I doubt it," Whitcombe said. "Why waste my time engaging in a challenge when it's offered freely elsewhere?"

Thorpe rolled his eyes. "Oh, spare us! I haven't avoided Houseman and his boasts about his talents at sleuthing just to listen to your bragging about your conquests in the bedchamber."

"*You're* no saint," Whitcombe retorted. "Weren't you shagging Lady Betty Grey?" He sipped his brandy, then let out a sigh. "Now *there's* a pair of thighs I'd like to dive between. She's the exception to the rule that a woman's allure fades with age."

"Lady Betty has the good sense to steer well clear of a man such as you," Thorpe said. "The one thing she values most is something *you'll* never be able to give her."

"Which is?" Whitcombe asked.

"Friendship."

Whitcombe wrinkled his nose. "Friendship—with a *woman*?"

"It's possible," Thorpe said. "Lady Betty and I have parted ways, but remain good friends."

"Why would you part company with that delectable creature?" Whitcombe asked."

"I have responsibilities to my ward," Thorpe said. "My niece, Beatrice."

"Ah yes—an orphaned niece can hinder a man's love life. Does she live with you?"

"The answer's no," Thorpe said.

"So she *doesn't* live with you?" Whitcombe asked.

"I'd give up, if I were you, Monty," Peregrine said. "If you value your balls, I'd steer clear of Lady Beatrice Thorpe."

"That's always been your problem, Whitcombe," Thorpe said. "You only think of a woman as a creature to seduce. But, if a man acts like an educated adult, rather than a rutting boar, he can maintain a friendship with his mistress. Granted, it requires a little more effort than simply discarding her with a slap on the buttocks and the toss of a trinket in her direction." He turned to Peregrine. "What say you, Marlow? It's possible to have a friendship with a woman, yes?"

At that moment, Peregrine was assaulted by the memory of the first friendship he'd ever experienced—not a friendship forged at school, but something far more precious than an exchange of conkers in the grounds at Eton.

My little Guinevere…

The vibrant little girl whose soul shimmered with energy and enthusiasm for life—who had looked up at him with adoration in her eyes.

He'd last seen her fourteen years ago, when they'd playacted at sword fighting and conquering dragons in the woods near Father's estate. Then she had disappeared, never to be seen again. And never to be spoken of. Father had threatened to whip Peregrine when he asked about her, declaring her father a treacherous criminal who'd attempted to ruin him, but in doing so had become ruined himself. It was only in later years that Peregrine had learned the truth, pieced together from snippets of London clubroom gossip. His little Guinevere was Viscount de Grande's daughter. De Grande had been notorious among Father's circle of acquaintances. The man had involved himself in fraudulent investments, and had attempted to draw Father and several others into his scheme. But justice had prevailed. De Grande suffered the consequence of his machinations and disappeared, as if he'd never existed. In fact, over the years, Peregrine would've begun to wonder whether the man—and his daughter—had been figments of his imagination, had it not been for the entry in *Debrett's*.

"Viscount de Grande."

That name, uttered in Whitcombe's deep baritone, brought Peregrine out of his dreams and snapped him back to the present.

"De Grande?" Peregrine asked—a little too loudly.

"Are you all right, old chap?" Thorpe asked. "You look like you've seen a ghost."

"You know de Grande?" Whitcombe asked. Then he shook his head. "Of course—his ancestral home's in Surrey."

"Surrey's a large county," Peregrine said, "but I do happen to know of de Grande. He's not been seen for some years, if I recall."

"Nearly fifteen," Thorpe said. "Ever since he lost his fortune at the gaming tables."

"I heard he lost his fortune due to an investment scandal," Whitcombe said.

"No—definitely the gaming tables," Thorpe replied.

"The fool!" Whitcombe scoffed. "No man should wager what he cannot afford to lose."

"Is that why you'll never marry, Monty?" Thorpe teased. "Because you're afraid you'll lose your heart?"

"He'd have to be in possession of a heart to begin with," Peregrine said. Then he turned to Thorpe. "So, you're acquainted with de Grande?"

Whitcombe let out a snort. "They have a...*mutual friend* in Lady Betty Grey."

Thorpe scowled.

"She's acquainted with de Grande?" Peregrine asked.

"Visits him regularly, I hear," Thorpe said.

Peregrine's stomach curled into a knot, and he tightened the grip on his glass.

Where had his little Guinevere gone? Perhaps she'd been married off. Or worse—with a wastrel for a father, it might have fallen upon her to earn a living...

"Do you know where they live?" he asked, steadying his voice despite the turmoil in his mind.

"Some poky little cottage on a cousin's estate," Thorpe said, "or so Betty let slip one evening."

"What the devil is de Grande doing *there*?"

"How should I know?" Thorpe replied. "I'm only surprised he still lives—I heard he'd taken ill."

"D-did he not have a daughter?" Peregrine asked, painfully aware of the tremor in his voice.

"Betty let slip something about a young woman," Thorpe said. "She's been attending a number of country parties, but I'd be surprised if she made it as far as London." His eyes narrowed. "Why the sudden interest, Marlow?"

"Nothing—I'm just curious."

Peregrine averted his gaze, aware of a pair of blue eyes on him. Then he was saved by the clock on the mantelshelf over the fireplace, which struck six.

Thorpe drained his glass and stood. "Duty calls."

"Ugh—duty!" Whitcombe sighed. "I don't know why you bother, Thorpe, when there's better ways to occupy our time."

"With an estate nearing ruination, and an orphaned cousin in my charge, I've enough to occupy myself with," Thorpe said. "Frivolity leads to weakness."

Whitcombe drained his glass and leaped to his feet. "That's *my* cue to depart," he said. "The moment a man lectures me on the benefits of a dutiful life, I fear I'll be tainted with the urge to be responsible. I'm subject to enough henpecking already from the mater. I'll see you anon."

He set his glass down, gave Peregrine a quick salute, then strode out of the clubroom. Thorpe followed, leaving Peregrine alone with his drink, and his thoughts.

Thoughts of *her*.

His little Guinevere.

So—she had been attending Society parties. Might he see her again? Would he recognize her if he did? In any case, Father would object. Father, who harbored resentment at the slightest folly—his hatred for de Grande would only have increased over the years.

But Peregrine could dream. A man needed a little pleasure in life. Not, perhaps, to the extent that Whitcombe indulged in. He needed to strike a balance between duty and pleasure. Duty was the burden undertaken in order for pleasure to be savored without guilt.

Yes—a little pleasure was to be allowed, even if it compromised his duty toward his estate, his friends, and his father.

And if he happened to stumble across his little Guinevere, where would the harm be in that?

CHAPTER SEVEN

As Lavinia returned home, she heard voices coming from the parlor—Papa and Lady Betty.

Over the past fourteen years, Lady Betty had proven herself to be the best of friends. Her sunny disposition helped temper Papa's melancholy, and she had proven invaluable to Lavinia due to her extensive acquaintance—and her discretion.

Lavinia entered the parlor, and Lady Betty rose, arms outstretched.

"Lavinia, *darling!*" she cried. "I'm so glad to see you. I'm leaving for London shortly, and feared I'd miss you."

Lavinia wrinkled her nose. "Aunt made me stay until I completed the alphabet sampler to her satisfaction. I had to unpick the final letter twice before she declared it fit to be seen."

"Your aunt knows what's best for you," Papa said. "To succeed in Society, you must make a good impression. She told me how disappointed she was with your behavior at Lady Francis's dinner party the other week, when you disappeared to the privy for half an hour during coffee. You must behave better in London."

"Dickie, don't be ungenerous," Lady Betty said. "Lavinia's delightful as she is. Nobody cares about that sort of thing anymore."

"Then what do they care about?" Papa asked.

"Dowries and titles, darling," came the reply. "It's always

been about birth and bounty. The pursuit of accomplishment is what my sex undertakes in order to delude themselves into believing they have control of their destiny."

"That sounds awfully depressing," Lavinia said.

"But," Lady Betty said, her eyes twinkling with merriment, "a clever creature such as yourself can outwit them all. Besides—as a viscount's daughter, you'll be deemed acceptable before you even set foot in London."

Papa sighed. "You mean a *disgraced* viscount."

"Dickie darling, it may disappoint you to learn that you're *not* the talk of Society," Lady Betty said. "More titled gentlemen than you think are required to give up their estates these days. Take poor Lord Danbury, for instance…"

"One of your many lovers, I suppose," Papa growled.

"Don't be churlish, Dickie," Lady Betty admonished him, in the manner of a nursemaid chiding her charge. "Danbury's downfall resulted from his weakness for the card tables. I'm not in the habit of toying with a lover's money, or his affections. I sent him back to his wife with his heart intact, I assure you."

"I intend to keep *my* heart intact when I go to London," Lavinia said.

"Sensible girl," Lady Betty replied. "When do you leave?"

"Aunt's taking me on Saturday," Lavinia said. "I wish I wasn't going."

"You'll love it, darling. It's a little overcrowded, but the parks are delightful."

"Aunt Edna's forbidden me to venture out until I'm fit to be seen," Lavinia said. "I'm to spend my first day stuck in a modiste's shop, being inspected like livestock and stabbed with pins. Then I must endure some dreadful party."

"What party?"

"Lady Foxwell's. Have you heard of her?"

"I met her once," Lady Betty said. "A rather insipid creature on the surface, but Lord Foxwell says she's an assertive little thing in the household. I rather admire her for that. We may live in a world of men, but a woman can carve out her own little world within which she can enjoy as much freedom as she wishes."

"It seems as if *I'll* have no freedom at all in London," Lavinia said. "Aunt's insisting on accompanying me everywhere."

"That's what's required in London," Lady Betty said. "As a new arrival, you'll come under much scrutiny. But you'll come to no harm, provided you do nothing to scandalize yourself."

"You must be careful, Lavinia," Papa said. "There are brigands aplenty, intent on stealing from the unwary."

Lavinia met her father's gaze. If he harbored any suspicions over her…*pursuits*, he showed no sign.

She glanced about the parlor. The ginger jar she'd appropriated from Lady Francis's bedchamber was not on display.

"I wonder, Lavinia, dear," Lady Betty said, "might you favor me with your company in a little sojourn about the garden before I depart? I believe your poor papa would like a little respite from my chatter, and I recall your saying in your last letter how beautifully Mr. Bates was tending to the rose garden. Perhaps you'd permit me to cut a bloom or two, to brighten up my home?"

"With pleasure," Lavinia replied.

Betty adjusted the blanket on Papa's knees, then led Lavinia out of the parlor and into the garden.

"I hope to see you while you're in London," Lady Betty said, "though I'd understand if you're unable to visit. Your aunt might not approve."

"What—of my calling on a titled widow?" Lavinia laughed. "Outwardly, at least, Aunt Edna must acknowledge your rank." She glanced toward the cottage, then lowered her voice. "Have you found someone to make the necklace?"

"When have I let you down, darling?" Lady Betty replied. "The necklace proved to be a little challenging, with the rather unusual design. But I know an excellent craftsman on Hatton Garden who owes me a favor." Her eyes glittered with mischief. "I tell all my gentleman friends to pay him a visit before returning to their wives. His pieces adorn some of the finest necks in the *haute ton.*"

"And…the painting?"

"That's proving problematic. My acquaintance can fashion a frame, but the artwork itself requires a considerable degree of talent, an excellent memory, and an eye for detail. When a painting is in a private collection, it's more difficult to replicate without attracting attention."

"A frame would suffice," Lavinia said. "Perhaps, when I come to London, we might seek out an artist together."

Betty arched a beautifully plucked eyebrow. "That painting is well known among experts who can spot a fake immediately."

Lavinia approached a rosebush and focused on the blooms. "I've no intention of procuring a perfect replica," she said. "It only needs to fool the untrained eye."

"You seek to deceive? Of course, forgery is prevalent among Society. A titled family struggling with the upkeep of their estate will often sell their treasures, replacing them with replicas. Sir William Moss—do you know him?—has had replicas made of all his wife's jewelry, and sold the originals to fund his profligate lifestyle."

"Such as patronizing you?" Lavinia asked.

"Oh, darling!" Lady Betty laughed. "I'm wealthy enough in my own right, and am much less of a strain on my lovers' resources than the gossips think. Besides, I must *like* my lovers, at least. Sir William thinks too much of himself. His son—Heath Moss—seems to think his prowess is determined by the number of men he cuckolds. I hear he's carrying on with Lady Francis."

Having caught the couple in question *in flagrante delicto* two nights ago, Lavinia opened her mouth to agree. Then she closed it again. The less Lady Betty knew about the true extent of her exploits, the better.

"I've no intention of making money," Lavinia said. "I know it's unlikely that we'll return to Fosterley, or retrieve what we lost—but if I can provide Papa with replicas of the most beloved items, then they'll bring forth the memories that he tries to cling to. Memories of Mama." She let out a sigh, and her breath caught at the memory of her mother—the gentle, fragile creature on whom she and Papa had doted.

A warm hand took hers, and Lavinia turned to see Lady Betty's brown eyes focused on her.

"Dickie's lucky to have you as a daughter," Lady Betty said. "You're the light of his life, and the image of your dear mother. If she were alive, she'd be so proud of you. It breaks my heart that you've been motherless for so long."

Her voice caught, and Lavinia took her other hand. *"You've* been a mother to me, Lady Betty."

"Dear child!" Lady Betty cried. "Your Aunt Edna would object to hear such a thing."

"Aunt Edna!" Lavinia scoffed. "There's more to motherhood then enforcing rules, and if you were to marry Papa…"

"Oh, darling!" Lady Betty cried. "If I married Dickie, it would do him—and you—no good. I value my freedom too much."

"You'd counsel against matrimony?"

Lady Betty nodded. "Do you believe in soul mates, Lavinia?"

"Soul mates?"

"Someone without whom you are incomplete—someone who can never be replaced. My Maddock, God rest his soul, was my true mate. He loved me despite my faults, and though it's been nearly twenty years since his passing, I miss him still."

Lady Betty slipped her arm through Lavinia's. "Of course, darling, if you're as fortunate as I to meet your soul mate, then your heart will thrive."

"Is that likely?" Lavinia asked.

"Oh yes, darling. He's out there somewhere—you just need to find him. Perhaps you'll discover him in London. Now, I've taken a fancy to those blood-red roses by the sundial, if you'd permit me to take one."

"Of course," Lavinia said.

Arm in arm, they returned to the cottage.

My soul mate…

What if she'd already met her soul mate—her own King Arthur—only to have lost him? The only things she could recall were the color of his eyes and the warmth of his voice.

And, in all likelihood, he'd have forgotten *her* altogether and found love with another—a woman who was not the daughter of an impoverished, disgraced viscount.

Perils there may be in London, but Lavinia's heart was not for the taking, because it would always belong to him—her *soul mate.*

So, she could venture forth into London, her heart encased in armor, and continue her quest to restore Papa's peace of mind.

CHAPTER EIGHT

S HE WAS THE loveliest thing Peregrine had ever seen.

The young woman standing at the entrance to Lady Foxwell's drawing room, accompanied by a sour-faced, sharp-nosed matriarch, lacked the air of superiority that rendered creatures such as Lady Irma Fairchild unpalatable. She was too tall to be considered as delectable as the likes of Lady Jersey, and her manner exuded discomfort. Rather than the brittle porcelain skin of the finely bred debutante, her face bore a rosy glow of health and vibrancy. A straight nose—a little too long to render her classically beautiful—sharp, well-defined eyebrows, and a stubbornness about the chin were the marks of a hellion.

As for her eyes…

A rather unremarkable shade of brown, they carried a look of discomfort as she swept her gaze about the room, as if searching for predators. They reminded him of the expression in a falcon's eyes—a bird that had been trained to return to her master's hand, but still yearned to soar into freedom as mistress of her world.

To the untrained eye, she was like any other young woman. But Peregrine could sense her unease. Perhaps she was a commoner's daughter, or mayhap a fog of doubt surrounded her parentage. Whatever her history, she believed herself an outsider.

And, to Peregrine, there was nothing more intriguing than a misfit—a free spirit who would not be tamed by the kind of flattery that rendered most women malleable in a man's hands.

Her gown was exquisite, yet she wore it with neither pride nor pleasure. A soft shade of pink, it caught the light and shimmered as she crossed the drawing room floor, the matriarch at her side. The fluidity of her skirts enabled a man to glimpse her form as she walked—long, shapely legs, which flared at the hips into delectable curves.

His gaze lingered over the curve of her throat. Her lace tuck preserved her modesty, but the mere thought of the treasures beneath was enough to warm his blood…

Bloody hell!

He drew in a sharp breath at the surge of powerful lust. He was a grown man, for heaven's sake, not a lusty lad of fifteen, eager to stroke himself to pleasure at the notion of a pair of breasts.

A very delectable pair of breasts…

…and a pair of delightful buds poking at the silk of her gown, just waiting to be tasted…

I've abstained for too long.

Yes, that was it. Since relieving himself of his mistress almost a month ago, he'd experienced a drought.

It was time to drink from the oasis once more.

And the intriguing young woman was unlikely to agree to a quick shag. Doubtless, the purple-clad crow accompanying her would have his balls if he so much as spoke to her out of turn.

And Peregrine wasn't in the mood for *courtship*—a tedious exercise in which a man pranced about like a prize pony to ingratiate himself with a chaperone, then endured protracted negotiations to determine how much compensation he'd be given to take a girl off her father's hands. Then came the far less palatable prospect of *marriage*, where he'd have to listen to a vicar droning on about the sanctity of a union, then bed a shivering, screaming virgin whose mama had schooled her into believing that the act was a sordid encounter to be endured out of duty— and as infrequently as possible.

No, a wife was not something Peregrine wished to saddle

himself with. By the time a young woman was old enough to enter Society, any free will had been schooled out of her—like a falcon bred in captivity, she knew no better.

But, occasionally, there existed a falcon who could never quite be tamed. Docile she may be at first, but if a man lowered his guard, she'd drive her beak into his flesh.

He glanced up and caught his breath.

A pair of eyes was trained on him. The brown, which he had at first dismissed as being unremarkable, was a soft hazel that shimmered with tones of green and gold. Her lips—plump and round—parted slightly. Then she flicked out her tongue, running the tip along her bottom lip until it glistened.

Peregrine's breeches grew a little too tight for comfort. He shifted position in an effort to conceal his growing manhood and lifted his hand to adjust his collar. Her eyes darkened, and his heart tightened, as if an invisible thread linked the two of them. The expression in her eyes seemed familiar, as if her soul called to his…

Then her eyes widened, almost as if in fear. Her hand flew to her mouth, and she stepped back.

He grinned to himself.

I've not lost my touch, if my potency can render a woman awestruck.

A hand touched his sleeve, and he turned to see Lord and Lady Francis. "I say, Marlow, I'm glad you're here," Lord Francis said. "I've been wanting a word."

"Lord Francis, Lady Francis." Peregrine inclined his head. "I didn't know you were here tonight."

"Foxwell and I were at Oxford together," Lord Francis said. "Bloody good shot, he is—bagged thirty birds in a single afternoon at my house party last month. Which reminds me—"

A shrill female voice interrupted him.

"Dinner is served, *mes amis!*"

Lady Foxwell stood in the center of the drawing room, wearing a silk gown in a toothache-inducing shade of orange. She raised her fan, as if in salute, then, with a flick of her wrist, snapped it shut.

"*Suivez moi, s'il vous plaît!*"

"Bloody hell—*quick march!*" Lord Francis muttered.

Lord Foxwell approached the intriguing young woman with her purple-clad chaperone, while Lady Foxwell sauntered toward Peregrine and his companion.

"Lord Francis, would you escort me to the dining room?" she asked. "I believe you're my dinner companion for tonight. Shall we lead the way?" She nodded to Peregrine. "Lord Marlow, you're partnering Lady Francis at supper."

Lord Francis grimaced, then offered his arm to the lady and let himself be marched into the dining room. With a sigh, Peregrine followed, Lady Francis clinging to his arm.

⇶❮❮❮

"Lady Edna—might I escort you and your niece to dinner?"

"Oh, Lord Foxwell, you're too kind! Is he not, *child?*"

Lavinia grimaced. Why did Aunt Edna have to behave as if they were in the schoolroom? Always picking at her headdress, telling her not to fidget, and whispering instructions on how to behave.

And now, she had to endure her aunt's company at dinner. Aunt Edna, while professing to be an expert in table manners, had the unique ability, when consuming soup, of conjuring the image of a litter of piglets drinking from a trough. Why was it was socially acceptable to *slurp* soup, but a capital offense if she dared touch the edge of the bowl with her spoon?

There was no respite from Aunt Edna. Hostesses were supposed to separate husbands and wives during dinner parties to ensure any marital altercations weren't carried through into the dining room to discompose the other guests. However, unattached young ladies must always remain tethered to their chaperones.

Lavinia glanced about the drawing room, but there was no sign of her friends—the two young ladies she'd met during Lady Stiles's tea party earlier that week, Henrietta Redford and Eleanor Howard. It seemed that neither Henrietta nor Eleanor had been invited to tonight's party. A pity—they were the only two young women Lavinia had met in London who didn't look upon her with distaste, primarily because, like Lavinia, they did not fit into Society's ideal of what a young woman ought to be.

Then her gaze settled on the gentleman who'd caught her eye when she arrived, who was now arm in arm with Lady Francis. Tall, with an athletic frame, he wore a close-fitting jacket of a dark, imperial green. An embroidered silk waistcoat was visible beneath the lapels, and a smooth silk cravat caressed his throat, pale against his tanned skin. His breeches left little to the imagination—soft cream fabric stretched across his thighs, serving to emphasize the powerful muscles that rippled faintly as he moved.

He reminded her of Samson, a stallion in his prime—the epitome of masculinity and virility.

And he knew it.

In fact, everyone in the room knew it. The atmosphere seemed to shift around him, as if the world declared its willingness to bend to his will.

Lavinia had smiled to herself at the frank admiration in their hostess's gaze. In fact, every woman he spoke to seemed transfixed, their eyes filled with a hunger to match that of Mr. Bates's pointer bitch when faced with a particularly tasty offcut from Mrs. Bates's roast beef.

But then he'd turned his gaze on Lavinia, and she was assaulted by a wave of powerful need—a flame that coursed through her body. A deep recognition filled his gaze, as if her soul was stripped bare before him, until she became his prey, a rabbit caught in a predator's gaze—trembling and vulnerable, only to be devoured moments later.

And devoured *willingly*.

Heavens!

He wasn't a man—he was a god.

Was this what Lady Betty meant when she spoke of the desires of the flesh—the intensity of pleasure that could only be achieved at the hands of a true master of seduction? Was this what a man could do to her with a single glance? If Aunt Edna was aware of the wicked sensations rippling through her, she'd have her thrashed—or exiled to a nunnery to scrub her mind of such unsavory ideas.

But as he strode across the room, Lady Francis on his arm, the turmoil of longing in Lavinia's heart morphed into a stab of envy. The lady clung to his arm, her elegant curls shifting in the candlelight, the diamond necklace glittering at her throat, then they laughed together, as if they were the best of friends.

Perhaps they were. Lady Francis—the same woman Lavinia had caught debauching herself with Heath Moss. An elegant creature, always dressed in the finest silks, who always knew the right thing to say in a social situation, and had men flocking around her like flies round a sweetmeat.

Curse her!

The party filed into the dining room, and Lavinia's envy heightened as the man pulled out a chair for Lady Francis, then took the space beside her.

During dinner, while Lavinia was stuck at one end of the table, subjected to Lord Foxwell's accounts of how many birds he'd blown out of the sky at a house party—"Much as I'm loath to speak of my prowess, Miss De Grande, the regent himself has remarked on my superior marksmanship"—Lady Francis bathed in the demigod's presence, while he tended to her with the diligence of a lover. Each time she held up her empty wineglass, he gestured to a footman for it to be filled. When she gestured toward the salt cellar, he passed it with a warm expression in his eyes. And when her napkin fluttered to the floor, he reached down for it, then placed it on her lap with a smile, seemingly oblivious to the fact that she'd dropped it on purpose.

Could the woman be any more obvious?

And could he be any more attentive?

As Lord Foxwell droned on about his shooting prowess, the servants cleared the plates, then placed tall, thin-stemmed glasses etched with a delicate pattern in front of each guest. They contained what could only be described as a pale pink snowball.

"Sorbet!" Aunt Edna cried. "*Such* a rare treat this time of year. My son's icehouse was depleted last month. What do you think, child?"

Lavinia picked up the long-handled silver spoon beside the glass, dipped it into the sorbet, and took a taste.

Ugh.

Why did everyone feel the need to smother everything in sugar? Strawberries, in particular, tasted foul when overly sweetened.

She wrinkled her nose and forced a smile.

"I've never tasted anything the like," she said. "Most...*extraordinary*."

Which—as Aunt knew full well—was how Lavinia described anything she loathed.

"Lavinia, my dear..." Aunt Edna began, but she was interrupted by a shrill voice from the opposite end of the table.

"Don't berate your niece, Lady Edna, I beseech you," a female voice said. "Given her circumstances, she's unlikely to have tasted it before."

The young woman who'd spoken leaned forward and smiled at Lavinia, her eyes glittering with cold superiority. "We must always be more...*charitable* to those among us who are unused to luxuries."

It was Lady Irma Fairchild, the Season's premier debutante.

Irma's beauty was undeniable, and her appeal on the Marriage Mart came from her title and fortune. It certainly wasn't due to her character—both Henrietta and Eleanor loathed her, and though Lavinia preferred to make up her own mind about a person rather than be persuaded by the views of others, she had yet to witness any redeeming qualities in Lady Irma Fairchild—nor, for that matter, Irma's equally loathsome friends, Lady Arabella Ponsford and Miss Juliette Howard. How Lavinia's dear friend Eleanor could have a sister such as Juliette was a mystery. Eleanor was all sweetness and humility, painfully shy, yet with a loving heart unmatched by anyone of Lavinia's acquaintance. Juliette was the exact opposite of her elder sister.

"I trust you'll enjoy the sorbet," Lady Irma continued. "You must savor every spoonful, in case the opportunity does not come your way again."

Lavinia fixed her gaze on Lady Irma, took another spoonful, then wrinkled her nose.

"I find it overly sweet," she said. "Not to my taste..." She glanced toward their hostess. "I mean no disrespect, Lady Foxwell. I'm afraid my tastes would be considered somewhat outré in a Society where most young ladies prefer to overindulge in sweetness."

"Not at all," their hostess replied. "I'll always value honesty over flattery, particularly when communicated with such civility."

"Well, I *love* the sorbet, Lady Foxwell," Irma said. "Your cook is a marvel. When I've secured a home of my own, the one element I shall not compromise on will be the quality of my cook." She glanced up and down the table, and Lavinia suppressed a smile at the uncomfortable expressions in the eyes of the single men, as if they feared that they were in danger of being singled out by Lady Irma as the man to provide her with the home of which she spoke.

"An abundance of sugar is never to be sneered at," Irma continued. "The sweeter the dessert, the better, in my opinion, even if *certain individuals* would disagree with me."

"I'm not so uncharitable as to refuse to acknowledge that there are those who benefit from an excess of sweetness in their diets, Lady Irma," Lavinia said. "Some individuals are in far greater need of sweetening than others in order to render themselves palatable."

Lady Irma's brow furrowed, and confusion clouded her expression. Aunt Edna—and one or two others who'd caught her meaning—drew in a sharp breath. But Lavinia was safe from public admonishment that would, if delivered, only advertise the insult.

Ignoring Aunt Edna's glare, Lavinia took another spoonful of the sorbet, then she heard a noise at the opposite end of the table that sounded suspiciously like a suppressed laugh, followed by a low cough. She glanced up to see a pair of clear hazel eyes trained on her.

Once again, that unfathomable sense of recognition rippled through her body. Then he lifted his hand and dragged it through the mane of thick honey-blond hair that framed his face—a firm, square jaw, cheekbones that could have been chiseled by Michelangelo himself, and lips…

Sweet Lord! Lips, full and sensual, curved into a smile of seduction. The corners of his mouth puckered as his smile broadened. Then he dipped his spoon into the sorbet and lifted it to his mouth. A moist pink tongue flicked out and curled around the tip of the spoon before he slipped it between his lips. His eyes darkened, then he closed them for a moment, his nostrils flaring. When his eyes opened, they sparkled with need. Slowly, he withdrew the spoon, his gaze fixed on her. As the tip of the spoon emerged, a bead of sorbet glistened in the corner of his mouth. He ran the tip of his tongue along his lower lip, which glistened in the candlelight. Then he licked the edge of the spoon, caressing it lovingly with his tongue, narrowing his eyes as if he fought to control the raw pleasure of such an act. A low rumble reverberated in the air, the almost primal growl of a ravenous beast enjoying his first taste of his prey, ready to devour the rest.

"Are you enjoying the sorbet, Lord Marlow?" Lady Francis's voice cut through Lavinia's fog of need.

"Oh *yes*," he replied in a deep baritone, his gaze fixed on

Lavinia.

His voice, warm and rich, resonated in Lavinia's bones, and heat swelled within her, giving rise to unfathomable, and positively *wicked*, sensations.

"I've never sampled anything more delicious, Lady Francis," he continued, maintaining his gaze on Lavinia. "Every connoisseur will tell you that we feast with our eyes first and foremost, all the more to heighten the pleasure when we come to taste, and devour, the delicious dessert presented before us."

"And how does the sorbet taste?" Lady Francis asked.

A sparkle of mischief shone in his eyes. "A little sweet for my taste," he said. "However, I'm sure there are other delights that would taste better than anticipated."

Lavinia drew in a sharp breath, then looked away. The expression in his eyes was that of a ravenous beast, and though a wicked voice whispered in her mind of the pleasurable prospect of being devoured by him, her head told her that he was her superior in the game of seduction, and would leave her tattered and broken once he'd taken his fill.

But a part of her yearned to be seduced—to be *taken*—by him.

With a combination of relief and loss, she heard Lord Foxwell declare the meal concluded, then he invited the men to join him for port and brandy. Only when the men had risen and taken their leave did she dare look up to see the object of her desires as he bowed gallantly over Lady Francis's hand, then followed the rest of the men out of the dining room. Lady Francis lifted her hand to her lips and gave a smile of triumph, and a ripple of jealousy through Lavinia threatened to expel the sickly-sweet sorbet.

He had been toying with her, enjoying her discomfort, while also, presumably, adding his name to the list of Lady Francis's conquests.

He was a rogue. All Society gentlemen were rogues. But her disappointment would fuel her resolve to continue her quest for vengeance against the unfeeling Society responsible for Papa's downfall.

Let them all think her an insignificant chit—it would make her task all the easier. For who would suspect that the Phoenix was a woman?

She would teach them a lesson—including the man who stirred her senses and ignited unwanted desires in her body with a single glance.

CHAPTER NINE

PEREGRINE USUALLY RELISHED the moment, during a dinner party, when the men separated themselves from the women. Tonight, however, was the exception.

Who was she?

Her remarks disparaging the sorbet had been refreshing in their frankness, but such an explicit declaration wasn't generally regarded as appropriate. Certainly not when coming from the lips of a young woman.

No matter how lush and delectable those lips were.

What might they taste like?

As a rule, women's lips tasted of strawberries and honey—a delicate sweetness with a promise of greater depth elsewhere. But the young woman at the opposite end of the dining table, subjected to Lord Foxwell's boasts about his prowess with a gun, could not be described as sweet. There was a determined sharpness to her demeanor, visible even to the untrained eye.

And Peregrine's eye was decidedly *not* untrained. Since entering manhood, he'd gained an understanding of women. They might say one thing, but their bodies often conveyed something else entirely. A courtesan, for example, to heighten a man's desire, might speak of her disapproval of his attempts to seduce her, while at the same time shifting her thighs to part them—not enough to be an overt offer of the goods she had to sell, but enough to heighten a man's need.

He sipped his brandy, savoring the sweet, sharp taste on his tongue, and his mind wandered to the sweet, sharp taste he might encounter elsewhere…

"Gentlemen," Lord Foxwell declared, "it's time we graced the ladies with our presence. It doesn't do to leave women to themselves for too long." He chuckled at his weak little joke, then led the company into the drawing room to join the ladies.

Peregrine caught his host's sleeve and gestured toward the purple-clad matriarch and her charge.

"I say, Foxwell, who's the formidable-looking creature in the purple? I don't believe I've seen her before."

"That's Lady Edna Yates—the dowager countess from Springfield. Have you heard of it? Charming little estate. She's here with her niece, who I hear is something of a handful. Lady Edna has a task on her hands. Miss de Grande, for all her charms, is severely lacking in propriety."

Peregrine drew in a sharp breath.

Miss…*de Grande?*

Lavinia de Grande?

He stared at the young woman, willing her to look up. Then she did, and their eyes met.

Is it you—really you? My little Guinevere?

"I say, old boy, are you all right?" Foxwell asked.

Peregrine nodded. "Yes," he said. "I wonder, would you oblige me and introduce me to—"

A hand touched his elbow. "Marlow, might I have a word?"

Frowning, Peregrine turned toward the owner of the voice.

"Lord Francis." He acknowledged the man with a nod. Then Lord Francis steered him toward an unoccupied corner of the drawing room.

Peregrine glanced back, but Miss de Grande was occupied with Lady Foxwell, her chaperone standing beside her like a watchful jailer.

Lady Francis approached, followed by a footman, bearing a tray with two coffee cups. Peregrine took one and sipped the dark, bitter liquid.

"Sugar, sir?" the footman asked.

"No thank you," Peregrine said, raising his voice. "I dislike overly sweet things."

The young woman at the far end of the room stiffened and glanced toward him. Then her chaperone nudged her elbow and she resumed her attention on Lady Foxwell.

His quarry was as aware of him as he was of her. Had she recognized him?

"I hear from Mr. Houseman that you've agreed to investigate *the crime,*" Lord Francis said as soon as the footman left.

Peregrine suppressed a snort. Francis had the tendency to overexaggerate. The emphasis on those last two words implied that a heinous offense had taken place, rather than what was more likely the simple misplacement of a trinket.

"The Phoenix?" Francis prompted.

Ah yes—my other quarry.

"Mr. Houseman said you'd agreed to investigate," Francis continued.

"I have," Peregrine replied. "What has the Phoenix relieved you of?"

"A vase—stolen from my estate in Surrey."

"Is it a family heirloom?"

"My late father acquired it at auction, I believe," Lord Francis said. "My steward found the papers in his desk."

"Which auction house?"

"I can't recall, but I doubt it's relevant."

"Everything's relevant," Peregrine said. "Not even the slightest observation should be overlooked. Theft is undertaken for a reason. Whether it be an opportunistic act undertaken out of a need, such as hunger in the destitute, or the restoration of honor, or spite against an enemy."

"You think my husband has an enemy?" Lady Francis asked.

"I cannot rule anything out," Peregrine said. "When was it stolen?"

"Last week, during a house party," Lord Francis said. "Right under my wife's nose. Isn't that right, Augusta?"

The lady inclined her head.

"Do you suspect any of the guests?"

"Good heavens, no!" Lord Francis cried. "Not even that young whippersnapper Mr. Moss would behave so badly."

Lady Francis colored and looked away. Peregrine made a mental note of her discomfort.

"Is there anything remarkable about the vase?" he asked.

Francis shook his head. "That's the thing, Marlow—it's practically worthless. The pater said he'd picked it up for next to nothing. A shilling—no, two, if I recall. Anyway, the wife took a fancy to it. I wouldn't normally bother with it, but she made quite a fuss when she discovered it was missing."

"Can you describe it?" Peregrine asked. "The color—the pattern?"

"Damned if I can remember," Lord Francis said.

Lady Francis shot her husband a look of irritation. "It's a charming little piece," she said. "A ginger jar—thirteenth century, I believe. It has a beautiful image of a dragon painted in blue on the belly—and the lid has flowers painted along the rim. I quite adore it."

Thirteenth century? That didn't sound right, if the vase had only cost a shilling or two at auction. Unless it was a fake, in which case, the Phoenix wasn't as clever as the rumormongers believed.

"For my wife's sake," Lord Francis said, "I would see the villainous Phoenix brought to justice."

A low cry made Peregrine look up, and he drew in a sharp breath.

Miss de Grande stood before him, flanked by Lady Foxwell and her chaperone.

"Lord Marlow," Lady Foxwell said, "might I introduce you to Lady Edna Yates and her niece, Miss de Grande?"

Peregrine clicked his heels together and bowed. "Lady Edna."

The matriarch offered her hand, and Peregrine took it. Bony

fingers enclosed his in a tight grip as he bowed over her hand. Then she released him and fixed her yellowing eyes on him.

The young woman beside her seemed to have paled, and the earlier defiance in her eyes was gone, replaced by vulnerability. Then she glanced toward Lord Francis.

Something about the man discomposed her. Though what, Peregrine couldn't fathom. The man was as dull as a bucket of wet earth. Rumor had it that on his wedding night, Lady Francis had to show him *what went where*—and after having performed his duty of siring an heir and a spare, he devoted his time to polishing his shotguns and re-enacting the Battle of Trafalgar with his collection of toy ships. He was, among the predatory males of Society, the very last man who could ever be considered a threat to a woman's virtue or person. So what did Miss de Grande have to fear from the man?

"Miss de Grande—Lord and Lady Francis you know, of course," Lady Foxwell said. She gestured toward Peregrine. "This is Lord Peregrine Marlow."

Miss de Grande paused, then she dipped into a curtsey. Peregrine offered his hand, and she stared at it.

"Lavinia…" the matriarch said.

She took his hand and stiffened. A crackle of need ignited where their palms touched, and Peregrine's breath hitched. He glanced at her neckline, and a pulse of fire throbbed in his groin as he spotted two little peaks straining against the smooth silk of her gown. Her chest rose and fell as her breathing quickened. She parted her lips, and her eyes widened.

Sweet Lord, she was aroused! And there was nothing more delectable than an innocent experiencing the first flush of arousal. Her body might know what was happening, but her mind had yet to be opened to pleasure. A courtesan, practiced in the art of seduction, knew how to use her body to invite a man to claim her. But even the most skilled courtesan paled into insignificance next to a young woman whose body responded, by instinct, to the pure, primal need that lay deep within every creature.

The need to be thoroughly pleasured.

CHAPTER TEN

S WEET HEAVEN—WHAT WAS happening to her?

One moment, Lavinia had been listening to unintelligible talk about how the width of the ribbon in a young woman's hair indicated her superiority of taste, then she'd found herself steered by Aunt Edna and Lady Foxwell across the drawing room, toward the very man who'd addled her senses at the dining table.

But she composed herself, recalling Aunt Edna's instructions.

Stature, Lavinia, dear. Stature. Glide across the room as if you were a swan—silent and poised. In a woman, silence is always to be applauded.

If only Aunt knew! Lavinia had already perfected the art of creeping about in silence—or, at least, the Phoenix had.

Then a male voice spoke, and her gut twisted in horror.

"I would see the villainous Phoenix brought to justice."

Lord Francis stood beside the demigod. Both men bowed as she approached them. After introducing Aunt Edna, Lady Foxwell gestured toward Lavinia.

"Miss de Grande—Lord and Lady Francis you know, of course. This is Lord Peregrine Marlow."

The demigod offered his hand, and Lavinia's breath caught in her throat. Her body willed her to take the hand, but her mind was in a turmoil.

Aunt Edna gave her a sharp nudge.

Lavinia reached forward, and her stomach somersaulted as

long, lean fingers encased her hand in a powerful grip.

"L-Lord Marlow," she whispered. "A…a pleasure."

"The pleasure is all mine, I assure you."

At first glance, he had been handsome. But at close quarters, he was nothing short of breathtaking. His eyes, laden with promise, were a warm, rich brown, with shades of green and gold that shimmered in the candlelight, offering the promise of wicked pleasure.

Stop it, you fool!

She withdrew her hand, and for a moment, hurt flickered in his eyes. Then she shook her head.

She must have imagined it. He was an expert seducer—a man capable of using her innermost desires to tempt her into sin.

But how exquisite the sinning would be!

Lady Francis broke the spell. "Lady Edna, what a pleasure to see you again!" She wrinkled her nose at Lavinia. "And your charming niece, of course, who regaled us all with her eccentricities last month."

"Lady Francis, a pleasure, as always," Aunt Edna replied.

"Are you being treated to a London Season, my dear?" Lady Francis asked Lavinia with a slight sneer on her lips. "Your cousin Earl Yates is a most generous man, is he not? How fortunate it must be to have charitable relatives."

"Thank you, Lady Francis," Lavinia said. "You're as generous as Lady Irma Fairchild in your compliments. I find myself disposed to like you just as much as I like her."

She heard a suppressed snort. The demigod lifted his hand to his mouth, then cleared his throat. "Forgive me, ladies," he said. "This coffee is overly sweet for my taste."

His eyes sparkled as he glanced toward Lavinia, and she found herself smiling in return.

Heavens—what kind of a man was he? His wicked sense of humor was enough to befuddle her, let alone what his very maleness was doing to her body.

"Miss de Grande," he said. "You have not yet been furnished

with coffee. Might I pour you a cup? I assure you it's palatable if taken without sugar." He offered his arm, and, acting on instinct, she took it. Then he steered her toward the table where a footman stood to attention beside a large silver coffee pot and a tray of sweetmeats, fashioned into the shape of flowers, in colors that could only be described as *eye-watering*.

"Marzipan." He plucked a piece from the pile and popped it into his mouth. "A little on the sweet side, but you can, at least, taste the almonds—unlike that sorbet, where I'm afraid the poor strawberry had succumbed to the assault of the sugar well before it had reached the table."

He gestured toward the tray. "Permit me to select one for you. You can be assured that it's safe, now I've survived."

Lavinia couldn't help smiling. "You took the risk, on my behalf, that it would poison you?"

"If you like."

"What if it had been disgusting?" she asked. "Would you have swallowed it to maintain the appearance of civility, or spat it out?"

"What would you have me do?"

"Aunt Edna says that if a lady inadvertently eats something unpalatable, she must swallow it to maintain her poise," she replied. "In extreme circumstances, she may expel the offending item into her handkerchief, provided the rest of the company believes her to be merely dabbing her mouth, or suppressing a cough."

"Does it work?"

"Most of the time." She grinned at the memory. "Though when Aunt discovered an abundance of salt in her custard last night, she almost failed in her endeavors."

He let out a laugh. "Miss de Grande, you are quite the misfit."

His words stung, and she moved away from him and crossed the floor to the tall, glass-paneled doors that led out onto a balcony overlooking a vast, manicured garden. On seeing the balcony unoccupied, she slipped through the doors and drew her shawl around her against the evening air.

She heard footsteps and the rattle of crockery.

"You forgot your coffee, Miss de Grande."

Lord Marlow stood in the doorway, coffee cup in hand. He held it out.

"Will you accept a peace offering?" he asked. "I spoke out of turn, and for that, I apologize."

His voice carried a note of sincerity, and his eyes betrayed no subterfuge. She took the cup and lifted it to her nose. The aroma of coffee caressed her senses. Deep, rich, and exotic, it was something that Papa could no longer afford. Lavinia recollected the aroma from her childhood, but she'd never been permitted to taste it.

"Perhaps you'll forgive the incivilities of an old friend," he added.

"What do you mean, an old friend? I haven't met you before tonight."

"Don't you recognize me?"

"If this is an attempt at flattery, it won't work on *me*, sir," she said.

Once again, she caught a flicker of hurt in his eyes. Then he shook his head. "Perhaps it was too much to expect you to remember after so long," he said, "but I have never forgotten my little friend—my little Guinevere."

Guinevere...

Her heart skittered in her chest, and the cup slipped from her grasp. He darted forward, grasped the cup, and took her hand. She drew in a sharp breath as the fizz of desire rippled through her body at his touch.

Then she looked up and met his gaze.

Those eyes...

"No—it can't be," she said. "You *can't* be my Arthur..."

"Would you pierce my heart and tell me that you don't re-member the knight who swore to protect you until he drew his last breath?"

"Of course I remember!" she cried. "But are you *really* he?"

He squeezed her hand, then held it against his breast. "Don't be sad, little Guinevere," he said. "I swear to protect you from dragons and brigands, on my honor, according to the codes of chivalry."

Her heart fluttered as he spoke the same promise that her King Arthur had uttered long ago.

Perhaps that was why her body had reacted when she saw him tonight, because it recognized whom she had been longing for in her dreams.

"It's been fourteen years," she said. "How did you recognize me?"

His eyes crinkled into a smile. "Did I not say I'd always watch over you?"

But he hadn't, in the end. He'd abandoned her and Papa, just like everyone else, save Lady Betty.

She turned her head away. What had Lady Betty said about placing a man on a pedestal?

No man deserves to be worshipped as if he were a god, darling Lavinia. For, when faced with the ultimate test of their mettle, they invariably fail. The demands of Society—the attractions afforded by their rank and fortune—will render them far too selfish to be worthy of our adoration.

Lady Betty was right. Men were weak souls who preyed upon each other like scavengers fighting over a carcass.

Papa's ruination had opened Lavinia's eyes to the ways of the world. And it had shown her who her true friends were—not the sycophants who would have liked her merely for her dowry and social position, but the rare individuals, like Lady Betty and her new friends Henrietta and Eleanor, who truly cared.

But Arthur—*her* Arthur—the boy she'd idolized, stood before her, now, as potent a man as ever there could be. Yet even he had proven to be a disappointment.

In the end, hope always surpassed reality.

Lavinia blinked, and tears clouded her vision. She moved

toward the terrace doors. But a hand caught her sleeve.

"Miss de Grande—little Guinevere—have I said aught to distress you?"

"You never came to see us after we left Fosterley Park," she said. "You abandoned me, just as Papa's friends abandoned him."

He shook his head. "Is that what you think? I had no idea where you'd gone after Lord de Grande's ruination. My father said—"

"There's no need to tell me what he said," she replied. "I know the contempt with which a ruined man is viewed by his former friends. I shall loathe every one of those former friends for all eternity, and I would have my vengeance if I could."

He recoiled at the hatred in her voice.

"Forgive me." She sighed. "Sometimes I feel so—*angry*—at the world."

"Many men suffer ruination," he said, gesturing toward the terrace doors. "I'll wager most of the guests here tonight faced ruination at some point. Men of the aristocracy are notorious for having a lack of understanding of the need to balance one's finances. I happen to know that it's only by virtue of having an excellent steward that Lord Francis remains solvent. Lady Francis likes to entertain a little too often, to maintain the appearance of status."

"You're acquainted with Lord Francis?" she asked, keeping her voice as smooth as she could.

"My father and his attended Harrow together."

"Aunt and I attended a dinner at his house a month ago," she said, "but I didn't see you there."

He laughed softly. "Lord Francis is at liberty to invite whom he wishes. A man isn't obliged to invite all of his acquaintances to every social function he holds, or he'd grow heartily sick of them, would he not? The benefit of acquaintances, as opposed to family, is that you can keep them at a healthy distance. With family, we have no choice in the matter, and are burdened no matter what."

"I would not be without my father for anything in the world,"

Lavinia replied. "I'd *never* think him a burden."

He bowed his head. "Forgive me, I meant no offense. Your father—is he well? I'm ashamed to say that I recall very little of him. Then, when you moved away..." He colored and looked away, then, after a pause, resumed his attention on her. "Is he in London?"

She shook her head. "He remains in the country. Springfield, if you know it?"

"In Sussex, if I recall," he said. "Less than a day's ride from London, so it would be no trouble for your father to travel. I hope to see him in London soon."

"He's not in good health," she said. "I'm afraid traveling is out of the question."

"I'm sorry to hear that," he replied. "But a visit to London might be beneficial. There are many excellent physicians on Harley Street. Or he might consider a vacation on the Continent? My own father resides in Italy, and the warmer weather does wonders for his—"

"It's quite impossible," she interrupted. Was the man a fool?

"I fail to see why—"

"My father was *ruined*," she said. "He does not have the means to afford a London physician, or a vacation in Italy."

Curse him! Curse the lot of them!

Lady Francis's spiteful words came back to taunt her. Was she nothing but a charity case, here by the grace of Cousin Charles and his benevolence?

To his credit, Lord Marlow looked ashamed.

"I meant no offense," he said. "I recall so little of Lord de Grande, and I'm not in a position to give an informed opinion on his circumstances."

"His *circumstances*, as you call them, are that he was betrayed by those he called friends, by men he had the misfortune to trust, and I wish nothing but misfortune on *them*."

"May I ask who has inspired such hatred?" he asked.

Hatred...

An ugly word—filled with evil. Did she hate them, the faceless men who had ruined her life? Perhaps not for her sake, but for Papa's. His ill health had been brought about by their machinations. The once virile man on whom she'd been able to lean had been reduced to a shell.

"No," she sighed. "I don't hate them—except, perhaps, for one. The man Papa holds primarily responsible for all his misfortunes."

"Who is that?"

"It would serve no purpose if I were to tell you his name."

He squeezed her hand, and she closed her eyes, fighting the deep-seated need that had lain dormant in her soul—the need to have a friend to trust. But she had to remember that Papa had once trusted a friend—and that friend had brought about his destruction.

"You *can* trust me, you know, Miss de Grande," he said.

"How can I?" she asked. "We might have been…acquainted when we were children. But we're strangers now. Perhaps we were strangers even then, for I never knew your real name."

He caressed the back of her hand with his thumb, and she drew in a sharp breath as her skin tightened in response.

"Then let me introduce myself properly," he said.

"I am aware of your name now, Lord Marlow."

"Peregrine," he said, pulling her close. "My name is Peregrine."

"Like the falcon?"

His lips curled into a soft smile—a smile that reached his eyes, which gleamed with warmth and friendship.

"Aye, that's right," he said. "Don't you recall that I once told you how King Arthur gave his Guinevere a falcon as a gift, Miss de Grande?"

"Lavinia," she said. "My name is Lavinia."

He lifted her hand and brushed his lips against her skin, and a warm shiver rippled through her at the thrill of his touch.

What might it be like to feel those lips on hers?

"I'm delighted to make your acquaintance, Lavinia."

His tongue curled around her name, as if he savored each syllable.

How could a man render her powerless at the mere mention of her name? Or was it the heady combination of his warm, rich voice resonating in her body and the aroma of masculine spices?

Sweet heaven—she had dreamed of the boy, but the man was far more potent—a virile beast capable of devouring her.

And a part of her wanted to be devoured.

He released her hand, and she shivered at the sense of loss. "Perhaps we should begin our relationship anew," he said. "Then I can prove to you that I'm as chivalrous as you believed me to be when we were children. If your father's ruination was at the hands of others, perhaps I might be able to bring them to justice."

"How so?" she asked.

"I consider myself something of an investigator," he said. "I studied art history and classics at Cambridge, and I now spend much of my time investigating the authenticity of antiquities."

"While languishing at your country estate?"

He let out a soft laugh. "We're not all wastrels, Miss de Grande. A solid education does wonders for a man. Without it, he cannot rise above the savage, or help the world."

Lavinia swallowed the flare of envy. How she'd longed to be given an education! Not Aunt Edna's tutelage in the correct way to hold a teacup, but a proper education that challenged and expanded the mind. But, by virtue of Papa's ruination—and of Lavinia's sex—it had been denied her.

"How does an understanding of the authenticity of antiquities help the world?" she asked.

"You doubt me, Miss de Grande?" He smiled, and her heart somersaulted in her chest. "A clear understanding of antiquities can assist greatly when investigating a crime—such as theft."

Her stomach tightened. "Theft?"

He nodded. "A recent spate of thefts among Society has been brought to my attention. My understanding of the pieces that have been reported stolen, and the link between them, will assist in bringing the criminal to justice."

"The…*criminal?*"

His expression hardened. "Would you defend a thief, Miss de Grande?"

"O-of course not," she said, "but what makes you think there's a link between the thefts? People steal for all manner of reasons—perhaps because they're hungry and need money for food, or coal. It happens all the time on London's streets."

"Perhaps," he said, "but a theft of a particular item from a country mansion, or a London townhouse, is not an opportunistic crime perpetrated by a hungry beggar. Rather, it's a deliberate act to suit a particular purpose."

"Which is?"

He shrugged. "I've yet to ascertain that. But I'm by no means discouraged. A pattern will emerge eventually—it's merely a matter of time. I have a feeling that the case I'm investigating now is of a very personal matter."

"In what way?"

"You seem to have a particular interest in the thief, Miss de Grande."

Her heart fluttered at the intensity of his gaze.

Damn—she'd shown too much interest. Why couldn't she behave like an empty-headed debutante and restrict her conversation to ribbons and lace? He was not a man to be fooled with—his expression spoke of a keen mind and a sharp wit.

"Miss de Grande!"

Lavinia jumped at the shrill female voice.

"What are you doing outside in the cold?" Lady Francis stood in the doorway, next to her husband. "Has your aunt not told you that wandering about creates a most undesirable impression? I wouldn't want you to ruin… Oh!" She let out a cry. "I didn't see you there, Lord Marlow. I do hope Miss de Grande isn't plaguing you too much."

"Lady Francis, do you impugn Miss de Grande's honor—or

mine?" he asked.

"O-of course not, Lord Marlow. I know *you'd* never behave in an untoward manner."

"Quite so." He gestured toward the cup in Lavinia's hand. "Miss de Grande fancied taking the air, and I brought her a cup of coffee."

"So I see."

"And the terrace doors have been open all the time, with Miss de Grande's chaperone within earshot," he continued.

"My wife meant no offense," Lord Francis said. "Did you, my dear? You often venture onto the terrace during a ball, do you not? You're always complaining of overheating. I recall Lady Hardstone's ball, when Mr. Moss escorted you outside."

Lady Francis blushed. "Yes, yes!" she cried, irritation in her voice. "We're not here to make idle chatter." She turned to Marlow. "My dear Lord Marlow, do say you've agreed to help me."

"Help you?"

"In finding that brigand, of course!" she cried. "The falcon—is that it?"

"The *Phoenix*," Lord Francis said. "Damn the man!"

"The—Phoenix?" Lavinia couldn't help asking, though her stomach twisted into knots.

"Lord Marlow is *so* clever, Miss de Grande," Lady Francis said. "I daresay he'll have ensnared the criminal before the month is out."

"I look forward to seeing him behind bars," Lord Francis added. "It's a pity theft isn't a hanging offense."

Cold fingers brushed against the back of Lavinia's neck. "Surely you wouldn't want a man to hang for stealing a vase?" Three pair of eyes focused on her, and she cursed herself. "L-Lord Marlow said something about a vase having been taken. Did you not, Lord Marlow?"

"Lord Marlow is a veritable wonder," Lady Francis said. "He was instrumental in solving the theft of Lady Wadchester's tea set two years ago. It had foxed the authorities, but Lord Marlow hunted it down—where did you find it, again?"

"An establishment in Lombard Street, Lady Francis."

"Quite so. Poor Lady Wadchester was most put out—it had been a gift from her godmother on her wedding day. It's a hideous thing, of course, but the tray alone is worth a fortune, and she must value it for that."

"I'd have thought she'd value it more because it was a gift from someone she loves," Lavinia said.

Lady Francis let out a snort. "What sentimental nonsense! But one can hardly expect *you* to understand. Perhaps, in time— and assuming your cousin's charity enables you to remain in Society for a little longer—you'll learn to understand what must be valued and what is beneath our attention."

She approached Lord Marlow and slipped her arm through his. "Meanwhile, my husband and I wish to discuss the matter with Lord Marlow in private—if you'd be so kind, Miss de Grande?"

"With pleasure, your ladyship," Lavinia said. "It's grown overly cold, and I swear I can smell a frost in the air." She dipped into a curtsey, then crossed the terrace and slipped back inside the ballroom.

When she reached the solitary footman guarding the punch bowl, she waved at him, and he filled a glass and handed it to her. She drained it in a single gulp.

You should never meet your heroes, Lavinia darling.

Lady Betty had spoken the truth. The boy Lavinia had idolized was a figment of her imagination, an ideal formed in her dreams. The reality was something completely different. He was a man—a virile man who had the power to consume her, not save her.

He was a hunter—the man who pledged to bring the Phoenix to justice, no matter how long it took.

And, though he didn't know it, she was his prey.

CHAPTER ELEVEN

WHY DID LADY Francis have to be so shrewish, venting her spite on those she deemed beneath her? Was she so insecure about herself that she needed to tear down others? Perhaps that was why she was rumored to have multiple affairs—in order to make herself feel desirable. But a woman who spread her legs for multiple men would never be anything but a harlot, no matter that she had a title.

By the time Peregrine had shaken off the undesirable couple, Miss de Grande had returned to her chaperone and was deep in conversation with their host. Her skin, which had bloomed a delicate shade of rose when he'd called her his little Guinevere, was now flushed a darker shade of red—a similar shade to that of Lord Foxwell when he'd taken a little too much brandy.

As he watched her, she lifted a glass to her lips and drained the contents. Then, excusing herself, she made her way around the perimeter of the room toward the punch bowl and waved her glass at the footman, who nodded and filled it.

To give her credit, she made a good effort at disguising her inebriation—head upright, body straight, smooth, even footsteps. But the glimmer in her eyes and the flush on her cheeks, which extended to the tips of her ears, told him all he needed to know.

She was well on her way to becoming drunk.

What the devil was she doing? The slightest transgression and her reputation would be in tatters.

He made his way toward the coffee and, dismissing the foot-man's offer of help, poured a cup and dropped four lumps of sugar into the brown liquid. Then he approached his quarry.

"Miss de Grande," he said. "I believe you're in need of this." Before she could protest, he plucked the glass out of her hand and held out the coffee cup.

She opened her mouth to protest.

"I'll take no refusal, Miss de Grande."

Her eyes widened at the anger in his voice. Then, her hand trembling, she took the cup.

"Drink."

She took a sip. "It's too sweet," she said. "I prefer—"

"It was not a request," he said. "How many glasses of punch have you had?"

She glanced toward the punch bowl.

"Look at me when you respond," he said.

"Why?"

"Because I find a perpetrator is more likely to respond honest-ly when forced to look his inquisitor in the eye."

"I…" She shook her head, then blinked, and moisture glim-mered in her eyes. "I shouldn't have come tonight," she said. "I told Aunt I didn't want to. I feel sick."

"I'm not surprised," he said. "You are aware what an overin-dulgence of liquor does to a woman?"

She shook her head.

"Drink the coffee," he said. "The sugar in it will settle your stomach. And it might revive you enough to disguise your condition to your aunt."

"My condition?"

"You're drunk, Miss de Grande," he said, "which is most unseemly for a young lady."

"Then you and Lady Francis can revel in your superiority," she retorted, bitterness in her tone.

"Pay no attention to Lady Francis," he said. "She's hardly the sort of woman you'd want as a friend."

"I can't see *anyone* here I'd want as a friend."

"Not anyone?"

She shook her head. "They're all pompous asses."

"What about your King Arthur?" he asked softly.

"He was a dream," she said. "He's no more. I am friendless—as is my father."

Her distress was so tangible, he could almost taste it. He steadied her hand and guided the coffee cup to her lips, and she swallowed a mouthful.

"Better?"

She nodded. "I don't know what came over me."

"I do," he said. "Lady Foxwell's punch. It's notorious—there's at least three bottles of brandy in every bowl." He paused. "I meant what I said about having a friend. I may not be the boy you remember, but you can trust me."

"So you'll help me find my enemy?"

"If it's in my power," he replied. "Who is it?"

She drew in a deep breath and sighed. Then her eyes darkened with hatred.

"Earl Walton."

His gut twisted at the name.

Father...

"Do you know him?" she asked.

"I-I've not seen him for some years," he said.

At least that was true—Father hadn't set foot in England for years, and Peregrine had no inclination to visit the old bastard.

"Do you know where I can find him?"

"Not in England, I can assure you," he replied.

"A pity," she said. "I'd like to put a bullet through his heart."

He recoiled at the loathing in her voice. "You hate him that much?"

"I do!" she said through gritted teeth. "Earl Walton set about ruining us after Mama died, by preying on Papa's grief. If that's not the definition of evil, then I don't know what is."

"Your father *told* you this?"

A tear splashed on her cheek, and she wiped it away angrily. "I overheard him talking to Lady Betty—the one friend who stood by us. From that day, I swore vengeance."

He took her hand. "Take care, little Guinevere—vengeance often causes greater harm to the perpetrator."

"I have to do *something*."

"Perhaps," he said, "but I'd counsel you to desist from speaking of Earl Walton—or even thinking of him. I can see it gives you pain, and I would not have you in pain."

"You wouldn't?" Vulnerability shone in her eyes. He longed to take her in his arms, but in a drawing room full of guests, it would compromise her as surely if he'd been caught rutting her on the terrace. The liquor had lowered her defenses, and he was not a man to take advantage of a woman who'd drunk herself out of her wits.

"If I may be so bold, may I suggest something else?" he asked.

"Of course."

"Avoid the punch bowl at parties. One never knows how much liquor has been poured into it until it's too late."

"Is that why the world tipped onto its side earlier?" she asked. A spark of mischief twinkled in her eyes, and he let out a laugh.

"That's more like it!" he cried. "Do you promise to follow my advice?"

"Your advice on *what*, Lord Marlow?" a sharp voice said.

Lady Yates stood before them. Miss de Grande stiffened, and her smile disappeared.

"I was advising your niece on the need to take sugar in her coffee after a rich meal," he said. "Lady Foxwell's sorbet was a little overwhelming, and your charming niece was just telling me that she'd felt obliged to clear her plate for fear of insulting our hostess."

"Is that true, Lavinia?"

"Your niece is too polite to be frank with you," he said. The dowager stared at him, disbelief in her expression, but she made no protest.

"Perhaps it's time you took your niece home, Lady Yates?" he suggested.

The dowager glanced at Miss de Grande. "Lavinia?"

Miss de Grande gave her a watery smile. "Would you mind, Aunt?"

"Of course not," came the reply. "I was going to suggest it myself."

Peregrine waved over a footman. "Would you have Lady Yates's carriage brought round?"

"Very good, sir."

Their host and hostess approached, making a fuss of Miss de Grande and bidding Lady Yates farewell. As they left the drawing room, Miss de Grande turned, met Peregrine's gaze, and mouthed a silent address.

Thank you.

But she had little to thank him for. He had deceived her. In promising to investigate her father's ruination, his motive had been to prevent her from discovering that his own father was the object of her hatred.

She must never discover whose son he was—for if she did, her bitter hatred would be directed at him.

CHAPTER TWELVE

As Lavinia stepped into the breakfast room, a sharp voice sliced through the morning air, and her temples throbbed with pain.

"*There* you are, child! I was wondering if you were ever going to favor me with your presence."

Lavinia's stomach churned at the odor of fried bacon, and she slipped into her seat, nodding thanks to the footman in attendance.

"A little bacon for my niece, Wilkins," Aunt Edna said. "And perhaps some tea, with a splash of milk."

Before Lavinia could respond, a plate of bacon, together with a cup of tea, was placed in front of her. At home she could eat what she liked, and take her tea how she preferred—but under her aunt's watchful eye, she found her meals restricted, both in size and variety. Proper young ladies, according to Aunt Edna, demonstrated self-restraint by eating as little as possible, to maintain the appropriate silhouette. And on no account should she serve herself. According to her aunt, it simply wasn't done among the older families. A buffet was an outré concept favored by the *nouveaux riches*.

Lavinia stared at her bacon—thick pink strips interspersed with gelatinous white streaks. She picked up her fork and pushed a rasher across the plate. The strips of fat wobbled, and she set her fork down, swallowing the tide of nausea.

"Child, it's not seemly to play with your food."

"I'm not hungry, Aunt," Lavinia said, "and I have a head-ache."

Aunt Edna let out an unsympathetic snort. "I'm not surprised. Lady Francis said you took far too much punch last night. Haven't I said that…"

She rattled on, reciting a catalogue of Lavinia's faults. While Lavinia longed to protest against a world that required women to adhere to preposterous rules, it would be a futile exercise where her aunt was concerned. Better to remain silent, give the impression of meekness, and let Aunt *have her say*. No matter what, she would always *have her say*. Then, with luck, she'd leave Lavinia alone.

"Is that not a good idea?"

Lavinia glanced up.

Oh no…

What had Aunt Edna said? If Lavinia nodded, she'd avoid admonishment for disagreeing, but she might end up committing herself to something hideous, such as another lesson in deport-ment or yet another bloody alphabet sampler. She shifted in her seat, her thigh aching from when she'd collided with the banister while negotiating the staircase en route to her bedchamber last night.

She opted for a more neutral response.

"I suppose so, Aunt."

"Good—I suggest you practice your instrument for the re-mainder of the morning, then I'll send Tilly to help you dress."

"I'm already dressed, Aunt."

"Lord spare me!" Aunt Edna cried. "It's as if you refuse to listen to a single word I say. I'll not have Mrs. Howard look down on us.

"Mrs. Howard?"

"Tiresome child! I've already told you, we're taking tea with her later today, and I'll not have you looking like a guttersnipe. Though Mrs. Howard's the daughter of a viscount, her husband's in trade; therefore, we must assert our superiority of rank, which means wearing a gown worthy of your station—not *that*"—she gestured to Lavinia's gown—"which has seen better days."

"Very good, Aunt," Lavinia replied. "May I be excused now? I'm eager to practice."

Aunt Edna's eyes narrowed with suspicion, but though Lavinia loathed the necessity of practicing an instrument merely to satisfy Society's rules, it was preferable to spending the rest of the morning in her aunt's company. Though she heartily disliked Mrs. Howard, the woman had one redeeming quality.

Her eldest daughter Eleanor—one of the sweetest young women in London.

Lavinia rose and approached her aunt, who turned her face to one side in expectation. She kissed her aunt's cheek.

"Very good, you may go," Aunt Edna said. "But I'll be listening, to make sure you practice *properly*. I was most disappointed that you were unable to play at Lady Francis's dinner last month."

"I doubt Lady Francis cared," Lavinia retorted.

"That's not the attitude, child!" Aunt Edna cried. "Lady Francis's friendship is much to be desired. And we must think kindly toward her. The poor woman is most distraught about the theft of her vase."

"The—theft?" Lavinia's skin tightened in apprehension. The last thing she wanted was her aunt showing an interest in the stolen ginger jar, not when it resided in Papa's chamber at Springfield Cottage.

"The culprit will be rooted out soon enough," Aunt Edna said. "Lord Marlow's been assigned the task. I hear he's to interview all the guests who attended the house party during which the vase disappeared. Lady Francis told me that if that yielded no success, he might have to interview every guest she's invited in the past month—which includes us." She let out a snort. "A waste of time, if you ask me. Doubtless a servant stole it—you know what *they're* like."

Aunt Edna rattled on, opining on the lower classes, and Lavinia exited the breakfast room.

A secret thrill coursed through her at the prospect of Lord Marlow visiting. But it was tempered by fear—would she be able to withstand his questioning?

All because of that meddlesome woman, Lady Francis— who'd so pointedly looked down on her.

As if *she* were a paragon of virtue!

Ride me like an Arabian stallion...

Wasn't that what she'd cried out while the lecherous Mr. Moss rutted her from behind? Perhaps if her infidelity were discovered, she'd be shown up for the hypocrite she was.

Lavinia entered the study, but instead of sitting at the pianoforte, she approached the writing desk.

It was time for Lady Francis to receive a little private correspondence.

Sitting at the desk, Lavinia pulled out a piece of paper, dipped a quill into the inkpot, and began to write.

My dear Lady Francis,

While it is not my wont to impugn a lady's honor, I find I must write to express my admiration for the extraordinary level of stamina you displayed not a fortnight ago at your country seat. Your turn of phrase was particularly enlightening.

"Ride me like an Arabian stallion, Mr. Moss!" Such an instruction to a lover is to be remembered. And, while the cuckolded husband was blissful in his ignorance, you must agree that ignorance in a gentleman is not to be borne. I understand your ladyship is most distressed at the loss of a particular item of porcelain. But, perhaps, if you indulge in a little nighttime sport, it's no wonder that items of a fragile nature are at risk of being broken.

A ginger jar from the thirteenth century, procured by your husband's late father, is just such an item. As is a lady's reputation. Were it to become known that Mr. Moss indulges in nighttime equestrian activities, not to mention the identity of the mare he mounts, the readership of the London Daily *would be furnished with a subject of gossip for the season.*

If, however, Lord Francis were to be made aware of the mishap that occurred when his wife accidentally smashed the vase, and how deeply she regrets her attempts to persuade him that she was a victim of the infamous Phoenix, then the readers of the London Daily *need never know what it was like to observe a lady being ridden by an Arabian stallion.*

I remain your most humble servant.

Yours,
P

Lavinia finished with a sketch of a bird rising from the flames. Then she folded the note and tucked it into her reticule.

Just in time. The tap-tapping of her aunt's cane echoed in the corridor outside. She slipped across to the piano stool and ran her fingers up and down the keyboard, playing a few scales. A shadow appeared at the foot of the door, and Lavinia opened the music book and began to play a Bach canon—the one piece she'd been able to master. Shortly after, the shadow moved and her aunt's footsteps faded into the distance.

Neither Aunt Edna nor Lady Francis—nor, for that matter, Lord Marlow—would get the better of *her*.

CHAPTER THIRTEEN

"LADY SPRINGFIELD AND Miss de Grande!"

The footman announced Lavinia and her aunt as if they were being presented at court.

Sitting on a chaise longue in a room furnished in shades of blue and gold was a tall, thin woman dressed in a gown of dark blue silk, her hair piled atop her head in a mass of curls. Next to her sat a young woman in a plain gown of white muslin, her hair fashioned into a pale shadow of her mother's elegant style. Her curls seemed to have already come undone, with loose tendrils either side of her face, almost completely concealing her eyes.

The younger woman would, by Society's standards, only ever be described as *unremarkable* in appearance. But, to Lavinia, Eleanor Howard was intelligent, charming, and the most interesting creature in the whole of London. Appearance often belied the truth—and no more so than in the Howard family. Eleanor's younger sister, Juliette, had all the appearance of an angel, and her beauty was lauded among Society. Yet she had the temper of a viper.

Mrs. Howard rose. Then she frowned at her daughter. "Show some manners, child!"

Eleanor stood, her cheeks flaming.

"Mrs. Howard, how kind of you to invite us to tea!" Aunt Edna cried. Then she glanced at Eleanor. "And Miss Howard, of course. But where is dear Juliette?"

"My youngest is dining at Lord Fairchild's tonight, as Lady Irma's friend," Mrs. Howard replied. "Lady Arabella Ponsford has also been invited—such a *charming* girl! I'm excessively proud of dear Juliette."

Eleanor flinched, but Mrs. Howard, seeming not to notice, continued. "Of course, *we've* been invited to Lady Houghton's ball next week. Eleanor is delighted, are you not, Eleanor?"

Eleanor mumbled a reply, looking anything but delighted.

"We've been invited also," Aunt Edna said, taking a seat. "Lady Irma would make a fine friend for my niece, considering they're of a similar rank."

Lady Howard's smile slipped at the oblique reference to her inferior status.

"Have I not said so, Lavinia?" Aunt Edna continued. "That Lady Irma would make a suitable friend?"

"I'm content with the friends I have," Lavinia said. She crossed the floor and sat next to Eleanor.

"A young lady will not further herself by merely being *content*," Mrs. Howard said. "Is that not so, Eleanor?"

"Yes, Mother," Eleanor replied, her voice devoid of emotion.

"I'm sure Miss de Grande would agree also," Mrs. Howard continued. Eleanor's blush deepened.

"Opportunities for betterment are certainly not to be sneered at," Lavinia said. "The broadening of one's intellect, through education and experience, for instance, is always to be admired. However, when it comes to the choice of a friend, I believe in constancy. Good friends are few and far between, and I am fortunate to have secured a friendship in London that I intend to maintain and nurture."

"With whom?" Aunt Edna asked.

"With Miss Howard, of course," Lavinia said, smiling at her friend. Eleanor lifted her head and met Lavinia's gaze. Two clear green eyes regarded her with fondness and gratitude.

"It is to be hoped," Mrs. Howard said, "that an association with you, Miss de Grande, will enable Eleanor to advance herself in Society, even if I cannot expect her to reach the heights to which my Juliette aspires."

Aunt Edna frowned. To her credit, though she valued her position in Society a little too much, Lavinia's aunt also valued common courtesy and kindness.

The door opened, and a maid appeared with a tea tray and set it on a side table.

"Eleanor, serve the tea," Mrs. Howard ordered her daughter. "Lady Yates first, of course."

"Yes, Mother." Eleanor leaped to her feet, as if she'd been whipped, then approached the table and poured a cup. Her hand shook and some of the brown liquid splashed onto the saucer. Aunt Edna, usually a stickler for tidiness, merely smiled.

"Thank you, my dear."

Eleanor gave a quick, tight smile, then continued to pour the tea, spooning sugar into her mother's cup before handing it to her.

"Did *you* want sugar, Lady Yates?" Mrs. Howard asked. "I'm afraid Eleanor forgot to offer—"

"Your daughter has done well to recall that I take no sugar in my tea," Aunt Edna interrupted. "An overindulgence in sugar is not to be encouraged—not at my age, at least."

Eleanor resumed her seat and focused her attention on her cup.

Mrs. Howard rattled on about Juliette's accomplishments, and how Lady Irma Fairchild was to be admired, but Lady Arabella Ponsford, despite having lost her parents, was not to be pitied, for she had inherited a sizeable fortune that she would come into upon reaching her majority.

Poor Eleanor remained silent throughout the conversation, responding only when instructed to lend agreement to everything her mother said.

Aunt Edna might be a stickler for propriety, but at least she lacked Mrs. Howard's cold ambition. She, in her own way, loved Lavinia, and tutored her out of a genuine belief that an elevated position in Society, together with a good marriage, would make her happy. Mrs. Howard seemed incapable of love—at least toward Eleanor.

"Eleanor!" Mrs. Howard snapped. "Is it not time to show Miss de Grande about the gardens?" She turned to Aunt Edna. "I despair of her, Lady Yates. She'd rather hide in her chamber than venture outside." She resumed her attention on her daughter. "Eleanor, do as I bid."

Blushing, Eleanor rose. "M-Miss de Grande? Shall we take a turn outside? The rose garden is particularly fine at this time of year."

Eleanor might as well have been reciting a laundry list. Most likely, her little speech had been dictated to her by her mother.

"I'd be delighted." Lavinia took her friend's arm, and they exited the parlor.

As soon as they stepped into the garden, Eleanor gave a sigh of relief. Her whole body seemed to relax, then blossom, like a flower bud opening its petals to reveal the beauty hidden within.

"Heaven save me from Society tea parties!" Lavinia cried. "I cannot think of anything more dull. Such inane chatter about subjects that matter so little."

"Mother is always telling me to engage in conversation," Eleanor said, "but I never know what to say."

"It's quite simple," Lavinia replied. "All you need do is remark on the weather—not too often, mind—and compliment the senior ladies in the room on the cut of their gowns, telling them that tastes and styles may change over the years, but will never improve. And, perhaps, say something about how private tea parties are preferable to public ones, where one might be forced to converse with people with whom one would usually have nothing to do."

Eleanor's eyes widened. "How do you *know* all that?" she asked. "I can never think of something to say that will not be laughed at. By the time I have thought of something, the conversation has usually moved on, and I must start thinking all over again."

"Well, never mind that," Lavinia said, squeezing her friend's arm. "I didn't come here to take tea with your mother—I came here to see *you*. Shall we indulge in the rose garden and, I might add, better company, now there's just the two of us?"

"Your aunt is charming," Eleanor said.

"There's no need for civility," Lavinia replied, "or I might be obliged to reciprocate and say something complimentary about your mother, which I'm afraid would be a challenge."

Eleanor giggled. "Mother despairs of me," she said. "When Juliette's around, I'm largely ignored—except by Papa, of course."

"You don't deserve to be overlooked."

"Oh, I prefer it, I assure you," Eleanor replied. "Better to see than be seen. But not even Papa can talk Mother out of making me go to so many parties. I *loathe* parties. I'm dreading the prospect of Lady Houghton's ball. And Mother's been complaining that we've not been invited to the house party at Hythe Manor next month. I can't think of anything worse—being stuck in a house filled with noisy people for three days!"

Hythe Manor…

The location of Papa's painting, procured by Lord Hythe at auction.

"I hear Hythe Manor has an impressive collection of art," Lavinia said, "including a piece by Peter Lely, or so I've heard."

"Oh yes!" Eleanor cried. "It's rather famous."

"You know the portrait?"

Eleanor nodded. "It's of the fifth Lady Hythe. She was rumored to have been a mistress of Charles II, which is likely to be true, if Sir Peter Lely painted her portrait. He was the royal portraitist, you know."

Lavinia smiled. Eleanor had an obsession with art, particularly portraiture and paintings of horses, and she knew all manner of insignificant facts about art history. Sadly, by virtue of her sex, she would never be valued for her knowledge—except by those who loved her.

"You've seen the painting?" Lavinia asked.

"Once," Eleanor said. "I painted a replica last year after Lady Hythe gave us a tour of the gallery."

"Did Lord Hythe permit you to copy it?"

"I painted it from memory."

"And—it's a true likeness?"

"Of course," Eleanor began, then she colored and looked away. "Forgive me. Mother's always telling me that a lady must show humility."

"Are you denying your talent for art?" Lavinia laughed. "You forget, I know you well enough to believe that, if anything, you'd rather hide your talents than advertise them. So, you can replicate a painting?"

Eleanor nodded. "When I see something I like, I can commit it to memory—when I close my eyes, it's as if it's there before me. Would you like to see the picture? It's in my study."

"Of course!"

Eleanor's expression illuminated with joy, and her eyes sparkled as she met Lavinia's gaze. Eleanor spent most of the time staring at her hands or feet—anything to avoid looking at the people around her. But in the rare instances that she looked at Lavinia in the eye, it was as if she entrusted Lavinia to safeguard her soul.

Eleanor's study was a peculiar combination of tidiness and disorder. At one end was a pile of books, placed such that the gold embossing on the spines perfectly aligned to form a pattern. At the other was a table and desk covered with papers—sketches, watercolors, and an array of painting tools. Eleanor approached the desk, opened the second drawer down, and pulled out a canvas.

The painting was exquisite. A lady with pale skin reclined in a wing-backed chair. Her eyes, a deep liquid brown, seemed to shine with mischief. The gown, a soft pink color, had a modest neckline trimmed with lace, and a full skirt that fell in folds about her legs, catching the light in soft ripples.

Lavinia reached out to touch the painting, almost expecting to feel the soft silk.

"Is it identical to the original?" she asked.

"Almost, except for the size and the signature," came the reply. "It's half the size of the original."

"Are you sure it's a good likeness?" Lavinia asked. "I've not seen the original—I've only heard about it."

Eleanor opened another drawer and pulled out a sketchbook. "If you don't believe I can draw likenesses, perhaps you'll recognize these," she said, flicking through the pages. She stopped at one, then passed the sketchbook over.

Lavinia drew in a sharp breath. It was like looking into a mirror. "It's me!"

The likeness was uncanny—right down to the small mole beside the corner of her mouth, and the almost invisible scar over her eye, sustained as a child when she'd fallen out of a tree.

Lavinia flicked through the book, admiring sketch after sketch—one of Henrietta, a handful of sketches of maids and footmen—until she came upon a series of sketches of a man with thick, dark hair, strong features, and liquid eyes that seemed to absorb the light.

"No!" Eleanor grasped the sketchbook, closed it, and clutched it to her chest. Then she thrust the book into the drawer and slammed it shut.

"Eleanor…" Lavinia took her friend's hand.

"Please tell no one what you saw," Eleanor said. "I-it's a passing fancy—nothing to regard."

"Of course I won't tell!" Lavinia cried. "But you must admit your drawings are exceptional. Does no one know of your talent?"

"Papa has seem some of my drawings. Mother would rather I painted landscapes for her friends' drawing rooms, but I cannot paint in the style she prefers. Juliette's work is more to her liking."

Bloody Juliette! Her *everything* was more to Mrs. Howard's liking.

"What about your replica of the Lely portrait?" Lavinia asked. "Your mother cannot object to that."

"You're the first person I've shown it to."

An idea formed in Lavinia's mind. "Do you think you'd be able to reproduce the original Lady Hythe painting, but full size?" she asked. "Enough to fool the untrained eye?"

Eleanor nodded. "Of course. Is it for a joke?"

"No," Lavinia said. "It's for justice."

"Then I'll do it," Eleanor said. "There's too little justice in the world, and if I can never find it for myself, I can at least help my best friend."

"Thank you," Lavinia said. "I'll return the favor if I can.

And she meant it. Except for Papa, nobody deserved justice—in an unjust, judgmental world—more than Eleanor Howard.

CHAPTER FOURTEEN

"WAIT HERE, YOUR lordship. I'll tell the master you're here.

The footman ushered Peregrine into a parlor, gestured toward a leather-backed armchair, then scuttled away.

Though elegantly furnished, the parlor showed evidence of neglect. The armchair creaked with age, the arms crackling at the seams, and the fabric on the sofa by the window had thinned such that the pattern had blurred into obscurity.

As for the curtains—the thick brocade frayed at the edges and the border at the hem had several tassels missing, reminding him of the mouth of a gap-toothed crone.

If the rumors were true, Lord Francis was in need of funds. He lacked the intelligence to run his estate wisely. His wife's intelligence surpassed his, but she employed it in outwitting her husband over her numerous affairs.

The door opened and the man himself appeared.

"Ah, Marlow." Francis gestured to the footman beside him. "Fetch some tea—there's a good chap." He gave Peregrine an apologetic smile. "I'd offer you brandy, but Lady Francis is to join us, and she frowns upon my taking liquor at this hour."

Peregrine glanced at the clock on the mantelshelf—a quarter to ten in the morning.

"Tea will do perfectly," he said. "It's better to keep a clear head when discussing business."

Moments later, a maid appeared with a tea tray. She set it on a table, then bobbed a curtsey.

"Fetch your mistress!" Lord Francis said irritably.

"Yes, m'lord." The maid colored, then fled.

"You must forgive my wife," Lord Francis said. "I fear she's a little delicate this morning, on account of supper last night."

"Did your cook commit a transgression?" Peregrine asked.

"We dined with Lord and Lady Fairchild. Their cook has a somewhat ostentatious approach to the fare—a few too many rich sauces and fine wines."

So, Lady Francis was nursing a sore head.

Peregrine smiled to himself. Perhaps Fate was punishing the woman for her spiteful remarks toward Miss de Grande.

Miss de Grande…

He drew in a deep breath to temper the little surge of lust at the memory of her hand in his—that smooth skin, the delicate aroma of rose as he'd brushed his lips against the back of her hand…

…and that lush, ripe body that had quivered almost imperceptibly with need as he'd drawn close.

He shifted position, and the leather creaked as he crossed his legs to hide the bulge in his breeches.

Lord Francis let out a chuckle. "She's a pretty little thing, aye?"

Shit.

Peregrine squeezed his thighs together.

Francis gestured toward the door. "I don't approve of seducing servants, but there's no harm in *looking*. There's something about the uniform."

Peregrine frowned. "I wouldn't be so crass as to pursue a servant."

"Dreaming of another, then? You can tell me, old chap—I'm the model of discretion."

The arrival of Lady Francis saved Peregrine from having to respond.

"Lord Marlow," she said, sweeping into the parlor. "Do forgive me. I've been very busy this morning."

Lord Francis let out a snort. Ignoring him, she approached the table. "Ah, tea. How do you take it, Lord Marlow?"

"A little milk, no sugar."

She poured a cup and handed it to Peregrine, then she served her husband. Finally, she poured a cup for herself, spooned sugar into it, then glided across the floor to an armchair in the shade and sat.

"Wouldn't you prefer to sit in the sun, my love?" Lord Francis asked.

She shook her head. "My health is a little delicate. Bright lights often bring on a megrim when one has dined on a rich meal—do they not, Lord Marlow?"

Peregrine lifted his teacup to hide his smile and nodded.

"We dined with Lady Fairchild last night," she said. "Such a charming woman! Her drawing room has been newly fitted out—oh, you should see it, Lord Marlow! I've never seen anything so elegant. The curtains alone, I heard, cost at least—"

"My dear," Lord Francis interrupted. "Our guest is not here to discuss soft furnishings."

"But—"

"Nor is he here to be enlisted in your quest to persuade me to refit this house. He's here to discuss business—or rather, the stolen vase. Isn't that right, Lord Marlow?"

Peregrine nodded. "I take it you have the papers for me?"

With a rattle of crockery, Lady Francis leaned forward in her seat and nearly dropped her teacup. "Papers?" she asked, her voice tight.

Lord Francis pulled a sheaf of papers from his pocket and handed them to Peregrine.

"I had Bunting bring these over from my country seat," he said. "They say that Pater acquired the piece at Griffin & Sons—have you heard of them?"

Peregrine nodded. Then he glanced over the front sheet.

Griffin & Sons, Bond Street

Bill of Sale September 17th, 1800

Lot 120. One ginger jar, presumed 13th century, Yuan Dynasty, ceramic, complete with lid, decorated in blue

Hammer price: two shillings

Auctioneer's commission: sixpence

Total to pay: two and six

"Half a crown," Peregrine said. "Is that all? A genuine Yuan Dynasty piece would be expected to secure significantly more at auction."

"Perhaps there were no other bidders," Lord Francis suggested.

"Unlikely, given that Griffin & Sons is one of the foremost auction houses in town. Collectors travel from all over the country to attend their sales."

"Perhaps it was a fake."

"Even less likely," Peregrine said. "Mr. Griffin's an expert in his field, and he'd never risk a lawsuit by offering an item for sale were its authenticity in doubt. No—your late father was either exceedingly fortunate, or…"

His voice trailed off as his train of thought split into two, considering the possibilities, then split again at each step, until an array of scenarios stretched before him. But none of them made sense. While this was, most likely, a routine case of theft, a small voice whispered in the back of his mind that something was amiss. And, in his experience of investigating the disappearance of antiquities, the voice of doubt should always be heeded.

He might have dismissed a piece bought at auction for a vastly reduced price compared to its value. He might equally have dismissed a theft of a single item in a vast residence. But both together? He did not believe in coincidences.

"You look like a bloodhound that's picked up a scent," Lord Francis said.

Peregrine traced the words on the page with his fingertips. "Perhaps. The Phoenix must have a motive. Mayhap this vase is the key to discovering it."

"George!" Lady Francis cried, leaping to her feet. Peregrine and Lord Francis followed suit.

"What is it, my dear?" Lord Francis asked.

"Shouldn't you be at the House this morning? I swear you told me there was a bill on servants' rights that you intended to vote on."

"That's not until later this week."

"You should still make an appearance," she said, "to persuade those who are as yet undecided to listen to your viewpoint." She moved toward him. "You know how good you are at presenting an argument."

He took her hand and lifted it to his mouth. "My dear, if I didn't know you better, I'd wonder if you weren't trying to rid yourself of me for the day."

"I'm thinking of *you*, my dear."

Lord Francis drew out his pocket watch, nodded, then snapped it shut. "Would you excuse me, Marlow?" he asked.

"Of course."

"Please don't leave on my husband's account, Lord Marlow," Lady Francis said. "You've not finished your tea."

"Yes, do keep my wife company," Francis said. "I'm afraid I always abandon her when a matter at the House piques my interest."

After Francis had exited the parlor, Lady Francis resumed her seat, and Peregrine did likewise.

She set her teacup aside, rattling the crockery as her hand shook. "I'm afraid I must beg your forgiveness, Lord Marlow."

"What for?" Peregrine asked.

"For wasting your time." She looked away. "I've been somewhat foolish. You see—the vase was never stolen."

"Did you break it, Lady Francis?"

She gave him a thoughtful glance, as if she were working

something out in her mind. Then she nodded, slowly.

"A shame," he said. "A piece like that can never be replaced. But if it were purchased for half a crown, it's no material loss to you."

She exhaled, as if sighing with relief, then drained her teacup.

"More tea, Lord Marlow?"

He nodded and rose as she glided toward the table and re-filled both cups.

"I find myself intrigued as to the price your late father-in-law paid for the vase," he said. "I should still like to inspect it, if you'd be so kind."

Her eyes widened, and panic flared in her expression. "I-it's in the country," she said. "And it's in pieces. You'd not be able to make anything of it."

"I flatter myself that I'm well placed to ascertain the authenticity of a piece, even if it's been smashed into a hundred shards," he replied. "I beg you to indulge me."

She colored and looked away again. What the devil was going on?

"I..." She seemed to shake with distress. Then she let out a sigh. "I'm afraid I sold it."

"You sold it?"

She nodded. "I-in London. I brought it here and sold it."

"At a pawnbroker's, I assume," Peregrine said. "Can you recall which one?"

"A—a what?" she replied. "Oh—yes, I suppose so. No—I'm afraid I quite forget. They all look the same, don't they?"

Peregrine fixed his gaze on her, but she seemed to be particularly interested in flicking a speck of dirt off her cuff.

After a pause, she glanced up, met his gaze, then looked away.

"What about the Phoenix?" he asked.

She made a dismissive gesture. "My husband has fanciful ideas."

Peregrine drew out a piece of paper from his pocket, unfolded it, then held it up.

"How do you explain this, Lady Francis?"

She stared at the paper, with its drawing of a bird in flames, and paled. "I—"

"I believe this was discovered on an occasional table in your bedchamber," he said. "The Phoenix's calling card."

"Are you impugning my honor, sir?"

"Not at all." He tapped at the image on the paper. "I find it somewhat unusual, given that only the Phoenix, and his victims, have seen this drawing. So, I take it that the ginger jar *was* stolen, but you'd rather Lord Francis believe otherwise?"

She stared at him for a moment, then let out a sigh. "My husband tells me you're a man of discretion," she said. "Can I rely on that discretion now?"

"Of course."

"And I have your word that you'll not repeat what I'm about to say to you now? Not even to my husband?"

"You have my word, as a gentleman."

Her shoulders slumped a little, as if she were about to shed a burden.

"I had a note from—*him* yesterday."

"From the Phoenix? How do you know?"

"At the bottom was"—she gestured toward the drawing in his hand—"that."

Peregrine nodded. "I take it the contents of the note are the reason why you'd prefer the world to believe that the vase wasn't stolen?"

She nodded. "I would have sent for you yesterday, but we were at Lady Fairchild's for dinner."

Which, no doubt, explained why Lady Francis had drunk a little too much of Lady Fairchild's wine, and was suffering from it now.

"Do you have the note?" he asked.

"I burned it—I trust you'll understand why. But you have my word that it was from *him*."

Her meaning couldn't be plainer.

The Phoenix was blackmailing her into silence. Clearly the ruffian wasn't above dishonor—as much as Lady Francis wasn't above a little extramarital indulgence.

"Then," Peregrine said, seeing the path clearing in his mind, leading toward his quarry, "we can assume that the Phoenix is among your acquaintance. Lord Francis said you discovered the vase missing during a house party. Might he be one of the guests?"

"My closest friends? I hardly think they'd be so treacherous. It must be one of the servants."

"Unlikely, given that he's struck elsewhere," Peregrine said. "A servant has not the means to travel. But it could be a guest you admitted at an earlier date, perhaps?"

"I cannot inquire further, Lord Marlow," she said.

"Then let *me*. If you're able to provide me with a list of all your guests for, say, the past three months?"

She nodded. "I can write the names down for you now, if you like," she said. "I have my journal upstairs, if you'd excuse me while I fetch it?"

AN HOUR LATER, Peregrine sat in his study, poring over a list of members of the *ton* that anyone wishing to enter into High Society would give their right arm to befriend. There were over sixty names, including the delectable Miss de Grande and her aunt, as well as Lord Thorpe, the Duke and Duchess of West-bury, and the duke's sons—his natural son. Mr. Drayton, and his heir, Lord Ravenwell. Lord and Lady Houghton, who were hosting a ball next week, were there, as were Lord and Lady Hythe—to whose house party Peregrine had been invited.

"One of you is the Phoenix," he said, "and I'll not rest until I've discovered who."

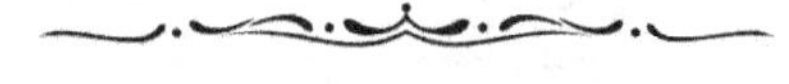

CHAPTER FIFTEEN

"Over here, Lav!" a voice cried.

Lavinia's heart leaped with joy as she caught sight of her friends. Henrietta stood at the edge of the ballroom, Eleanor sitting beside her.

She navigated her way around the dancers who were indulging in a gavotte that was a little too lively for her tastes. In fact, Juliette Howard had tripped over the hem of her gown twice—though whether that had been a deliberate ploy, Lavinia couldn't tell. Juliette had, each time, fallen into the arms of the Duke of Dunton.

Could Juliette be any more obvious in her quest to bag a titled husband—no matter how repugnant he was? How could such a creature be related to the quiet, gentle Eleanor?

As Lavinia reached her friends, Henrietta pulled her into an embrace.

"Dear Lavinia! We'd hoped to see you tonight, didn't we, Elle?"

Eleanor nodded, and Lavinia sat beside her. "I see your sister's displaying her intentions toward the Duke of Dunton."

Henrietta let out a laugh. "Juliette Howard cares not who she cleaves herself to, as long as he's a duke!" She snorted. "She was eyeing up Whitcombe earlier, as if he were a prime fillet of streak she wished to sink her teeth into—wasn't she, Eleanor?"

"I-I hardly noticed."

"You must have done," Henrietta continued. "You were staring at them earlier when they were over by the fireplace."

Eleanor flushed scarlet.

Lavinia came to her rescue. "Perhaps Eleanor was looking at the painting hanging over the mantelshelf."

Eleanor glanced toward the fireplace. "You mean the Stubbs?"

Henrietta cocked her head to one side. "Stubbs?"

"He painted horses, Hen," Lavinia said. "Didn't you know that?"

"Horses are for *riding*, not looking at," Henrietta said. "One horse is the same as any other."

"I doubt Mr. Stubbs would have agreed with you," Eleanor said, taking on a rare note of animation. "Horses—like people—are individuals, each with their own distinguishing features. The difficulty with the horse is that we are more used to studying faces of men and women, and therefore are less able to distinguish one horse from another. Stubbs understood that more than any man. He studied the anatomy of horses to such an extent that he was aware of every bone, every sinew beneath the pelt, which is why his likenesses are so remarkable, as if he captured the horse's soul, and—"

She paused, then looked away. "Forgive me," she said, more quietly. "Mother is always admonishing me for rattling on."

Henrietta let out a snort. "Your mother's a *fine* one to talk—she rattles on a great deal about how perfect your sister is, when Juliette is nothing but a..." She drew in a sharp breath. "Oh, forgive me, Eleanor. I meant no insult to your family."

Eleanor let out a giggle, then stifled it with a cough.

The dancing continued, and Lavinia followed the dancers with her gaze as they moved to and fro in time to the music. Juliette clung to her partner while he wheezed his way across the dance floor. Lady Irma Fairchild's partner seemed a little more appealing, a young man dressed in a flamboyant ensemble— bright green jacket and cream breeches—that belied his dull features and witless expression. Close by, Lavinia caught sight of the haughty profile of Lady Arabella Ponsford with none other than Heath Moss. Did that sour-faced miss know that her partner was working his way through the beds of the bored wives of London Society?

A hand caught Lavinia's sleeve.

"I've finished the painting. Shall I bring it round tomorrow?"

"Hush, Eleanor!" Lavinia said, giving her friend a nudge. "It's our secret, remember?"

"Even from Henrietta?"

"From *everyone*."

"What are you whispering about?" Henrietta asked.

Eleanor flushed scarlet.

"My necklace," Lavinia said. "What do you think of it?"

Henrietta's eyes narrowed with suspicion. Then she nodded and glanced at Lavinia's necklace.

"It's a little unusual," she said. "Is that a *real* emerald in the center?"

"What do *you* think of it, Eleanor?" Lavinia asked. "You could paint it, if you like."

Eleanor shook her head. "It's pretty enough, but it lacks the depth of shine you'd normally see in an emerald. Are you sure it's real, Lavinia?"

"Eleanor!" Henrietta cried. "Must you be so brutally frank?"

"I'm only speaking the truth," Eleanor replied. "The only color I see is green."

"Emeralds *are* green, Eleanor," Lavinia said.

"They're not merely *green*," came the reply. "I've a ring that belonged to my grandmother, and the stone has many shades of green, and blue—like an ocean. When I look at your stone, I see only green."

Lavinia covered the necklace with her hand to conceal it from her friend's observant eye. The stones in the necklace—which had arrived last week, the direction on the parcel written in Lady Betty's clear hand—were most decidedly *not* real.

"Oh dear," Eleanor said, a stricken expression on her face. "I've done it again, haven't I? Forgive me. I meant no insult."

"None taken, my dear friend," Lavinia said. "Brutal honesty is always to be favored over flattery."

She glanced about the ballroom. The dance was in full swing, bodies colliding with each other as they whirled around. The dancers were occupied with each other and the rest of the guests were either focused on their drinks, or observing the dancing. None had any interest in the small group of women hiding like wallflowers at the edge of the ballroom.

Her time had come when she could slip away unnoticed to embark on her quest.

She rose to her feet. "Would you excuse me?" she asked. "I must…see to my needs."

"Your—needs?" Eleanor asked.

"I drank a little too much water before coming tonight," Lavinia said. "Would you tell my aunt, if she asks, that I've gone to take the air?"

Eleanor nodded, then lowered her gaze to the floor.

Lavinia skirted the perimeter of the ballroom, making her way to a small side door, through which she could slip out unnoticed. According to Lady Betty, who had once indulged in a tryst with Lord Houghton, Lady Houghton's dressing room—the obvious location of Mama's necklace—was on the first floor, somewhere in the east wing. With all eyes on the dancers, her friends ready to make her excuses, and a folded piece of paper bearing the Phoenix's calling card in her reticule, her time had come.

She was fewer than ten paces from the door when a male voice spoke in her ear.

"Miss de Grande. Where are you going?"

She turned and looked up to see a pair of clear hazel eyes staring directly at her—accusation in their expression.

"L-Lord Marlow!"

He tightened his grip and pulled her toward him. "Did you

think you could escape me?"

His eyes darkened, and her heart flip-flopped in her chest.

"E-escape?"

"Why else would you scuttle across the ballroom?" he asked.

"Must you respond with a question of your own?" she asked. "And, I don't *scuttle*—or do you think me a black beetle?"

"There are worse creatures to be—real and mythical."

Her stomach clenched, twisting into knots.

He knows.

Then his mouth curled into a smile, and he bowed his head.

"Forgive my forwardness, Miss de Grande, but when a gentleman approaches a lady to ask her to dance, he cannot be condemned for feeling a little hurt on seeing her flee from him like a fox from a pack of hounds."

"So, I'm a fox, now?"

"Were you not running from me?" he asked. "Or…" His eyes narrowed again. "Perhaps you're up to no good?"

Curse him! Why did he have to be so sharp-eyed?

But boldness, not fear, was her best defense.

"I fear I'm constantly up to no good tonight," she said, "at least in my aunt's eyes. She's been lecturing me all day about the absence of names on my dance card, so I decided that the only way to avoid her disapproving looks would be to take a turn about the terrace."

"Then permit me to restore your reputation—at least in the eyes of your aunt." He offered his hand. "Shall we?"

She glanced toward the door—so tantalizingly close, yet so far out of reach.

"Miss de Grande?"

There was no denying the thrill that rippled through her body at the feel of his hand on her arm.

He arched an eyebrow, possession and hunger glittering in his eyes. Lavinia doubted that any woman had refused his offer to dance—nor, in all likelihood, refused an invitation to share his bed.

He was not a man used to denial.

And he was not a man to be denied.

Before she could stop herself, she took his hand and laced her fingers through his, relishing the feel of his skin on hers. His rich, masculine scent filled the air, and she drew in a deep breath, savoring the heady combination of woody spices and man…

Pure, virile man.

She lowered her gaze to his lips—full, sensual lips—and a little pulse of need throbbed in the center of her belly, sending a wicked heat between her thighs.

"I'm not in the habit of taking a woman unwilling, Miss de Grande," he said, his voice a low rumble. "You must give me your consent if I am to claim you."

She drew in a sharp breath as an image floated before her mind's eye—of this man claiming her as a woman ought to be claimed.

Sweet heaven—what was happening to her?

She flexed her hand, sliding her fingers along his, and he drew in a sharp breath.

"You must voice your consent, Miss de Grande."

She lifted her gaze to his, and her skin tightened at the raw hunger in his eyes. A hunger that matched her own.

"Y-yes," she whispered.

Then, without warning, he caught her waist and pulled her into the throng.

"We—we're dancing?" she said, her voice hoarse.

"Of course," he replied. "Did you think I had something else in mind?"

She caught a glimpse of mockery in his eyes. Cheeks flaming, she averted her gaze.

"Eyes on *me*, Miss de Grande. You belong to me—at least for the next few minutes."

"Do not laugh at me, sir."

"Believe me, Miss de Grande, what I wish to do with you tonight has nothing to do with ridicule."

He lowered his gaze to her neckline, and he licked his lips.

She glanced down, and the heat in her cheeks intensified. *Sweet heaven*—a rosy bloom had spread across her décolletage, and—if she were not mistaken—two little peaks poked at the muslin of her gown, just below the neckline.

"Such unusual treasures, Miss de Grande," he said. "If it's not too forward of me, may I take a closer look at them?"

Sweet Lord! Such impertinence—and yet a wicked deliciousness coursed through her.

"At…*what?*" Her voice came out in a squeak.

"The gemstones in your necklace. A rather unusual combination—rubies and emeralds."

"Oh," she said, fighting the rush of disappointment.

"It's not a conventional piece," he said.

"It is rather old, I believe."

"You don't wear it well."

Indignation rose with her. "Do you intend to insult me, Lord Marlow?"

"Of course not—but you look a little uncomfortable, as if it weighs heavily on you."

She glanced away. How could he be so perceptive? At all costs she must rid herself of him, despite how she relished the feel of his hands on her, the warmth of his body heat as he drew her close…

He led her across the dance floor, past Lady Irma and her partner. Irma glanced at Lavinia and wrinkled her nose, though she smiled sweetly at Lord Marlow—*curse her.*

"I wear the necklace because it reminds me of my mother," she said. "After she died, Papa gave it to me as a keepsake. It's all I have of her."

The dance concluded, and the couples dispersed. He bowed and escorted her to the edge of the room where Eleanor sat, alone.

"I'm afraid I've disappointed you," Lord Marlow said, "and a gentleman should never leave a lady unsatisfied."

A thrill rippled through her at the prospect of receiving *satisfaction* at his hands.

"Perhaps you'd permit me to atone, if you'd favor me with a second dance?"

"Perhaps later."

She withdrew her hand, then sat beside Eleanor.

"May I fetch either of you ladies something to drink?" Marlow asked.

"No, thank you," Lavinia said. Eleanor opened her mouth to speak, then she stiffened. A blush spread across her cheeks, and she curled her hands into fists.

Lavinia placed a hand over hers. "Are you all right?" she whispered.

"I say, Marlow—it is you!" a deep voice boomed.

A tall man approached in long, confident strides and clapped Marlow across the shoulders. "Some congenial company at *last*," he drawled. "You'd think Lord Houghton's home would be a little less—*provincial*, wouldn't you? I've spent half the evening trying to avoid our hostess and her horse-faced progeny."

"Miss Houghton's charming," Lord Marlow, said, glancing toward Lavinia. "I say, Monty, have you met the honorable Miss de Grande?"

The man raised his eyebrows, then glanced toward Lavinia and Eleanor, noticing them for the first time. But rather than show remorse at his ungentlemanly words, he resumed his attention on Marlow.

"No," he said. "I have not."

Nor did he want to, given the sneer in his voice.

What an uncivil creature! But he looked oddly familiar—a strong jaw, thick, dark hair—a little too long to be respectable—and wickedly dark eyes.

Savagely handsome, and he knew it.

Where had she seen him before?

Beside her, Eleanor trembled, distress in her expression, as if she were a rabbit caught in a fox's stare. Her hands curled into fists, she clutched at her skirts. Her chest rose and fell rapidly, and she looked as if she were about to faint.

"Lord Marlow," Lavinia said, "I have no wish to dismiss you and your friend, but there's something I wish to discuss with *my* friend. In private."

The newcomer let out a snort of derision, turned his back, and strode off. Lord Marlow bowed, then followed.

"What an unbelievably rude man!" Lavinia cried. "Who the devil is he?"

"Montague, eighth Duke of Whitcombe."

Eleanor spoke in barely a whisper, as Lavinia followed the man with her gaze.

Then she noticed it.

Of course!

He was the man in the portrait—or rather, *dozens* of portraits—in Eleanor's sketchbook.

"Heavens!" she cried. "The likeness—it's extraordinary. If you know him, Eleanor, why didn't he acknowledge you?"

"W-we've never been introduced."

"But the sketches—they…"

"They were drawn from memory, not from life."

"And you have an interest in the subject?"

Eleanor sighed, stretching her long fingers. Then she smoothed her skirts. "He'd never look at someone like *me*."

"Then it's his loss," Lavinia said. "But if you've yet to be introduced, that can be remedied. I could ask Lord Marlow to introduce you?"

"No, please—I couldn't *bear* it."

Eleanor's voice, usually devoid of emotion, had lifted in pitch and was filled with distress. Lavinia placed a hand over her friend's. "I didn't mean to upset you, Eleanor—but I now see the extent of your talent. If you can draw such perfect likenesses of someone to whom you've never been introduced, that leaves me in no doubt as to your ability to replicate that painting."

Eleanor nodded. "It's finished. I can bring it over next time I come for tea."

"Excellent," Lavinia said. The music struck up again, and a number of couples filled the dance floor, including Lord Marlow partnered with Miss Houghton.

Lavinia smiled to herself. Perhaps he'd offered to dance with her as consolation for his friend referring to her as being *horse-faced*. Though, she had to admit, the young lady's face was a little on the long side, and her teeth a little too large—all the better to chew hay with.

But with his attention fixed on his partner, Lavinia was, at least, free from his observant gaze. After ensuring that Eleanor would be content on her own, Lavinia rose to her feet and sidled toward the door. This time, she was determined to succeed in her quest, and nobody—not even Lord Marlow—would stop her.

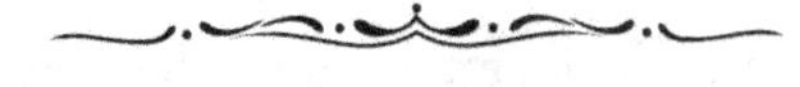

CHAPTER SIXTEEN

THERE IT IS!
Nestling on a cushion of red velvet, tucked away in the back of a drawer, together with a number of other boxes, was the necklace.

Mama's necklace.

Lady Houghton's dressing room was filled with boxes of jewels. Gaudy trinkets, most of them—overly bright colors, overly large stones, row upon row of pearls, each necklace showier than the last.

Lavinia had almost given up hope, until, after searching in the sensible places that a prized necklace might be, she began looking in the least likely locations, such as an underwear drawer, where all manner of interesting items were to be found.

Lady Houghton clearly had a laudanum habit, which, given that the bottles were tucked away among her silk drawers, Lord Houghton knew nothing about.

As to her other habit…

Nestled among Lady Houghton's stockings was a wooden item resembling part of the male anatomy. Not that Lavinia had seen a man's…but Samson had once displayed something similar when Cousin Charles's mares were in season.

She'd resisted the temptation to inspect the wooden piece—heaven knew where it had been. By now, she'd been absent from the ballroom for almost half an hour. She couldn't rely on poor

Eleanor to furnish Aunt Edna with excuses forever.

She plucked the necklace from its velvet cushion and held it in her hands, feeling the weight.

"Hello."

Smiling, she ran her fingertips along the metalwork, tracing the outline of the jewels, until she reached the central emerald, which felt almost warm to the touch, as if it were alive.

She reached into her reticule and pulled out a piece of paper bearing a single image—the outline of a bird rising from the flames. Then she removed her necklace and held it beside the genuine article that it had been imitating all night.

Side by side, the differences were more apparent. The clasp on the original was more ornate, with a filigree design that matched the metalwork linking the gems. As for the gems themselves...

Eleanor had been right. The genuine emerald outshone the fake as the sun outshone a dying candle. Eleanor always said that there were more shades of green than blades of grass in a field. Lavinia had dismissed the remark as part of Eleanor's obsession with painting. But as she held the necklace to the light, she saw a hundred different variations of the color, ranging from the warm, fresh green of a leaf illuminated by summer sunshine, to the deep, cool green of an endless ocean.

She put Mama's necklace on, relishing the feel of it against her skin, and placed the replica in the box. Then, on noticing a bureau at the far end of the room, she picked up the quill, dipped it into the inkpot, and scratched two drawings beside the phoenix. A bottle, bearing the label "laudanum," and a male part.

It was almost too easy. Lady Houghton, like Lady Francis before her, had a guilty secret that Lavinia could use to her advantage to ensure her silence, were she ever to discover that the real necklace was missing.

She tucked the piece of paper beneath the fake necklace, then closed the box and pushed the drawer shut. Then she crept to the door and peeked outside.

The coast was clear. Placing a hand over the necklace around her throat, she crept along the corridor and returned to the ballroom, as a dance was coming to a close.

The couples dispersed. Henrietta passed by, arm in arm with her partner. Eleanor stood next to her mother at the far end of the ballroom—red-faced and downcast, most likely being lectured for not having secured as many dance partners as her younger sister.

Aunt Edna sat with a gaggle of matriarchs, drink in hand, engrossed in gossip.

Lavinia smiled to herself. The Phoenix had struck again, and nobody was the wiser.

"What *are* you about, Miss de Grande?"

Her stomach flipped at the familiar, deep voice.

"Lord Marlow—this is becoming a habit," she said. "Do you always accost young women from behind?"

"Only to heighten their pleasure, Miss de Grande." A wicked glint shone in his eyes. "Did you forget you'd promised to give yourself to me? For another dance, at least."

Once again, Lavinia found herself being led onto the dance floor before she could protest.

The music began, and the couples moved across the dance floor, myriad colors gleaming in the candlelight—bright silks, nodding feathers, and glittering jewels. Lady Houghton glided past on her husband's arm, a necklace around her throat that could only be described as dripping with diamonds. No wonder Mama's necklace had been discarded and thrust into a drawer. It was insufficiently grand for Lady Houghton's taste. But no matter. The necklace would be reunited with those who appreciated and loved it.

"Your necklace."

Lavinia's stomach somersaulted, and she glanced up to see her partner staring directly at her.

"I-I beg your pardon, Lord Marlow?"

"I was remarking on how different your necklace looks compared to earlier," he said. "Almost as if you've changed it."

Her gut churned with fear. At that moment they were separated by the dance, and she found herself in the company of one of the Meredith twins for the next few steps. Handsome enough, but with an expression that was, at best, benign—or, if she were feeling particularly wicked, *witless*.

Which only emphasized the superiority of Lord Marlow's mind.

Did he suspect she'd swapped necklaces?

When he rejoined her, she felt her body tighten with apprehension, and she lost her footing and stumbled against him. He took her hand in a firm grip and steered her around in time to the music.

"I realize why you look so different from when we danced earlier," he said.

"Oh?"

"It's not the necklace itself, but how you're wearing it."

His insight unsettled her.

"It's around my neck, Lord Marlow," she said, "as it was earlier this evening."

"But it looks like it's a part of you now," he replied. "You seemed uncomfortable wearing it earlier."

"Is that so?"

"Yes," he said. "And, if I were you, I'd be very careful."

Her gut twisted into knots. "C-careful?"

"Yes, there's a thief about," he said.

Lavinia tilted her head to one side and narrowed her eyes.

"Ah yes, the"—she hesitated—"falcon, wasn't it? Or griffin?"

"The Phoenix."

"And you think I'm in danger of being robbed in the middle of a ball?"

"The Phoenix is capable of striking anywhere," he said, "and he steals for a very specific purpose."

"Does he?"

"Oh yes," he replied, "and once I've discovered that purpose,

I'll catch him."

"How will you manage that?" she asked.

"That's simple," he replied. "A pattern exists between the items he's stolen. More complex than that of a common thief, I'll grant—but a pattern, nonetheless, like a series of steps in a dance."

"I-I don't understand."

"Consider this dance, Miss de Grande. We may be, at first, unfamiliar with the steps—but, by careful observation of the dancers, we can discern a pattern such that we can anticipate the steps. The Phoenix is leading me on a dance, but soon I'll be able to anticipate his moves and play him at his own game."

A game! How dare he liken the restoration of her beloved papa's peace of mind to a game!

"You think it a game?" she cried. His eyes widened at her outburst. Then he nodded.

"I do, Miss de Grande—a game that relies on wits and luck. But do you know what they say about wits and luck?"

"What do they say?"

"That a man cannot survive on wits alone," he said, twirling her around as the dance came to an end, "and luck always runs out in the end."

She shivered at the determined set to his jaw and the darkness in his eyes.

"Why do you suppose he calls himself the Phoenix?" she asked, forcing a lightness in her voice. "Is he a lover of mythology?"

"I believe it's more personal," came the reply. "He steals with a purpose. Doubtless he's chosen his title with equal purpose. My guess is that something he valued was destroyed—and he's risen from the ashes of his misfortune to seek vengeance."

How the devil could he have worked *that* out?

She bit her lip to stem the sharp intake of breath. "Your imagination seems a little lively tonight," she said.

"Perhaps, but one needs an imagination in order to outwit a

clever adversary." He pulled her close and lowered his voice. "Shall I let you in on a secret, Miss de Grande?"

"Please do."

"I'm closer to catching the Phoenix than many believe."

"Y-you are?"

"I've reason to believe that he's a member of the *ton*. I've drawn up a list, and I'm certain that one of the names on that list is my adversary."

"How many names are on the list?"

"Around sixty names—including *yours*, Miss de Grande."

A cold hand clutched at her insides. "M-*my* name?"

"Your aunt's name is there also."

She forced a laugh. "The world would ridicule you for believing that the Phoenix is a *woman*."

"I must cover every eventuality," he said. "But, at least, I can pursue the Phoenix in relative comfort. His hunting ground is the ballrooms and drawing rooms of Society. Therefore, it shall be my hunting ground also. Beginning with the Hythes' house party next month. If he strikes there, I'll be waiting."

Lavinia's heart tightened in her chest. The Hythes' house party—where she planned to steal the painting.

"Are you all right, Miss de Grande? You look a little flushed."

"I'm finding the dancing tiring, and the conversation tiresome," she said. "I didn't come here to discuss brigands, or the men who seek to entrap them."

"Entrap?" He laughed. "You sound as if *I'm* the one in the wrong, Miss de Grande. The Phoenix is the criminal, and he shall suffer for his crimes. But, as you say, there are pleasanter topics of discussion than a brigand, are there not, my little Guinevere?"

He slid his fingers between hers, and her body shivered with need at his touch.

How the devil was she to resist him without being caught? She would have to be on guard morning, noon, and night. Papa's honor—and her liberty—was at stake.

And, she feared, her heart.

CHAPTER SEVENTEEN

"OH, ELEANOR—IT'S BEAUTIFUL! I cannot thank you enough."

Lavinia held the canvas up until the afternoon light from the parlor window illuminated the detail, and she could pick out the brush strokes.

"Are you sure it's a true likeness?"

"It's close enough," came the reply. "Did you doubt me?"

"Not really," Lavinia said. "Your likeness of the Duke of Whitcombe—"

"May I have more tea?" Eleanor interrupted, a little loudly.

Lavinia nodded and rose to refill her friend's teacup.

"My apologies," she said. "I didn't mean to distress you. It's only that your ability to recall detail is extraordinary—akin to witchcraft."

"Hardly witchcraft," Eleanor said, "though I do notice things others find insignificant. Such as..." She hesitated, then set her teacup down and focused her clear blue eyes on Lavinia.

Eleanor so rarely looked anyone in the eye that her direct gaze was somewhat unsettling.

"What were you going to say?" Lavinia asked.

Eleanor hesitated. Then she leaned forward and lowered her voice.

"Are you the Phoenix?"

Lavinia's breath caught. Her teacup rattled against the saucer, and hot liquid splashed onto her skirts.

"Do forgive me," Eleanor said. "I meant no offense—but last night, at Lady Houghton's ball… The necklace…"

"What necklace?" Lavinia asked.

"The one you were wearing," Eleanor said. "It looked…*different* at the end of the evening, compared to the beginning."

"Perhaps that's because you were tired," Lavinia said. "Everything looks different when we're tired."

Eleanor frowned. "I wasn't tired, and I'm not stupid. You were wearing a different necklace. The emerald looked more *alive* at the end of the evening. At first I wondered if it was the light, but it was a much deeper shade of green, with notes of blue. And the rubies surrounding it were more even in size. Earlier in the evening, the rubies on the left side of the emerald were a little smaller than those on the right." She set her cup aside. "Then, when you were dancing, I knew for sure that it was a different necklace."

"How so?"

"The clasp was different. When you were waiting in line for the dance with Lord Marlow, you had your back to me. The clasp had a pattern etched into it to match the rest of the necklace. Yet the necklace you wore at the start of the evening had a plain, smooth clasp."

"And because of that you think I'm the Phoenix?" Lavinia asked.

Eleanor leaned back, her cheeks flaming. "Forgive me. I meant no offense," she said. "But when you disappeared, then returned wearing a different necklace, I wondered if you'd stolen it. Everyone's talking about a thief called the Phoenix. I wondered if it might be you."

Sweet Lord…

"I'm right, aren't I?" A broad grin spread across Eleanor's face. "Tell me I'm right!"

"Hush!" Lavinia said. "You must promise not to breathe a

word of it."

"On my honor."

"In which case, it *is* me," Lavinia confessed. "Do you think I'm in danger of anyone else discovering me?"

"Perhaps not," Eleanor said. "I have a habit of noticing detail that others miss. It's landed me in trouble before, when Mother has scolded me for being impertinent, so I often keep my observations to myself. Was it you who stole Lady Francis's ginger jar?"

"Yes, that was me."

"Marvelous!" Eleanor cried. "How did you manage it? It disappeared during Lady Francis's house party, didn't it? But you weren't there at the time."

"I climbed in through a window in the middle of the night."

Eleanor choked on her tea, sending droplets of liquid into the air. "You *what?*"

Lavinia leaned back and set her cup aside. "It was a risk, but I had luck on my side."

"It was a *huge* risk!" Eleanor cried. "The ginger jar must have a particular significance to make you go to such lengths. Like the necklace—most people would have simply stolen it, rather than have a replica made to swap it with."

Lavinia stared at her friend. Beneath Eleanor's rather dull, almost slow-witted exterior lay a sharp mind with a talent for observation. There was no sense in concealing the truth from her.

"The ginger jar and the necklace have a personal significance," Lavinia said.

"Are they family heirlooms that your father lost, along with his fortune?"

Lavinia nodded. "Papa was led to ruination by five of his friends, who each took something precious from him. I am taking back what's rightfully his."

"How marvelous," Eleanor said. "It's so romantic—a quest to restore your family honor."

"And your painting will further my quest."

Eleanor narrowed her eyes. "How can that be? That Lely painting has been in the Hythe family for generations."

"I'm not going to steal *that* painting," Lavinia said. "I intend to outwit my pursuer—to throw him off the scent."

"Like a fox outwits the hounds?" Eleanor shook her head. "The fox is always flushed out in the end, and you know what happens then—she's torn to pieces by her predators."

"Nevertheless, I owe it to Papa to seek retribution on the men who destroyed him, the worst of all being—"

The door opened to reveal Aunt Edna, together with a footman.

"Aunt!" Lavinia rose, dropping her shawl on the sofa to conceal the canvas. "Would you like to join us for tea?"

"Not at this hour, child. I never take tea after five, and it's almost six."

"Oh dear!" Eleanor cried, leaping to her feet, almost sending her teacup flying. "I hadn't known it was so late. Mother expressly said she wanted me home by six."

The distress in Eleanor's expression tore at Lavinia's heart, in the knowledge that she'd receive a dressing-down from an unsympathetic mother.

"Shall I walk you home, Eleanor?" she asked. "I can explain to Mrs. Howard that I kept you late."

"We can do better than that, my dear," Aunt Edna said. She turned to the footman. "Have the carriage brought round for Miss Howard."

"Oh, you mustn't, Lady Yates," Eleanor said. "I-it'd be too much trouble on my account."

"Nonsense!" Aunt Edna cried. "The horses relish the exercise. I'm afraid ferrying me back from Lady Thorpe's wasn't enough for them. I'll take no refusal, my dear."

"Very well, thank you, Lady Yates." Eleanor draped her shawl around herself and bade Lavinia goodbye.

Moments later, Lavinia and Aunt Edna were waving the carriage off.

"Your friend's a charming girl," Aunt Edna said.

"I thought you didn't like her, Aunt."

"She's a little difficult to get to know, certainly, but when she's overcome her shyness, she's quite pleasant," Aunt Edna said. "But she'll have to sparkle if she wants to secure a husband—especially with that sister of hers outshining her at every turn. It's a pity she's not more accomplished. Now—it's time for my nap before supper."

Lavinia slipped her arm through her aunt's and escorted her upstairs. After depositing her safely in her bedchamber, Lavinia retrieved the canvas and retired to her own chamber, where her trunk was almost packed, ready for Lady Hythe's house party. She lifted the lid and dropped the canvas inside, on top of the empty picture frame she'd placed there yesterday.

She smiled to herself at the thought of the mischief she would make at Hythe Manor, where the Phoenix would strike again.

But, as she folded her undergarments and placed them over the canvas to conceal it from her maid's inquisitive eyes, Eleanor's words returned to haunt her.

The fox is always flushed out in the end, and you know what happens then—she's torn to pieces by her predators.

CHAPTER EIGHTEEN

PEREGRINE STARED OUT of the window, watching the other guests arrive, while his valet scratched about in the dressing room next door. Lord and Lady Hythe greeted each guest with the customary aristocratic insincerity, before liveried footmen shepherded each guest inside.

He drew in a sharp breath as a carriage bearing the Yates crest arrived and rolled to a halt. The carriage door opened, and Peregrine caught a glimpse of a gloved hand.

Miss de Grande...

"Lord Marlow, sir!"

Peregrine turned to see his valet holding an array of cravats.

"Do you have any preference for dinner, sir? The cream silk is a little creased, but I can—"

"I'll leave the choice to you, Lawson."

"But sir, you always say—"

"I care not which bloody cravat, Lawson!" Peregrine cried.

"Very good, sir."

The valet arched an eyebrow, then retreated into the dressing room, and Peregrine returned to the window.

Miss de Grande stood beside the carriage, while their hosts greeted her aunt. She dropped her reticule and, before a footman could retrieve it, crouched down and picked it up. Her aunt snapped at her in a sharp, crisp voice, and she nodded, slumping her shoulders.

To the unobservant, she was merely a young lady who'd committed a *faux pas* in retrieving a dropped item rather than expecting a servant to pick it up for her. But her lack of decorum most likely came from her upbringing in poverty.

His conscience pricked at him. Had his father been instrumental in Lord de Grande's downfall? Peregrine had written to Father for an explanation, but he'd not replied. Languishing in Italy with an array of harlots to service his whims, Father was all too fond of the life of idle luxury to spare a thought for his son. Or his estate, for that matter. And Peregrine had no intention of spending a single day in that bloody mausoleum.

Would she direct her hatred at him when she discovered whose son he was? He smiled at the irony. He loathed the old bastard as much as she—perhaps more. But there was no reason to tell her whose son he was—not unless they reached a level of intimacy that would require an introduction.

Intimacy...

His cock twitched in his breeches at the notion of intimacies shared with her—that divine, lithe body pressed against his...

He closed his eyes to relish the memory of her body's response when they'd danced at Lady Houghton's ball. Her skin had flushed a delicate shade of rose as the first sign of arousal, then her body bloomed as she'd arched her back. And when he lowered his gaze, he'd almost spent in his breeches at the swell of her breasts straining against her neckline, below which two delectable little peaks poked insistently against the fabric, as if to offer their sweetness to him.

Each night since, he'd gone to sleep stroking his length at the memory of her arousal. What could be more alluring than an innocent whose body was ready—eager—for him, though her mind was still unaware? How he longed to awaken her to the pleasures they could share!

No longer his little Guinevere, she was a woman—all woman.

Lavinia...

At that moment, she glanced up. Her lips curved into a smile of satisfaction. Her hair in disarray, cheeks flushed, she looked like a pagan goddess.

How might she look after a bout of lovemaking, her hair spread about the pillow while she lay in his bed—naked, pliant, and willing?

His manhood surged against his breeches, and he drew in a sharp breath, then lowered his hand to ease the ache...

"Sir?"

Bloody hell!

He removed his hand and whirled around. "Damn it, Lawson—must you creep around like a thief in the night?"

The red-faced valet stood in the doorway, holding aloft a dark green riding jacket. "Begging your pardon, sir, but I wondered if you still intended to take a ride before dinner?"

Peregrine opened his mouth to refuse, then closed it again. A good, hard ride, and a dose of fresh air, was the perfect remedy to cool his ardor.

"Yes, thank you, Lawson," he replied.

"Very good, sir—I've set out your boots."

Lawson was a good enough chap. Ordinarily, his ability to move about unheard was to be lauded—no man wanted a valet who crashed about the place. But the last thing one wanted was his valet to catch him stroking himself while whispering the name of the woman he wanted to fuck.

But Lavinia de Grande was not merely a woman to be fucked. The childhood friend from his memories had blossomed into an alluring, intelligent young woman.

And one with whom he was in danger of falling in love.

PEREGRINE SPURRED HIS mount into a canter and veered into the woods at the edge of the estate, concentrating on retaining his seat, rather than letting his mind wander toward the delectable

Miss de Grande.

The sunlight, broken by the trees, formed a dappled pattern on the ground, highlighting the occasional frond of bracken. He reined his mount to a halt, then closed his eyes, relishing the voice of the forest—the rush of the wind in the trees, the birdsong, and the occasional scuffle of a creature in the undergrowth. His horse gave a small snort, and he patted the animal's mane.

"Steady there, Poseidon. I only want to enjoy the peace and quiet for a moment. Can you understand that?"

The horse dipped its head up and down, as if in acknowledgement.

Peregrine tipped his head toward the sunlight and smiled at the gentle warmth caressing his face. If only he could remain here all afternoon! Why the world preferred to amass in drawing rooms to indulge in tea and gossip, or across the countryside, shooting every bird in their path, when such joy could be had in the simple pleasure of feeling the sun on one's face, he'd never understand. Society was merely a collection of men and women who believed themselves superior to the rest of the world by virtue of their birth, and who sought to attract a partner by selling their lineage to the highest bidder.

When he found a wife, he wouldn't want some brittle debutante desperate for a title. He wanted a woman to match his soul, someone who cared nothing for Society and its rules—a free spirit who challenged him on her own terms.

He stiffened as a voice drifted across the breeze.

"Hello there, little fellow! What might you be doing out in the open?"

Little fellow? He was hardly that. His athletic, muscular physique meant he'd had his pick of the courtesans last summer, and Poseidon was a good seventeen hands.

"It's not safe there," the voice continued.

He glanced around, but there was no one to be seen.

Laughter echoed through the forest. "Dear chap! There's

nothing to fear from *me*. But I fear you're in danger of being eaten by another."

Peregrine's skin tightened in recognition.

That voice—he'd know it anywhere.

It was *her*.

He squeezed Poseidon's flanks and headed deeper into the wood, until the owner of the voice came into view.

Crouched on the ground, holding a stick, in the middle of a clearing, she seemed to be talking to a clump of bracken. A beam of sunlight illuminated her with a soft, golden glow. Wisps of hair, in disarray, formed a halo about her head.

Had he not recognized her voice, he might have mistaken her for a wood nymph—a faerie creature illuminated in an ethereal light.

Sweet Lord—since when had he become so poetic? Whitcombe would laugh his arse off if he said such a thing at White's.

But here, surrounded by nature, with the loveliest woman he'd ever seen—such words didn't seem out of place.

"Miss de Grande."

She looked up, her eyes widening, then she frowned and held her finger to her lips.

"Shush! You'll scare him."

He swung one leg over the saddle and dismounted. "Scare who?"

"My friend."

He cocked his head to one side. "Well, I'm glad you've cleared *that* up."

She rolled her eyes, then rose, slowly, to her feet and held up her hand.

"Don't come any closer—I don't want him coming to any harm."

"Who?"

She pointed toward her feet. "The adder."

His stomach knotted and he stepped back. "The—*what?*"

"It's a snake."

"I know damned well what an adder is," he said, "and you're worried about *it* getting harmed? Back away, you fool—you're in danger of getting bitten!"

She placed a hand on her hip in the manner of an exasperated nursemaid. "He's perfectly harmless," she said. "I see adders all the time at home."

"Then it's a wonder you're still alive," he said. "Why the devil are you playing with an adder?"

"Now *you're* being a fool, Lord Marlow," she said. "I'm not playing. The poor creature's more afraid of us than we are of him. Out here he's exposed to predators—I was merely trying to shepherd him to the safety of the bracken."

"What if it bites you?"

"He'd only bite if a clumsy oaf trod on him by mistake," she replied, "which is why *you* should stay back."

"Are you calling me a clumsy oaf, Miss de Grande?"

A ripple of mirth bubbled inside his throat at the expression of horror in her eyes.

Then she resumed her attention on the ground, and a smile curved her lips.

"He's moving!" she cried. "There you go, little chap. I suggest you remain concealed in the bracken." She dropped the stick and wiped her hands.

"Why bother with the creature?" Peregrine asked. "Most people would either run from a snake, or try to kill it."

"*All* creatures deserve a chance," she replied, "and the misunderstood doubly so."

"How so?"

"Because they must fight harder to survive." She gestured toward the bracken. "I was merely giving one of my fellow misfits a helping hand, to protect him from those who might misunderstand him merely for what he is."

His heart ached at her meaning. Did she consider herself an outcast because of her father's ruination?

"Your slithery friend is most fortunate to have you as his

champion," he said.

"Are you mocking me, Lord Marlow?"

"Not at all," he replied. "And you needn't fear for your friend's safety. There are surprisingly few oafs in this part of the estate. Present company excepted, of course. Our host said something about rain clouds, and the whole party elected to remain indoors."

"*I'd* rather be outdoors than stuck inside listening to tittle-tattle," she said, "even if under the threat of rain."

"I'm sure your aunt, and the other ladies, would object to their conversation being referred to as *tittle-tattle*."

"I daresay they would—as would the gentlemen who tittle-tattle just as much." Smiling, she took one last glance at the undergrowth, then approached Peregrine, her hand outstretched. He drew in a sharp breath in anticipation of her touch.

But she passed him and approached his horse.

"Be careful," he said. "Poseidon doesn't take to strangers."

"Poseidon?" She arched an eyebrow. "God of the sea, and tamer of horses."

"You *know* that?"

Her smile slipped, and she resumed her attention on the horse. Peregrine tensed his body, but rather than rear up, Poseidon dipped his head and let out a low snort. She placed her hand on the horse's forehead and caressed his nose.

"There's a beautiful boy!" she cooed. "*You* wouldn't reel in shock at the notion of my having read the classics, would you?"

"Forgive me," Peregrine said. "It's just that a young lady is not—"

"Let me guess," she interrupted. "A young lady is not usually educated in anything other than embroidery, drawing room gossip, and the ability to glide across the floor with her nose stuck in the air to portray her superiority."

"I meant no offense," he said.

She met his gaze, mischief gleaming in her eyes.

"You spoke the truth, Lord Marlow," she said. "And the truth will always be preferred to flattery. I'm afraid I've been a disappointment to my poor aunt. While she did her utmost to school me in the manners of a lady, I preferred other pursuits."

"You seem to have a way with horses," Peregrine said. "Do you ride?"

She nodded. "Our horse Samson is an excellent mount. I ride him every day at home." She let out a sigh. "How I miss him!"

"Isn't he with you in London?"

She colored and looked away. "We cannot afford the livery."

"Surely Lord Yates—"

"Cousin Charles would have paid had Papa asked," she said, "but Papa dislikes taking charity. He's determined to restore our fortunes without relying on handouts." Her expression hardened. "Papa never wishes to be beholden to another—or rely on another—again."

"Then you must ride Poseidon while you're here," Peregrine said. "I'm sure Lady Hythe's head groom would find a suitable saddle, and Lady Hythe might lend you a habit."

"*Now* who's offering charity?"

"It's not charity when it's an offer from a friend."

"I barely know you, Lord Marlow."

"But we played as children, did we not, little Guinevere?"

"Children grow up," she said. "Look at you—I can recall you trotting about on a little gray pony. Now you have a stallion who must be sixteen hands, if not more."

Peregrine closed his eyes at the memory of Sir Lancelot—the pony who'd been his constant companion as a child, until...

"What happened to him?" she asked. "Lancelot, wasn't it?"

"I shot him."

Her eyes widened. "You—*what?*"

"About a year after you and your father disappeared," he said, swallowing the pain of the memory. "I was teaching him how to jump. He fell at a fence and broke his leg."

"You rode him too hard."

He turned away at the accusation in her voice. "You cannot

admonish me any more than I admonished myself," he said. "When Father found out, I expected a thrashing, but he had a worse punishment in store."

"What could be worse than a thrashing—unless he cut your allowance, of course?"

He couldn't mistake the sneer in her tone. "He made me shoot him."

She drew in a sharp breath. "He did *what?*"

"He fetched his pistol, then dragged me back to where Lancelot lay in the field and ordered me to shoot him."

"Couldn't you refuse?"

He shook his head. "The poor creature was in pain—the noises he made haunted my dreams for months afterward. Father gave orders that none should shoot him but me, and if I was too cowardly to do the deed, then he'd thrash me, confine me to my chamber, and let Lancelot die in his own time." He let out a sigh. "I could already see crows circling ahead, ready to pick at him in his final hours. So, to end his suffering, I did as my Father ordered, and shot him between the eyes. I would have taken ten beatings if Lancelot could have lived."

He closed his eyes, trying to dispel the memory of his beloved pony's eye staring into his own at the final moments, while the spark of life flickered and died.

A hand took his, and he opened his eyes to see her soft hazel gaze filled with compassion.

"You did the right thing," she said.

"It's my fault he was lamed."

"Accidents happen."

"I was twelve—old enough to know better."

"Twelve!" She shook her head. "You were still a child." She lifted her free hand and placed it on his cheek, and his heart fluttered at the feel of her skin on his. "Lancelot would have been grateful. You eased his suffering."

He caught her hand, and her eyes widened. Then he lowered his gaze to her lips. Would they taste as sweet as they looked? He only need dip his head a fraction, and he could claim them…

She withdrew her hand.

"Forgive me," she said. "I should not have asked about your pony."

"There's nothing to forgive. What's done is done. Father was…"

He broke off, unwilling to speak further, lest he reveal his father's identity. The last thing he wished to see was the bitter hatred return to her eyes—not when the compassion that he saw in them now swelled his heart.

"Is your father dead?"

"He's very much alive. But he lives abroad. We don't get on."

"I'm sorry," she said. "I cannot imagine not loving a parent. My papa is everything to me. I only wish he could have come to London."

"But his health prevented it."

She nodded. "Each day with him is a gift. I was unwilling to leave him, but he told me it was his greatest wish for me to have a Season in London—and I'd do anything to make him happy again."

The vehemence in her tone, and the love in her eyes, tore at his heart. What might it have been like to have enjoyed such a bond with his own father—to have loved him so deeply that he'd do anything to make him happy?

But he could never love that bitter old bastard.

"I should be getting back," she said. "Aunt will be wondering where I am."

"May I walk with you?"

She laughed. "I doubt your companion would be agreeable to that. He looks restless. You should finish your ride."

He glanced toward Poseidon. The horse tossed his head up and down, shifting on the ground with pent-up energy. Even though Peregrine had ridden him all the way over to Hythe Manor, the horse had yet to tire, and needed a good, long gallop.

"Will you be safe on your own, Miss de Grande?"

She let out a laugh. "I was on my own when you came upon

me, Lord Marlow. I have no need of a man to take care of me." She offered her hand. "I'll see you at dinner."

He took it, curling his fingers round hers. "Perhaps you'd favor me with a dance after supper."

Her eyes crinkled into a smile. "I'd like that."

He lifted her hand to his lips, then released her. Then he mounted Poseidon and set off. He turned to see her following along the path. She waved, and he raised his hand in salute. Then he urged Poseidon forward and emerged from the forest into a wide-open field.

Had he remained in that forest with her a moment longer, he would have pulled her into his arms and kissed her into oblivion. The urge to claim her had almost overpowered him, but he would find some release in the ride.

He pushed Poseidon into a gallop. As he approached the edge of the field, he leaned forward and steered the animal toward the hedge lining the field. In a smooth, graceful movement, the horse leaped into the air and sailed over the hedge. Peregrine leaned back as Poseidon landed on the other side then raced across the landscape, relishing the freedom that could only be experienced when away from the rest of the world—at one, with his horse.

By the time he arrived at the stables, Poseidon had lost his restlessness. Peregrine dismounted and led the horse toward a stall. A groom came running and took the reins.

"That's a fine animal you have there, sir."

Peregrine nodded his thanks, then approached the main house. He spotted a familiar, tall figure running across the lawn— the muslin of her gown clinging to her form, doing nothing to conceal the shape of her legs.

Miss de Grande.

A free spirit who followed her own path—a young woman who would shepherd a little snake to sanctuary with no thought for her safety. She was the embodiment of love—a loyal soul who placed the happiness of another before her own indulgences. She cared nothing for Society and its rules.

She was his perfect match.

CHAPTER NINETEEN

Lavinia made her way to the edge of the drawing room and sipped her coffee. Why did the sound of ladies talking make her ears feel as if they were being turned inside out? She'd almost rather visit Dr. Williams to have a rotten tooth pulled. No—she *would* rather have a tooth pulled, where the brief spike of pain would at least be followed by blessed relief. When ladies gathered to gossip, there was no relief to be had—the torture was perpetual.

The door opened and the men filtered into the drawing room, accompanied by the aroma of brandy and cigar smoke. The shrill voices of the ladies rose in pitch as they greeted the men, then settled into a murmur, this time tempered by the lower pitch of the men's voices.

"And not a moment before time!" Lady Hythe trilled, a petulant tone to her voice. "I was just saying to Lady Francis that the gentlemen had been neglecting us. What can you have found so interesting to discuss that you'd abandon us for so long?"

Anything would be interesting compared to your inanities, Lady Hythe.

Lavinia suppressed the urge to giggle, and sipped her coffee.

Their hostess's outburst was followed by a volley of apologies from the gentlemen, who eased her petulance by flattering her over the cut of her gown and the excellence of her choice of dinner menu, until she sparkled once more, and basked in their praise.

Ugh.

Lavinia wanted none of it. Lady Hythe—and every other woman in the room—measured their worth by the opinion that the men in the room had of her, rather than the value she gave to the world.

But, most likely, Lady Hythe gave no value to the world whatsoever. These women of Society, who fancied themselves superior to the rest of the world, spent their lives in desperation, securing the attention and approval of the men who dictated their lives.

Perhaps, had Papa not been ruined, Lavinia herself might have grown up to become like the rest of them. Shallow, spiteful, and only concerned about how many trinkets she had about her neck, or how many fine gowns she had in her wardrobe, looking down her nose at the less fortunate. Hardship had given her a better understanding of the world.

Perhaps she ought to thank Earl Walton for what he'd done—if she hadn't spent the past fourteen years hating the man.

Lady Hythe issued an order, and two footmen rushed forward and began moving chairs about, clearing a space in the center of the room. Then she made a great show of approaching the pianoforte.

Footsteps approached, and Lavinia wrinkled her nose at the onslaught of cologne—so powerful that its owner must have drenched himself in it.

"Miss de Grande—would you partner me for this dance?"

She looked up into a pair of pale blue eyes in a sharply handsome face framed by soft blond hair.

Heath Moss stood before her.

Ugh.

She'd had the misfortune of sitting opposite him at dinner, where he'd spent much of the meal leering across the table at her. She'd felt his eyes on her while she fixed her attention on the elderly Reverend Pilcher, feigning an interest in seventeenth-century ecclesiastical texts while the vicar droned on in a voice soporific enough to render an entire congregation unconscious.

Moss might possess the sort of attractiveness that enticed most ladies. But he knew it, and that knowledge gave him an air of arrogance, as if he believed that no woman would refuse him.

"Well?" He held out his hand.

"No, thank you," she said.

His eyes widened. "I—beg your pardon?"

"I said no!"

"Well!" he exclaimed. "Of all the—"

He broke off as Aunt Edna approached, and the anger in his eyes disappeared.

"Lady Yates." He bowed. "May I fetch you something to drink?"

"A little coffee, thank you," Aunt Edna said. Then she settled into the seat beside Lavinia.

A few notes rang out as their hostess ran her fingers along the pianoforte, and a handful of couples lined up in the center of the room.

"Miss de Grande," a familiar, deep voice said, and Lavinia's breath hitched as the tall form of Lord Marlow appeared, brandy glass in one hand and a coffee cup in the other. "Would you favor me with this dance?"

"I'd be delighted."

"Excellent." He bowed, then approached a footman, who relieved him of the glass and cup.

Aunt Edna leaned over and hissed in Lavinia's ear.

"That wasn't very civil, child."

"What—accepting Lord Marlow's invitation to dance?"

"No—refusing Mr. Moss's invitation."

"Can't I dance with whom I like?"

"You must observe propriety," Aunt Edna said. "If a young woman refuses an offer to dance from a gentleman, she's honor bound to refuse offers from others."

"Why?"

"Heavens, girl!" Aunt Edna cried. "You never listen to a thing I say. A refusal to dance would be taken as a direct cut, were you subsequently to accept the hand of another. Mr. Moss has every right to feel aggrieved."

"I was polite in my refusal."

"That's of no consequence. You've shown Mr. Moss that you have a marked preference for another, instead of merely being disinclined to dance."

"I fail to see anything wrong in refusing to dance with a man I dislike," Lavinia said. "Why should I be honor bound to dance merely because I was unfortunate enough to have *him* be the first to ask me?"

Before Aunt Edna could respond, Lord Marlow returned, hand outstretched. Lavinia rose, and he led her toward the center of the room where the couples had lined up. On the way, they passed Moss holding a cup of coffee. He scowled, his eyes darkening, and a shiver rippled across Lavinia's skin at the dislike in his expression. Then he approached Aunt Edna, flashing a smile, and presented her with her coffee.

The dancing began, and Lavinia resumed her attention on her partner. The melody was barely discernible, obscured by discordant notes that jarred the senses.

"Lady Hythe's talents for music are to be commended," Lavinia said, fighting the urge to giggle.

Her partner arched an eyebrow. "I think, perhaps, the melody would be a little easier on the ear if her lapdog were at the pianoforte instead. As a rule, ladies are accomplished, able to bring forth the most melodious of tunes from an instrument. I'm afraid, however, that Lady Hythe is the exception to that rule."

"All ladies?" Lavinia asked.

"Is that not what ladies occupy themselves with—music and needlework?"

"Surely you cannot believe that!" she cried. "Why can't a woman distinguish herself as a man does?"

He let out a laugh. "Have I pricked your pride, Miss de

Grande? Do you think the gentlemen in the company tonight have distinguished themselves?"

"Most likely not," she said, "but they've been provided with opportunities that a woman can only dream of—even if they choose to squander those opportunities languishing in luxury while others see to their estates."

"Careful, Miss de Grande—you're dangerously close to demonstrating advocacy for the common man."

"The *common man*, by your definition, is one who earns his living."

"And I salute him, for he enjoys freedoms that a titled gentleman can only dream of."

"A titled gentleman has more freedom than anyone else, Lord Marlow."

"I must beg to disagree," he replied. "A commoner has no obligations to maintain an estate that he is responsible for merely due to his birth. Nor is he burdened by duty to furnish the title with an heir."

She let out a snort. "Hardly a duty when he has the pick of the debutantes and their dowries."

"Take care, Miss de Grande," he said. "I would not have you melancholy when I've been looking forward, all day, to dancing with you."

He ran his thumb over the back of her hand, and a ripple of need caressed her skin. Then they were separated from the dance, and she found herself partnered with Lord Hythe for the next few steps.

Yellow-eyed, wheezing, and with a brittle, bent frame, he hardly looked the embodiment of villainy. Yet he was one of the men who'd conspired to ruin Papa.

He flinched as another discordant note rang out, and Lavinia smiled to herself. Perhaps the Almighty had punished him for his role in Papa's downfall by giving him his wife.

"Are you well, Lord Hythe?" she asked.

He fixed his milky gaze on her. "Forgive me—you are...?"

"Miss de Grande," she said. He frowned, as if in concentration. "I believe you knew my father, Viscount Richard de Grande, formerly of Fosterley Park?"

His frown deepened. "I recall the name, but…" He shook his head. "Are you enjoying the dance, Miss…?"

"De Grande."

"De Grande, yes—that's it," he said. "So many new names for a man to contend with. Delighted, I'm sure."

Another clash of notes rang out as Lady Hythe made her best attempt at the chorus, and as the dancers changed partners, Lavinia found herself once more with Lord Marlow.

"You must forgive me, Miss de Grande," he said.

"What for?"

He smiled. "For discomposing you earlier. A woman should enjoy the same freedoms as a man to choose how she lives her life."

"Ah, but if a woman displays too much freedom, she is vilified by Society."

"Are you thinking of any woman in particular?" he asked. "Lady Betty Grey, for instance?"

She drew in a sharp breath. How did he know that she had Lady Betty in mind?

"You're very perceptive, sir."

"I overheard your aunt sharing her opinion of Lady Betty over dinner," he said.

"Lady Betty is a dear friend," Lavinia said.

"Then I applaud your generosity toward her. Most ladies would give her the cut direct. It's a common fault of your sex."

How dare he!

"I disagree, Lord Marlow," she replied. "It's the fault of *yours.*"

"How so?"

"It's perfectly simple," she said. "Men rule women by manipulating them into turning against each other."

He let out a laugh. "Are you saying that we persuade women

to fight? Somewhat preposterous, don't you think?"

"When a man is unfaithful to his wife, Lord Marlow, whom does Society blame? Not the husband—*he's* applauded for exercising his rights as a man, and proving his virility. His wife is blamed for not satisfying him such that he's forced to look elsewhere. And his mistress is blamed for playing the temptress and bringing discord into the harmonious family unit."

"Then, perhaps, the wife should admonish her husband, rather than direct her disgust at the mistress," he said.

"And what do you suppose the husband would do if the wife admonished him?" she asked. "Most likely he'd punish her by exiling her to the country while he entertains his mistress elsewhere."

"Then the mistress—"

"Is merely seeking a living," she said. "She's not to blame for her actions. She is a function of the world in which she lives—a world ruled by men."

They turned in the dance, and she moved forward, treading on his toe.

"I consider myself duly admonished, Miss de Grande," he said. "The sweet child I once knew is no more."

"Perhaps you didn't know me at all," she replied. "After all, I could never recall your name."

"You wound me, Miss de Grande!" he cried. "A man may wish to be many things—but *forgettable* is not one of them."

"Do not underestimate the power of anonymity."

"Anonymity is for cowards," he said. "Such as the Phoenix."

Lavinia stumbled against him. He caught her, and their eyes met.

"Do you wish to stamp on my other foot, Miss de Grande? Or have I discomposed you by speaking of the infamous thief?"

She averted her gaze, her cheeks warming. If he looked into her eyes, would he discern her thoughts? Did he suspect her? Perhaps he knew, by some devilish means, of the picture frame concealed in her trunk, ready to set her plan in motion.

"Why should I be discomposed by talk of a thief, Lord Mar-low?" she asked.

"This particular thief has a penchant for striking in country houses," he said. "His next victim might be Lord Hythe."

She forced a laugh. "His next victim might be *you*."

"He'd be a fool to steal from the very man who's been engaged to catch him."

"Perhaps he doesn't know that."

"Oh no, Miss de Grande," he said, fixing his gaze on her. "I'm sure that he *does*."

She swallowed her fear. Was he toying with her?

"Wh-why do you say that?"

"Because he's a clever fellow, and he's a member of the *ton*. He steals for a very particular purpose. I merely need to ascertain that purpose, and I'll be one step closer to catching him."

"He could just be stealing on a whim, with no thought attached to the items he takes."

He shook his head. "No, Miss de Grande. There's a pattern, I know it."

"If he's as clever as you say, he might be toying with you, making you *believe* there's a pattern, to outwit you."

"No man has outwitted me," he said. "I will catch that slippery devil—it's only a matter of time."

Fear rippled through her at the determined set to his jaw. Did he already suspect her? Would he, at any moment, expose her in front of the whole company?

The dance concluded and the music stopped, followed by a collective sigh of relief. Lady Hythe stood to polite applause.

"Another dance, perhaps?" she asked.

Lord Hythe rushed to her side. "I think, my dear, you should take your rest. Let me fetch you a brandy."

Lavinia suppressed a giggle. The man may be losing his wits, but even he had the presence of mind to act when his guests' ears were under threat of further assault.

Her partner steered her toward the edge of the room. "Forgive me, Miss de Grande," he said. "I was overly harsh. You are not to blame for my frustration."

"Your frustration?"

"I'd hoped to have caught the Phoenix by now, but he continues to elude me. Perhaps I should take a lesson from your philosophy, Miss de Grande, and consider the Phoenix to be a woman."

Her heart leaped in her chest, and she caught her breath.

"Do I shock you, Miss de Grande?"

"A-a little."

"Then I must beg forgiveness for displaying further ungallantry toward your sex. The Phoenix's actions are not those of a woman."

"Why? Because they're outwitting you?"

He laughed. "No—I believe his motive is far simpler than the desire to outwit another."

"What do you believe it to be?"

"Vengeance," he said. "A game that any woman would consider too dangerous."

"What about justice?"

"Justice and vengeance are entirely different," he said. "Take yourself, for instance."

Surely he didn't mean…

"Few, if any, would go out of their way to ensure the safety of a creature capable of killing them for the cause of justice," he continued. "It takes great courage to place yourself at risk, when others would not."

He lifted his hand and brushed a stray tendril of hair from her face. She tipped her head up and met his gaze. The color of his eyes softened to a moss green, with flecks of brown. Such an extraordinary shade! Then he lowered his gaze to her lips, and she caught a flash of hunger in his eyes—a craving to match her own.

She lowered her gaze to his lips. Full and rounded, with a firm, determined shape, they were the lips of a man who would not brook denial.

How many women had those lips kissed? What had he said about men having to exercise their rights as *men*—to prove their virility?

He flicked his tongue out, and she caught sight of the moist pink tip running along the seam of his lips. Then he parted his lips and sighed. His warm breath caressed her face, and her skin tightened with want and anticipation. She moved closer until she could feel his hard body against hers.

Then he spoke, his voice vibrating against her chest. "Are you placing yourself at risk *now*, Miss de Grande?"

"A-at risk of what?"

Hunger flashed in his eyes, and he brushed his knuckles against her neckline. Desire fizzed through her, and to her shame, she felt her nipples hardening, straining against the fabric of her gown. He only need lower his gaze, and he'd see them. She shifted position, and an uncomfortable heat bloomed between her thighs.

He circled her arms with his hands, long, lean fingers curling possessively around her flesh.

Then he pushed her back and broke the spell.

"You look a little overheated, Miss de Grande."

Unable to speak, she nodded.

He glanced over his shoulder, then lowered his voice. "Perhaps I might venture to say that a criminal resides here tonight, in this very room."

Her stomach somersaulted.

He knows.

"Wh-who do you mean?"

His eyes twinkled with mirth.

"I believe Lady Hythe may be guilty of a crime far worse than theft," he said, gesturing toward the pianoforte at which their hostess was settling down once more. "Herr Mozart has my sympathies, for I fear he's about to be murdered again."

Lavinia let out a laugh of relief.

"Do I amuse you, Miss de Grande?"

"The piece we were dancing to earlier was a Bach canon."

"Then I must applaud your greater intellect," he said. He glanced toward the pianoforte. "Perhaps I should ask a footman to fetch me the remains of the cheese from dinner."

"So you can distract yourself by eating?" she asked.

"So I can stuff it into my ears."

She let out a snort, caught sight of Aunt Edna glowering at her from across the drawing room, then turned it into a cough.

"Miss de Grande, are you well?" he asked in mock concern. "A most unusual cough."

Torn between the urge to laugh and the desire to slap him on the arm for his impertinence, she shook her head. "I'm in need of a little fresh air. The balcony beckons."

"Quite so—Lady Hythe's particular form of torture cannot pass through closed doors. But perhaps you'd like a brandy, to dull the senses further, as a precaution?"

"Thank you, sir."

He bowed, then approached a footman, weaving his way around the dancers. He paused beside Aunt Edna, obscuring her from view for a moment, at which point Lavinia slipped outside through the balcony doors. She closed them behind her, then approached the edge of the balcony and leaned over, surveying the landscape bathed in moonlight.

The sounds of the night overcame the strains of music and idle chatter. An owl hooted in the distance, and she caught sight of a ghostly form gliding through the air. Then it swerved and dived toward the ground. Shortly after, a squeal rose up.

She shivered—some poor creature had met its end. But the difference between the owl and a man was that the owl knew no different—he hunted his prey in order to survive. Whereas a predatory man...

The door opened and closed, and soft footsteps approached from behind.

Aunt Edna would most likely admonish her for yet another *faux pas*, but the prospect of being in Lord Marlow's arms was worth any punishment her aunt would mete out. Though she struggled to reconcile him with the boy she'd known fourteen years ago, the admiration in his gaze that afternoon in the forest, and the mischief in his eyes tonight, elicited the same sensation of friendship. Only now she was a grown woman, and those sensations had developed from a childhood fancy to something more…

Something more *visceral*.

She closed her eyes, her mind searching for the familiar scent of him—the aroma of wood and spices.

But instead, a different scent assaulted her senses.

The sickly-sweet odor of cologne.

She turned, and the newcomer approached, a lazy smile on his lips, cold blue eyes gleaming in the moonlight.

"Miss de Grande."

His tongue rolled over her name as if he were devouring it. She stepped away until her back hit the balcony railings.

"Mr. Moss," she said, keeping her voice even. "Are you taking the air?"

He shook his head slowly and took another step forward, and she wrinkled her nose at the onslaught of cologne. Did he think the stench attracted women like flies? Or, perhaps, he sprayed himself with it to disguise other, unsavory odors.

"I'm most disappointed in you, Miss de Grande," he said. "Such a lack of decorum—what would your chaperone say?"

"Very little, I suspect, given that I've not acted untoward," she said. "Whereas *you*—"

She stopped herself. This was not the time to taunt him about his affair with Lady Francis.

"Whereas I what?" he sneered. "*I'm* the injured party here, Miss de Grande."

"In what way have I injured you?"

"Don't be a simpleton!" he scoffed. "Did you mean to insult me so publicly tonight?"

So, that was it. She'd pricked his pride by accepting Marlow's offer to dance.

"I had already promised the first dance to Lord Marlow," she said tartly. "Therefore, I committed no transgression in refusing your offer."

He shook his head. "In an impromptu dance after dinner, there's no prior claim."

He stepped closer, and the moonlight highlighted his blond hair as if he were surrounded by a halo.

With his sharp cheekbones and perfectly proportioned features, he looked like an angel.

Then he smiled, revealing white, even teeth.

"A young woman with your unfortunate background can be forgiven."

"I'm not ashamed of my background, Mr. Moss," she said. "I'm the daughter of a viscount."

"An impoverished fool who brought about his downfall and nearly ruined his friends—or so I heard. A lifetime in obscurity in the countryside can render a person somewhat savage. Had you been a man, I would have called you out."

She let out a laugh. "All this because I didn't wish to dance with you, Mr. Moss?"

"Do you prefer to ride a gelding," he said, "when you could have partnered a stallion?"

Ride me like a stallion—an Arabian stallion!

Lady Francis's words echoed in Lavinia's ears, and a tide of nausea swelled within her, exacerbated by the stench of cologne.

She pushed him aside, but he caught her wrist.

"Unhand me, Mr. Moss," she said.

"Not until I've had satisfaction."

"You'll get no satisfaction from me, I assure you."

He tightened his grip, then pulled her hard against him.

"Let me go!" she cried.

"Nobody insults me without suffering the consequences," he hissed.

"And nobody molests me without suffering the consequences, Mr. Moss," she retorted. "One scream from me, and you'll have the whole party witnessing your disgusting behavior."

"Be my guest," he said, his eyes glittering with triumph. "My reputation will remain intact, whereas *yours…*"

Her gut twisted in fear. He spoke the truth. Were she to cry out, they would be discovered, and she would be compromised. And she knew enough of Society, from Aunt Edna's warnings, to realize that a young woman caught in a compromising position with a man was often forced to marry him.

He drew his face close, his eyes gleaming with lust. His breath stank of stale cigar smoke and rotting meat. No wonder he drenched himself in cologne.

The strains of music and chatter grew louder, and she froze.

"That's better," he said. "My clever little mare—my beautiful mare."

She swallowed the urge to retch as he used the same words he'd uttered the night she caught him rutting Lady Francis. Surely he wasn't going to—

"All I ask is a kiss," he whispered, lowering his tone in what she presumed was an attempt to appear alluring. "One sweet kiss."

Disgusting creature! Yet he held the power, and he knew it. But the merest thought of his touching her—she could not allow it. She reached up and grasped his arms.

"Oh yes," he rasped. "While I relish a struggle, the sweetness of surrender is always to be preferred."

Lavinia closed her eyes and braced herself, shifting her weight onto one leg, while the other she tensed to thrust upward. A swift knee to the groin would soon put an end to that disgusting bulge in his breeches.

"What the bloody hell's going on?"

She opened her eyes to see Lord Marlow standing on the balcony, a brandy glass in each hand. Raw fury glittered in his eyes.

Moss glanced over his shoulder. "What does it look like,

Marlow? The lady and I are enjoying a little *tête à tête*."

"Somewhat unwillingly, on her part."

"She encouraged me," Moss said. "You know what women are like."

Marlow barked out a laugh. "Do you take me for a fool? You were eyeing her up over dinner as if she were the dessert."

"That doesn't mean to say my attentions weren't reciprocated."

"Miss de Grande is far more discerning than you may think," came the reply. "I believe she prefers the attentions of a *man*, not a boy."

Geldings, stallions, men, boys… Was this how men fought over a woman—as if she were the mare to be claimed by the strongest?

"Can I not speak for myself?" She pushed her assailant aside. "Please leave, Mr. Moss," she said. "As I've already said, your attentions are unwelcome."

Moss jerked his head toward Lord Marlow. "You think you can spread your legs for him because he has a title?"

"Damnation!" Lord Marlow cried. He flung the brandy glass aside, and it struck the wall, shattering on impact. His hands were fisted at his sides, and his body shook with fury. "Get out of my sight, Moss," he hissed, "before I throw you over that balcony."

Fear glittered in Moss's eyes, then he lifted his chin and spoke, a thin layer of bravado barely disguising his cowardice.

"Why don't you call me out?" he asked. "Is it because you doubt the lady's virtue?"

"I don't doubt Miss de Grande for a moment," Marlow said. "It would give me great pleasure to shoot you at dawn, but I've no wish to bring further attention to Miss de Grande after she's had the misfortune of suffering your notice. Leave, now, and I'll say no more about it. But do not approach her again if you value your head."

"Is that a threat?"

Marlow took a step forward, his tall frame dwarfing Moss's.

"No," he said. "It's a promise."

Fear rippled through Lavinia at the quiet determination in his voice. A man who possessed such ice-cold control over his anger was not a man to be crossed.

"There's nothing to stop me from telling everyone that she threw herself at me," Moss said.

"There is, if you wish your little liaison with Lady Francis to remain a secret."

Moss hesitated, then let out a bark of laughter. "My—*What?* You have no proof."

"You had a witness," Marlow said in the same quiet, even voice. "In the good lady's bedroom during Lord Francis's house party."

"Wh-what witness?"

Marlow wagged his finger. "Tut-tut, Mr. Moss—you expect me to betray an informer? I'm a model of discretion—and I'll remain so as long as I see fit. Unless your actions persuade me otherwise."

Moss glanced toward Lavinia, and she fought to restrain her laughter at the horror in his expression—the blackmailing bully being bested at his own game.

"Lord Francis can be a somewhat jealous man," Lord Marlow continued. He glanced toward Lavinia and winked—he actually *winked*!

The temptation was too much to resist.

"I've also heard that he's an excellent shot," Lavinia said.

Moss glanced from her to Marlow.

"He bagged thirty birds during a shooting party on Lord Fossett's estate," Marlow said.

"And he's not averse to shooting the occasional weasel," Lavinia added.

"So, you'd best take care, Mr. Moss," Marlow said. "Francis can hardly be admonished for ridding the world of vermin."

"I...I—" Moss stammered.

"Quite so," Marlow interrupted. "You should return to the

dancing. But I'd refrain from asking Lady Francis to dance while her husband's in the same room."

Moss retreated toward the balcony doors, then slipped inside.

Lord Marlow approached Lavinia, and his warm hands enveloped hers. "Miss de Grande—are you all right?"

She nodded, but found herself shaking, and he drew her into his arms.

"Forgive me," he said. "I shouldn't have left you."

"You weren't to know Mr. Moss would follow me outside."

"But I pledged to protect you," he whispered, his warm breath caressing her hair. "Am I not your Arthur, little Guinevere?"

"That was a long time ago," she said. "We were children, and I hardly remember it."

"I declared myself your champion."

Surrendering to her need, she relaxed into his arms.

"Miss de Grande," he whispered. "Lavinia…"

She drew in a deep breath and sighed. He placed his fingers under her chin, gently coaxing her until she tipped her head up, bringing her lips close to his.

His full, sensual lips…

"Lord Marlow," she breathed.

"I think we've gone beyond the formalities," he whispered. "Can you not speak my name?"

He lowered his face until their mouths were almost touching.

"Peregrine," he whispered. "My name is Peregrine."

The name suited him. Like the falcon, he was sleek and swift—an accomplished hunter who used intellect and accomplishment rather than brute force.

In which case, she was his prey—a willing prey, placing herself at his mercy.

"Lavinia…"

His breath caressed her lips, and she drew in a deep breath, relishing his rich, warm scent.

"Shall I kiss you, my little Guinevere—my sweet Lavinia?"

How she longed to taste those lips! They filled her mind with their promise of pleasures untold—pleasures she could only imagine that a man and a woman shared. Pleasures the want of which, according to Lady Betty, drove a creature to madness. Until now, she couldn't imagine being driven insane for want of pleasure. But as she savored being in his arms, her body thrummed with need, and heat radiated through her body, until a thick ache pulsed between her thighs.

She lifted her gaze to his, and her heart jolted at the expression in his eyes. She'd expected desire—but in their depths she saw something else.

Something akin to…

"I'll not kiss you without your consent," he whispered. "You must ask." She nodded, awaiting the pleasure. But he shook his head. "No—you must say my name."

"Peregrine…"

As if she had unleashed the beast, his mouth crashed against hers. She parted her lips in a gasp, and his tongue slipped between them. The assault was not unwelcome—the soft, velvety weapon coaxed and teased, promising pleasure, and she relished the taste of him—hot, strong spices, with an undercurrent of wickedness.

Suppressing a cry of surprise, she surrendered to his claim of ownership.

With long, slow, sweeping gestures, his tongue stroked her mouth, and her body roared into life. How could something so simple as a kiss elicit such wicked sensations? Pleasure swelled, and she squeezed her thighs to ease the ache. Then he placed a hand at her throat, caressing her skin in a tender gesture that belied the savage mastery of his tongue. Her breath hitched, and he lowered his hand to her neckline. Gentle, insistent fingers began to explore the skin of her breasts, which strained against the neckline of her gown.

A cry swelled in her throat, and she curled her tongue around his, indulging in a slow, sensual dance.

Peregrine murmured his approval.

He stilled his hand. Chasing the pleasure, she arched her back to brush her breasts against his fingertips, and let out a soft mewl, urging him to touch her.

Then he slipped his hand beneath her neckline. Her nipple tightened in anticipation, and he flicked it with his thumb. A fizz of pleasure coursed through her, and she threw back her head.

She let out a cry. "P-Peregrine!"

He gave a long, low growl—a beast ready to take his mate.

Sweet Lord! Was this what it was like to be claimed?

The glorious ache in her center intensified, and she pressed her body against his, seeking relief.

"Please…" she gasped, "I-I…need…"

Then he released her. A rush of cold air rippled over her, and she shivered.

"Shit!" he cursed. "I shouldn't have done that."

She winced at the profanity. He shook his head, and the desire in his eyes faded. Her heart sank as she caught regret in his expression…

Regret—and disgust.

The pleasurable ache in her body began to fade. Willing it to return, she moved toward him.

"No!" He gripped her arms, pushing her back, and held her at arm's length. "Forgive me, Miss de Grande. What I've done is reprehensible—worse, even, than Mr. Moss."

"How can you say that?" she cried. "You can't compare yourself to him? He disgusts me—but you…"

"Don't say it." He glanced toward the doors. "Tidy yourself up and return inside—quickly! I'll follow a moment later. While Mr. Moss is unlikely to say anything, it's best we don't arouse suspicion. The last thing I want is to be seen compromising you."

"What if I had no objection to being compromised?"

He shook his head. "You cannot mean that, Miss de Grande. You know as well as I that a woman's reputation is irreparable. If we were caught, I'd be forced to marry you."

Forced?

Her gut twisted with the shame of his rejection, and she wrenched herself free.

"I see," she said, fighting the urge to scream at him. "We cannot have that, can we? What a disaster that would be for *you*."

"Miss de Grande, I only meant—"

"I know full well what you meant," she retorted. "I'm well aware of my inferiority due to my circumstances, and I thank you for reminding me."

"That's not it at all," he said. "I—"

"Spare me!" she interrupted. Then she strode toward the door.

"Take care!" he cried.

"Don't worry—I will," she said bitterly.

"No…" He pointed toward the stone floor beside the doorway. "The broken glass."

What was broken glass compared to a shattered heart?

She sidestepped the shards of glass and returned to the drawing room.

The dancing was still in full swing, but the music was a little less excruciating—mainly due to Lady Francis now occupying the stool at the pianoforte. Lord Hythe was partnering Aunt Edna, the two of them doddering about the room, bumping into the rest of the party. Lady Hythe danced with Moss, pressing her bosom against him and eyeing him seductively. Perhaps *she'd* be the one demanding he ride her like a stallion tonight.

Lavinia gestured to the footman standing guard beside the brandy bottle. "Pour me one, would you?"

He splashed a quantity of brown liquid into a glass and pushed it toward her. She took it, drained the contents, then held it out.

"And another."

"Miss, I hardly think—"

"I asked you to give me a drink, not to think."

He gave a disapproving glare, then splashed a small quantity into her glass. She fixed him with a cold stare, then he relented and tipped the decanter up again, half filling the glass. She snatched it, then retreated to the corner of the drawing room.

She took a sip and glared at the company.

Society was rotten to the core, filled with self-indulgent, self-important fools who had no use in the world other than to bark orders and look down their noses at others. Moss only wanted to rut every woman in the room. Lord Hythe had taken a part in Papa's downfall.

As for Lord Marlow…

She spotted him across the room, speaking to Lord Francis. As if he sensed her looking at him, he glanced up. She averted her gaze and drained her glass. The liquor burned her throat, and she fought the urge to choke. But she swallowed it, and a raw, sharp warmth spread through her chest, dulling the pain of her humiliation.

Heath Moss made no pretense at decency—anyone could see he was a rake at first glance. Lord Hythe, by virtue of what he'd done to Papa, had shown his villainy. But Peregrine—Lord Marlow—*he'd* tricked her into believing he was different. And, fool that she was, she'd fallen for it.

She set her glass aside and smiled to herself. Her plan was already in motion. And, with one small adjustment, she would show the three of them—Moss, Hythe, and Marlow—that she was no fool.

The Phoenix would teach them *all* a lesson—beginning to-night.

CHAPTER TWENTY

PEREGRINE ADJUSTED HIS cravat and descended the main staircase. Voices came from the breakfast room, and his stomach growled at the aroma of kedgeree.

My favorite.

A footman approached him at the breakfast room door.

"Lord Marlow, would you follow me? The master wishes to see you in his study."

"What the devil for?"

The servant lowered his voice. "It's important, sir. Something's happened."

For a glorious moment, Peregrine visualized Moss lying in a flowerbed, having been tipped over the balcony. It was plain that he'd intended to cuckold Lord Hythe last night. Though why would any man be attracted to Lady Hythe, if her lovemaking had a similar degree of competence to her musicianship?

"Very well," he said, "lead the way."

The footman led Peregrine to a room at the end of the hallway, where Lord Hythe sat behind a large, squat mahogany desk.

Hythe glared at the footman.

"I'm glad to see you're capable of following *one* order, at least, Bradley," he snapped. "Now, go."

The footman scurried out.

"Incompetent fool!" Hythe said.

"What's he done?" Peregrine asked.

"Nothing—more's the pity. It's what he's *failed* to do."

"Forgive me, Hythe—but what has this to do with me?"

"It's your thief—what's his name—the Phoenix? The bastard's struck again!"

Peregrine stiffened. "What—here?"

"Last night."

"How can you be sure?"

"Because a painting's been stolen!" Hythe spluttered, his face reddening with rage.

"And you know it was taken last night?"

"I saw it when I retired," Hythe said. "I always walk through the gallery with the dogs. But that cursed fool Bradley"—he gestured toward the door—"burst into my dressing room this morning to say it had been stolen."

Hythe rose to his feet. "Come and see."

Not waiting for a response, he exited the study and led the way to the picture gallery that Lady Hythe had been so eager to show the party yesterday.

"There—look!"

Halfway along the hallway was an empty frame.

Peregrine approached the frame and inspected it. A modern piece, though the distress marks suggested otherwise, as if the maker had deliberately scuffed the wood to give it an appearance of antiquity.

Then he saw it—a small, folded piece of paper, tucked inside the bottom corner of the frame. He picked it up, unfolded it, and let out a low hiss as he recognized the drawing.

"It's the Phoenix, isn't it?" Lord Hythe said.

Peregrine nodded. "Can you recall the painting?"

"Of course I bloody can!" Hythe looked like he was going to burst with rage. "It's priceless—a family heirloom! A gift from the king."

"The present king?"

"No. It was gifted to the fifth Lady Hythe—painted by none other than Sir Peter Lely."

"Ah—then it must be Charles II," Peregrine said. "Lely was the royal painter." He shook his head. "No—that can't be right—the painting would be over a hundred years old, but this frame looks new."

He caught the scent of fresh wood shavings. Definitely a modern frame—he wouldn't be surprised if it had been made within the past month. And had the canvas been taken out of its frame, there'd be signs of tampering. Which only meant one thing.

Peregrine glanced at his host. "This isn't the original."

"Don't be a fool!" Hythe scoffed. "The painting's been in my family for generations."

"The frame's a replica," Peregrine replied. "Granted, a good one—made to look older than it is—but it's been fashioned in isolation. Frames are usually built around a canvas, and there would be evidence of damage had the canvas been removed."

"What are you trying to say, Marlow?" Hythe asked.

"That, in all likelihood, the thief has stolen the entire piece intact—canvas and frame together."

"Then why go to the trouble of hanging an empty frame in its place?"

Why, indeed?

Peregrine smiled to himself. The Phoenix had attempted to outwit him. But the quarry had underestimated the hunter.

"Lord Hythe, would you permit me to interview your guests?" he asked.

"Surely you don't believe one of my *guests* is the thief?"

"I'm afraid I do," Peregrine replied. "He thinks he's outwitted me, but if you grant me leave to interview the guests, I'll root out your thief before the morning's out."

"Then you have leave to do whatever you wish," Hythe said.

Smiling, Peregrine strode back toward the breakfast room, from where he could hear gay chatter and laughter.

One of those voices belonged to the Phoenix.

Laugh all you like, my friend. Soon, you'll never laugh again.

CHAPTER TWENTY-ONE

"LORD MARLOW—ARE YOU out of your wits?" Moss's voice vibrated with indignation. "How you can make such an accusation is beyond me. How much of our host's brandy did you take last night?"

"Sit down, Moss!" Peregrine snapped. "I'm serious. The culprit is among us."

"Do you include the ladies in your accusation, Lord Marlow?" Lady Hythe asked.

"Gertrude, my dear, of course he doesn't include *you*."

"I'm afraid everyone's a suspect, Lord Hythe," Peregrine said, "man and woman alike."

"A *woman?*" Lady Francis asked. "I cannot believe that."

"You'd be surprised, Lady Francis," Peregrine said. "Some women have a little intellect."

He heard a snort, followed by a volley of coughing, and caught sight of Miss de Grande at the far end of the table, holding a napkin to her mouth, her shoulders shaking.

"B-but, we're *victims!*" Lady Hythe cried. "Rather than accusing us, you should be looking for the painting."

"I intend to do exactly that, Lady Hythe," Peregrine said. "I wonder, would your guests object to my searching their chambers?"

"Whatever for, Marlow?" Moss asked. "Didn't you say there's an empty frame in the gallery? The canvas could be concealed anywhere—it'll be impossible to find."

"That's what the Phoenix wants us to believe," Peregrine said, "but the frame's a fake. The entire piece has been stolen. I suspect it's still in the building."

"Don't be a fool!" Moss scoffed. "Who'd steal a painting and keep it here?"

"Someone trying to trick us," Peregrine replied.

"I agree." Miss de Grande had recovered from her coughing fit. She leaned forward, eyes bright. "If the painting's in the building and the thief is a guest, he'll have hidden it somewhere familiar—such as his bedchamber, or even his trunk."

"I'll not have someone rifling through my possessions!" Moss cried.

"Have you something to hide, Mr. Moss?" Peregrine asked.

"Of course not! But I'll not tolerate such disrespect."

"Stealing a priceless painting is notably *less* respectful," Peregrine said. "All I wish to do is eliminate your name from the list of suspects."

"Well, *I* have nothing to hide," Lady Yates declared, "and neither does my niece. You may search my chamber, but only if both I and my maid are present. You may doubt my honesty—permit me to doubt yours also."

The old crone had a point. A frost had descended in the atmosphere as several hostile pairs of eyes stared at him.

Then an unlikely ally came to his aid. Miss de Grande rose to her feet.

"Let *me* be the first to submit my chamber for inspection," she said. "May I also suggest that you have the carriages searched, and the servants' quarters? The culprit might have coerced their valet—or maid—into concealing the painting."

"Well—really!" another voice said. "This is most objectionable."

"I shall conduct the searches with the utmost discretion, Lady Withering, I assure you," Peregrine said. "I like it no more than you—but it must be done to stop the Phoenix. You and Lord

Withering might be his next victims."

Lady Withering colored. "Oh, very well," she said, "but I like it not."

"Do you approve of this, Hythe?" Lord Francis asked. "It's your house that's about to suffer violation."

Lord Hythe nodded. "With reluctance, I do. I want the culprit found and punished."

Lord Francis sighed. "In which case, I suppose it's best to submit, then once this humiliation is over, we might enjoy the rest of the weekend."

"Once this is over, I'll stand each of you drinks at White's," Peregrine said. "Except the culprit, of course."

A murmur of laughter rippled through the party.

Miss de Grande rose and approached Peregrine. "You may inspect my chamber first—and Aunt Edna's." She turned to her companion. "Aunt—shall we?"

Nodding, the dowager took her arm, and the two women followed Peregrine and Lord Hythe out of the breakfast room.

As they approached the staircase, Miss de Grande paused.

"Might I make a further suggestion, Lord Marlow?"

"Lavinia!" Lady Yates said. "What have I said about speaking out of turn?"

"Please—speak," Peregrine said.

"I wonder, as a precaution, whether the gallery should be guarded—in case the thief returns."

"The painting's already been stolen, Miss de Grande," Lord Hythe said. "He'll not strike again."

"But if the Phoenix is as clever as you say"—she glanced toward the breakfast room, then lowered her voice—"that's what he'd *expect* you to think. As Lady Hythe explained on our tour of the house yesterday, the gallery boasts a number of extremely valuable works."

Peregrine stared at her, unable to suppress his admiration. "The young lady has a point, Hythe," he said. "Perhaps you should set a footman at each end of the gallery to watch over it tonight. But I'd suggest we not speak of this to the other guests. We might catch the Phoenix in the act."

"Very well," Hythe said. "I'll set *two* footmen at each end, and at every door leading outside. I'm taking no chances." He nodded to Lavinia. "Thank you, young lady. Perhaps Marlow should employ you as an assistant."

"Oh, no, Lord Hythe!" Lady Yates cried. "I wouldn't have my niece engage in anything so vulgar."

Peregrine exchanged a smile with Miss de Grande. Relief washed over him at the warmth in her eyes. He'd acted like an arse last night. Not only had he come close to compromising her, he'd pushed her away, too occupied in containing the erection in his breeches to have any concern for her feelings.

And, he'd discovered, her feelings—her happiness—were as important to him as catching the Phoenix.

⟫⟫✳⟪⟪

"THAT'S THE LAST of the trunks, sir."

Peregrine glanced up from his notes to see his valet in the doorway. "I take it the painting was nowhere to be found?" he asked.

"I'm afraid not, sir. Lord Hythe won't be pleased."

"I daresay he won't." Peregrine gestured to the seat opposite the desk. "Sit, Lawson. Take a little brandy."

"No, sir, I couldn't possibly…"

"Nonsense." Peregrine took the decanter, splashed brandy into a glass, then pushed it across the desk. "I think you've earned it after your little…*discoveries* this morning."

Lawson colored. "It's not something I expected to do during my tenure with yourself, sir—rummaging through ladies' undergarments."

"Particularly when said ladies' undergarments were found in one of the gentlemen's chambers?" Peregrine asked. "Something tells me, from the expression on Mr. Moss's valet's face, that not even *he* expected to discover a pair of lace drawers in his master's trunk. It's perhaps somewhat fortunate, then, that the man was not present when we searched Lady Francis's chamber, given that an identical pair was found in *her* trunk."

The valet's blush deepened, and he shifted in his seat.

"Come, Lawson—you're not so weak-bellied as to take offense at the contents of Lady Francis's trunk."

"Not Lady *Francis's* trunk, no…" The valet trailed off, and his blush deepened.

Peregrine leaned forward. "Aha!" he cried. "You made a discovery after all? Another stolen item, perhaps?"

"I doubt it—at least, I cannot imagine Lady Withering—"

"The lady who objected so vociferously to our searching the trunks?"

"I ought not to say."

"You must agree that one who objects the most to having their belongings searched has, in all likelihood, the most to hide."

Unlike Miss de Grande and her aunt—whom he had to thank for their willingness to submit their chambers to a search, which helped mollify the other guests. Had it not been for them, none of the other ladies would have agreed—even if it had all been for naught, for the painting was still missing.

"So," Peregrine said, "does Lady Withering possess undergarments designed to outperform Lady Francis in making a rake's pulse quicken?"

"Not undergarments, no, sir, but pictures… A book of pictures."

"What kind of pictures?"

But he had no need to ask. The valet's blush deepened so much that the tips of his ears were almost glowing.

"A little—ahem—*anatomical*, were they?" Peregrine asked.

The valet nodded.

"There's a market for a certain type of art," Peregrine said. "Drawings depicting a glimmer of flesh to titillate the rake—

though I'm surprised a *woman* has such material in her possession."

"These drawings left nothing to the imagination," the valet said. "My father was raised on a farm, so the drawings are nothing I've not seen the animals partake of—b-but the *other thing!* What would a lady have need of *that?*"

Peregrine stifled a laugh at the discomfort in the usually stoic valet's expression. "In need of what?"

Lawson shook his head. "I-I cannot bring myself to say, sir."

"You've come this far, Lawson," Peregrine said, tipping another measure of brandy into the man's glass. "You might as well see it to the bitter end."

Lawson stared at the glass, then he picked it up and drained it in a single gulp.

"A-a male...*appendage.*"

"From a man?"

"No—marble. I-it was carved out of marble. I thought it was a candlestick, at first, until I picked it up"—the valet shuddered and drew in a sharp breath—"and felt the detail on the end. I... Oh dear... I fear I've shocked you, sir. Of course, I-I put it back right away."

Ah.

"And, of course, I washed my hands afterward, sir. One never knows where such things have been."

On the contrary—Peregrine knew *exactly* where it had been.

"Why do you suppose Lady Withering placed such a-an item in her trunk?" the valet asked. "Unless it was Lord Withering's doing. Do you suppose her ladyship knows he put it there?"

"I daresay she does," Peregrine said, "each and every time."

"Sir!"

"Forgive me, Lawson. I'll say no more on the matter. Suffice it to say, I suspect Lord Withering's a lucky man. The secret to a good marriage is..."

Filthy pictures.

"Is what, sir?"

Marble cocks.

Peregrine cleared his throat. "Compatibility." He gestured to the decanter. "Another brandy?"

"I really shouldn't, sir—not a cognac of that caliber."

"I find one brandy much the same as any other.

"It's a Martell 1802 Cordon Noir, if I'm not mistaken," Lawson said. "Somewhat expensive. His lordship has a cellar full of the stuff."

"So he's not in need of cash."

"No, sir—his valet was only too quick to regale me with a whole catalogue of Lord Hythe's liquor collection."

Is that what valets did: play sport with each other, comparing their masters' attributes—the size of their estates, the value of their wine cellars, the number of mistresses they kept…

…and, perhaps, even the length of their manhoods—marble or not.

"You needn't worry, sir—*I'm* not one to indulge in petty one-upmanship."

"Of course not." Peregrine rose. "I suppose we must disappoint our host—the painting remains missing. Thank you, Lawson—you may go."

The valet bowed and scuttled out of the study, and Peregrine went in search of Lord Hythe.

He found him in the morning room, with the other guests. The conversation died as soon as he entered, and several pairs of eyes focused on him. Moss fidgeted, shifting from one foot to the other. Lady Withering stared at him, a delicate bloom on her cheeks and a saucy smile in her expression—to match that of her husband's.

Lord Withering—you lucky, lucky bastard.

Peregrine gave the man a conspiratorial wink, then cast his gaze over the remainder of the guests.

Had he been determined to identify the Phoenix based on a guilty expression, he could have accused any one of the company.

Except Miss de Grande. Clear-eyed and relaxed, she sat beside her aunt, a soft smile on her lips. Their eyes met, and she gave him a nod of encouragement.

Perhaps the hardships she'd suffered meant that she lacked the air of conceited outrage the other guests possessed. She was the only one among them who didn't believe that she was beyond reproach by virtue of her status in Society.

And because of that, she was the brightest jewel in the room, though the rest of the world was blind to her shine.

"What did you find, Lord Marlow?" Lady Hythe asked.

"Nothing," Peregrine said. He glanced at Lady Francis, then to Moss, and back again. "At least, nothing that merits further public discussion."

"Of course, that means the painting is still missing," Lord Francis said.

"We mustn't let that ruin the rest of the party," Lady Hythe said. "Come along, *mes amis*—it's time for our excursion in the park."

Lord Hythe scowled at his wife—but the perfect Society hostess never let a little thing like a stolen painting spoil her house party, lest it soil her reputation. The party rose and followed their hostess out of the morning room.

Peregrine hung back, and took Lord Hythe to one side.

"So, is that it?" Hythe asked. "You disrupted my house for nothing?"

"Of course not," Peregrine replied. He lowered his voice. "The Phoenix is toying with us. Unless he's spirited the painting into thin air, it's still in the building, in which case it's likely he'll move it tonight."

"Slippery bastard," Hythe said. "A priceless family heirloom— the estate's trustees will give me a dressing-down."

"I doubt it'll be missing for long," Peregrine said. "Most experts will recognize a Lely portrait—as soon as our thief attempts to sell it, he'll be caught. I'll alert my contacts in London when I return. Perhaps, in stealing a painting of renown, the Phoenix has made his first mistake."

"I'll wring his bloody neck," Hythe said through gritted teeth.

"Do you have anyone who would wish you harm?" Peregrine asked.

"Enemies, you mean?"

"People can bear grudges."

"I've always had a wide circle of friends," Hythe said, "many of whom I've known since boyhood. Your father among them. We were at Cambridge together. St John's, you know." He gestured ahead to the rest of the party. "As was Francis's late father. And Caldicott's father."

Francis, Caldicott…

"Francis has been robbed," Peregrine said, "and Caldicott lost a sword last month. Who else was in your set?"

Hythe frowned. "Lord Houghton. Has *he* had something stolen?"

"Not that I'm aware of."

"Then it can't be anything to do with us," Hythe said. "Besides—other people have been robbed. Didn't the regent lose a set of spoons?"

Hythe was right. The connection between the robberies still eluded Peregrine.

But it was only a matter of time until the Phoenix played one game too many.

He was all the more determined to catch the Phoenix and see the man brought to justice. Then, once he'd achieved his objective, he'd turn his attention to his other quarry.

Miss Lavinia de Grande.

Chapter Twenty-Two

L AVINIA GLANCED AT the clock on the mantelshelf. The days following the house party at Hythe Manor had been filled with dull events and inane activities. But today, she had something to look forward to. Aunt Edna was snoring in her chamber upstairs, after a heavy luncheon with the dowager Lady Thorpe, and Eleanor was due for tea any minute.

Better still, Papa—dear Papa—was due to arrive in London tomorrow morning. Lady Betty had written to say that his health had improved, and he was insisting on spending a few days in London before the summer was over. The timing could not be more perfect, for Lavinia had another gift for him.

She glanced at her needlework basket beside the sofa and smiled at the thought of what lay inside, and how she'd fooled everyone. As far as she was aware, nobody had noticed its disappearance. They were all looking for the wrong painting.

She smiled to herself, imagining Lord Marlow parading up and down the streets of London searching for a painting that he would never find.

I have bested you, my friend.

Then the image of his expression swam into her mind—eyes filled with desire, which had darkened as he caressed the skin of her breasts. A tiny pulse of longing throbbed in her center, and she shifted position, squeezing her thighs together.

Peregrine…

But he'd withdrawn from her, as if her touch burned him.

The door opened and a footman appeared.

"What is it?" she asked sharply.

"Ahem…" The footman hesitated. "Begging your pardon. Miss Howard is here."

He stepped to one side to reveal Eleanor, discomfort in her expression.

"I'm sorry," she mumbled. "Have I come at a bad time?"

Lavinia leaped to her feet. "No, dear Eleanor!" she cried. "Come in, please." She turned to the footman. "Would you be so kind as to bring us some tea? And perhaps some cake for my guest?"

"Very good, miss." The footman bowed, then retreated, closing the door behind him.

"Sit, do," Lavinia said.

Eleanor hesitated for a moment, then crossed the floor and took a seat. "Have you heard the news?" she asked. "Henrietta's to be married."

Lavinia nodded. "Lady Thorpe told Aunt Edna today. I can't imagine Henrietta and Giles together—she's so full of adventure, while he's such a stuffy creature, though I confess his cousin Beatrice is delightful."

"Perhaps their union was not unexpected," Eleanor said. "The two of them were always at odds—isn't that supposed to be a sign of love?"

"Is it?"

"Oh, yes," came the reply. "An adversarial relationship is often driven by a deeply rooted attraction that both parties strive to deny. Their struggles manifest in outward conflict."

"So, you're saying that we must find our ideal partner by arguing with him?" Lavinia laughed. "I cannot imagine you arguing with anyone, Eleanor!"

"*I'm* hardly likely to find a partner."

Lavinia's heart ached at her friend's stricken expression. In all likelihood, Eleanor had been subject to yet more criticism from her mother—and spite from her sister—about her lack of allure to the opposite sex.

The door opened and a maid entered, carrying a tea tray.

"Ah, thank you, Bessie," Lavinia said. "Put it on the table, would you?"

"Yes, Miss Lavinia," the maid said. "Cook said I was to bring a slice of her fruitcake, on account of Miss Eleanor being here— what with Miss Eleanor being one of her favorites."

Eleanor's face illuminated with a smile. "Please thank Mrs. White for me."

Bessie set the tray on the table, bobbed a curtsey, then slipped out of the room.

"Our cook has a soft spot for you," Lavinia said.

Eleanor colored. "I've met her once or twice while out walking. I rather wonder at her recalling it."

Lavinia smiled to herself. Mrs. White had regaled her with tales of how her friend was "the kindest young woman in London" after Eleanor had stopped to assist when she tripped in the street, suffering her mother's admonishments as a consequence. While Eleanor feared Society gatherings, she thought nothing of kneeling on the ground, in full view of the world, to help a servant she barely knew who'd fallen in the street, even though such an act of kindness risked her reputation.

After serving tea, Lavinia waited for her friend to shake off the awkwardness she always carried when entering into a social occasion—even an intimate tea between friends. At length, Eleanor, finished a slice of cake, then relaxed back into her seat, teacup in hand.

"That cake was delicious," she said. "It's not often I'm allowed any at home."

"Take another slice."

Eleanor shook her head. "Mother would never approve."

Doubtless she wouldn't. Mrs. Howard was the sort of woman who believed that a slender frame was the height of sophistication and that a healthy appetite was evidence of a lack of control.

Poor Eleanor, with her natural curves, was doomed to disappoint her mother.

Lavinia leaned forward. "Can I trust you to keep a rather wicked secret?"

Eleanor nodded. "Of course."

Lavinia opened her needlework basket and pulled out her bounty—a small painting, with a delicate gilt frame.

"What's that?" Eleanor asked.

Lavinia balanced the painting on her lap. "It's the Phoenix's latest treasure—appropriated from Hythe Manor. What do you think?"

Eleanor frowned. "That's not the painting you asked me to copy."

"That was a decoy." Lavinia grinned. "*This* is what I was really after."

Eleanor shook her head. "I don't understand. Where's the Hythe painting—the *real* one? Everyone's talking about it still being missing. And where's the copy?"

"The real painting never left Hythe Manor," Lavinia said. "As for the copy, I posted it. Or, at least, I gave it to a lad on the street to post—for a shilling."

"To whom?" Eleanor lifted her cup to her lips, and sipped her tea.

"Heath Moss."

Eleanor froze, her eyes widening.

"Of course, it might never reach him, though the boy looked like an honest sort," Lavinia continued. "Forgive me—I hope you don't mind my sending it to him. He'll never identify you as the painter, I'm sure, so you've naught to fear."

Lavinia glanced at the painting on her lap and smiled. Then she heard a splutter, followed by sharp cry. Eleanor convulsed, rattling her teacup in the saucer. Then she threw back her head and laughed.

"Eleanor?"

"Oh, do forgive me!" She wiped her eyes, then set her teacup aside. "I think the painting *did* reach Mr. Moss. Not only that, I suspect he believed it to be the real painting—and persuaded another to believe it, also."

"What in the name of the Almighty to you mean?" Lavinia asked.

Eleanor shook her head. "Oh, it's too amusing!" She leaned forward. "Juliette's been boasting about the gifts Mr. Moss has been lavishing her with," she said. "Sadly, her attempts to make me jealous failed, because I can't abide that lecherous dandy!"

"What can you mean?" Lavinia asked.

"Mr. Moss has been trying to court Juliette. Last week, he brought her a bouquet of orchids, every day, and when he took tea on Saturday, he spent the whole afternoon showing off the new pocket watch he acquired in Hatton Garden and telling us it cost over a hundred guineas."

"A hundred guineas? He's either a liar or a fool."

"Both, I imagine," Eleanor said. "Mother and Papa had this huge argument about it. Mother said Mr. Moss was a fine catch for Juliette, but Papa said he was an arrogant wastrel who lacked the intellect to hold a conversation with Uncle Hugh's prize sow, but clearly had enough cunning to persuade a watchmaker to give him credit, given that every tradesman in England knows that a promissory note from the Moss family is worth less than the paper it's written on."

"Your father said *that*?" Lavinia asked.

Eleanor nodded. "Word for word. Of course, I wasn't *meant* to hear."

"I daresay you couldn't help it," Lavinia replied. Eleanor's mother had the kind of voice that could slice through bank vaults.

Eleanor gestured toward the painting. "It's very pretty. May I see?"

"Of course." Lavinia handed it over.

Eleanor studied the picture. "J.R. 1765," she said, running her fingertips along the frame.

"Do you recognize the artist?" Lavinia asked.

"No, but she—or he—was very talented. The work's exquisite. Just a few simple brush strokes have captured the essence of the landscape—the effect of a field dusted with snow. Watercolor's the hardest medium, you know."

"I thought it was the easiest," Lavinia said. "Don't most ladies use watercolor?"

"It's easier to use than oil paints, but it's more difficult to produce a work worthy of note. A mistake on a watercolor cannot easily be rectified—it turns the color to mud. But with oils, you can paint over any mistakes."

"Papa's due to arrive tomorrow," Lavinia said. "I can't wait to see the expression on his face when he's reunited with the painting. Of course, Aunt Edna mustn't see it—but given that Papa's bringing Lady Betty with him, Aunt will either confine herself to her room, or go out."

"Do you think it's wise to show your father the painting so soon after you stole it?" Eleanor asked. "What if someone recognizes it?"

"Papa won't say anything—and nor will Lady Betty."

Eleanor shook her head. "It's still dangerous—what if you're discovered?"

"I've not been discovered so far—and there's only one item left to acquire. Then the Phoenix can return to the ashes and disappear forever."

"You ought to be careful," Eleanor said. "There's people investigating the thefts. Sooner or later, they'll catch you."

"Everyone believes that an entirely different painting has been stolen. By the time Lord Marlow discovers what's really happened, I'll have completed my quest, and nobody will know who outwitted them."

"What about Mr. Houseman?" Eleanor asked.

"Who the devil's that?"

"He's offered a reward of ten guineas for information leading to the capture and arrest of the Phoenix. It was advertised in the *London Times* last week—didn't you see it?"

"So—some fool thinks he can catch a thief, and has set the whole of London blundering about in search of one," Lavinia scoffed. "Every man on the street eager for ten guineas will be plaguing him with tales of shadowy figures creeping about the streets. If anything, that'll lessen the chances of my being caught, for while they're bumbling about the place, I can slip into Walton's estate unnoticed."

Eleanor stiffened. "Walton? Did you say *Walton?*"

Lavinia nodded. "Yes, Earl Walton, the blackguard. Papa's worst enemy—the man who has Papa's clock, the final item. I've left the worst enemy till last. In fact, when Papa comes, I'm going to ask him—"

"No!"

"What's the matter?" Lavinia asked. "Surely you don't think I'm in danger of getting caught?"

"Oh, Lavinia!" Eleanor said. "I hadn't realized…" She shook her head. "No—you're playing a dangerous game. Do you have any idea what they'll do to you if you're caught? The article said that Mr. Houseman is eager to see the Phoenix suffer the harshest punishment possible. I didn't think much of it, but *Walton!* You mustn't steal from him, Lavinia, for your sake."

"Eleanor, there's no danger, I assure you—"

"Please," Eleanor whispered. "You cannot steal from Walton. Don't you know he's—Oh!"

The door opened to reveal the footman.

"You have a visitor, miss," he said. "It's Lord Marlow."

Sweet Lord! Lavinia glanced at the stolen painting on the chair, for all the world to see. There was no time to hide it.

She'd been caught.

CHAPTER TWENTY-THREE

PEREGRINE GLANCED AROUND the morning room where Lord Yates's footman had ushered him in to wait. The curtains were fraying at the edges, and the two-seater sofa by the window had long since lost its luster.

Was this what Viscount de Grande and his daughter had been reduced to? Living off the charity of a cousin barely able to maintain his townhouse? And yet Miss de Grande remained cheerful—her father's ruination had failed to crush her spirit.

He'd come here today, on impulse, to see her, having no other reason than the need to be near her again. He couldn't remove her from his mind. Each night as he'd climbed into bed, he dreamed of having her lie beside him—and each morning he'd woken with a cockstand so painful that he thought he might die from it. And though he could ease the pain with his own hand or, heaven forbid, the attentions of a doxy, nobody would satisfy the need like Lavinia de Grande.

He would claim her as his. But before that, he had to tell her the truth:

That his father was Earl Walton, her father's bitter enemy and the man she had declared to hate above all others. Better it came from his lips than any other's. Then, once he had declared himself to her—both the truth and the feelings of his heart—the two of them could build a future together, side by side, a match of equals.

The door opened, and he rose to his feet, ready to drop to one knee and propose that instant. But it was the footman.

"Miss de Grande has another visitor, but she'll see you now."

"Are you sure I'm not inconveniencing her?" Peregrine asked. "Or Lady Yates?"

"Her ladyship is resting. Miss de Grande is in the parlor upstairs—if you'd like to follow me?"

The footman led the way out of the morning room to a parlor at the end of the hallway on an upper floor. Then he knocked on the door and pushed it open, announcing Peregrine's arrival.

Two young women occupied the parlor. Perched on the edge of their seats, backs straight, bodies stiff—they bore an air of guilt.

Peregrine bowed. "Miss de Grande," he said. "Thank you for admitting me."

She rose, then dipped into a curtsey. "Lord Marlow—a pleasure, as always. You know Miss Howard?"

"We've yet to be formally introduced," Peregrine said, "though I had the pleasure of seeing her at the Houghtons' ball, of course."

Miss de Grande gestured to her friend. "Eleanor—may I present Lord Marlow?"

Miss Howard colored and rose, a little unsteadily. Then she lowered herself into a curtsey, her gaze fixed on the floor.

"Delighted to meet you, Miss Howard," Peregrine said, offering his hand.

She took it. "Thank you."

"I'm already acquainted with your sister, of course," he said. "Miss Juliette—a charming, elegant young woman."

Miss Howard stiffened, then withdrew her hand. "Lavinia, I must be going," she said. "Mother will be expecting me."

"But Eleanor—"

"Please!" Miss Howard glanced toward Peregrine.

"Of course." Miss de Grande nodded toward the footman. "Wilkins, Miss Howard wishes to go home. Would you send for her maid? Then, perhaps, see if my aunt is awake?"

"Very good, miss."

The two young women embraced, then the footman escorted Miss Howard out.

Peregrine drew in a deep breath. His time had come.

Miss de Grande gestured to a chair. "Please, sit, Lord Marlow."

"So formal?" he asked. "Will you not call me Peregrine, now we're alone?"

"My aunt may come at any moment."

"You're quite safe from me, I assure you."

She returned to her seat, stopping to adjust the lid of the basket beside the sofa.

"Don't tell me you've succumbed to Society's greatest vice?" he asked.

She glanced up, a spark of fear in her eyes. "Vice?"

"Needlework." He gestured toward the basket. "Did you not once say that the pursuits of an accomplished lady were the greatest vice of all, for they perpetuated a patriarchal Society?"

She let out a sigh. "I believe I did."

"May I see the fruits of your sin?"

She placed her hand on the basket and shook her head. "The basket contains the work of another."

"Miss Howard, perhaps?"

"Miss Howard is more accomplished than I," Miss de Grande replied. "But it is her misfortune that her attributes are too often overlooked by those who don't understand her. What did you think of her?"

"She seems pleasant enough," he said. "But I'm not here to talk about Miss Howard."

"Eleanor is my friend, Lord Marlow."

"Then I shall resolve to like her for *your* sake."

She met his gaze, and a smile danced in her eyes.

The time had come. "Miss de Grande..." He hesitated. "Lavinia—may I be permitted to tell you something?"

Her eyes widened, and he could swear he glimpsed fear in

their expression.

"I'm afraid I've been less than honest with you," he continued, "but I value you too deeply to continue the deception."

A delicate bloom spread across her cheeks. "You—*value* me?"

"Can you be in any doubt?"

Before she could reply, footsteps approached, together with the tap-tapping of a cane. The door opened, and Lady Yates strode in.

"Lord Marlow," she said. "What a pleasure." She glanced toward her niece. "Lavinia, is Miss Howard not here?"

"She left, Aunt, which is why I asked Wilkins to send for you."

"Quite so. I'm glad to see you're capable of observing propriety, though not as often as I'd like." She fixed Peregrine with a stare. "Are you here to see me, Lord Marlow, or my niece?"

He found himself blushing under her gaze—a look as sharp as a knife, capable of filleting a hindquarter of pork at twenty paces.

Then the corners of her mouth lifted into a smile of satisfaction.

A ripple of relief surged through him. If Lady Yates approved of him as suitor for her charge, then the battle was half won. Many chaperones tasked themselves with directing their charges toward the suitor of whom they approved the most.

"Lord Marlow is here to see *both* of us, Aunt," Miss de Grande said. "Is that not right, your lordship?"

She cast Peregrine a saucy smile. He returned the smile, then lowered his gaze to her neckline, below which two stiff little peaks poked against the fabric of her gown.

Sweet heaven! Were it not for her aunt's presence, he'd be fighting the urge to leap across the parlor and take her on the sofa. He closed his eyes as the image flooded his mind—Miss de Grande, her skirts about her waist, parting her thighs to offer her sweet pink flesh to him... Her mouth opening into a wide O of surprise when he thrust into her, claiming her as his... The little mewls of pleasure while her body tightened and rippled around his cock...

"Lord Marlow!"

He startled and leaned back in his seat, crossing his legs to hide the evidence of his arousal.

Sweet Lord—he was ready to burst in his breeches like a lad of fifteen! If the mere thought of taking her caused such a sensation, what would the act itself do to him?

"F-forgive me, Lady Yates," he said, his voice strained.

"You seem a little...discomposed," the dowager said. "Perhaps you thought my invitation somewhat forward?"

"Your invitation?"

"To dine with us tonight. My niece and I are sorely lacking in male company, though we expect Lord de Grande to arrive tomorrow."

Miss de Grande nodded.

"Just an informal family supper, mind," Lady Yates continued. "I find them preferable to elaborate dinners—don't you? An abundance of rich foods lies heavy in the stomach."

"And on the *nose*," Miss de Grande added, "especially when one is forced to sit next to the Duke of Dunton."

"Lavinia!" Lady Yates admonished her niece, but mirth flickered in her expression. "His Grace demands your respect."

"Not after he's consumed a plate of beef ragout and cabbage, Aunt. You didn't have to sit next to him at Lady Ross's dinner. I almost fainted at one point."

Peregrine stifled a laugh. "Perhaps that's why the gentlemen and the ladies separate after dinner—to enable the...*atmosphere* to dissipate among the gentlemen, while the ladies are enclosed in safety in the drawing room. We suffer for the benefit of your sex."

Miss de Grande gave him another smile. "That's very gallant of you, sir."

"Tell me, Lord Marlow," Lady Yates said, "are you making progress in catching that thief—the Phoenix?"

"I believe I am," he said. "I must thank you both for your

assistance at Lord Hythe's house party. I doubt the other guests would have been so accommodating had you not taken the lead."

"H-have you found the painting?" Miss de Grande asked.

"No, but I'm confident that I shall."

"Oh?" Her voice had risen in pitch.

"I'm close to discovering the pattern that connects the stolen items," he continued. "Or I should say *we*, since there are several of us working on the case."

"S-several?" Miss de Grande clasped her hands together. There was no doubt about it—something distressed her.

"I trust the punishment will be severe when you catch him," Lady Yates said. "Were I the magistrate, I'd—"

"Aunt, please!" Miss de Grande interrupted. "I'm sure our guest has no wish to discuss the Phoenix."

"Anyone in Society could be his next victim, Lavinia. We must all be vigilant, must we not, Lord Marlow?"

"I think, perhaps, *you* may be safe from the Phoenix, Lady Yates—and your niece, of course," Peregrine replied.

"How so?" Miss de Grande asked, her voice tight.

"Because the Phoenix, whom I consider to be an intelligent adversary, would be a fool to attempt to steal something of yours. He may be too clever for most of Society, but I believe that *you* are too clever for *him*."

"You flatter my niece too much, Lord Marlow," Lady Yates said.

"On the contrary, ma'am, I don't flatter her enough. But I'll gladly remedy the situation, if she consents."

Lady Yates drew in a sharp breath. Peregrine glanced toward Miss de Grande...

Lavinia...

Did she understand his meaning as well as her aunt?

"Or perhaps," he added, fixing his gaze on her, "if Lord de Grande would consent."

Her eyes widened, and he caught a spark of hope in her expression.

Hope—and desire…

She was his for the taking. He only need ask.

A door opened and closed in the distance. Then footsteps approached and they heard voices outside the parlor door.

Lady Yates glanced at her niece. "You're not expecting more visitors, are you, Lavinia?"

Before Miss de Grande replied, the door opened to reveal the footman, accompanied by a man, and a woman clad in a deep purple gown, hair piled elegantly on top of her head.

Peregrine would have recognized Lady Betty Grey anywhere.

As for the man standing beside her, he looked like a relic from a bygone era. His jacket, fashioned from blue silk and edged with gold brocade, exuded the faded elegance of the previous century. It hung on his frame as he hunched over a silver-topped cane. Wisps of white hair were visible beneath a powdered wig, framing a face that was creased with weariness and pain.

The man needed no introduction. The years may not have been kind to his body, but the sharp intelligence in his eyes was exactly the same as it had been the last time Peregrine set eyes on him at Fosterley Park.

"Good heavens—Richard!" Lady Yates cried. "What are you doing here at this hour? We weren't expecting you until tomorrow." She wrinkled her nose. "And…I see you've brought *that woman*."

Lady Betty inclined her head graciously, maintaining her smile. Doubtless she'd weathered worse insults.

Miss de Grande was not so circumspect. She leaped to her feet and ran toward the newcomers.

"Papa—Lady Betty!" She kissed her father on the cheek, then embraced Lady Betty.

"Lavinia, darling!" Lady Betty replied. "I see London agrees with you."

"Child!" Lady Yates snapped. "Must you show such a lack of decorum toward that woman?"

"Edna—show a little more respect, please," Lord de Grande

croaked. "Were it not for Lady Betty, I'd not even—"

He broke off as his gaze fell upon Peregrine.

"Who the devil is *that*?"

"Papa, let me introduce Lord Marlow," Miss de Grande said. "Aunt and I have invited him to—"

"Marlow, you say? Marlow…" De Grande cocked his head to one side, frowning as if in concentration.

Then recognition rippled across his expression and the confusion morphed into hatred.

"Marlow!" he cried. "How *dare* you show your face here, you…you *blackguard*!"

"Papa?"

De Grande rounded on his daughter. "Is this how you repay me, child—with *betrayal*?"

Lady Yates approached the old man. "Richard, calm yourself." She glared at Lady Betty. "Is this what your company has done to him—addled his wits? You're not welcome in my home. You—"

"Don't be a fool, Edna!" de Grande cried. "Lady Betty is a loyal friend—unlike the vermin you've invited into our midst."

"Papa, Lord Marlow's a friend also," Miss de Grande said. "Don't you recall my childhood friend from when we lived at—"

"Is this why you came to London, Lavinia—to *betray me*?"

"Papa, I-I don't understand."

"I take it you know who this man is?"

"Of course, Papa," she said. "He's Lord Marlow."

"And do you know who his *father* is?"

She glanced toward Peregrine, doubt in her eyes. "I know he's the heir to an earldom—so his father must be Earl Marlow, though I've not met him."

"Ignorant fool!" de Grande spat. "And you!" He jabbed a finger at Lady Yates. "Did you not *think*?"

"Lord de Grande," Peregrine said, "if I might explain—"

"Spare me your lies, Marlow," de Grande said. "After what your father did, do you think I'd believe a single word you say?"

Miss de Grande glanced toward her father, then back at Peregrine. Then a flicker of understanding glimmered in her expression, and Peregrine's heart cracked at the horror in her eyes.

"Wh-who is your father, Lord Marlow?" she asked.

"I can explain…" he began, but she raised her hand to silence him.

"Who is he?"

"His father is Earl Walton," de Grande said. "The man who set out to ruin me, and didn't stop until I'd lost everything—the man who, with his friends, saw me hounded from my home, humiliated, and disgraced. The man responsible for everything you have suffered, Lavinia." He shot Peregrine a look of venom and jabbed a finger in his direction. "*That* is whose son he is."

She shook her head. "No…"

"Lavinia, let me explain—"

"There's nothing to explain!" she cried. "Why didn't you say who you were?" She shook her head. "I trusted you! I told you what happened to me—to my father—and you listened, knowing the part you played in our downfall."

"I tried to tell you."

"No, you didn't!" she said. "When I told you how much I loathed Earl Walton for what he did to us, why didn't you say anything? Or did you delight in deceiving me, knowing that your family had destroyed mine?"

"Lavinia, I—"

"How *dare* you address my daughter in such a familiar manner!" de Grande said. "Leave—now—before I put a bullet in your heart!"

"Richard, I fail to understand what Earl Walton has to do with any of this," Lady Yates said. "He's not been seen in England since—"

"Since he ruined me!" de Grande cried.

"How did *he* ruin you? I thought—"

"Lady Yates," Lady Betty interrupted. "We should discuss this another time. I fear we're distressing Lord de Grande."

"How dare you speak to me, you *hussy!*"

"Aunt, please!" Miss de Grande said. "Lady Betty doesn't deserve—Oh!"

Lord de Grande let out a strangled gasp and pitched forward, clutching his chest. His cane clattered to the floor.

Lady Yates stood, face ashen, while Miss de Grande caught her father before he fell to the floor. Lady Betty took hold of de Grande's arms, then hailed the footman.

"You there—Wilkins, is it? Help us—hurry!"

Between them, the two women and the footman carried the old man to the couch and laid him down. Lady Betty placed a cushion beneath his head and pressed her fingers against his neck.

"Papa!" Miss de Grande cried. "Papa—forgive me! I didn't know."

"Brandy," Lady Betty said. "Quick, now!"

The footman darted across the room toward a bureau, then returned with a glass half-filled with a dark brown liquid.

"Give it to me," Miss de Grande said. She kneeled beside the couch and held the glass to her father's lips, which had turned blue against the gray pallor of his skin. His chest rose and fell in a sigh. He lifted his head, took a sip, then fell back.

"Can't…br-breathe…" he gasped.

His daughter clasped his hand. "Don't panic, Father," she said. "Remember what we did the last time you had a seizure? Breathe in slowly and count to three—then out slowly, counting to five. Ready?"

He nodded, and she kissed his hand.

"Wilkins—fetch a doctor," Lady Betty demanded.

The footman shuffled uncomfortably from one foot to the other.

"Quickly!" she cried. "Take my carriage—go to Dr. McIver, number fifty-three Harley Street. Tell him I sent you, and it's to be charged to my account."

"Very good, ma'am."

Lady Yates stood in the center of the room, body shaking. She hadn't moved since Lord de Grande had collapsed. Lady Betty poured a brandy and handed it to her.

"You've had a shock, Lady Yates," she said. "Let's sit you down."

The dowager curled her fingers around the glass, then let Lady Betty escort her to a seat. By now, both Lady Betty and Miss de Grande spoke in confident, quiet tones. Peregrine found himself admiring both women—especially Miss de Grande. Despite her evident distress, she forced herself to remain calm for the father she loved.

If only he'd had such a relationship with his own father!

His father. *Bloody hell!*

That old bastard had a lot to answer for.

Peregrine approached the couch where Miss de Grande had placed a hand on her father's chest.

"How is he?" he asked.

A ridiculous question, given that the man had suffered a seizure—but, accompanied by two strong women willing to take charge in a crisis, Peregrine felt his own inadequacy keenly.

She glanced up at him. "His breathing has eased. His heart's still racing, but provided he's not distressed any further, he should recover."

Guilt jabbed at Peregrine's heart as he watched the old man struggling for breath. If only Father could see what he'd done! But then, that old bastard wouldn't give a damn.

De Grande's eyes fluttered open.

"Papa," Miss de Grande whispered. "It's me, Lavinia." She leaned over him and kissed his cheek. "Must you always make such a dramatic entrance, Papa?"

A smile slid across his thin lips. Then his gaze met Peregrine's and the smile disappeared.

"I told *you* to go," he croaked.

"But..." Peregrine protested.

"Go—please," Miss de Grande said.

"I cannot help who my father is," Peregrine said.

"His blood runs in your veins," de Grande wheezed. "He's—" He broke off in a fit of coughing, jerking his thin body while he fought for breath.

"Just go!" Miss de Grande cried. "Even if I could forgive your ancestry, I cannot forgive your deceit—not when I had grown to feel…" Her eyes glistened with moisture. "Please—*Peregrine*," she whispered. "Can't you see you're distressing my father? I cannot see you again. I'm sorry."

He reached toward her face, and she closed her eyes. Then she jerked away and turned her back to him, focusing her attention on her father.

A hand touched his elbow, and he looked up to see Lady Betty, her warm brown eyes staring at him with understanding.

"You should go," she said. "I'll take care of him now." She glanced toward Miss de Grande. "I'll take care of them *both*."

The time had come to admit defeat. He nodded, then gave Lady Yates a stiff bow and exited the parlor, the footman in his wake.

As he stepped out into the street, the cold air washed over him. But rather than relish the freshness of the outside, he only felt the cold—a cold to match his heart.

Lavinia—his little Guinevere—would never forgive him. Tonight, he'd entered the house, an eager suitor hoping to win the hand of the woman he loved. But now, he was leaving that house having lost all hope of securing her heart. In all likelihood, she would hate him forever.

CHAPTER TWENTY-FOUR

T HE DOCTOR DROPPED his instruments into a black medical bag, snapped it shut, then wiped his hands on a cloth.

"You gave your family quite a shock, Lord de Grande."

Papa let out a sigh, while Lady Betty tucked a pillow behind his back where he lay watching over his audience like a monarch acknowledging his subjects. A single candle illuminated the bedchamber, flickering in the air as Lady Betty had moved to and fro, following the doctor's instructions with quiet efficiency. It cast sharp shadows across Papa's face, emphasizing the wrinkles around the corners of his deep-set eyes.

Lady Betty and the doctor had, between them, carried Papa into the bedchamber, while Lavinia brought a washbowl and cloth. The doctor's instructions, delivered in crisp, professional tones in his Scottish brogue, served to soothe Lavinia's fear, forcing her to focus on the task at hand. Aunt Edna had languished on the parlor sofa, overcome by shock. But now, having recovered, she sat beside Lavinia while the doctor examined his patient.

"How is he, Dr. McIver?" Lavinia asked.

"He's recovering, miss. His pulse is stronger than it was, though still a little uneven. I don't see why he shouldn't be up and about in a day or two. But…" He turned toward the patient, his tone growing stern. "You must take things easy, Lord de Grande. No more excitement—and I wouldn't recommend traveling for a few days."

He gestured to the phials on the table beside the bed. "Don't forget now—two spoonsful of that tonic, three times a day. The laudanum is to be taken sparingly, and only if you have trouble sleeping."

"Have no fear, doctor," Lady Betty said. "We'll take care of him."

Aunt Edna opened her mouth to protest. Frowning at her aunt, Lavinia rose to her feet.

"Is there anything I can do?" she asked.

"No more than usual, lass. You might want to ensure that he takes his medicine."

"What should I give him?"

The doctor smiled. "Anything he wants."

"Good," Papa said. "I'm hungry."

"Dinner will be spoiled now," Aunt Edna said. "But you're welcome to stay, Dr. McIver. I'm sure the cook can salvage something edible."

"Och no, Lady Yates, I wouldn't put you to the trouble. I'd best be going."

"I'll show you out," Lady Betty said. "It's time I left, also— Lord de Grande is in good hands."

"No," Aunt Edna said, rising to her feet. "I should like you to stay."

Lady Betty's eyes widened. Then she nodded. "That's most kind, Lady Yates. I'd be glad to." She turned to the doctor. "Let me see you out, Dr. McIver, and we can discuss your account."

The doctor exited the chamber, followed by Lady Betty.

"Aunt…" Lavinia began, but her aunt held up a hand.

"It's perfectly natural to invite to dinner one who has done our family a service, child," she said.

Lavinia smiled. Aunt Edna would never admit Lady Betty into her social circle. But Lavinia recognized the olive branch her aunt offered for what it was—a gesture of friendship that could never be openly acknowledged.

Aunt Edna turned to the figure sitting upright in the bed. "Richard, shall I send Sarah up with a tray? The ragout would lie heavy on you, but Cook makes a tolerable broth."

"Very well, Edna," Papa sighed, and Aunt Edna swept out of the bedchamber.

Lavinia approached her father and took his hand.

"You gave us all a fright, Papa. You shouldn't have come to London if you weren't feeling well. I could more easily have come to Springfield Cottage."

"I wanted to visit London one last time," Papa said breathlessly, "to see you enjoying the Season, as you deserved—the Season I always feared would be denied you. You're my world, Lavinia—you know that, don't you?"

"Dear Papa!" Lavinia stroked the back of his hand, running her fingertips across the translucent, papery skin, beneath which she could discern faint blue veins.

"And..." He drew in a deep breath, fighting for air. "The doctor was right about giving me what I want."

"Don't worry, Papa—I'll make sure Sarah brings you a bowl of ragout once you've finished your broth. And"—Lavinia leaned forward and lowered her voice—"Cook has prepared lemon syllabub—your favorite. If you promise not to tell Aunt Edna, I'll bring you a bowl myself."

"I wasn't referring to dinner," Papa said. "I was referring to *that man.*"

Lavinia's heart twisted at the loathing in his voice. "You mean Lord Marlow?"

"Don't speak his name!" Papa hissed. He leaned forward, spasming into a cough.

"Hush," Lavinia said, stroking his hand. She placed a kiss on his forehead and eased him back onto the pillow. His eyes glistened with moisture, and her gut twisted with guilt at having inadvertently resurrected the pain he'd suffered when his friends betrayed him.

The door was knocked upon softly, and a maid's head appeared.

"Supper is served, Miss Lavinia—Lady Yates awaits you in the dining room."

"Tell them I'll have my supper with Papa," Lavinia said. She squeezed her father's hand. "I'm going to take the best care of you while you're in London."

"Don't be a fool," he said, affection in his eyes. "You should be enjoying Society while you're here."

"I've seen enough of Society to be able to afford some time for whom I love best in the world," she said, smiling. "Besides, it'll do Aunt Edna good to dine alone with Lady Betty."

"You mustn't be too harsh on your aunt," Papa said. "She's from a different generation—brought up to believe that women should be content not to have the same freedoms as men."

"And *you*, Papa? What do you think?"

He squeezed her hand. "I think that a little independence in a woman is no bad thing—provided, of course, she heeds the advice of a loving father."

He leaned back and sighed. "My darling daughter," he whispered. "Everything I want—and do—is for you."

And I you, Papa.

"I have a surprise for you," she said.

His eyes widened, and his mouth creased into a smile. "I think I've had my share of surprises tonight."

"This one, I promise, you'll enjoy."

"Very well." He patted her hand indulgently. Lavinia kissed him once more, then exited the bedchamber and made her way to the parlor. She heard female voices and the clattering of crockery in the distance. Good—Aunt Edna and Lady Betty were safely in the dining room.

She picked up the needlework basket, then returned to Papa's chamber. The aroma of wine and herbs filled the air, and the room was bathed in a soft, warm glow. Someone had lit the candles and placed a tray on the table beside the bed, with a plate of ragout and a bowl of broth from which wisps of steam rose.

"What's that you have there?" Papa asked. "Has your aunt finally succeeded in persuading you to embroider cushion covers—or whatever young women are supposed to do?"

She let out a laugh. "I'm afraid not, Papa. I have no embroidered nightshirt for you in here—but there *is* something I believe you'll very much like. Though I fear it may overexcite you."

"I'm willing to take the risk," Papa said.

"We should eat our supper first, before it goes cold," she said. "Then, if you finish your broth, you may have your reward."

"Dear child!"

Lavinia set the tray on her father's lap, then sat at the table and ate her supper, watching him as he dipped his spoon into the broth. By the time he'd finished, the color had returned to his cheeks.

After removing his empty bowl, Lavinia sat beside the bed and placed the needlework basket on her knees.

"Your reward." She reached inside the basket, pulled out the painting, and held it up.

Papa grew still, confusion in his expression. Then recognition glimmered in his eyes. He reached out, his hand trembling, to touch the painting, then ran his fingertips along the deep brown wooden frame flecked with gold, as if caressing a long-lost love.

"*The Snow Field*," he whispered. "Do my eyes deceive me?"

"It is as you see, Papa," Lavinia said. "Your painting—finally back where it belongs."

"B-but—I don't understand. How did you persuade Lord Hythe to part with it?"

"You needn't concern yourself with that, Papa."

He narrowed his eyes. "What do you mean? You didn't disgrace yourself, did you?"

She avoided his gaze. "I did no such thing, Papa. Lord Hythe took little to no persuasion. Would you like to look at the picture more closely?"

He nodded, and she passed it over. He held the painting in his arms as if cradling a beloved child and ran his fingertips over the features—distant hills painted in a delicate purple, with a man and a boy in the foreground, sheltering beneath a tree beside a gate that led to a field dotted with cattle.

"It was your dear mother's favorite," he said.

Lavinia nodded. Papa had told her years ago that he'd procured the painting at an auction in London shortly after Mama accepted his hand—and that she had treasured it ever after.

Footsteps approached outside, and Lavinia snatched the painting back and slipped it into the basket.

Papa narrowed his eyes with suspicion.

"Aunt Edna wouldn't appreciate it if she knew I'd been engaging in the purchase of a painting," Lavinia said. "I paid considerably less than it's worth, and I fear she'd disapprove."

Papa let out a snort of derision. "You've done no worse than that blackguard Hythe—not to mention that bastard Walton." A tear rolled down his cheek. "Much as I love the painting—and the other items you've brought back to me—I cannot be at peace knowing that your mother's clock is still in that bastard's filthy hands."

The door opened, and a maid appeared. "Begging your pardon, your lordship, Miss Lavinia. Will you be wanting anything else?"

"Perhaps later, Sarah," Lavinia said.

"Very good, miss." The maid cleared the plates, then bobbed a curtsey and exited with the tray, closing the door behind her.

Lavinia took her father's hand, an idea forming in her mind. "Don't despair over the clock, Papa," she said. "Perhaps I can persuade Lord Marlow to sell it to us."

Papa shook his head. "Walton would never sell it—not to me."

"He needn't know," Lavinia said. "I'm sure if Peregrine knew how much it meant to us, he'd—"

"*Peregrine?*" Papa sat up. "*Peregrine?* You address him with such familiarity, knowing whose son he is?" His face colored, and his breathing grew labored.

Lavinia placed a hand on her father's shoulder and eased him back onto the pillow. "Please, Papa, don't distress yourself!"

"Then speak no more of that blackguard—or his spawn."

Lavinia flinched at the hatred in his voice. "Hush, Papa," she said. "You should get some rest."

She reached for the bottle of laudanum, but Papa caught her hand, curling bony fingers around her wrist.

"I'll not be denied this, child," he croaked. "Did not the good doctor instruct you to ensure I was given what I wanted?"

"Yes, Papa."

"Then be a dutiful child and do as I bid. Do *not* speak to Lord Marlow again—and don't mention his name in my presence. Is that understood?"

She nodded.

"I shall instruct your aunt to ensure he's not admitted again."

A shard of pain spiked at her heart.

Peregrine might have deceived her, but he'd not set out to harm her. But, as she pressed her hand against Papa's forehead— her own fears rising at how cold his skin was—she could not defend him. He was their enemy's son, and as such, she could not see him again.

"Lavinia—my darling daughter," Papa whispered, clinging to her as if he clung to life. "M-make me a promise. Swear, on the life of your dear, departed mother, that you'll not fraternize with my enemy."

She closed her eyes, but the image of Lord Marlow—and the desire in his eyes—threatened to overpower her. She opened them again to find herself confronted by Papa's strong gaze.

"I swear," she whispered, ignoring the pain in her heart.

He lessened his grip, his body relaxed, and a soft smile curled his lips.

"That's my darling girl," he said. "You've always been loyal to your dear papa—when others betrayed me, you were my salvation. Your mother would have been so proud of you." His chest rose and fell on a sigh. "I think, perhaps, London is no longer the place for me. I'll return to Springfield Cottage as soon as I'm able. London is for the young—the hale and hearty—but it is also where treachery lies, and I no longer want any part of it. I wish to live out my days in peace, surrounded by those who love me—and the memory of my one true heart." He stroked her hand. "I cannot thank you enough for returning the painting to me."

"I would do it again, a hundred times over, to restore the balance of justice," she said. "Now, how about I venture into the kitchen and bring you a bowl of syllabub? A small bowl, mind, so Cook doesn't miss it."

"Have you taken to thieving, daughter?"

Her heart fluttered, but she merely smiled. "A little thievery can be forgiven if it's for a good cause, Papa."

"Perhaps," he replied, "but only if the thief evades capture."

"You need not fear," she said. "I'm always careful."

He fixed his gaze on her, then glanced toward the painting, and she caught a flicker of understanding in his eyes.

"I think I'll return to Springfield the day after tomorrow," he said. "Then I can display the painting. It would look very pretty in the parlor, but I'll keep it in my chamber. Now—be off with you. I'm rather tired, would relish the quiet, and I'm sure Lady Betty would value your company, rather than be subjected to your aunt all evening. And don't trouble yourself over the syllabub. While I'm sure your skills as a thief are exceptional, all thieves are caught in the end. I think, perhaps, from now on, you should restrict yourself to more...*honest* means of procurement, however honorable your intentions. In fact, I'd like you to return to Springfield with me when I leave."

Lavinia kissed her father's hand, then slipped the painting back into her workbasket and exited the chamber.

He knows.

Papa was no fool.

And he was warning her to stop.

But her heart had almost cleaved in two at his look when he

spoke of Walton, and his eyes had moistened with sorrow when he mentioned his beloved clock. Try as he might to persuade her not to, she owed it to him to see her quest through to the end.

One more item—and then her quest would be complete, and Papa would have the peace of mind that had been denied him for so many years.

And perhaps…

Perhaps, once his precious treasures were restored, Papa might think more kindly of the man she had grown to love.

For she *did* love Peregrine—the pain when she'd learned who his father was told her that. Had she cared nothing for him, it wouldn't have mattered.

But the boy she'd idolized as a child, had dreamed of while she grew into a woman, and the man who had captivated her and brought her to pleasure…

She had fallen in love with him.

CHAPTER TWENTY-FIVE

"THERE'S TWO GENTLEMEN to see you, sir," Peregrine's footman said. "One of them is Mr. Houseman."

What did that arrogant arse want?

The footman ushered Houseman into the study, together with a thin, white-haired man dressed in a threadbare coat, holding a cloth cap in one hand and a packet in the other.

"To what do I owe the honor?" Peregrine asked.

Houseman gave a satisfied smile. "This morning, I received a visit from someone in my network of contacts."

Arrogant fool! A handful of ne'er-do-wells who frequented the inns in the less palatable parts of London was hardly a *network*.

"And?" Peregrine prompted.

"A painting signed by Peter Lely was discovered in a curiosity shop."

Peregrine caught his breath.

"Aha! I *knew* that would get your attention," Houseman said. "I took the liberty of bringing the proprietor with me. Mr. Camp—this is Lord Marlow."

His companion bowed his head. "A pleasure, your lordship."

"And—you claim to have a Lely?" Peregrine asked. "I find that somewhat unlikely."

Camp held up the packet. "I have it here, your lordship."

"How did you come by it?"

"A man sold it to me about a fortnight ago."

"Can you describe him?"

Camp glanced toward Houseman. "When do I get my payment? You promised—"

"Just answer the question!" Peregrine snapped.

"There's no need to take that tone," the man began, but Peregrine raised his hand.

"There's every need. Theft is a crime, Mr. Camp—as is handling a stolen painting. I take it you'd rather avoid a spell in Newgate."

"I don't know nothing about no stolen painting, sir," Camp replied. "He said it was a family heirloom—I bought it off him in good faith. Cost me ten pounds, that did."

"Can you describe him?"

He gestured toward Houseman. "I already told him."

"You must tell *me*."

"Very well. He was a gentleman, and an arrogant one at that. Pale hair—almost white—and blue eyes."

"Anything else?"

"A bit of a dandy, if you must know," Camp continued. "Not like *you*, sir—he seemed overly fond of bright silks. He wore a pink waistcoat—not something you see in my part of London, I can tell you. Drove a hard bargain. At least, he thought he did." A smile of smug satisfaction curled the man's lips. "Any fool could see the painting's worth twice what he wanted for it. You only need look at the quality."

"There's plenty of dandies in London," Peregrine said.

"This one reeked of cologne," Camp replied. "Overwhelming, it was. I almost lost my breakfast. Mrs. Camp had to open all the windows to dispel the stench after he left—didn't want it putting off my customers."

Peregrine caught his breath. Only one man of his acquaintance reeked of cologne.

Heath Moss.

Moss was arrogant enough to believe himself above the law, but he had all the intelligence of a boiled egg. Surely he couldn't be the Phoenix?

"Has the gentleman visited you before, Mr. Camp?" Peregrine asked.

The man nodded. "Last year, he came with a boxful of trinkets—watches, snuffboxes, and the like."

"Anything more recently—within the past six months?"

"No, your lordship."

"You're sure?" Peregrine asked. "What about a ginger jar, or a sword?"

The man frowned. "I bought a dagger off someone a few months ago," he said. "An odd little thing—Moorish in design. But I know the man who sold it to me—a sailor who's often in with trinkets he's picked up. He's as honest as I am."

Not necessarily the best accolade.

Peregrine gestured toward the packet. "Show me."

The man pulled out a canvas from the packet and unrolled it on the desk.

Peregrine leaned forward and studied the painting. It was a portrait of a young woman dressed in a gown of pale blue silk, sitting on a bench under an oak tree, the façade of Hythe Manor in the distance. Her hair, an elegant mass of blonde curls, was piled on top of her head and adorned with feathers matching the color of her gown. Two white-stockinged feet peeked out from the hem of her skirt with black, buckled shoes.

He ran his fingertip along the painting, and his cheeks warmed as he traced the neckline of her gown, cut scandalously low, to reveal the swell of her milky-white breasts. Then he traced the outline of her gown, following a line across the ground, until he reached the signature in the corner.

Lely, 1664.

"Well?" Houseman said, pride in his voice. "Have I not succeeded where others have failed?"

Peregrine looked up, fighting the urge to obliterate Houseman's smug grin with his fist.

"The brushwork is exquisite," he said. "But, I'm afraid, this isn't the painting that we're looking for."

"Nonsense!" Houseman cried. "It fits the description—and that's Hythe Manor in the background."

"I'm not disputing that," Peregrine said. "Nor am I disputing that this is a painting of the fifth Lady Hythe."

"I don't understand," Houseman said.

"It's perfectly simple," Peregrine replied. "This painting is a fake."

"A *what?*"

"See here?" Peregrine gestured toward the background. "The scenery's too light in tone. The background of the original was darker. And the blue in the gown is too bright. Modern pigments weren't available in Lely's time—the tones of the original were much more muted." He ran his fingertip along the edge of the canvas. "There's no fraying around the edge," he said. "Nor are there any of the marks you'd expect from a canvas that has been removed from its frame. What's more..." He leaned forward, almost pressing his nose on the canvas, then inhaled deeply. "That confirms it."

"What the devil are you doing?" Houseman asked.

Peregrine rose and rang the bell for the footman. "I'll wager it was painted less than a month ago—two, at most. I can still smell the paint." He rolled the canvas up, then opened the top drawer of his desk and pulled out a sheaf of notes. "Ten pounds, you say?"

"I'm selling it for twenty," Camp said.

"Ten pounds," Peregrine said, "or a visit to the magistrate, Mr. Camp—you decide."

Camp scowled, but snatched the notes, folding them and stuffing them into his pocket. "Bloody toffs."

"If you'll both excuse me, I must pay a visit."

There was a knock, and the footman appeared.

"This is *my* investigation," Houseman protested. "You cannot visit Lord Hythe without me."

"I'm not visiting Hythe," Peregrine said, "though whom I visit is none of your business. But you may accompany me when I return the canvas to Lord Hythe—even if it's not the one he's looking for. Now—if you'll excuse me?"

Houseman hesitated, but like all bullies, he was a coward, and at length, he scuttled out of the study, Mr. Camp in his wake.

As soon as they'd gone, Peregrine rang the bell for the carriage. Hythe could wait—but first, he had to pay Heath Moss a visit.

⁂

"I'M AFRAID MR. Moss is out, sir—perhaps you'd like to call another time."

The footman shuffled from one foot to another, and Peregrine smiled to himself. He'd interviewed enough criminals to know when a man was concealing the truth—or, in this case, uttering a falsehood.

"Mr. Moss's availability may be dependent on the matter I wish to discuss with him," Peregrine said. "We have a mutual acquaintance—a Mr. Camp, of Drury Lane. Perhaps you could check again whether Mr. Moss is receiving visitors?"

The footman hesitated, then bowed and disappeared. Shortly after, Peregrine found himself being ushered into a small parlor at the back of the house, where he found Moss leaning against the mantelshelf over the fireplace, in a stance meant to convey complacency.

But the expression in his eyes betrayed his apprehension.

"Lord Marlow," he said. "What a pleasure. I cannot think what my man was up to when he said I was unavailable." He glanced at the footman. "You can go," he said sharply. "Do not disturb us unless sent for."

As soon as the door had closed behind the servant, Moss gestured toward a decanter on a side table. "Perhaps you'd like a brandy."

"This isn't a social call," Peregrine said, "as I'm sure you're aware."

Moss shifted on his feet as if he had a nest of ants in his breeches. "I'm afraid I've no idea…"

"Pay me the compliment of refraining from falsehoods, Mr. Moss," Peregrine said. "I'm here to determine how that painting came to be in your possession."

"Wh-what p—"

"Kindly drop the façade," Peregrine interrupted, wrinkling his nose at the stench of cologne. "Mr. Camp was most obliging in his description. I gather you've paid him several visits. Short of funds, are we?"

Moss colored. "I don't see how that's any business of yours."

"It is, if you're profiteering from theft," Peregrine said, "but ten pounds is a paltry sum for such a valuable painting."

Moss opened his mouth to reply, then his shoulders slumped.

"Did you honestly think you'd get away with it?" Peregrine asked.

"I didn't steal it," Moss said.

"Why should I believe you?"

"Because I'm a gentleman!" Moss cried. "A gentleman wouldn't stoop to such behavior."

"Neither would he sell a stolen painting rather than returning it to its rightful owner," Peregrine said. "Ye gods, man—that painting's been in the Hythe family for over a hundred years! Lord Hythe would have paid you a handsome reward for returning it."

Moss let out a snort. "Hythe's a miser. At most, I'd have received a hearty thank-you. Most likely he'd have accused me of theft—much as you're accusing me now."

"I doubt he'd have accused you of anything, given that the painting you sold to Mr. Camp was a fake."

Moss blanched. "A-a what? No—you must be jesting."

"I'm afraid not," Peregrine said. "It's an excellent likeness—

enough to fool the untrained eye."

Moss stared at him, his eyes widening. Then he shook his head.

"What the devil is Hythe playing at, behaving so dishonestly?" he asked. "Is this a trick to entrap me? No—this will not do!" His face darkened to a deep shade of puce, and he rocked to and fro, puffing out his cheeks.

Peregrine suppressed a smile—at any moment, the man might spontaneously burst into flames. "I rather think you're in no position to accuse another of dishonesty," he said. "Now, might you enlighten me as to how the painting came to be in your hands?"

Moss let out a sigh. "It arrived here by post, shortly after I returned home from Hythe's house party."

"And you took it to Camp's Curiosity Shop on Drury Lane and sold it for ten pounds?"

"Keep your voice down!" Moss said. "*I'm* the victim here. Somebody sent me a fake in order to make sport with me."

"Nevertheless, a crime has been committed, which you are party to."

"And I suppose you're going to tell the pater—and Lord Hythe?"

"It would serve you right if I did," Peregrine said, "but given that I doubt you're the Phoenix, I see little reason to."

"Of course I'm not the Phoenix!" Moss cried. "I have too much honor."

"And too little intelligence." Moss frowned and opened his mouth, but Peregrine continued. "I'll keep your secret, provided you return the money."

"What money?"

"Ten pounds, Mr. Moss."

"I hardly think that's proper—a gentleman does not deal with money."

"He does when the alternative is being questioned in relation to theft," Peregrine said. "Did you know that Lord Stiles—the magistrate—is a friend of mine? A fair man, if ever there was one, but he's known for being overly stern, particularly when the perpetrator of the crime is a gentleman who, as he puts it, 'should know better, and therefore deserves to be made an example of.'"

Moss cursed under his breath. In all likelihood he didn't have any cash on him. Doubtless he'd spent the money as soon as Camp handed it over.

"Very well," Peregrine said. "If you're unable to raise the funds, I must seek satisfaction."

"S-satisfaction?"

"I'm paying a visit to Hythe Manor in a few days' time. Shall I pass him your compliments?"

"I say, old chap—you wouldn't tell on me, would you?"

"A man of honor is safe from me," Peregrine said, smiling. "I would never tell on a man who refrained from taking that which did not belong to him, such as a painting, a trinket, or"—he fixed his gaze on Moss—"another man's wife."

Moss colored and lowered his gaze. Then Peregrine drew out his pocket watch. "I say—is that the time? I really must be going. A pleasure as always, Moss."

He bowed and exited the parlor, striding across the hallway, where the footman stood beside the front door, then stepped outside and climbed into his carriage.

He leaned back in the seat and closed his eyes, rocking to and fro with the motion of the carriage.

Curse you, Phoenix!

He could almost hear the man's laughter—whoever the devil he was.

The Phoenix was toying with them all. Why go to such an elaborate deception as to have a fake painting made—and send it to Moss? Unless he'd slipped up and wanted Peregrine to believe that he'd sent Moss the original painting.

No—the Phoenix was too clever by half. He'd *expected* Peregrine to discover the fake—of that he was certain.

In which case, where, and how, had he disposed of the *real* painting?

Unless…

He sat upright, his heart hammering in his chest.

Of course! Why had he not considered it before?

Unless…the painting had never left Hythe Manor.

CHAPTER TWENTY-SIX

THE CARRIAGE TURNED a corner, and the expansive façade of Hythe Manor came into view. Peregrine leaned back while Houseman stared out of the carriage window, his eyes filled with the spiteful envy of those not born into privilege who, instead of wanting to further themselves, preferred to languish in their own self-pity and a sense of entitlement, and turn their bitter resentment toward others.

How different Houseman was to Lavinia! *She* had more reason than Houseman to be resentful. Yet though she harbored hatred for his father—perhaps rightly so—she didn't resent those with fortunes of their own. Instead, she focused her efforts on her own betterment, and the care of a father she loved dearly.

What Houseman preferred to ignore was the burden placed upon men such as Lord Hythe—not only the upkeep of a crumbling mansion that was forever draining a man's resources, but the familial burden to produce an heir to perpetuate the family line.

Peregrine wanted children of his own, but he wasn't so desperate for a son and heir as to seek a wife the moment he set foot in London, to act as nothing more than a broodmare.

No—for a wife, he wanted a woman who would make him a better man—a woman to challenge him, and make him happy until the end of his days…

A woman not just to warm his bed, but to ignite it with a

flame of passion hot enough to engulf his soul.

He knew just the woman—but in all likelihood, she hated him.

All because of his cursed father.

Damn!

"Is anything the matter, Marlow?"

Houseman's nasal voice returned him to the present, and he turned to see his companion staring at him.

"Disconcerted that you've yet to catch the Phoenix?" Houseman asked, and it sounded almost like a taunt. "I can explain the circumstance to Lord Hythe, if you prefer."

"That's not necessary," Peregrine said, "unless you know the whereabouts of the real painting?"

"I suspect it's long gone," Houseman said. "Mr. Camp said many of the items he sells are shipped overseas, and I often hear from my network of contacts that—"

"I daresay you're right," Peregrine interrupted. He had no wish to endure further boasts about Houseman's *network of contacts.*

The carriage arrived and drew to a halt. Houseman climbed out and looked over the building. "Hythe's a lucky bastard to live in a place such as this."

"Envy does not become a man," Peregrine retorted.

Houseman scowled, but said nothing, and he followed Peregrine to the entrance, where a footman stood waiting.

They found Lord Hythe in his study—the very place where Peregrine had conducted his fruitless attempt to catch the Phoenix red-handed.

The irony was not lost on him.

"Sit, please," Hythe said. "I understand you're nowhere closer to finding the painting. I have to say I'm disappointed—as is my wife."

"Shall we see Lady Hythe today?" Peregrine asked.

"My wife is taking the waters in Bath. She's suffered megrims since the theft." Hythe leaned forward. "I'm willing to put up a reward for the return of the painting, and the capture of that scoundrel. What say you to one hundred guineas?"

"*How* much?" Houseman cried, his eyes glittering with greed.

"I don't think a reward will help," Peregrine said.

Hythe gestured toward Houseman. "I suspect your friend would be willing to capture the Phoenix, dead or alive, for such a sum."

"Dead or alive—yes, indeed," Houseman said with a degree of relish that reminded Peregrine of a crow picking at carrion.

"Theft isn't a hanging offense," Peregrine said. "Besides, that's not why I'm here today."

"Then why *are* you here?" Hythe asked.

"To ask you to indulge me, Hythe," Peregrine said. "I have a theory, and have come to put it to the test."

"And your theory is…?"

"That the painting was never stolen."

Hythe's face darkened. "Exactly what are you accusing me of, Marlow?"

"Nothing," Peregrine replied. "But I believe the painting may still be here." Hythe's eyes widened, and Peregrine continued, "If you were to conceal the painting, Hythe—where would you do so?"

Hythe shrugged. "In the attic, I suppose—or one of the out-buildings."

"What if you had little time, and were concerned you'd be caught?"

"Then I'd hide it somewhere closer." Hythe made a dis-missive gesture. "This is all conjecture, of course—and damned preposterous with it. Why would I hide my own painting? My wife is distraught! Do you think I'd deliberately torment her?"

"Then where do you think the *Phoenix* would have hidden it?" Peregrine asked.

Hythe frowned. "Damned if I know."

"Would you mind if we went to the gallery?" Peregrine asked. "My theory is that our adversary hid the painting close by—perhaps even in plain sight."

"Very well." Hythe rose and led the way to the gallery. Two footmen stood at the entrance, bowing as they passed.

The missing portrait had been replaced with a still life—a pewter plate laden with fruit beside a dark green bottle. It was a marked contrast to the generations of long-dead Hythes who stared out from their canvases, overseeing their ancestral home.

Peregrine strode along the gallery, stopping to inspect each portrait. "I take it each of these paintings is in its rightful place—except the still life, of course."

Hythe nodded. "We never move them, except when the chimneys are being swept. Even then, the larger paintings we'll cover with a dust sheet, rather than go to the trouble of taking them down." He gestured toward the marble fireplace halfway along the gallery. "You wouldn't believe the soot and ash that comes out of that fireplace, given how infrequently it's lit." He let out a snort. "Enough ash for twelve phoenixes to rise from."

The Phoenix from the ashes…

Peregrine glanced at the fireplace.

"Surely not," he whispered to himself.

"Marlow?" Hythe asked. "What is it?"

"The fireplace."

"What of it?"

Houseman glanced at Peregrine, then at the fireplace, and back again.

"Bloody hell," he muttered.

Hythe flinched at the profanity. "What?" he asked.

"The phoenix rises from the ashes of his predecessor," Peregrine said. "Perhaps he concealed his bounty in his birthplace to taunt us?"

"Don't be a damned fool!" Hythe said. "Nobody in their right mind would hide a painting in the *fireplace!*"

"We've seen enough of our slippery friend's handiwork to know that he's capable of doing what we least expect," Peregrine said. He strode toward the fireplace—a monstrosity carved out of marble, its wide, gaping hole covered by an embroidered fire screen depicting a peacock in vibrant colors.

Peregrine pushed the fire screen aside.

"Careful!" Hythe cried. "That's my wife's handiwork."

"And very pretty it is, too," Peregrine said.

The mouth of the fireplace was big enough to fit ten men, and was flanked by a brass coal bucket on one side, and a tall jar containing a poker and rake on the other. Peregrine stepped forward, his eyes adjusting to the darkness. At the back of the fireplace, near the chimney wall, was a large, rectangular shape, covered in brown paper.

It didn't take much intellect to work out what it was.

"You clever bastard."

"Have you found something, Marlow?" Houseman asked.

Peregrine lifted the object out of the fireplace and pulled away the wrapping paper to reveal the portrait inside.

"Well—I'll be damned!" Hythe cried.

At close quarters, the original Lely painting was even more exquisite than Peregrine remembered. And though it was different to the copy, the likeness between the two was remarkable.

How the devil did you do it, my friend?

"Is it the original?" Houseman asked.

"Of course it is!" Hythe exclaimed. "I'd swear on the fifth Lady Hythe's grave."

"Then we're no closer to catching the Phoenix," Houseman said. "Nothing's been stolen."

"We can't be sure of that," Peregrine said. "The Phoenix left his calling card, and each time he strikes, an item goes missing."

"But the painting's been found," Hythe said. "And while I'd like to horsewhip the man from here to Inverness, I'm only relieved that I'm not on his list of victims."

"Not as far as you know," Peregrine said.

The Phoenix must have planned this for some time. But for what purpose? He'd thrown everyone off the scent by making them all believe that the Lely painting had been stolen. Then he'd done it again, by sending the fake to Moss. Why would he create so many diversions?

Unless…

"Lord Hythe," Peregrine said. "Has anything else gone missing in the past few days?"

"Not that I'm aware of, Marlow, but we have a large estate here. It's unlikely that we'd notice anything missing for some time."

"It might be something very particular," Peregrine said, "given that our friend went to such trouble to steer us in another direction. I believe he's taking objects that have a particular meaning."

"Such as?"

"Lord Francis, of course, had a ginger jar stolen at the beginning of the season."

"A *ginger jar*, you say?" Hythe said. "Now, what does that remind me of?"

"And the sword," Houseman said.

"A sword?" Hythe's eyes widened.

"Lord Caldicott had a Medieval sword stolen."

"And there's the apostle spoons taken from the regent's Brighton residence," Houseman said. "A heinous crime if ever there was one.

"I'm still of a mind to put *that* one down to carelessness on Prinny's part," Peregrine said.

Or, perhaps, even a tall tale spun to garner sympathy. Parodies depicting the regent as a hog continued to circulate in London's morning rooms. Prinny wasn't the kind of man to understand that the theft of one of his many treasures, while half of the populace of London starved, was unlikely to elicit sympathy from anyone.

"I wonder…" Hythe began, then he shook his head. "No— that's impossible."

"Nothing's impossible," Peregrine said. "Any information you have, however trivial you consider it, might be the key to unlocking this mystery."

"No—it'll still be there."

"What will?"

Hythe averted his gaze, as if he were ashamed of something. "It's nothing," he said. "A mere trinket—a landscape in one of the second-floor parlors. A snowfield, if I recall. Pretty enough, but it's not at all valuable. I paid a shilling for it—no, two, I believe."

"Two shillings? No trader in his right mind would sell it for such a pittance."

Hythe colored. "I acquired it at auction, some years ago. I-I thought Lady Hythe might appreciate something pretty, but she wasn't much fond of it—you know what women are like."

Bought at auction for two shillings—just like the stolen ginger jar. That seemed too unlikely to be a mere coincidence.

"Can I see the painting?" Peregrine asked.

"Very well," Hythe said. He gestured to the footman. "You there! Make sure the Lely portrait is restored to its rightful place on the wall."

The footman bowed, then Hythe led the way out of the gallery and up a small flight of stairs, to a parlor in a side wing of the house. Peregrine wrinkled his nose at the odor of damp. Most of the furniture was covered in sheets, save a table by the door, which bore a thin layer of dust.

Hythe strode toward the wall at the far end of the room that was covered in paintings, inspecting each one until he stopped short beside a miniature silhouette.

"The blackguard!" he cried, pointing to the miniature. "He's stolen it!"

"What do you mean?" Houseman asked.

"The painting was there the last time I saw it—I *swear it!*"

Peregrine plucked the miniature from the wall. "You recognize this?"

"Yes, it's ours," Hythe said, "but I don't recall seeing it *there*. It's usually set on the table—see where the dust's been disturbed?"

"Then it's not a fake," Peregrine murmured. He turned it over in his hand to inspect the back, then froze. "Gentlemen," he said, "I believe we have unearthed the true theft."

"What do you mean?"

He held up the miniature.

Houseman let out a low whistle, while Hythe swore.

Tucked inside the frame, at the back, was a piece of paper—with a drawing of a bird rising from the ashes.

CHAPTER TWENTY-SEVEN

THE WATERS OF the Serpentine glistened in the afternoon light, tiny diamonds dancing across the surface. Standing beside Lady Betty, Lavinia watched a pair of swans glide downstream. She drew her shawl around her shoulders and sighed.

"You seem a little melancholy, Lavinia darling," Lady Betty said. "Is something amiss? Your father's health is much improved. He's certainly well enough to weather the journey when you return to Springfield Cottage."

"I know," Lavinia said, "and I'm looking forward to returning home. It's just…"

"You've grown fond of the town," Betty said.

"A little."

"Or perhaps"—Lady Betty moved closer and lowered her voice—"you've grown fond of London's residents—one in particular?"

"I-I don't know what you mean."

"Of *course* not, darling," Lady Betty said, her eyes twinkling. "I quite understand your reluctance to declare a liking for him, given your father's aversion toward him—or rather toward his father." She placed a light hand on Lavinia's arm. "There's no sin in being *fond* of someone, you know. Lord Marlow's nothing like his father."

"You knew Lord Marlow's father was Earl Walton?" Lavinia

asked.

"*Everybody* knows it. I'm surprised *you* didn't."

"How could I be expected to know?" Lavinia asked. "His name is Marlow—not Walton. I spoke to him of Earl Walton several times—of how the man betrayed Papa, and how much I detested him. Why didn't he tell me then that Walton was his father?"

Lady Betty slipped her arm through Lavinia's. "My poor, dear child—isn't it obvious?"

"Not really."

Lady Betty gave a soft laugh. "Darling Lavinia, your naïveté does you credit, as does the absence of the pride that other young women in Society have in abundance. Lord Marlow can only have had one reason—that he had no desire to lessen your opinion of him. And, given that most men in his position care little for the opinion of any member of our sex, I can only surmise that he's in love with you."

Lavinia drew in a sharp breath, and her stomach tightened at the delicious notion. Then she shook her head.

"I-I cannot believe that."

Lady Betty smiled. "You fear such belief because you love him in return."

Lavinia opened her mouth to voice her denial, then closed it. There was no deceiving Lady Betty—a woman of the world who possessed a sharp eye and a quick wit.

"There's no shame in loving another, Lavinia."

"I *can't* love him," Lavinia said. "To love him would be to betray Papa."

"A man should not suffer for the sins of his father—especially since, if I recall, he's been estranged from his father for some years."

"They're estranged?"

Lady Betty nodded. "He never visits the estate—Marlow Park. He prefers to remain in London."

"And...Earl Walton?"

"He resides in Italy, if I recall," Lady Betty said. "Marlow Park is somewhat neglected. Has your father not spoken of it? It's barely ten miles from Springfield."

Ten miles…

It was riding distance. Was Mama's clock there? Or had Walton taken it to Italy?

"Such a pity it's neglected," Lady Betty continued. "The grounds are beautiful. Your father visited it often when your dear mama was alive."

"Did Earl Walton visit Papa"—Lavinia hesitated—"at Fosterley Park?"

"Several times," Lady Betty said. "They were great friends, until…" She waved a dismissive hand in the air. "No matter. That's in the past. But he often brought his son with him—I saw them, once, when my late husband and I used to visit your mama and papa. They always came on horseback, when Lord Marlow was old enough to ride."

Lavinia closed her eyes to bring forth the memory of the boy. And his gray pony, Lancelot, the beloved companion his father had forced him to shoot.

No wonder he'd not admitted who his father was.

Oh, Peregrine!

"Lavinia…"

Her heart fluttered at the sound of her name uttered in that familiar voice—the voice of the boy she'd adored, and the man she had fallen in love with.

"Lavinia."

She drew in a deep breath, inhaling the aroma of male spices. Then she heard a sharp cry from Lady Betty and snapped her eyes open.

Peregrine stood before her.

"You shouldn't be here, sir!" Lady Betty said. "Nor should you address my friend in so familiar a manner."

"Forgive me, Lady Betty, but I must beg an audience with Miss de Grande."

Lavinia's skin tightened with need at the timbre of his voice—the sweet, familiar voice that had visited her dreams only last night. Then she blushed with shame at the memory of how she had touched the intimate place that she dare not speak of, to reignite the delicious, wicked pleasure that he'd given her…

…and how her body had responded, rippling deep inside her center as she ran her fingertips across her flesh, imagining they were his…

She squeezed her thighs together and felt her cheeks warm with shame at the wanton reaction borne of primal female instinct. Since when had she turned into such a weak woman as to almost swoon with desire at the mere sight of him?

"Miss de Grande," he said. "May I beg an audience with you?"

Lavinia met his gaze, and her breath caught at the expression in his eyes—a desire so raw that she could almost taste it.

He offered his arm.

"Lavinia, darling," Lady Betty protested, "I hardly think your papa would approve."

"Did you not just lecture me on the faults of filial culpability—and of filial obedience?" Lavinia asked.

Lady Betty sighed. "Oh, very well." She released Lavinia's arm. "I trust you'll observe propriety, Lord Marlow, with regards to my charge."

"I will." A firm, strong hand took Lavinia's and placed it on an equally firm, solid arm. Her stomach flipped at the vow, so often spoken in church, and she curled her fingers around his arm, relishing his solidity.

They set off, Lady Betty a few paces behind. The swans glided ahead on the water, two serene figures side by side—like any devoted couple enjoying an afternoon constitutional.

"Filial culpability?" he asked.

"The expectation that a son should bear the responsibility for the sins of his father," Lavinia replied.

"And…filial obedience?"

"The expectation that a daughter should accede to the demands of *her* father, whether or not she wishes to."

She glanced toward him. Though he stared straight ahead, seemingly entranced by the swans, a smile curved his lips.

"I've been coming to Hyde Park every day, in the hope I'd see you," he said.

"Did you not consider paying us a visit?"

"I doubt I'd have been welcome."

"You might return with us now," Lavinia said. "Papa is taking his rest. Aunt Edna has no objection to your company—and she's entertaining Lady Thorpe today. Do you know Lady Thorpe?"

"Lavinia, darling," Lady Betty interjected, "I hardly think that's appropriate. Whether or not you agree with him, you must respect your father's wishes. He'd never grant Lord Marlow entrance."

"Papa needn't know."

"What if he found out? His constitution couldn't weather another upset." Lady Betty shook her head. "I can't condone it."

"Lady Betty's right," he said. "But perhaps you would take tea at my house—both of you. It's a short walk from here to Grosvenor Square."

"I-I don't know," Lavinia said. "Papa and I leave for the country in a few days, and I promised Sarah I'd help with the packing."

He squeezed her hand. "There are certain things that must be said, and I would not have them remain unsaid if you are to leave London."

Lady Betty watched Lord Marlow with a thoughtful expression in her dark eyes.

"Perhaps, Lavinia, your papa wouldn't object to your taking tea with an acquaintance before you leave," she said.

"Do you object?" Lavinia asked.

"Not at all," Lady Betty said. "And if I might impose upon Lord Marlow a little further, I would release you into his care for the rest of the afternoon, provided he returns you safely home before suppertime." She cast a hard glare at Lord Marlow. "That is, of course, if he can be trusted with your welfare."

He raised an eyebrow, then nodded. "Of course, Lady Betty," he said.

Lavinia approached her companion and lowered her voice. "Is that not improper?" she whispered.

Lady Betty nodded. "Perhaps—but true love should outrank propriety. Lord Marlow is an honorable man, and who am I to deny you the opportunity to spend a little time with him before you leave London? Who knows when the two of you might meet again?"

"But Papa…"

"What your father doesn't know won't hurt him." Lady Betty gave a conspiratorial wink. Then she resumed her attention on Marlow. "I'm entrusting you with my charge, sir, but do not take my trust as leave to do as you wish—if you harm her in any way, you'll have me to answer to. And though you may consider me a weak woman, let me remind you that I have weathered widow-hood and vilification. I care little for my reputation, which renders me a danger to those who value theirs. My extensive acquaintance among the members of White's enables me to reduce a man's desirability among the demimonde to almost nothing by a mere word or two about flaccidity brought about by the pox."

What the devil was she saying? But as Lavinia glanced toward Lord Marlow, she saw shock in his expression, followed by understanding, and finally respect. Then he threw back his head and laughed.

"My dear Lady Betty, you're wasted on London Society, for they don't appreciate you as much as you deserve. If only all chaperones were like yourself. While it would render Society somewhat…*wicked*, it would make for a more amusing Season and, I suspect, happier unions."

Lady Betty's eyes sparkled in the sunlight. "I see we under-stand each other, Lord Marlow."

She slipped her arm through Lord Marlow's free one. "Come," she said. "Let us take a stroll before I place my charge into your care."

CHAPTER TWENTY-EIGHT

THE AFTERNOON LIGHT streamed in through the windows overlooking the street and stretched across the Aubusson rug.

There wasn't a speck of dust to be seen—not even in the beam of sunlight, where dust motes continually swirled in the air in Cousin Charles's townhouse. The gilded wood in Lord Marlow's parlor gleamed, as if servants polished it daily.

In all likelihood, they did—probably twice daily, given the number of servants that had been milling about the place when Lord Marlow ushered her inside after they took their leave of Lady Betty.

He approached the window, teacup in hand. The sunlight illuminated his hair, forming a halo about his face, as he regarded Lavinia with a blend of apprehension and desire.

This is a mistake. I shouldn't be here.

He held out the cup. "Tea?"

Her hand trembling, Lavinia took the cup, which clattered against the saucer.

"You're wrong," he said quietly.

She lifted her eyebrows in question.

"You *should* be here," he added. "This room is better with you in it."

Then he shook his head. "Forgive me—that was a crass thing to say, even if it's true."

Sweet heaven—was he nervous? He sounded like a naïve young man seeking the approval of his…

His what—his intended?

Don't be a fool.

"You're safe here with me," he said. "I won't bite."

She took a sip of her tea, then set the cup aside.

"Unless, of course," he continued, "you *want* me to."

A wicked smile curled his lips. Then he colored and looked away. "Forgive me, Lavinia. I didn't invite you here to take advantage of you—I wanted to apologize."

"What for?"

"For my father." He sat beside her and offered his hand. "May I?"

She nodded, and he took her free hand, interlocking their fingers. Her stomach fluttered at the feel of his skin, and a crackle of need fizzed inside. He lifted his free hand and cupped her chin. Then he tilted her head until her eyes met his.

"I believe you might have spoken the truth when you said my father was instrumental in your father's ruination."

She flinched. "I *might* have spoken the truth?"

"You misunderstand me, Lavinia," he said softly. "I'm not accusing you of falsehood—in fact, I admire your honesty."

She flinched again—but this time out of shame, rather than indignation.

"My father always said that Lord de Grande lost his money speculating on ventures in the South Seas, and that he tried to help your father, but was refused. But…" He hesitated. "Now I wonder whether rather than helping your father, he helped himself instead."

He lowered his head, and his warm breath caressed her skin. She only need move her head a fraction and their lips would meet.

"Oh, Lavinia," he whispered. "My sweet little Guinevere— the delightful girl from my childhood has grown into a lovely young woman. I can no longer conceal my feelings."

Her heart fluttered as his eyes darkened with desire.

He lowered himself to the floor and kneeled before her. "Lavinia," he whispered, curling his fingers around hers, "my love…"

"Please, do not say it!" she cried.

A flicker of hurt rippled across his expression, and she ached with the need to ease it.

"Have I misunderstood you, Lavinia? Is my love not returned?"

She shook her head. "Oh, Peregrine, it's impossible," she said. "Can you not see that? My father would never allow it. He insists I have nothing to do with you again. I'm betraying him merely by sitting here."

"And yet Lady Betty had no objection."

"Lady Betty is a dear friend. She wants me to be happy."

"And your father wants you to be miserable?"

The pain in his eyes tore at her heart—for it mirrored her own. "You don't understand," she said. "Papa has suffered so much. After Mama died, he clung to her memory. But when he was ruined, even *that* was taken from him. He might have forgiven the loss of his wealth—but, to him, what your father did was like losing Mama all over again, because it desecrated her memory."

"How so?"

The expression in his eyes sharpened, and she caught a glimpse of the intelligence that had shone there the day the Hythe painting disappeared. Was he, even now, ruled by his determination to catch the Phoenix?

Which was another reason why she must deny him.

"I-I only meant the loss of his home—of Fosterley Park, where he was so happy with my mother," she said. "Papa is not the man he was. His health has deteriorated over the years, and the last thing I want is to distress him further."

"Your devotion to your father does you credit," he said. "But, perhaps, I might be able to persuade him?"

She shook her head. "You saw how he reacted—I cannot risk it. I-I would never forgive myself if he fell ill again."

"But don't you deserve to be happy?" he asked. "Don't you love me?"

Moisture stung her eyes, and a tear splashed onto her cheek. "I love my father," she whispered. "Everything I do is for him. His hatred for your father runs too deep."

He curled his fingers around hers, then brought her hand to his lips and pressed a soft kiss on her palm. Her heart threatened to break at the tender, gentle gesture, and another tear splashed onto her cheek. He lifted his hand and wiped the tear away.

"Don't be sad, my love," he whispered.

"I don't know what is to be done."

He held her hand against his chest, where his heart beat faintly against her palm.

"Do you feel my heart?" he whispered. "It beats for you, and will do so until I draw my last breath. I pledge myself to you, here and now."

"But we cannot be together—I cannot do that to Papa."

"I *love* you, Lavinia," he said, his voice thick with emotion. "Perhaps, in time, your father will come to understand that. But if not, I will wait for you—I'll wait until the end of days to claim you as my wife, if need be."

He cupped her face, his lips close to hers, and she surrendered to her need—the need that had tormented her from the moment she'd stepped into his home.

"Peregrine…"

She reached toward him, and he pulled her close, circling his arms around her until she found herself kneeling beside him on the soft rug.

"Will you end my torment, dearest Lavinia, and consent to be my wife?"

Yes—oh yes!

She closed her eyes, willing her head to conquer her heart, but her heart won out, surrendering to the warmth of his arms, the solidity of his body, and the deep, woodsy aroma of his very maleness.

Oh, Papa—forgive me…

She placed her head on his chest and suppressed a sob.

"Hush, my darling," he whispered. "All will be well. I promise, I'll not do, or say, anything to distress your father. We can make our pledge in secret, and only declare our love to the world at such a time when…when your father no longer objects to our union."

A sob escaped her lips as she caught his meaning.

"I'll say nothing to disturb your father's peace of mind," he said. "But I declare myself as yours—and yours I shall remain. When you have need of me, I'll be there."

She lifted her head, blinking through the tears, to see him gazing down at her, his own eyes glistening with moisture. He smiled.

"Did I not declare myself to you once before, when we were children? I, King Arthur, pledged my love to Guinevere, that I would serve and protect her for all my days."

"A childish game," she said.

"Childish it may have been at the time," he replied, "but perhaps we were destined for each other."

He traced the outline of her face with his fingertips, then followed a path along her throat until he reached her neckline. His fingertips brushed across the swell of her breasts, causing her nipples to stiffen to painful, needy points that ached for his touch. She arched her back against him, willing those expert fingertips to ease the ache.

"Lavinia," he whispered, his voice hoarse, "I fear I'm in danger of compromising you, and I made a promise to Lady Betty that I would do no such thing."

"If I recall," she said, "you promised not to harm me." She caught his hand, then guided it toward her breast. A low growl rumbled in his throat, and he cupped her breast with the eagerness of possession, flicking his thumb over the distended nipple through the muslin of her gown. "I feel no harm, sir," she whispered, "only pleasure."

"Sweet Lord, you tempt a man so!"

"I am no temptress, Lord Marlow," she said, leaning into his touch. "The temptress heightens a man's desire while refraining from delivering that which she has promised. I assure you, sir, that I am more than willing to fulfil any obligation on my part to deliver that which you see before you."

He leaned over her. "I find myself completely at your mercy," he whispered, "a situation that I intend to reverse."

"What can you… Oh!"

She drew in a sharp breath as he slipped his hand inside her gown. He flicked her nipple again, sending a jolt of desire through her body, a brief spike of pain followed by a deeper pulse of pleasure, and she clung to him.

A deep yearning swelled in her center, and she tilted her hips, seeking his touch, in an instinctive quest for release. Pleasure flared as she felt his hardness against her belly, and she parted her thighs to shift closer to him.

He let out a low growl in response—a primal beast voicing his approval. "So good," he whispered. "So responsive…"

Sweet heaven—since when had she turned into such a wanton? She opened her eyes. Skin flushed with need, he had tipped his face to the heavens—eyes closed, a smile of pure pleasure on his lips. She leaned forward and placed a kiss on his throat, and he shuddered. His hardness swelled, and she drew in a sharp breath at the delicious heat of him against her belly. She peppered his chin with kisses while he murmured soft words of praise. The heat intensified. She only need ride the wave to reach the moment of dissolution.

With a soft, undulating motion, she rocked against him. Her instincts took over, as they had done when she touched herself at night. She gripped his arms and thrust her hips against him, riding the wave, nearing the crest, and he mirrored the motion, shifting his hips against hers.

One more thrust, and she would find the pleasure she sought…

"Lavinia—stop!" he cried.

Two hands gripped her arms and pushed her back, and she let out a cry of frustration as the wave receded.

She looked up to see his face contorted in agony, eyes tightly closed, jaw bulging as he gritted his teeth.

"We…cannot…" he said, his voice strangled.

Tears of frustration and despair stung her eyes, and she looked away.

"You must understand," he said. "I want nothing more than to give you pleasure—but I fear I'll lose control. If we continue, I shan't be able to stop."

"Don't you want me?"

"Oh, Lavinia!" he cried. "There's nothing I want more than to bury myself inside you—but I cannot ruin you."

"Did you not pledge yourself to me?"

"Aye, my love, but I value your honor over my desires."

"And what of *my* desires?"

"I cannot ruin you."

"How can it be ruination to seal our love?" She placed her hands over his. "Did I not say that I want you to bring me to pleasure, not harm? Can you not give me this—so that I might have something to hold on to while we wait? I'm leaving London next week. Who knows when we might meet again?"

"I fear I'll hurt you," he said. "A woman experiences pain her first time."

She dipped her head and kissed his knuckles. "I trust you," she said. "Would you deny me this one request?"

"Oh, sweet Lord—you unman me!" He drew her to him and kissed her, slipping his tongue inside to stake his claim. She responded in kind.

He let out a groan, and she lay back on the rug, pulling him against her. Desire flared once more, and she shifted her thighs wider. He deepened the kiss, and low growls resonated in his chest, growing in intensity as he devoured her mouth. Then strong, insistent fingers tugged at the skirts until her legs were exposed, and she felt a rush of cool air against the hot skin of her thighs.

She blushed with shame at the sensation of moisture pooling between her thighs. Then he slipped his hand along her skin, moving his fingers slickly across the folds of her flesh, where the ache had grown so intense that she feared she might die of it.

"Sweet heaven, woman! You're ready for me—so ready. I never could have believed such a delectable creature existed…and you're mine—all mine."

He fumbled at his breeches, then she felt him, hard and hot, against her thigh. The scent of man thickened in the air—spicy and musky, with sharp top notes, followed by sweet, earthy undertones. She tilted her head back and drew in a long, slow breath, drinking her fill.

Then she reached down and touched him—tentatively at first, caressing the soft skin of his shaft.

"Oh, sweetness…"

She curled her hand around him. His member moved eagerly in her hand, and he let out a low groan.

"Do I pain you, Peregrine?"

He dipped his head, burying it against her shoulder. "Oh, no, my love. I've never felt such pleasure."

Emboldened by his praise, she gave a gentle squeeze.

"I-I can wait no longer—sweet Lord!" he cried. He grasped her wrist and moved her hand away. Then he took her other wrist and shifted on top of her, pinning her to the floor. She parted her thighs to welcome him, and felt the tip of him shift against her flesh. Heat met heat, and she let out a low mewl of need. Then he gave a gentle thrust, slipping his manhood along her center, and the wave began to swell once more. But this time, it was thicker, higher—threatening to engulf her whole world.

Then he slowed, and she bucked, thrusting her hips upward to chase the wave.

"Are you ready for me, Lavinia?" he whispered.

"Yes."

"Do you want me inside you?"

"Yes!"

"Say it again."

"Yes!" she cried. "Sweet Lord, Peregrine—*please*! I want you inside me!"

He thrust forward and speared her with a swift, sharp movement, slamming his hips against hers to claim her fully. She let out a cry at the sharp spike of pain, and he grew still, his breath coming in sharp puffs against her cheek.

"Be still, my love," he said. She opened her eyes to see him looking at her, tears glistening. "It pains me to hurt you, but it will only hurt the first time, I swear. Is it very painful?"

She lifted her head and placed a kiss on his lips. "Only a little," she said, "but I trust you."

"Your trust is the greatest gift you can give me."

She clung to him, trembling, until the pain lessened as her body began to stretch around him. Then he placed another kiss on her lips and began to withdraw, slowly. A low growl of ecstasy escaped her lips, and he quickened the pace, thrusting in and out. The pain faded, to be replaced by pleasure—faint at first, but intensifying with each delicious thrust, swelling, pulsating, until the whole world faded and she became aware of nothing but the pure sensation of him deep inside her, as if the two of them had formed a single creature, a primal beast formed of a pure, instinctive need.

The need to mate.

His breath was coming in deep, hoarse pants, now—raw and primal.

Then he let out a roar and thrust forward. A burst of heat ignited deep inside her, as if she were engulfed by a flame, and her body exploded into shards.

"Peregrine—oh, Peregrine!"

She threw back her head and cried his name. Wave after

wave of intense, exquisite pleasure ripped through her body, and she rode the waves, soaring toward the heavens. She reached the crest, then plunged toward the world below, not caring whether she fell to her death.

Then a strong pair of arms caught her, enveloping her in soft, gentle warmth—a warmth that promised to protect her from harm. Together, they floated through the air, then drifted back toward the ground, where they settled in each other's arms and lay together, their hearts beating in unison.

When she opened her eyes, she saw him staring down at her.

"Th-that was…" She drew in a deep breath, unable to articulate the sensations that had torn her to pieces, then rebuilt her. "It was like…" She shook her head. "I-I cannot describe it."

His eyes crinkled with a smile, and a tear spilled onto his cheek. "Like dying and being reborn," he said.

"Is it always like that?" she asked.

"Not always."

She swallowed the flare of jealousy at the notion that he'd experienced pleasure with others. But what man of Society had not taken a mistress, or visited a bawdy house, at some point in his life? They were generally expected to indulge.

"I never felt such pleasure before today," he said. "Perhaps that's because I have never been in love—until now."

Cold air brushed across her thighs, and she grew aware of their surroundings. She was on her back, her legs spread like a harlot, on the floor, with her lover inside her. She tried to move, but he held her firm.

"Be still, my love," he whispered. "We shan't be disturbed—and I wish to hold you for a while longer."

He rolled onto his side, taking her with him, and she nestled into his embrace, her head on his chest, listening to the slow, languorous rhythm of his heart.

"I shall miss you every day," she said.

"I'm sure you'll have much to occupy yourself with in the country," he said. "I envy you the freedom."

"What will you occupy yourself with in London?" she asked.

"My continued search for the Phoenix. I believe the net is closing in on him—it's only a matter of time before he's caught."

"Can't your colleague pursue him instead?"

"No," he replied, and she shivered at the steel in his voice. "The Phoenix is *my* quarry, and though he deserves to be brought to justice, I cannot leave the matter to Houseman."

"Why not?"

"Houseman is, I'm afraid, the sort of man who'll stoop to anything to further his own ends. He's not interested in justice— he merely relishes the chase. And, like a dog, he'll relish the kill even more."

Her stomach tightened with fear. "The…kill?"

"Aye," he said. "Houseman is determined to see the Phoenix subjected to the harshest punishment possible. I fear that, if apprehended by Houseman, the Phoenix will suffer at his hands."

A ripple of dread rolled through her.

"Is all well, my love?"

"Of course," she said. "But I…I almost feel sorry for the Phoenix—whoever he is."

"Don't," he replied. "Clever he may be, but he's broken the law, and must therefore reap the rewards of his sins." He placed a kiss on her forehead. "But let us not speak of him while there are more pleasurable pursuits to indulge in. I fear I have acted abominably by taking you on the morning room floor. Perhaps, when I am ready for you again, we might enjoy a little sojourn to my bedchamber."

She nodded, then turned away to disguise her disappointment.

She couldn't ask him to help her return Mama's clock to Papa. In doing so, she'd run the risk of revealing her identity as the Phoenix. Though she could trust him with her body and her heart, she could never trust him with her secret.

She would have to steal Mama's clock, as originally planned. The Phoenix would complete one final quest before disappearing into obscurity forever.

CHAPTER TWENTY-NINE

"Y OU HAVE A visitor, Lord Marlow."

Peregrine set his fork down and glanced at the footman in the doorway. "At this hour?"

"It's Mr. Houseman."

Bloody Houseman. Didn't he know the impropriety of visiting while a man was supposed to be enjoying his breakfast?

"He was somewhat insistent," the footman continued.

And, in all likelihood, angling for a free breakfast.

Peregrine sighed. "I suppose you'd better let him in."

Moments later, the footman ushered Houseman into the breakfast room. He glanced at the buffet table and raised his eyebrows.

Peregrine nodded to the footman. "Would you set a place for my...*guest?*"

"I've no wish to inconvenience you, Marlow," Houseman said, his nasal tone grating on Peregrine's senses.

Yet I find myself inconvenienced.

Without waiting for an invitation, Houseman took a seat opposite Peregrine. When the footman returned and placed a plate in front of him, he stared pointedly at it, then back at the footman.

"You help yourself," Peregrine said, gesturing toward the buffet. "Something I'm sure you do on a regular basis," he added in a low whisper.

"I beg pardon?"

"I *said*, help yourself. I recommend the bacon."

"Oh…yes…of course." Houseman approached the buffet and piled several rashers of bacon onto his plate, followed by a spoonful of eggs. Then he returned to the table and began eating.

Peregrine pushed his plate aside. Not only did he have to endure the man's company, he was also subjected to an assault on his senses—did the man not know it wasn't the done thing to chew with one's mouth open?

"To what do I owe the pleasure, Houseman?" he asked.

"I've made a breakthrough in our quest to find that ruffian," Houseman said through a mouthful of bacon.

"Which is?"

"The spoons have been found in a pawnshop on Hatton Garden."

Peregrine frowned. "Spoons?"

"The regent's apostle spoons."

"The spoons that were stolen in Brighton?"

"The very same," Houseman said, and Peregrine cringed at the pomposity in his voice. "They were brought in by a young man." He pulled out a piece of paper and unfolded it. "Yes, that's right," he said, tapping the paper with his fingertip. "A young man, the proprietor said. Handed over the spoons in return for twenty guineas. He was dressed in a footman's livery, and wearing a cloak, despite it being a warm day."

"And when was this?"

"July fifteenth," Houseman said, studying the paper. "A few days after they were reported stolen."

Peregrine let out a snort. "I wouldn't be surprised if the regent returned to London from Brighton on the fourteenth. Have you checked the Court and Social announcements?"

"What are you saying?"

Peregrine suppressed a laugh. "Isn't it obvious? The regent himself pawned the spoons. He's been strapped for cash this summer."

"The regent himself is demanding the Phoenix be brought to justice," Houseman said. "That's what I came to tell you. He's offered a reward of ten guineas."

"For the return of the spoons?"

"No—for the successful incarceration of the thief," Houseman said. "The pawnbroker was only too delighted to hand over the spoons for nothing."

"I'll wager he was, given who'd asked for them," Peregrine said. "Clever bastard."

"The Phoenix is not so clever."

"I didn't mean the Phoenix."

"But one of the stolen items has been found," Houseman said, "and now, thanks to my investigation, we have a description of the Phoenix."

"Good heavens," Peregrine replied. "I thought you were in possession of greater intelligence. The Phoenix didn't steal the spoons."

"Why do you believe that?"

"First, it doesn't fit the pattern—the Phoenix has stolen items from country estates, not royal residences. Secondly, it's clear that the Phoenix's motive isn't money. And thirdly, not even the Phoenix would be so bold as to deposit his bounty in a prominent pawnbroker's where it would almost certainly be discovered. But our glorious regent has, in all likelihood, managed to increase his personal funds by twenty guineas, earn himself sympathy for being the victim of a crime, and earned a reputation for generosity in offering a reward which he expects never to have to pay."

Understanding glimmered in Houseman's expression—together with a flicker of greed.

"If we catch the *real* Phoenix, then His Royal Highness will be obliged to pay the reward."

Hoofbeats echoed outside, and shortly after, Peregrine heard a knock on the main doors. Was the whole of bloody London out to disturb his breakfast?

The footman disappeared, then returned shortly afterward,

his wide-eyed, shocked expression reminiscent of a man who'd seen a ghost.

"L-Lord Marlow," he stammered. "Y-you…have another visitor."

"Well—don't just stand there, show him in."

The footman moved aside to reveal an elderly gentleman who stood in the doorway, leaning on a cane with a silver top. His tanned, wrinkled skin reminded Peregrine of a well-worn leather saddle. He was thinner than when Peregrine last saw him, and the hair, once thick and blond, now formed wisps of gray that framed a face with a long, straight nose and sharp cheekbones. But the expression in his pale blue eyes was as sharp and critical as ever it was, and as Peregrine met his gaze, the past fourteen years seemed to fall away and he was, once more, an adolescent standing before an adult whose approval he constantly strove to earn, but had always been denied.

"What are you doing here, Father?"

Earl Walton twisted his mouth into a sneer. "You've not changed, boy," he said. "Still lacking respect for your elders and betters. This house still belongs to me, you know."

"And yet you haven't set foot in it for ten years."

The earl gestured toward Houseman. "Should you be insulting your father in front of a guest?" He wrinkled his nose. "Not that I approve of your inviting tradesmen to dine."

Houseman stopped chewing.

"Why don't you join us, Father?" Peregrine said. "Assuming Houseman has left you any bacon."

"Houseman, you say?" The earl took a seat, then glanced at their guest with interest. "You're the one investigating the thefts with my son?"

"How do you know about the thefts?" Peregrine asked.

"Lord Caldicott sent me a letter after his sword was stolen."

"He *wrote* to you?" Peregrine asked. "Whatever for? And why would that necessitate your coming here?"

"Don't be insolent, boy! Caldicott's an old friend." The earl glanced toward Houseman again. "We were at Cambridge together—St John's College. Have you heard of it?"

Houseman shrugged.

The footman approached the earl with a plate, but he waved it away. "Fetch me some tea."

"Very good, your lordship."

After the footman exited the breakfast room, the earl leaned forward. "As it happens, I returned because of the thefts. I fear I'm to be the next target."

"What makes you think that?" Peregrine asked.

"It's not your place to question me," the earl said. "Your duty is to do as I say."

Peregrine had begun to wonder whether he'd been uncharitable in his feelings toward his father. But now, sat next to the pompous, dictatorial old man, he understood why he'd felt nothing but relief when the old bastard retired to the Continent.

"Very well, Father—do you know what the Phoenix intends to steal from you?"

"A clock," Father said. "At Marlow Park."

"Any clock in particular?" Peregrine asked. "After all, there's several in the main building alone, let alone the whole of the estate."

The earl shot him a sour look. "A French mantel clock—it's in the drawing room."

Peregrine closed his eyes, trying to picture the interior of his ancestral home. But he'd not visited for years. "I don't recall it," he said. "Is it a family heirloom?"

"I purchased it at auction."

At auction…

Just like the other stolen items.

Something connected them. Perhaps Father was the link?

"*I* believe you, Lord Walton," Houseman said. "Lord Hythe knew which of his paintings had been stolen even before it had been discovered missing—didn't he, Marlow?"

The earl drew in a sharp breath. "Hythe, you say?"

"Yes—it was discovered missing almost a fortnight ago."

The earl snorted. "Hythe always was a lily-livered fool. No balls to speak of. Well, that settles it. We must go to Marlow Park forthwith to prevent the theft of the clock—though, perhaps, we may be too late."

"Or," Houseman said, a sly smile on his lips, "perhaps, for the first time, we're one step ahead of the Phoenix."

"What do you mean?" Peregrine asked.

"If the Phoenix intends to steal your father's clock, we could lie in wait and catch him in the act."

"It could be weeks before he strikes," Peregrine said. "Have some sense, man! We can't wait about the place in the hope that he might come."

"We could set a trap," Houseman said. "Flush him out like a pheasant. What say we put it about that your father is transporting the clock back to the Continent? If the thief is among your acquaintance, the news would reach him easily. He'd have to act quickly in order to secure it, and many a man has slipped up when acting in haste."

"You're suggesting we use the clock as bait?" the earl asked.

"Aye," Houseman said, "then, when the blackguard takes the bait, we can bag him."

A cold smile crept across the earl's lips. "I'd like that," he said. "Houseman—can you make the arrangements?"

"It would be my pleasure," Houseman said.

"Good," the earl replied. "The bastard deserves everything that's coming to him. With luck, he'll end up swinging from a gibbet."

Icy fingers brushed against the back of Peregrine's neck at the savage relish in his father's tone. He could almost have believed that Father knew who the Phoenix was—that he was an adversary he wanted to see destroyed…

Dear God!

His father had only one bitter enemy that he was aware of.

Lord de Grande.

CHAPTER THIRTY

Sussex, September 1814

LAVINIA SPREAD JAM on her toast and glanced at her father across the breakfast table. He lifted his teacup, stared into it, then set it down with a clatter.

"Would you like some more tea, Papa?" she asked, picking up the teapot.

"There's no need to do that, daughter," Papa said. "Bates can serve me."

"My arms and legs are still functioning," she replied, smiling. "Mr. Bates is seeing to Samson, and by the time we've summoned him, the tea will have grown cold. I'm sure we can forget propriety for the sake of keeping your tea hot."

"He's seeing to Samson?"

"I'm going for a ride after breakfast." Lavinia poured tea into Papa's cup, then dropped two sugar lumps in. "Samson had almost no exercise while I was in London."

"And," Papa said with a smile of mischief, "I suppose you'll be riding astride now that your Aunt Edna has gone to take the waters in Bath and is no longer here to teach you decorum." Then he gave a mock sigh of exasperation. "I swear, Lavinia, you're more fond of that horse than you are of your own father."

"Dear Papa!" she said. "There's no one in the world whom I love more than you."

"Not even…" His eyes darkened, and he stared at her, as if trying to read her mind. She flushed and looked away.

You know, don't you, Papa?

When she had returned from Peregrine's townhouse—the day they'd made love—Papa had been waiting for her in the morning room. And he'd looked at her…*differently*, as if he knew she'd changed forever.

She felt different—as if she'd been a mere child before, but now she was a woman—with a woman's understanding of her body's desires and how to satisfy them. Only now did she understand the vehemence with which the vicar at Springfield Church preached against the sins of Eve.

And how delicious that sin had been!

Her thighs had ached where Peregrine had taken her, but she had relished the discomfort, savoring the sting as she eased herself into the bath that night, reliving the feel of him inside her.

And last night, he'd come to her in her dreams, and she had caressed herself where he'd claimed her. But, try as she might, though the sensation had been pleasurable, she could not reach the same heights of ecstasy that she experienced at his hands.

Her world—and her body—had changed forever.

How would she survive without seeing him again?

Gravel crunched outside, heralding the approach of a carriage. Moments later, Mrs. Bates opened the breakfast room door.

"Lady Betty's here, sir."

Lady Betty swept through the door in a flurry of bright blue silk. "Thank you, Mrs. Bates," she said. "Dickie darling, I'm *so* sorry I'm late."

"I'll fetch a fresh pot of tea," Mrs. Bates said, "and more toast."

"There's no need to trouble yourself," Lady Betty said.

"But you must try some jam," Mrs. Bates said. "We had a good crop of raspberries this year, and it's my best jam yet, if you don't mind me saying."

"Then I'll be delighted, Mrs. Bates, thank you."

"Do sit, Lady Betty," Papa said. "I feel most uncomfortable with a lady standing in my presence."

Lady Betty smiled and took a seat at the table. Then she drew out a paper from her reticule.

"Ah—the *London Daily*." Papa extended his hand.

"Yesterday's edition, I'm afraid," Lady Betty said, "but you might want to take a look at page seven—the Court and Social."

Papa flicked through the paper, then stopped, his gaze wandering over the page. He drew in a sharp breath and looked up.

"Good God!" he cried, and Lavinia flinched at the blasphemy. "That bastard Walton's back in town—strutting about St James's Palace as if he hasn't a care in the world!" He gritted his teeth. "It says here that he arrived in London last week, and attended court. Then, after a brief visit to his country estate this week, he'll be leaving England and intends never to return."

Papa placed the paper on the table. "Well, I for one, will not mourn his leaving the country." He glanced toward Lavinia. "Perhaps he's taking that son of his with him."

Lavinia drew in a sharp breath at the stab of pain in her heart. Then she glanced toward Lady Betty, who gave her a smile of reassurance.

"I have it on good authority that Walton is leaving on his own," Lady Betty said. "Ah, Mrs. Bates, how kind," she added as the door opened once more and Mrs. Bates entered with a tray. She placed a fresh teapot on the table, together with a plate of toast and a dish of jam, and left the room.

Lady Betty leaned forward and resumed. "Lady Edgington says it's the talk of London."

"What is?" Papa asked.

"That Earl Walton has returned to England because he fears he's the Phoenix's next victim."

"The Phoenix?" Papa asked. "You mean the thief who's been causing such a furor—at least, according to Edna? Why the devil would a series of thefts induce that bastard to return to England?"

"I hear that he's concerned about one item in particular,"

Lady Betty said. She glanced at Lavinia and met her gaze. "A Louis XVI mantel clock."

Papa let out a low cry. The teacup slipped from his fingers and fell onto the saucer, shattering on impact.

"Oh!" Lady Betty said as hot tea splashed onto the tablecloth. "Mrs. Bates—Mrs. Bates!"

The door opened, and Mrs. Bates rushed in. "Bless me! What's happened, your lordship? Oh, look at you—you're shaking." She rushed toward Papa and took his hand.

"Stop fussing, woman!" he growled.

"I'll fuss as much as I see fit, sir. You must take the greatest care of your health, particularly given your constitution. I knew you shouldn't have gone to London, yet you would insist upon it. The journey might be a short one, but the roads are not well cared for—the ruts and bumps would jolt a person so. Not that I'm blaming Lady Betty, now. No—Lady Betty has your best interests at heart, but you were very persuasive, and she had no choice but to indulge your whims. But it's just like my Joe. When he has his heart set on something, nothing will deter him, and the easiest path is to placate him, then admonish him later when the consequences of his actions fall upon him. Men are all the same when they insist on something. Stubborn as oxen, they are. Now…"

"Spare me, woman, in the name of the Almighty!" Papa said. "I'll do whatever you command, provided you desist from speaking. Why do women chatter on so? It's all nonsense— everything they say is nonsense."

Lady Betty rose. "Do you really want to speak so disparagingly of our sex, Dickie darling, given that you're outnumbered?"

"Not you as well, Betty," he said. "Your redeeming feature has always been that you know when to keep your mouth shut. I really think… Aah!" He let out a cry and threw his head back, opening his mouth wide as if fighting for breath.

"Breathe, your lordship," Mrs. Bates said, massaging his hand. "Remember what I said? Deep, slow breaths—and count to ten.

Here—let me help you upstairs."

"But I have a guest."

"Who Miss Lavinia can tend to, I'm sure."

Papa glanced at Lavinia, then his shoulders slumped in defeat, and he let himself be led out of the room. As he passed Lady Betty, she placed a hand on his arm.

"Dickie—I'm so sorry if I said anything to distress you," she said. "I never meant—"

"I know, Betty dear." He took her hand and lifted it to his lips. "You've nothing to reproach yourself for. It's Walton—the bastard. It's *always* been Walton."

"Papa…" Lavinia rose to her feet, but he shook his head.

"I'll be all right, daughter," he said. "Mrs. Bates has become quite proficient in taking care of me while you've been in London, and I cannot rely on you forever. You enjoy the rest of your breakfast. Mrs. Bates wouldn't want to see that jam going to waste. But I'd like you to come and see me before you take your ride."

"Of course." She watched her father shuffle out of the room on Mrs. Bates's arm.

"Poor Dickie," Lady Betty said. "Perhaps I shouldn't have told him about Walton. I thought he'd want to know."

"He'd have found out eventually," Lavinia said, "and he'd have been more distressed if he knew you'd kept it from him. He dislikes secrets."

"Some secrets are best kept hidden," Lady Betty said. "*You* should know that."

"What do you mean?" Lavinia asked.

Lady Betty spread jam on a slice of toast, then took a bite. "Mrs. Bates is right," she said, pushing the plate of toast toward Lavinia. "This jam is exceptional. You must have some."

She leaned forward and lowered her voice. "Do you know why your father acted so strangely when I mentioned the clock?"

"I suspect he was upset on hearing Walton's name," Lavinia replied.

"No—there's something more," Lady Betty said. "I can see it in your eyes, Lavinia. I may no longer receive invitations to Society parties, but my acquaintance is extensive enough that I'm kept abreast of gossip, including the theft of a painting that was replaced by an empty frame at Lord Hythe's country seat."

"The painting in question was later discovered," Lavinia said. "It hadn't been stolen at all."

"But I hear that a *different* painting was stolen. Perhaps the empty frame was a decoy devised by the infamous Phoenix?" She finished her toast, then dabbed her mouth with a napkin. "Yes— this jam really is most delicious."

She looked at Lavinia and smiled. "The Phoenix really is a most remarkable man." She lifted her teacup. "Or perhaps the Phoenix is no man. After all, I've never known any man to be that clever."

"I've no idea what you're saying," Lavinia said.

Lady Betty sipped her tea. "Tell me, Lavinia, darling—have you stolen the necklace yet, or does the fake I procured for you still reside in your bedchamber?"

Lavinia sighed. "There's no point in my denying it, is there?"

"No," Lady Betty said. "I take it the clock has a particular significance, otherwise Earl Walton wouldn't have made such a fuss about wanting to retrieve it from his estate. By all accounts, he's there now."

"At Marlow Park?"

Lady Betty nodded. "And he'll be leaving on the nineteenth of this month—at dusk, or so Lady Edgington tells me—and will be taking the clock with him."

"That's two days away." Lavinia pushed her plate aside. "Why are you telling *me*?"

"I think you know why. I'm not about to warn you off—I know enough of your tenacity to understand the futility of that."

"You think I'm interested in the clock?"

Lady Betty leaned forward, her expression softening, and sadness flickered in her eyes. "We both know that the clock is your mother's, and you intend to restore it to its rightful owner—your father."

"Restore it to its rightful owner?" Lavinia asked.

"It sounds better than *steal*, darling. But while I'll do nothing to stop you, I feel I must counsel you. Be careful of Walton—he's a dangerous man."

"He can't harm me," Lavinia said, "and there's nothing more he can do to harm Papa."

"I wouldn't be so sure. I'll admit that most of Dickie's old friends were fools—the late Lord Francis was notorious for his lack of intellect. But Walton is a different man entirely—he was sharp enough to ruin your father. You'll not do anything rash, will you?"

"I won't," Lavinia said, "but for Papa's peace of mind, Walton deserves to be punished for what he did. Even if I cannot punish him as fully as he deserves, I can, at least, do something to restore the balance of justice."

Lady Betty took her hand. "Darling child—you're more like your mother than you know. She had a determined streak, and was utterly loyal to your father—as he was to her. Your father has the memory of your dear mother to cherish. Nobody—not even Walton—can take that away from him. Sometimes it's best to cherish what we have than yearn for more. Letting Walton go will prevent him from having any power over you—it's best if the man never sets eyes on you."

"He doesn't even know me," Lavinia said.

"You're the daughter of his worst enemy—for that alone, he would hate you." Lady Betty caressed her hand. "But, as unpleasant as Walton may be, his son is nothing like him. You have given your heart to a good man, Lavinia. If you wish to be with him, you must do nothing to attract his father's attention."

She glanced at the clock on the mantelshelf. "Forgive me—I really must be going," she said, rising from her seat. "Please give my regards to your father."

Lavinia rose too, and Lady Betty drew her into an embrace.

"Nobody could replace your dear mama, but let me give a mother's counsel," she said. "Loyalty to a parent is to be commended, but there comes a time when you must place *your* heart, and happiness, first."

After seeing Lady Betty out, Lavinia climbed the staircase and entered Papa's bedchamber. She found him reclining on the sofa beside the window. The sunlight shone on his face, illuminating his soft brown eyes and creased white skin. He turned and looked at her, then held out his hand.

"Daughter."

She approached him and took it. The skin was dry and paper thin, as if it might disintegrate at the slightest touch.

"Shouldn't you be in bed, Papa?"

"I prefer to sit by the window," he whispered. "I can feel the sun on my face and watch the world outside. Ah—there's Betty." He leaned toward the window and raised his hand in salute. "A good friend to me, she's been," he said. "Of course, nobody could ever replace your dear mother, but had I been inclined to ask another, Lady Betty would have been my choice—though she'd never have me."

"She might," Lavinia said. "*I'd* have no objection, if that's your concern."

He shook his head. "No. Betty might love me, but she's not in love with me. She lost her heart to another, years ago. And though I love her as a dear friend, she's not the person in the world I love best." He curled his fingers around hers. "That is you, dearest daughter. I may be a feeble old man, but I'm no fool. Nor am I blind."

She kneeled beside him and placed his hand against her cheek. "I know, Papa," she said, "and I love you too."

"That's not what I meant," he said. "The ginger jar…"

"What of it?"

"…and the necklace. The sword—and the painting. Did you really think I believed that you'd *purchased* them all?"

"Papa…"

"I won't admonish you for attempting to right whatever wrong you believe was done to me. I—" He broke off, his voice wavering, then stared out of the window again, the sunlight reflected in his eyes, which glistened with moisture. "The clock that Lady Betty mentioned—it means nothing to me."

"Was it not a gift that Mama gave you when I was born?" she asked.

"Was it?" He blinked, and a tear splashed onto his cheek. "I-I must be getting old, for I can't remember."

"But Earl Walton—"

"There's nothing to be gained from dwelling on Walton," he said. "Your mother married me—loved *me*. The clock is an inanimate object, a *thing*. What value can be placed on an object when there's memories to be had?" He tapped his head. "Walton can never take away what's in *here*."

He drew in a breath, and his body spasmed with a cough.

"W-water…" He gestured toward a pitcher and a glass beside the bed. Lavinia poured water into the glass and held it to his lips. He clutched her hands, shaking while she tipped the glass up. His throat bobbed as he swallowed, then he closed his eyes and pushed the glass away.

"Lily," he whispered. "My beloved Lily—I failed you, my darling."

Lavinia grasped his hands. "No, Papa—you've failed no one."

"I failed *you* most of all, daughter," he said. "But I'll keep you safe now. The clock means nothing to me—I swear. *You're* what's important. Promise me you won't put yourself in danger—not for my sake."

He broke off in another fit of coughing, and he clawed at his chest. "Can't…breathe…"

"Mrs. Bates!" Lavinia cried. "Help us!"

Footsteps approached, and Mrs. Bates burst through the door.

"Oh, sweet Lord!" she cried. "Joe—Joe! Get yourself up here, now!"

Shortly after, Mr. Bates entered the chamber.

"Get him into bed," Lavinia said. "Quickly!"

"Here, let me," Mr. Bates said. "He's as light as a feather, he is." He scooped Papa into his arms and carried him over to the bed, where Lavinia drew the bedsheet back.

"T-tonic…"

Mrs. Bates nodded, drew a phial from her pocket, and uncorked it. She held it to his lips. "Just a drop, now, sir." Then she drew back while Papa's breathing eased. At length, he lay still, his chest rising and falling to a gentle rhythm.

"Tonic?" Lavinia asked.

"Laudanum," Mrs. Bates said. "Just a drop or two settles him, poor man."

"Does he need it?"

"Not all the time, but he's been in need of it a lot more this past month. It pains me to say that his health is failing."

Mrs. Bates placed a pudgy hand on Lavinia's arm. "We must all face our time when it comes, miss," she said. "Your father's love for you has sustained him. But he misses your mama something bad. While you were in London, Mr. Bates and I would often wake at night to hear him crying out for her."

Lavinia looked away, blinking back the tears.

"Oh, forgive me, miss!" Mrs. Bates said. "I didn't mean to distress you."

"And yet ye have, woman," Mr. Bates grumbled. "I said ye shouldn't tell the lass."

"No," Lavinia said. "It's best that I know."

She glanced toward her father, who was now asleep, a peaceful expression on his face.

Forgive me, Papa, but I trust you'll understand why I cannot do as you ask.

"Mr. Bates, is Samson ready?" she asked.

"Aye, miss."

"Then if Mrs. Bates would be so good as to watch over Papa, I'll take him for a ride now."

Lavinia bent over Papa and placed a kiss on his forehead, then she exited the bedchamber and made her way to the study. She approached the desk and pulled out the bottom drawer. Buried under a pile of papers, where he'd hidden it since their arrival at Springfield Cottage, was Papa's pistol. She closed the drawer and headed toward the stables, where Samson stood waiting.

"Hello, boy," she said. "How do you fancy another sojourn to a country estate to check the lie of the land?"

Marlow Park was barely ten miles from Springfield. And if what Lady Betty said were true, in two days' time, a carriage would be leaving the house, bound for London—most likely containing Mama's clock.

And Lavinia was determined to retrieve it.

By any means necessary.

CHAPTER THIRTY-ONE

THE LONG GALLERY at Marlow Park was lined with portraits of Peregrine's ancestors—each more cadaverous than the last.

He reached the end and stopped beside an enormous painting in a thick wooden frame. The subject stared out from the canvas, his thick-jowled face showing a yellowish hue—though whether that was due to the pigment in the paint having faded over the centuries, or due to the subject's sickly constitution, he could not tell.

Most likely it was the former. Had the artist painted a true likeness, doubtless he'd have left the establishment missing not only his fee, but his head.

The subject sat stiffly in a deep leather armchair, his hands folded on his lap, staring out as if he thought the rest of the world undeserving of life. Fleshy fingers were adorned with an array of rings, including a thick, carved gold band bearing a single blood-red ruby that winked malevolently, mirroring the expression in the subject's eyes.

The ring that had been bestowed upon the subject by a grateful monarch. Father had always said that it was due to some act of honor, though Lord Hythe had jested years ago that it had been payment in lieu of delivering the earl's mother, and both of his sisters, to the king's bed.

Peregrine approached the painting, which was covered in a thin film of dust, and ran his thumb along the nameplate at the bottom of the frame.

Ignatius Henry Stephen, First Earl Walton.

"Well, Ignatius Henry Stephen," he muttered. "I wonder if Lord Hythe spoke the truth about you."

No—not Lord Hythe. As Peregrine continued to stare at the painting, the memory resurfaced.

It had been de Grande, during a dinner at Marlow Park. As a young child, Peregrine had slipped past his nursemaid and run through this very same gallery to the drawing room, hoping to see the woman who Father had said was the most exquisite creature in all of Christendom. Peregrine had glimpsed the party through a crack in the drawing room and overheard de Grande's remark about the first Earl Walton. De Grande had then announced that Lady de Grande was to furnish him with an heir. Father's voice had risen in pitch to the level Peregrine had recognized as that which preceded a beating, and he'd fled back to his chamber. The next morning, Father had refused to rise from his bed, and when Peregrine asked his nursemaid why, she shushed him with a clip round the ear, instructing him to be quiet and stay out of the master's way until he "recovered from his headache."

An air of apprehension lingered about the place—it had always intensified when Father was having one of his headaches.

Was it any wonder that Peregrine never returned after he'd left for Cambridge?

But now, the building seemed to have lost some of its oppression, leaving only an air of neglect, as if it were to be pitied, rather than feared.

It's not the building that makes a place a home—it's the people who reside within it.

She had said that.

His little Guinevere…

Lavinia.

He exited the gallery and made his way to his father's study.

The desk was covered in a mess of papers. Father must have attempted to tidy them, then given up. It served him right for neglecting the estate for years.

As I have also neglected it.

Peregrine sat at the desk and shifted through the papers, which contained nothing of interest. Then he pulled open a drawer. It was empty save for an inkpot, stained with deep blue ink at the rim. He closed the drawer and opened the one below. Another pile of papers. He rummaged through them until he found a bundle tied together, decorated with a familiar motif—a mythological creature, with the head and wings of an eagle, but the body of a lion.

A Griffin. Where had he seen that before?

He pulled out the bundle and read the front sheet.

Griffin & Sons, Bond Street. Auction, dated September 17th,
1800
Catalogue of lots

The same auction at which the late Lord Francis had purchased the ginger jar for two shillings.

Peregrine flicked through the catalogue until he reached a section entitled "ceramics," then ran his thumb along each lot until he spotted it. An item on the list, beside which someone had marked the page with a cross.

Lot 120. Ginger jar, presumed 13th century, Yuan Dynasty, ceramic, complete with lid, decorated in blue

That was it! The piece Francis had purchased for two shillings. He read the line below and caught his breath.

Guide price: one hundred to one hundred and fifty guineas

He flicked through the pages until he came to the section entitled "artwork." His gaze fell upon an item near the bottom of the page.

Lot 254: Landscape oil painting entitled "The Snow Field" framed with gilded mahogany, signed J.R. 1765. Guide price: twenty to thirty guineas

Beside the item was another mark—a tiny cross.
"Hythe…" he whispered.
Further along the list, in the "militaria" section, he came upon another marked item.

Lot 329: Sword bearing a crest with filigree design at the hilt, circa 12th century. Guide price: eighty to one hundred guineas

"Caldicott."
His heart hammering in his chest, he flicked back through the catalogue until his gaze rested on the item he sought, marked with a cross.

Lot 206: Louis XVI late 18th century ormolu boulle mantel clock. Guide price: fifty to eighty guineas

There was no doubt about it—the Phoenix had stolen items that had been purchased at the same auction, items that Father and his friends had purchased at a cost that was considerably below the guide price.
And Lord de Grande was somehow involved.
He flicked through the catalogue again in search of more marked items. There was one more, in the "jewelry" section.

Lot 47: Lady's necklace in gold, one central emerald, with six rubies in graduated sizes. Guide price: thirty to fifty guineas

Nobody had reported the theft of a necklace, but it sounded familiar. He'd seen something similar recently…
He closed his eyes to heighten the memory.
A central emerald with six rubies in graduated sizes—set in deep gold, adorning a long, slim neck of soft, creamy white skin—an emerald that had grown in intensity as the night wore on…

No—it can't be…

"Lavinia," he whispered. "What are you about?"

At that moment, a voice roared a summons.

"Boy! Where are you?"

For a moment he was, once more, a boy of five being summoned for a beating.

"Boy! Come here!"

The voice came from the breakfast room. Peregrine descended the stairs at the end of the gallery and made his way there. Father and Mr. Houseman were seated at the table—Houseman indulging in a plate of bacon.

Peregrine entered, then froze as he caught sight of the object in the center of the table.

It was a mantel clock, with a round, white enamel face and delicate ormolu hands, decorated with royal-blue Roman numerals. The body, curved and sensual, surrounded the clock face then tapered at the bottom, before flaring outward at the base. The whole piece had been ornately decorated with a design of interlocking leaves and covered in ormolu, and at the top was a golden cherub cradling a sundial.

Father gestured toward the piece. "Do you know what that is?"

"A Louis XVI late eighteenth-century ormolu boulle mantel clock," Peregrine replied.

"It's *bait*," Houseman said.

Peregrine picked up the clock and inspected it. Some of the gilding had faded. He held it to his ear, but could hear no ticking. Most likely, it had never been wound from the day Father left Marlow Park.

He turned it around in his hands and flipped open the back. Inside, the metal had been etched with an inscription.

To my darling Richard, with love, always, on the birth of our beloved daughter, Lavinia.

He drew in a sharp breath as his heart gave a little jolt and the answer to the riddle slid into place. Father had ruined de Grande out of jealousy, then taken the one thing that the viscount had of his late wife.

A clock was a living, breathing organism—a piece to be treasured and cherished. But Father only valued something in terms of how it gave him gratification—or how it could be used to exact vengeance on a man he envied. He would never understand the love and skill that had gone into creating such a beautiful piece.

Nor would he understand the love a man harbored for another—the love that de Grande felt for his late wife…

…and the love Peregrine felt for de Grande's daughter.

The key was still inside the clock. Peregrine slotted it into place and turned it three times. A gentle ticking began, as if the clock had been brought back to life.

"Put it back, boy," Father said. "I want to catch that bastard red-handed."

"What do you mean?"

"Houseman here thinks the Phoenix will attempt to steal it tomorrow night, when I leave."

"And if he doesn't?"

"Then he'll have missed his chance, but at least I'll have the satisfaction of knowing that he'll never see it again."

The earl rubbed his hands in glee, and his eyes glittered with malevolent triumph.

Peregrine shook his head. "Why is the clock so important to you, when you clearly place no real value on it?"

"Because de Grande humiliated me, that's why!" Father snarled. "He took the woman *I* wanted, snatched her from under my very nose. When your mother left me free to marry again…"

"You mean when she *died*," Peregrine said.

The earl waved a dismissive hand at him. "I wanted Lady Lily—and de Grande knew it. So I waited until the time was right, then I took everything he had. The fool was only too willing to augment his fortune with a little speculation."

"You mean you tricked him," Peregrine said. "Were you in

league with others—Hythe, Francis, Caldicott, and Houghton—by any chance?"

The earl paled, and his eyes widened. Houseman glanced at Peregrine, then back to the earl, his eyes gleaming with greedy interest.

"So, you acquired the clock through nefarious means, merely to spite de Grande."

"It was a legitimate transaction."

"Purchased at an auction for considerably less than it was worth?"

The earl looked away. "I-I don't know what you mean."

"I think you do," Peregrine said.

"It matters not, boy. The clock's mine to do with as I please. Nothing will stop me from taking it with me when I leave. And I insist on your accompanying me to London."

"With pleasure," Peregrine said. "If, at the end, I see you safely onto a ship bound for the Continent, never to return, it'll be a journey well spent."

"Forgive my son, Mr. Houseman," the earl said. "He possesses little loyalty, and even less honor."

Peregrine rose to his feet. "I'm happy to disappoint you, Father."

Then he strode out of the breakfast room. He had no wish to take part in Houseman's ridiculous plan to ensnare the Phoenix—his own desire for victory over his adversary had faded.

In fact, it had disappeared completely, now he suspected the Phoenix's identity.

Lavinia...

Foolish girl! What possessed her to embark on such a crusade—one that could lead her into danger?

And how much of a simpleton had he been to not have realized sooner that it was her?

The evidence had been before him at every turn. It was at her suggestion that the guests' possessions were searched at Lord Hythe's house party after the painting had disappeared. She had suggested Lord Hythe have the gallery guarded—which had diverted everyone's attention from the real painting she'd set out to steal from a different part of the house.

She had been present at the Caldicotts' house party when the sword had gone missing.

And then there was the necklace, which he'd seen her wearing at Lady Houghton's ball. He'd even remarked on how the shine of the emerald seemed to have deepened, looking richer at the end of the evening than it had at the beginning—almost as if it were a different stone altogether.

As it had been.

Lavinia de Grande must have stolen the necklace in plain sight, replacing it with the fake she'd worn to the ball, and Lord Houghton was none the wiser.

Peregrine suppressed a smile. What other woman would make such a bold move?

In all respects he should despise her—breaking the law, causing a scandal among Society with her antics. Theft was a dishonorable act.

Yet he found himself admiring her.

She was the most honorable woman he knew—not swayed by a desire to present herself in such a manner as to make herself desirable, or attractive among a shallow Society that valued appearance, wealth, and birth over goodness. Her acts of theft were driven by honor. Peregrine's father saw himself as the victim—as did Lord Hythe and the others. But they were the perpetrators of the true sin—the ruination of de Grande. Lavinia was attempting, in her own way, to right the wrongs that had been perpetrated against her father.

Was she, even now, plotting to steal the clock? If she were, a trap awaited her.

CHAPTER THIRTY-TWO

A N OWL SCREECHED in the distance, and Lavinia's mount stamped on the ground.

"Hush, Samson!" she hissed.

The sun had long since sunk beneath the horizon, emitting one final, fiery glow at the edge of the world before it was consumed by the darkness, as if swallowed by a giant beast.

Why did the onset of darkness always heighten her fear? And why were sounds always louder at night?

She heard a rustling noise on the path ahead, then a small shape scuttled across the road, barely discernible in the faint moonlight. A silent shadow swooped through the air and dived toward the ground. A squeal rang out, then was silenced.

The night hunters were going about their business.

And tonight, she had joined them.

She urged Samson forward, keeping to the side of the road to muffle the hoofbeats. The road curved around, and a dark shape grew visible—the main building of Marlow Park. It dominated the landscape, turrets and chimneys forming jagged shapes to pierce the night sky. The house was mostly in darkness save for occasional windows, lit from within, staring out across the landscape.

It's as if you're watching me.

A shiver rippled through her skin.

Tonight might mark the demise of the Phoenix, for her quest

would be complete.

Assuming Earl Walton was leaving tonight—assuming he had the clock with him.

And assuming her courage did not fail.

She drew Samson to a halt at the edge of the trees, where they would be concealed among the shadows. It was the perfect vantage point—she'd checked it the previous afternoon when she'd ridden Samson over to undertake a little reconnaissance. It gave a clear view of the road where it dipped some fifty paces ahead, to re-emerge two hundred paces away.

Like all hunters, she had the perfect cloak of concealment. Her coat—or rather Mr. Bates's coat, which she'd appropriated from the greenhouse—might be several sizes too big, but its dark color helped her to blend into the background. She pulled her tricorn hat—another gift from the unwitting Mr. Bates—low over her forehead and waited.

At length, she caught sight of a flickering light—no, *two* flickering lights—in the distance. They swayed from side to side in unison, two wraiths engaged in a dance, moving closer and closer. Then the crack of a whip echoed through the evening air, followed by the rumble of hoofbeats and rattle of wheels.

"They're coming, Samson," she whispered, and the horse let out a low snort.

The lights disappeared as the carriage reached the dip in the road.

Two hundred paces…

She pulled her neckerchief up until it concealed the lower half of her face. Then she slipped her hand into the coat pocket, seeking reassurance from the solid shape within. As her fingers met the smooth wooden handle and the cold, hard metal barrel, her chest tightened with fear, and her heart pounded in her ears in unison with the approaching hoofbeats.

Then the lights appeared again on the road ahead.

Fifty paces…

Grasping the reins, she steered Samson into the center of the road, in the path of the carriage.

"Whoa there!" she roared.

A voice cried out from the carriage, and it drew to a halt about twenty paces away.

Biting her lip to stem the tremor in her arms, she drew out her father's pistol and held it in the air.

"Stand!" she cried, lowering the pitch of her voice. "I demand you deliver your goods."

"Why, you—" the driver began.

"Silence!" she interrupted. "Or I'll shoot!" She gestured toward the driver with her pistol. "Drop the reins. Hands in the air where I can see them."

He complied, and she steered Samson closer, stopping a few paces from the carriage door, where she could make out the outline of the Walton crest.

"Step out of the carriage!"

For a moment, the carriage remained still. Then, with a creak, the door opened and a tall, thin shape emerged. It turned toward her, and she caught sight of a white face, creased with age and bitter hatred.

"Lord Walton, I presume," she said.

"Whoreson!" the man cried. "I know what you've come for—and you shan't have it!" He reached inside the carriage and brought out a bundle wrapped in a cloth. "Is this what you seek, *old friend?*"

He removed the cloth, and she caught her breath at the sight.

Mama's clock…

The memory resurfaced from her childhood—Papa winding the clock every night. After Mama's passing, he'd continued the nightly ritual, speaking softly to his wife as he lovingly tended to the precious timepiece, his eyes glistening with moisture. Until it had been taken from him.

"H-hand it over," she said, her voice wavering.

"What would *you* want with it?" Walton sneered. "It's practically worthless—I paid two shillings for it, and even that was too much."

His voice was laced with derision and triumph. The skin at the back of her neck prickled with apprehension. Why did he sound so confident?

"Why I want it is my business," she said. "Do as I say."

He let out a cold laugh. "Why would I wish to do *that*?"

"Just do it!" She placed her thumb on the hammer and cocked her weapon. "I insist you hand over the clock."

"Oh, *insist*, do you?" Walton chuckled. "Did you hear that? He *insists*—the insolent blackguard!"

The carriage dipped to one side, and a thick-set man climbed out. He stood next to Walton, then pulled something from his pocket.

Lavinia's gut twisted in fear as she caught the glint of the barrel of a pistol.

"I-I don't wish to harm anyone," she said. "I only want the clock—please."

"Please?" Walton said. "Oh, he's *so* polite! Go on, then, you bastard—shoot me, if you dare."

A third man stepped out of the carriage, and Lavinia let out a cry as she recognized his tall, lean shape.

Peregrine…

She curled her fingers around the reins, and Samson shifted beneath her, as if he sensed her distress.

"Drop your weapon," Peregrine said, the deep, warm voice she loved now cold and hard. "Do it now, or it'll be the worse for you."

Shaking, she tightened her grip on the pistol.

"I *said* drop your weapon!" he roared.

What a fool she'd been! Not only had she walked into a trap, but she'd placed her head inside the noose.

Walton let out another laugh. "Coward!" he taunted her. "You're not man enough to shoot me—you don't have the balls."

"That's enough, Father!" Peregrine cried.

"Ha!" Walton barked. "You're just as bad." He turned to Lavinia. "You're a fool to risk your neck for a worthless trinket, all for the sake of a whore! Lily de Grande let me fuck her—did you know that?"

Mama...

Hatred coursed through her—hatred for the man who'd ruined Papa, then attempted to desecrate her mother's memory—and she curled her forefinger around the trigger.

But she couldn't do it. Better if he lived out the rest of his life in bitterness, his own evil eating away at him from within like a canker.

She shook her head and lowered the pistol.

A flash flared in front of her, followed by a loud crack. An explosion of pain tore through her shoulder. Her fingers twitched, and the pistol in her hand jerked upward as it fired, emitting a puff of blue smoke. Pain radiated from her arm until her whole body resonated with it.

Houseman had shot her.

Clutching the reins in one hand, her father's pistol in the other, she glanced up. Houseman stood by the carriage, a smile of satisfaction on his lips, holding his spent pistol as the final vestiges of smoke emanated from the end of the barrel. Beside him, Walton stared at her, his face white with fury. He jabbed a finger in her direction. "You...murdering bastard!"

She glanced toward the footman's post at the rear of the carriage.

But the post was empty. Instead, on the ground beside the carriage was the prone body of a man wearing a footman's livery.

Cold fingers clawed at her stomach, and she leaned forward and retched.

Walton threw the clock to the ground and sprang forward. "I'll have you for that, you bastard!"

The instinct to flee took over, and she sat up and clawed at the reins. Her heart racing, she turned Samson in a tight circle, then spurred him on, urging him into a gallop.

Only when she'd reached home did she slow him to a trot and dare look behind. But there was no sign of pursuit.

She slid off Samson's back, turning her ankle as she landed, then led the horse into his stall. Biting her tongue to stem the pain in her arm, she fumbled at the straps on the saddle and removed it. Then she limped toward the cottage and slipped inside.

There was no sound, other than the faint snoring from the Bates's bedchamber at the back of the cottage. Feeling her way in the dark, Lavinia tiptoed through the parlor until her fingers met the squat, solid shape of the decanter. Then she climbed the staircase, taking care to miss the creaky step at the turn.

She paused at the top of the stairs, and the image threatened to engulf her, swelling with intensity like a great tide—a man in a footman's livery, lying on the roadside…

No—do not think of it!

She pushed open the door to her chamber, wincing at the creak of wood. Once inside, she checked that the curtains were drawn, then struck a flint and lit a candle. She peeled off her garments, and her stomach churned at the metallic stench of blood. Then she inspected her arm in the flickering candlelight. A shallow groove ran along the muscle of her shoulder, glistening with thick red moisture, but there was no sign of the lead ball. She reached for the decanter and soaked her shirt in brandy. Then she pressed it against the wound. She let out a low moan at the sharp sting that sliced through her flesh like a knife. But, at length, the pain subsided. Then she tore a strip from the shirt and wound it around her arm, securing it with a knot. While she worked, she focused her attention on the sounds outside. But the night was quiet, as if a shroud had descended over the world.

As silent as a grave.

A grave…

She reached for the decanter, then held it to her lips and tipped her head up, swallowing the fiery liquid. Perhaps if it lessened the pain on the outside, it would also numb the pain within. Then she bundled the garments into the closet, slipped her night rail on, and climbed into bed.

Safe at last—but the tide of horror that had been swelling against her conscious mind finally burst through, and she let out a cry.

Heaven help me—I've killed a man!

CHAPTER THIRTY-THREE

PEREGRINE STARED AT the road ahead where the rider had disappeared into the darkness. His gut twisted with horror. *Lavinia…*

He turned on Houseman. "What the bloody hell have you done?"

"My duty," Houseman said, pocketing his pistol, "which is what *you* should have done. That was the Phoenix, and the bastard got away."

"At least he didn't get the clock," the earl scoffed.

Peregrine winced at the bitter triumph in his father's voice. "Is that all you care about, Father—a bloody *clock*?"

"The clock's nothing."

"No, of course not," Peregrine said, gritting his teeth to temper the fury raging within. "You only care about ruining lives. As for you"—he turned to Houseman—"you didn't have to shoot her!"

Houseman's eyes narrowed. "*Her?*"

"Houseman had every right to shoot," the earl said. "Nobody's safe these days with highwaymen haunting the roads. They deserve to be shot."

"Not when they're lowering their weapons," Peregrine said. "Would you shoot someone who's unarmed?"

"If necessary—to protect what's mine."

"But the clock isn't yours, is it?"

"It *is* mine!" the earl snarled. "I've the bill of sale to prove it. It belongs to me, according to the law."

"I'm not talking about the law," Peregrine said. "I'm talking about justice."

"It's the same thing."

"No, it's not, Father. If we lived in a just world, you'd have been held to account for what you did."

"What did you mean…*her*?" Houseman asked.

"The man wasn't unarmed," the earl said, ignoring Houseman. He pointed to the prone figure of the footman. "He's killed a man. Would you advocate justice for a murderer?"

The figure moved and gave out a low groan. Peregrine rushed toward him, crouched down, and placed his hand on the man's forehead.

"He's alive," he said.

"That may be—but that highwayman shot him."

"By accident!" Peregrine cried. "Houseman shot first—he's the one who shot on purpose."

"Yes—to defend us against a murderous ruffian!"

Peregrine glanced up at Houseman. "You shouldn't have fired."

"*Her*?" Houseman asked.

"What?" Peregrine asked.

"You said, 'You didn't have to shoot *her*.'"

Shit.

"I said no such thing, Houseman," he said. "Your hearing's addled from firing your weapon. You shouldn't have shot…him."

"I hit him in the arm," Houseman said. "He'll not get far. With luck, we'll find him dead in a ditch along the road."

"Then we should follow him," the earl said. "Get back in the coach."

"What about the footman?" Peregrine asked.

The earl shrugged. "What about him?"

"We need to get him to a doctor."

"We shouldn't be wasting time on a *servant*."

"You bastard," Peregrine said. "You'd let a man die?"

Another groan, and the footman lifted his head.

"Don't move," Peregrine said, "not until we know where you've been hit. What's your name?"

"John, sir."

"Stay still, John," Peregrine said. "Houseman—come and help. Check his body for injuries."

"It's m-my ankle," the footman said. "I twisted it when I fell."

"Where were you shot?"

The footman hesitated, and Peregrine could swear he saw the color deepening on his cheeks, despite the darkness.

"I-I think I fainted, sir. With…with fright."

"Can you stand, John?"

The footman nodded.

Peregrine helped him to his feet. The footman's tricorn hat lay on the ground, and Houseman picked it up.

"There," he said, holding the hat up. "See?"

Peregrine glanced at the hat, which was silhouetted against the moonlight save for a perfect, round hole that glowed like a single white eye staring back at him.

Houseman lowered the hat and poked his finger through the hole. "A bullet hole," he said. "Evidence of the highwayman's intent to kill."

"I'm sure he didn't intend to kill anyone," the footman said.

"He shot you," the earl said.

"No, he didn't."

"Nevertheless, we should go after him," the earl said.

"No," Peregrine said. "We must go back. John needs a doctor, and the highwayman will be long gone. I'll search for him in the morning."

"This is nonsense," the earl said. "My ship sails tomorrow."

"You're going nowhere, Father," Peregrine said.

"I must agree with Lord Marlow," Houseman said. "You're a witness, Lord Walton. We'll need you to ensure the man hangs."

Hangs…

Peregrine swallowed the bile rising in his throat and glanced at his father, whose lips were curved into a cold smile of satisfaction.

"I should like that." The earl glanced at the footman. "Return to your position."

The footman retrieved his hat and placed it on his head. "Very good, your lordship."

"There's no need for that, John," Peregrine said. "Your ankle's hurt. Come inside the carriage."

"Where to, Lord Marlow?" the driver asked.

"Back to Marlow Park."

Ignoring his father's protests, Peregrine ushered the footman and Houseman into the carriage, then climbed in after them. The driver cracked the whip, steered the carriage in a tight circle, then set off in the direction in which they had come.

After they arrived at Marlow Park, Peregrine helped the footman out, followed by Houseman and his father.

"We should go after the highwayman," Houseman said.

"I'll go in the morning."

Houseman stared at him. "I'll come with you—unless you have a particular reason for wanting to go alone?"

Damn, the man was suspicious—and he had every right to be.

Peregrine spoke to the driver. "Make sure the carriage is ready in the morning. Houseman and I will begin our search then. Be ready at nine."

"As you wish, sir."

The driver cracked the whip, and the carriage rolled away.

"I think it's time for a brandy," the earl said. "What say you, Houseman?"

"Thank you, sir—I'd like that."

The two of them entered the building as if they had just returned from dinner at White's, leaving Peregrine with the footman.

"Shall I send for a doctor, John?" Peregrine asked.

"No, sir, my ankle's a little sore, but I'll live." The footman hesitated. "Don't be too hard on…him, sir."

"Who—my father?"

"No, the highwayman. The earl might want retribution, but in that highwayman's eyes I saw no evil—only fear."

Peregrine smiled. "Never fear, John," he said. "I know the difference between justice and retribution. Would you see to it that my horse is saddled and ready to ride tomorrow morning?"

"At nine, so you can travel with Mr. Houseman?"

"No," Peregrine said. "At six. Make sure my father and Mr. Houseman don't know."

"For what purpose?"

Peregrine closed his eyes, and the image of Lavinia's beautiful face floated before his mind's eye.

"I intend to see justice served."

CHAPTER THIRTY-FOUR

A VORTEX OF black and red swirled around Lavinia until it tightened her chest, pushing the breath from her body. A wraith floated in the air, glowing in the red light that smothered the horizon. She struggled to break free, but blackness pinned her to the ground.

The wraith turned to face her, and she caught sight of a skull bathed in red—two eyes as black as coal staring soullessly at her and a wide, gaping mouth fixed into a demonic grin. Skeletal arms reached toward her, claw-like hands sliding hungrily toward their prey.

Fate had come to claim her—a life for a life.

The wraith stepped forward, placing a foot on the ground with a sharp crack. It took another step—then another, and another…

She reached up to defend herself, and her hands dissolved in front of her, morphing into bones. The demon's grin broadened as it broke into a run, reaching for her throat…

Crack, crack, knock, knock…

With a scream, she sat upright, and the demon dissolved. She glanced at her hands and saw only pale skin, illuminated in the light of the morning sun.

She was in her bedchamber, bathed in the beam of sunlight that stretched across the bedsheet from the window where she'd forgotten to draw the curtains last night.

She jumped as the door was knocked again, followed by a female voice.

"Miss Lavinia? Your father sent me. It's gone seven, and breakfast's ready."

The door opened to reveal Mrs. Bates.

"Forgive me, miss, but I heard—" She broke off, her eyes widening. "Mercy me, miss! Whatever's the matter? You look very ill."

Lavinia shook her head. "No, Mrs. Bates, I'm quite well. I-it was a bad dream, that's all."

"Are you sure? You're as white as a sheet. I could send for the doctor."

"No!" Lavinia cried. Mrs. Bates flinched. "Forgive me, Mrs. Bates—I'm merely tired. I slept poorly."

"That's nothing a good breakfast won't cure," Mrs. Bates said. She gestured toward the closet. "Shall I help you dress?"

"No, I'll be all right. Tell Papa I'll be down directly."

"Very good, miss." Mrs. Bates tilted her head to one side and regarded Lavinia with a thoughtful expression. "Are you *sure* you're all right?" Lavinia nodded, and Mrs. Bates leaned forward and kissed her forehead. "If you say so, sweet girl," she said. "It breaks my heart that you've no mother to share your burdens. You're so strong for your papa—but who's there to be strong for you? If there's anything I, or my Joe, can do to help chase your nightmare away, you only need ask."

Dear Mrs. Bates! But what could an honest, hardworking—and god-fearing—couple do to help her, given that she'd...

No—do not think of it!

Mrs. Bates patted Lavinia's hand, then exited the room. Lavinia re-bandaged her wound, then dressed as well as she could, choosing a long-sleeved gown to conceal the bandage. The bleeding had stopped, but her arm had grown stiff, and the wound itched.

She found Papa helping himself to eggs from the side table. He nodded in greeting, then shuffled back to his seat.

"It's not like you to sleep late," he said. "Is anything the matter?"

"No—I'm quite well."

He cast a sharp glance in her direction, but said nothing. Lavinia approached the buffet and spooned eggs onto her plate.

"Perhaps you're tired from your exertions earlier this morning," Papa said.

Lavinia's stomach clenched and she dropped the spoon, which clattered into the dish.

"My—what?"

"I felt a little better this morning, so I went out to take the air before breakfast, and I happened upon the stables. Samson looked like he'd been ridden hard, and his saddle had been left in the stall, covered in mud." He eyed her with disapproval. "I told Bates to deal with it, but I'm surprised you didn't ask him yourself."

"I-I didn't want to wake him."

Papa resumed his attention on his breakfast. Lavinia took her seat and poured a cup of tea, and they ate in silence.

After a while, Papa spoke.

"A midnight ride is dangerous."

She glanced up. "A what?"

"Do you take me for a fool, daughter? The mud on the saddle was caked dry, as if it had been there for hours. Where the devil have you been?"

What could she say? Papa was the one person in the world who didn't deserve to be lied to.

"I should have known." He sighed. "You've been to Marlow Park to see Walton, haven't you?"

She recoiled at his insight. "H-how do you know?"

"I saw it in your eyes when Lady Betty said Walton was in England. Was there a particular reason for your going?" He leaned back and folded his arms. "It's unlikely to be a social call in the middle of the night."

"No," she said, gritting her teeth. Her arm flared with pain as she reached for her teacup. "It wasn't."

He stared at her for a moment. "You hate Walton as much as I, don't you?"

"Yes, Papa, I do."

"And his son?"

Her heart fluttered at the thought of *him*, and she looked away.

But Papa was too sharp. He leaned across the table and took her hand.

"H-he's not like his father, Papa," she said.

He stroked her hand. "Perhaps I've been too harsh. Lady Betty admonished me for it. My own father was a cad, so I'm the last person who should wish to see the son suffer for his father's sins." He smiled. "I recall the bright boy who came to visit when Walton and I were friends, before your dear mama passed away…" He gave a wistful smile. "He always used to take care of you. Most boys would have chased you away. At that age I'd never have wanted a younger child—let alone a girl—trotting around after me. But he was a better child than I—perhaps he's grown up to be a better man, also."

He placed a kiss on her hand. "You can speak the truth, Lavinia," he said, "and you can trust me to listen. You've been a good child—you've weathered our hardships better than I'd hoped, been a friend to Lady Betty when others would have scorned her. Perhaps I should trust you—though I would caution you not to get hurt."

Had the pain in her arm not been so intense, she'd have laughed at the irony.

Then he patted her hand again. "No matter," he said. "I take it your foray into the night was unsuccessful."

"I-I don't know what you mean, Papa."

He tutted in the affectionate manner he used to when she was a child. "Now, what did I say about trusting me with the truth, child? Do you think I believed your story about having *purchased* those pieces that adorn my bedchamber? Houghton would never have sold the necklace—and I overheard Mrs. Bates gossiping about the theft of Lord Hythe's painting."

"You did?"

"She has a niece in service at Hythe Manor," he said, frowning. "Gossip travels below stairs as well. I didn't know my daughter was a thief."

Overcome with shame, she withdrew her hand. "Forgive me, Papa."

His frown disappeared and a smile slowly crept across his face. "There's naught to forgive. In fact, I'm rather proud of your escapades. From what Mrs. Bates said, the Phoenix is the talk of the servants—a legend akin to Robin Hood."

She began to laugh, then the darkness of last night pushed to the fore.

The body on the ground…

There was *everything* to forgive—but what she'd done was unforgiveable.

Her vision blurred, and she blinked as the tears spilled onto her cheeks.

"Lavinia!" he cried. "What's wrong?"

She shook her head. How could she tell him?

Blinded by the tears, she withdrew her hand to wipe her eyes. Then she heard his chair scrape back, and two bony arms drew her into an embrace.

"It matters not," he said. "Your old papa will take care of you. As your mother used to say, 'Everything will be all right in the end.'"

If only she could be so sure!

A sob swelled in her throat, and she clung to him.

Then their peace was shattered by three sharp raps on the front door.

"Who the devil has come to see us at this hour?" Papa muttered. "It's barely seven o'clock." He let out a huff. "Unless it's the butcher's boy using the front door again—Mrs. Bates has already admonished him about that."

Mrs. Bates clomped along the hallway, then Lavinia heard the latch lift, and muffled voices.

Footsteps approached, and the breakfast room door opened. Lavinia rose to greet the newcomer, then froze as a familiar pair of hazel eyes stared directly at her.

Peregrine…

His powerful frame filled the doorway, seeming to block out the sunlight—the man who had pledged to bring the Phoenix to justice.

She opened her mouth, but no sound came.

Then he stepped forward and reached toward her. The image of the wraith from her dream flashed before her mind, and she gave a start.

"Lord Marlow, I don't recall inviting you here," Papa said, "and certainly not at this hour. Why have you come? I doubt it's because you wish to share my breakfast."

Peregrine glanced at Lavinia, and her gut twisted at the seriousness of his expression. Then he resumed his attention on her father and issued a deep bow.

"I am come to apologize, Lord de Grande," he said.

"For what, Lord Marlow?"

"For what my father did to you." He gestured around the breakfast room. "I apologize that your circumstances were reduced to *this*."

Papa straightened his stance, and for a moment his expression was proud. "The state of my circumstances depends on your perspective, Lord Marlow. I may have lost my fortune, but I have honor on my side, and I have my beloved daughter, two precious treasures that nobody could take from me—though your father took everything else, did he not?"

Peregrine nodded. "I know," he said quietly. "I suspected it, but didn't want to believe that my father could do such a thing. Even now, after so many years, he harbors no shame for what he did. He boasted of the bidding he'd fixed at auction with the others to secure your most precious treasures for a pittance."

He glanced toward Lavinia again. "It was there in front of me—the link between each item—and yet I did not see it."

Her vision blurred again. Peregrine reached toward her and caught her arm, and she let out a low cry of pain.

"Are you hurt, my love?"

Papa drew in a sharp breath.

"In one thing you're right, Lord de Grande," Peregrine said. "Your daughter is your greatest treasure."

He glanced at her arm, then his eyes widened. She looked down and almost let out a cry. The white muslin bore a stain, a small patch of red—insignificant at first, but it began to spread slowly, glistening in the sunlight.

"You are hurt!" Papa cried.

"Were you injured last night?" Peregrine asked.

"No—she was here all night," Papa said, a little too quickly. "I swear it."

But there was no use in denial. His voice was thick with the knowledge that he'd lied, and Peregrine was too clever a man to fool any longer.

"I almost caught the Phoenix last night," Peregrine said. "I thought, perhaps, my quest had come to an end."

"You've been hunting the Phoenix?" Papa asked.

Peregrine nodded. "For some weeks now, the Phoenix and I have been adversaries, pitting our wits against each other. But I can finally concede that the Phoenix has proven to be a cleverer man than I could ever have imagined." He released Lavinia's arm, then took her hand, interlocking his fingers with hers. "Or, perhaps, I should concede that the Phoenix is a cleverer *woman* than any could have imagined. She is to be admired, not censured, and I will always admire and love her."

"So…" Papa's voice wavered. "You came here today to tell us that?"

"And because I feared that the Phoenix was hurt last night."

Lavinia caught her breath as a ripple of nausea threaded through her, and she curled her fingers around his, drawing comfort from his strength.

"My fear is greater than yours, sir," she said. "I-I fear that another was hurt last night—at my hand."

"What do you mean, Lavinia?" Papa asked.

Peregrine lifted her hand to his lips. "Let me ease your mind on that score," he said. "The footman is unharmed."

A spark of hope ignited in her heart, then she dismissed it. "B-but I saw him—on the ground!"

"What's all this?" Papa asked, his voice sharp. "Have you been in an accident?"

"No, Father," she replied. "I..." A sob swelled in her throat. "I-I can't say—I'm so ashamed!"

Two strong arms pulled her into an embrace.

"Hush, my love." Peregrine's deep voice resonated in her body, and his warm breath caressed her cheek as he held her close. "I'll do everything I can to protect you."

"Peregrine, wh-what happened to the f-footman?" she stuttered.

"He fainted in fright," he said. "The only damage is a neat bullet hole in his hat—of which, I might say, he's rather proud."

Her heart swelled with hope. Beset with visions of being dragged into prison, she had prayed for herself as well as the footman. She set little value on the power of prayer as an entreaty, believing that the Almighty rarely saw fit to answer her prayers.

But here, and now, her prayers had been answered.

"Oh, thank heavens!" she cried as she drew her arms around him. "I feared the worst." She closed her eyes, safe, at last, in the arms of the man she loved, safe in the knowledge that he knew who she was—and what she'd done—and loved her regardless.

He held her tightly, almost desperately, as if he feared she would leave.

But she never would. She belonged to him—her King Arthur. She had always belonged to him, and he to her. Nothing would part them again.

She tipped her face up, and warm, soft lips brushed against hers in a kiss. Then he withdrew. She opened her eyes to see him gazing at her, his own eyes filled with tears.

But they were tears of sorrow, not joy.

"I'm sorry, my love," he whispered. "So, so sorry."

A cold, invisible hand of dread clawed at her insides. "Do you… Do you not love me now you know I'm the Phoenix?"

"Oh, sweet heaven, no!" he replied. "I love you more than anything—and nothing will change that, no matter what you've done. But…"

"What has my daughter done?" Papa asked.

"I-I'm sorry, Lord de Grande," Peregrine said. "I promise I'll do everything I can to protect her."

"Protect her from what?" Papa asked. "From Walton?"

"From the authorities, Lord de Grande," Peregrine said. "Your daughter held up a coach last night."

"Dear God—no!"

"In the eyes of the law," Peregrine continued, "it matters not that nobody was harmed."

"What do you mean?" Lavinia asked.

"Highway robbery is a hanging offense," Peregrine said. "The Phoenix now has a price on his head—dead or alive."

The invisible hand curled around her heart and crushed it.

She opened her mouth to cry—but no sound came. Her chest tightened, and the world began to spiral around her in a fury of black and red, pulsing to the rhythm of her father's cries.

She had been right—sometimes the Almighty did answer her prayers.

But today, that answer was *no*.

CHAPTER THIRTY-FIVE

THE WOMAN IN Peregrine's arms shuddered with horror.

The woman he loved.

What the devil had she been thinking last night? The Phoenix had always laid such careful plans, leading everyone on a merry dance with moves and countermoves. How much planning and ingenuity had the theft of Lord Hythe's painting taken?

But last night, seemingly on a whim, she'd committed an act of utter lunacy, for which, if convicted, she would hang.

Peregrine glanced up, and his eyes met Lord de Grande's despondent, milky gaze. His childhood memory of de Grande was a vibrant man with a charming, elegant wife and an exuberant, intelligent daughter. But the man before him now was a shadow of his former self—his body bent with age and pain, and his eyes filled with loss. The wife had long since died. As for the daughter…

Lavinia had risked everything in a desperate attempt to give the father she loved peace of mind, and she was now on the brink of losing all she had, including her life.

I'll not let that happen.

He'd pledged to bring the Phoenix to justice. But what justice would there be in handing her over?

He placed a kiss on the top of her head.

"Lavinia, you have nothing to fear," he said. "I'll protect you."

"What can *you* do, Lord Marlow?" de Grande asked. "You're just one man."

"One man is capable of anything for the woman he loves."

De Grande's eyes widened.

"That's right, sir," Peregrine said. "I love your daughter. I know you'll never approve of me—and I understand that. What my father did to you was unforgiveable, and you've every right to throw me out. But *I* don't matter here—what matters is your daughter. Hate me all you like, but that won't save her."

Tears stung his eyes. He blinked, and a bead of moisture splashed onto her hair. It glistened briefly in the sunlight, then dissolved.

Cradling Lavinia in his arms, he helped her back to her seat at the table. She blinked, her eyes glazed with fear. His heart ached to see it, and he placed a hand on her cheek.

"All will be well, my love," he whispered.

"Tell me what to do," Lord de Grande said.

Peregrine turned to see the old man standing behind him, body erect.

"Lord de Grande, this is my responsibility. I don't think—"

"No," the old man said, his voice filled with determination. "You're not the only one in the world who loves her. You may think me a sick old man, and perhaps I am. But she's my daughter. Since your bastard of a father nearly destroyed me, the one thing I've had, to give me hope, is her. Even as a child, she gave me comfort. She's been strong for me all these years. Now, it's time for me to be strong for her."

He stepped forward and held out his hand.

"Now, Lord Marlow," he said. "Tell me what I must do."

Peregrine took the proffered hand, and thin, bony fingers curled around his wrist in a surprisingly strong grip.

"What my father did to you was wrong," he said. "All your daughter did was try to right that wrong. You keep her safe here, de Grande. I'll make sure that the authorities won't come looking for her."

Lavinia stirred and slipped her fingers through this. "Th-they won't?"

Peregrine lifted her hand and brushed his lips against her skin. "You have my word," he said. "Trust me."

"Always."

"Lavinia," he whispered. "My little Guinevere. I have always loved you."

"And I you."

"I'll keep you safe," he said. "I'm yours, Lavinia. My heart, and"—he hesitated—"my hand are yours."

His heart almost sang at the hope in her eyes, after the crushing despair only moments before. She blinked, and tears rolled down her cheeks. But her lips—her beautiful lips—curled into a smile.

A smile for him.

He leaned forward and brushed his lips against hers, tasting the salt on her skin.

Then she stiffened and shifted her gaze to her father. The hope in her eyes faded.

"I can't, I…" Her voice caught, and she shook her head. "I'm so sorry, but I just can't. Forgive me."

"No, daughter," de Grande said. "Don't sacrifice your happiness for the sake of my desire for vengeance against my enemy. What purpose would that serve if it rendered my beloved daughter unhappy?"

She lifted her gaze. "Papa?"

De Grande leaned over and placed a kiss on her forehead. "My darling child, you cannot deny your heart's desire on my account. Whatever path you wish to follow to secure your happiness, you have my full blessing to embark upon that path."

Peregrine's heart swelled with hope, and he met de Grande's gaze.

The old man nodded. "Yes, my boy," he said. "You have my blessing."

A clock chimed in the distance, and Peregrine stiffened.

Half past seven.

"I must go."

"Peregrine, what's the matter?" Lavinia asked, her voice trembling.

"Houseman is conducting a search of the area," he replied. "If I leave now, I can catch him before he sets off, and prevent him from coming here."

"How will you do that without arousing suspicion?" de Grande asked. "Lady Betty's told me about Mr. Houseman. Overly obsequious, she said, and ready to do anything for his personal advancement."

"You needn't worry about that," Peregrine said. "I'll think of something."

Though what, he couldn't fathom.

He held her hand against his breast. "I must go now, my love, but I'll return as soon as I can." He glanced at de Grande. "I think, perhaps, Lavinia should take her rest. She's had a shock."

"Of course," de Grande replied. "Come, daughter, let me help you upstairs."

"No, Papa, I—" she replied, but he ignored her.

"Mrs. Bates!" he cried out.

After a suspiciously short time, the housekeeper appeared in the doorway. "Oh, my poor lamb!" she said. "Here, let me help you to your room. Some of my sweet tea will see you right."

She rushed forward and helped Lavinia to stand.

"Mrs. Bates, I'm perfectly well," she protested. "In fact, I— Ouch!" She let out a cry as Mrs. Bates took her arm.

"I thought as much," Mrs. Bates said in the manner of an exasperated nursemaid. "Let's get you upstairs, and I'll take a look at that arm of yours."

Lavinia's eyes widened. "Mrs. Bates, how did you know…"

"I know—and see—a lot, dearie. You think I didn't notice when my Joe couldn't find his gray coat this morning, or when he saw the state of your horse's saddle? Or when that little jar appeared in your papa's chamber the other month after you'd gone for one of your midnight rides—not to mention that ugly old sword, the necklace, and that pretty little painting you brought back from London?"

"Why didn't you say anything?" de Grande asked.

"Oh, mercy me, your lordship! It's not my place—and I know Miss Lavinia would have had a good reason. She's tended to you without a word of complaint, lovely young lass that she is." She glanced at Peregrine. "Go and do what you must, Lord Marlow. I'll help his lordship take care of Miss Lavinia, you have my word. And now, Miss Lavinia," she said, her voice growing stern, "let's tend to that arm, shall we? I can see it pains you."

She ushered Lavinia toward the door, like a mother hen bundling a lost chick back into the nest.

De Grande took Peregrine's hand.

"I'm trusting you to do what you can, Marlow," he said. "But trust does not come easy. The last time I trusted a man, it ruined me—and led my daughter to *this*. I may have given you my blessing to wed my daughter, but God help you if you betray that trust."

Peregrine nodded. "Understood."

Then he bowed and took his leave.

Poseidon stood waiting patiently by the cottage gate. Peregrine mounted the horse and set off on the return journey to Marlow Park. With luck he'd arrive before Houseman had set off. But de Grande was right—Houseman would go to any length to further himself, and the man was determined to capture the Phoenix. In all likelihood, Peregrine wouldn't be able to stop him. But de Grande and his daughter had given him their trust.

So he had to try.

CHAPTER THIRTY-SIX

BY THE TIME Peregrine returned to Marlow Park, his mount was showing signs of distress. And well he might. Poseidon had been bred for stamina, but Peregrine had ridden him hard. Sweat glistened on the animal's pelt, and his breath misted in the air.

As he sighted the stables, Peregrine could almost feel the relief in the animal's body. He leaned forward and patted Poseidon's flank.

"I'm sorry, my boy," he said. "I'm in love—and love is the most destructive of emotions, for it's often used to justify the mistreatment of others. But I've no wish for *you* to suffer."

He steered the animal into the stable yard. The uneven gait told him that Poseidon was favoring his rear left foot. A stable boy emerged from one of the stalls and took the reins.

"Lord Marlow, sir! I didn't expect you back so soon."

Peregrine dismounted. "He needs a good rub-down—and check his left hindquarter. He may be a little lame. I'm afraid I rode him rather hard."

You've ridden him too hard, boy!

The image flashed before his mind's eye of Lancelot, and his father's cold detachment as he'd ordered him to shoot the animal.

Curse you, Father!

"Beg pardon, your lordship?" The boy raised his eyebrows in question.

"Take particular care of him, please," Peregrine said. "I'll make sure you're compensated for my folly."

"Your folly?"

"In not treating my horse with the respect he deserves. He cannot speak for himself, and this morning I failed him. It won't happen again."

"Lord bless you, sir—you're the opposite of your f—" The boy broke off, blushing.

"Thank you," Peregrine replied. "I intend to be." He patted Poseidon's flank, then returned to the house.

He found his father in the breakfast room, a pile of bacon on the plate before him.

The earl glanced up and scowled. "Where the devil have *you* been, boy? You know breakfast in my house is served at eight."

"I'm no boy," Peregrine said, "and I've a house of my own in London."

"That house belongs to the earldom, therefore it belongs to *me*."

"*You're* not the earldom, Father," Peregrine said. "You're merely the present incumbent."

"Since when did you become so disrespectful of your betters?"

"My *betters?*"

Peregrine shed his coat and handed it to the footman beside the door. Then he took a seat. Another footman appeared with a platter of bacon, and Peregrine waved him away.

"Where's our guest?" he asked.

"Houseman? He's gone."

"Already? I thought he was leaving at nine."

The earl shrugged. "He changed his mind and left earlier. He'll be halfway to London by now. With luck, he'll find that blackguard bleeding on the road. But I hope he'll take him alive."

"Alive?"

"Yes," the earl said between mouthfuls. "We wouldn't want to be robbed of the satisfaction of seeing him swinging from a gibbet. Now, eat your breakfast."

Peregrine rose and scraped his chair back. "I find I lack the stomach for it."

His father snorted. "You always were a weakling."

"Better that than a thief."

"Don't be a fool!" the earl cried. "I've never stolen a thing in my life."

"Perhaps not in the eyes of the law," Peregrine said, "but you took everything from another, didn't you?"

"I don't know what you mean."

"Oh, yes you do." Peregrine gritted his teeth to suppress the urge to smash his fist into his father's self-satisfied face. "Persuading another to invest his fortune in a doomed enterprise may not be an offense that lands the perpetrator in jail, but it's an offense nonetheless—against decency, honor, and friendship."

"What would *you* know about decency, honor, and friendship, boy?"

"A damned sight more than you!" Peregrine cried. "You set out to ruin de Grande because you envied him. But you couldn't leave it at that, could you? Not content with relieving the man of nearly everything he owned, you saw fit to claim for yourself that which you knew he cared for the most—the token of his late wife's love."

"I don't know what you—"

"Oh, for fuck's sake!" Peregrine roared.

Crockery clattered, followed by a cry, as the footman dropped a tray laden with dishes, which shattered as they fell to the floor.

"You think I've never heard of bid rigging?" Peregrine continued.

The earl averted his gaze. "Heard of *what?*"

The old bastard was lying. Over the years of investigating thefts, Peregrine had learned that a man exhibited a certain type of behavior when attempting to spin a falsehood...a clearing of the throat, a tapping of the fingers, or a furtive glance to one side.

"Don't take me for a fool, Father," he said. "A Louis XVI mantel clock must be worth at least a hundred guineas, but you secured it with a bid of two shillings. How did you manage that?"

Father glanced to one side again. "Good fortune."

"A man makes his own good fortune," Peregrine said. "Isn't that what you told me when I was a child? But you…" He gestured toward his father. "You made yours at the expense of an innocent man."

The earl resumed his attention on the plate in front of him. "I care not what you think."

"You never did," Peregrine said, "but I'll wager the partners at Griffin & Sons would have something to say if they knew what you did. They don't take kindly to bid rigging. What did you do—collude with Hythe, Francis, and the others? Or did you threaten the other bidders at the auction?"

"I don't stoop to violence, boy!"

"That doesn't absolve you, Father. You're no better than the man on the street who robs a passerby. In fact, you're worse. You didn't do it to feed your family, or to save yourself—you did it out of gratification of seeing your former friend suffer."

"And what if I did?" the earl said. "De Grande had what I wanted!"

"He had *what* you wanted?" Peregrine shook his head in disgust. "To you, Lady de Grande was a commodity—a possession you envied, rather than a woman you loved. Dear God, Father—I always knew you were a bastard, but I had no idea exactly what kind of bastard you are."

He thrust his hand into his pocket, then drew out two coins and tossed them across the table.

"What's this?" the earl asked.

"Two shillings—in lieu of the clock."

"It's not for sale."

"It never should have been," Peregrine said. He turned and approached the door, shouldering past the footman.

"Where do you think you're going?" the earl demanded.

"Outside," Peregrine replied. "I'm in need of air. The atmosphere stinks in here, and I don't mean the bacon."

"But you'll be back?"

"No, Father. After today, I never intend to come back to this place—until the day I can be assured that *you'll* not be here to plague me."

The earl paled as he caught Peregrine's meaning. "Son, y-you don't mean that…"

"When have *I* ever lied, Father?"

Ignoring the plea in the old man's eyes, Peregrine exited the breakfast room. His father might be old, but age had not tempered his selfishness. The sooner Father left England, the better. Peregrine had no wish to set eyes on the man again.

Once outside, he drew in a lungful of fresh air. Though he longed to leave Marlow Park as soon as possible, he'd already ridden Poseidon to the brink of his endurance, and Houseman had taken the carriage. He'd have to remain at Marlow Park for another day. But that didn't mean he had to be in the same room as the bastard who'd sired him.

As he strode along the gravel path at the front of the house, Peregrine spotted a figure limping across the lawn. He raised his arm in greeting.

"John! How's the ankle?"

The footman stopped. "Morning, Lord Marlow."

"Should you be walking without a stick?" Peregrine asked. "You look like you're in pain."

"I'm as right as the rain, sir." The discomfort in the man's eyes belied his words.

"You don't look all right," Peregrine said. "I could find you something to support that leg."

"Don't go troubling yerself, sir. My Daisy says 'tis the best thing for a sprain."

"What—to endure the pain?"

"No—to keep moving." The man smiled, his eyes sparkling with mischief. "Doubtless she wants me outside so as I'm not under her feet all day. She says that when a man sits still, he takes up too much room in the house. And, if truth be told, I can weather a little pain if I'm free of her nagging for a while. She has a rare talent for finding work for idle hands—particularly the hands of a man she catches sitting in her kitchen. It's washing day today, and a man shouldn't be expected to scrub his wife's undergarments—pleasant though they may be to look at."

Peregrine couldn't resist a smile. John's voice was filled with the love he bore his wife—and the slight lift in pitch when he mentioned his wife's drawers spoke of a man well satisfied with every aspect of marital life.

"It's not meself I'm worried for, though," the footman continued. "That poor young rider was shot in the arm."

"The highwayman? You sound as if you have sympathy for…him."

"*Him?*" The footman's eyes widened. "If you say so. It was plain to see that he meant no harm. He didn't know one end of a pistol from the other. It was my fault I sprained my ankle—I fainted and fell off the carriage. As for the bullet hole in my hat— well, my Daisy sees it as a mark of my bravery. And let me tell ye, a wife knows how to reward a husband for his bravery."

Peregrine smiled. "I envy you, John, in having such an understanding wife."

"I'm sure ye'll find a wife to love ye just as well, sir." The footman cocked his head to one side, understanding in his eyes. "Is she badly hurt—Miss de Grande?"

Peregrine's breath caught in his throat. "H-how did you…"

"You might have a talent for rooting out secrets, sir, but secrets are passed below stairs as well as above."

"She's wounded," Peregrine said. "But it's healing."

The footman nodded. "I should have realized when your father insisted on taking that clock with him. And I recognized the horse right away—Samson, his name is. I thought the rider was Lord de Grande, until he—or rather *she*—spoke. I said to myself at the time—that's the voice of a woman, or my name's not John White."

"And you knew about the clock?"

"My cousin's housekeeper at Fosterley Park. She was head housemaid when Lord de Grande had to leave nigh on fourteen years ago. The new tenants kept the staff on—ever so kind they are, she says. She was there when the creditors removed some of the treasures in the building—not the items that were under trust, of course. She always said that Lord de Grande cared little for material objects, save a small number of items that it broke his heart to be parted from. But the creditors insisted, and took them anyway."

"Can you recall what those items were?" Peregrine asked, though he already knew the answer.

"The one my cousin said broke her master's heart the most to lose was a clock."

"The clock that currently resides in our morning room?"

"The very same. And there was a painting. My brother told me about it—a snow scene, which he said looked worth a lot more than it cost his master."

"Your brother?"

"He's head gardener at Hythe Manor, and his wife, who was one of the housemaids back then, always said it was a pity that such a pretty little painting should be hidden away in a side room, as if his lordship were ashamed of it. Then, when Robert wrote to say it had been stolen, I wondered if it were some form of retribution, and whether Lord de Grande had a champion, like Robin Hood from the tales my ma used to tell me. After all, the painting had been for sale at the same auction as the clock."

"The auction..."

"The one held in London after de Grande's ruination—at Griffin & Sons, if I recall."

Ye gods! Peregrine had been so busy fostering relationships with auctioneers, pawnbrokers, and proprietors of curiosity shops—not to mention the loathsome Mr. Houseman—that he'd completely ignored the most likely set of people to assist him with his inquiries.

"It seems I've been speaking to the wrong people," Peregrine said. "To further my investigations, I should have spoken to the servants, rather than the lords."

The footman let out a hollow laugh. "Who listens to the word of a servant?"

"*I'm* listening," Peregrine said. "What do you know?"

"You may not like what you hear."

"Why? Because it paints my father in an unflattering light?"

The footman colored and looked away.

"Trust me, John, I'd rather cast light on the truth," Peregrine said, "no matter how unflattering that may be."

The footman nodded. "Very well. Your father traveled to London for the auction. Lord Caldicott was in the carriage with him, as were Lords Francis and Houghton."

"But not Lord Hythe?"

"From what I overheard, there was some doubt over whether Lord Hythe would be joining them."

"What did they talk about?" Peregrine asked.

"The earl was boasting about his accomplishments in bringing about de Grande's ruination. And…" He hesitated. "You'll not like it, sir."

"Let me hazard a guess," Peregrine said. "They were plotting to fix the auction so they could procure de Grande's favored items for two shillings apiece."

"I don't know nothing about two shillings, but they had made an arrangement with someone at the auction house to ensure the bids remained low."

"How the devil do you know all this?"

The footman smiled. "Folks' tongues will loosen in front of a servant. To them, we're invisible. When we stopped to give the horses water, I overheard some of their conversation."

"And you didn't think to say anything?"

"And lose my position?" The footman blushed. "Daisy and I had a little'un on the way at the time. We'd have been tossed out on the street if I said anything. And what's to have stopped your father insisting Lord Hythe toss my brother out, also? To folk like you, we're disposable commodities, to be discarded when we give offense."

Guilt needled at Peregrine at the footman's words. The man was right—the wealthy and titled treated the less fortunate with contempt.

How many souls depended on the Marlow estate? Servants—tenants…

Yet Peregrine knew very few of them. As if they didn't matter.

"Begging yer pardon, sir, but that clock belongs in Lord de Grande's hands," the footman said. "The lass was merely trying to restore it to its rightful owner."

"You seem convinced of the rider's identity," Peregrine said.

A smile curved the man's lips, and he placed a hand on Peregrine's arm in the manner of a loving father—the loving father he'd never had.

"Aye, I do," he said. "And do you know what secured it in my mind as a certainty?"

"What?"

"It was the way you looked at her, sir. You recognized her right away. And when that fool Houseman shot her…" He shook his head. "I've never seen anyone so terrified."

"Anyone would be afraid after being shot."

"No, sir. I meant *you*. A man—or woman—may fear for their own life, but there's nothing so raw as the fear for the life of a loved one."

Peregrine caught his breath, and the footman nodded.

"I'll not betray her identity, sir," he said. "A sprightly little thing she was as a child. Whenever your father used to visit de Grande at Fosterley, she'd always come up to me, asking to help with the horses. The first time, I tried to deter her. 'Miss de Grande,' I said. 'You're a lady—and a lady doesn't bother herself with servants or animals. She only makes friends with other ladies, and your nursemaid would object.' And do you know what she said?"

"No."

"She looked me right in the eye and said, 'Then for today, you and the horses shall be ladies, so I can talk to you. And if Nursie objects, I'll give you one of her petticoats to wear—the horses, too.'"

Peregrine smiled to himself at the image of a determined little girl ordering the thick-set footman to don a petticoat—not to mention put one on a horse.

"Came to see us every time your father visited," John continued, "until you accompanied your father on your pony while you were home from school in the summer. Then she trotted about after you like a faithful hound—do you remember?"

"Yes," Peregrine said. "I do. I was only a boy myself, but I believe I fell in love with her that summer." He sighed. "I've loved her ever since."

"Then go to her, sir," John said. He gestured toward the main building of Marlow Park. "Leave this godforsaken place, with its bitter shades, take the clock, and go to her."

Peregrine nodded, his mind made up. As soon as his horse was fit to ride again, he'd do just that.

CHAPTER THIRTY-SEVEN

"**T**HERE, MISS LAVINIA! That's much better." Mrs. Bates finished bandaging Lavinia's arm and secured it with a neat knot. "Now—what would you say to some tea? I can bring a pot up."

"Please don't trouble yourself, Mrs. Bates," Lavinia said. "I can come down."

"Nonsense!" Mrs. Bates gestured to the writing desk by the window. "You'll want to finish your letter to your friend. And besides, you need to rest after your little adventure."

Hardly a *little adventure*—holding up a carriage in the middle of the night, and getting shot in the process. But Lavinia wasn't about to remind the housekeeper what she'd done. For the past two days she'd been on a knife's edge, anticipating a visit from the magistrate—or an angry Earl Walton. Each time a carriage drove past the cottage, her stomach tightened with fear.

"Where's Papa?" she asked.

"He's resting in the parlor before Lady Betty comes. He wanted to take a nap in the garden, but it's far too cold, with that chill he's caught. My Joe's lit a fire for him. Shall I send him up to light a fire for you, miss?"

"Don't trouble your husband, Mrs. Bates. Just the tea will do."

"Very good, miss. I'll bring up some of the shortbread I've made for Lady Betty's visit this afternoon—it's just out of the oven."

As soon as Mrs. Bates left, Lavinia crossed her bedchamber to the escritoire. That morning she'd received a letter from Henrietta—now the blissfully happy Countess Thorpe—informing her that she was soon to furnish her husband with an heir.

She settled into the chair and resumed reading the letter.

I'm astonished, dearest Lavinia, to have succumbed to the prospect of my confinement with little protest. But I imagine that is the effect that love has on a woman, even one as determined as I to defy the rules of Society. Giles, of course, is still a little overbearing in his determination to assert his place as head of the family, but I'm prepared to permit his little indulgences, particularly when he asserts himself so sweetly. He says I am a vessel, carrying the most precious cargo in the world. I, of course, tell him that his wits have been addled by the urge of the aristocratic male to be furnished with a male heir, and that I should summon the doctor to examine his head.

My dearest wish is to see you as happy as I. Though I wouldn't presume to suggest that a woman must secure happiness by entering the marriage state, I'm fully aware you hold a certain viscount in high regard compared to the rest of the baying bucks whose company we endured last Season. Do tell. In your last letter you said you'd danced with him twice at a party. As we all know, a gentleman asks a lady to dance when he wishes her to know she's the object of his interest. But when he asks her to dance a second time, he's declaring his interest to the whole room.

I must take my leave of you now, darling Lavinia. The modiste is due to arrive with my gown for Beatrice's wedding. I swear it grows tighter with each fitting. But I'm determined to attend the wedding, rather than languish at home. Beatrice is like a sister to me, as are you, and Eleanor, of course, and I trust that as soon as my child is born, you will oblige me with a visit, for I miss you terribly.

Yours,
Henrietta

Smiling, Lavinia pulled out a piece of paper. Then she picked up her quill and began to write.

Dearest Henrietta…

Hoofbeats on gravel crunched in the distance, and she glanced out of the window to see a carriage drawing to a standstill.

Lady Betty must be early.

Lavinia set her quill down and wiped her hands. Then she approached her dressing table and tidied her hair. Lady Betty might care little for propriety and a polished appearance, but Lavinia still wanted to make the effort for a woman she loved like an older sister—or a favorite aunt.

She secured a ribbon in place, then exited her bedchamber. Papa's voice could be heard coming from the parlor as she descended the stairs. He sounded animated—angry, even. What had Lady Betty done to upset him?

She pushed open the parlor door and froze.

Papa stood beside his chair, next to Mrs. Bates. In the center of the room stood three men. Two she didn't recognize—they had thick-set frames and wore identical dark attire. But the third…

The third was the man from the night she'd held up the carriage.

The man who had shot her.

He stepped forward, licking his lips. "Ah, so your daughter *is* at home, Lord de Grande. You must have been mistaken earlier." He nodded to his two companions, who moved to stand either side of Lavinia, blocking her exit.

Her gut twisted in fear. "Wh-what is this?" she asked. "Papa, who are these people?"

"I think you know precisely who we are," the man said,

"though, of course, I had no opportunity to introduce myself the last time we met."

Her skin crawled at the triumph in his tone. He stepped toward her and smiled, his teeth gleaming, as if he wanted to rip her throat out. Then he inclined his head in a bow, so slight as to almost be considered an insult.

"Mr. Houseman, at your service," he said. "I am also, of course, in the service of the Crown."

Lavinia drew in a sharp breath to combat the nausea swelling within her.

"Lavinia de Grande," he said, "you are charged with theft, highway robbery, and—"

"Don't be a fool!" Papa cried.

"*You're* the fool," Houseman said. "Take her!"

A hand grasped her arm, where the wound was still healing, and she cried out at the flare of pain.

Houseman's eyes widened. "I *knew* it! I shot a highwayman in the arm, just before he shot a footman in cold blood."

Papa's eyes widened. "You have no proof," he said. "Leave my daughter alone—how dare you insult our good name?"

"Oh, I have proof, your lordship," Houseman said. "Both Earl Walton and Lord Marlow have been very forthcoming, and have furnished me with enough evidence to convict you."

Lavinia's heart withered at Houseman's words.

Lord save me—Peregrine!

He had betrayed her.

"Your *good name* was ground into the dirt years ago, de Grande," Houseman sneered. He gestured about the parlor. "You've only to look at this hovel to see how far you've sunk."

Lavinia tried to free herself, but the hand on her arm tightened its grip, and another spike of pain shot through her body. A second hand took her free arm.

"This is outrageous!" Papa cried. "Mrs. Bates, fetch your husband!" He stepped forward, but Houseman drew a pistol out of his pocket.

"Stay right there!" he barked. "I'm authorized to shoot if necessary, and my reward will be the same whether I deliver the Phoenix alive or dead. Alive is preferable—we wouldn't want to be denied the satisfaction of a trial, or an execution."

Lavinia fought to draw breath. A roaring sound thundered in the distance, intensifying until her mind almost burst from the agony of it.

"Lavinia!" Papa pitched forward, and Mrs. Bates rushed forward to support him.

As Lavinia slipped into unconsciousness and felt herself being dragged away, she heard Houseman's words, muffled by the blanket of oblivion, accompanied by a wail of despair from her father.

"Accept my condolences, Lord de Grande, for the loss of your daughter."

CHAPTER THIRTY-EIGHT

PEREGRINE DREW POSEIDON to a halt outside Springfield Cottage, then dismounted. The horse's leg seemed to have healed, but nevertheless, despite his desire to see Lavinia again, he'd kept to a steady pace on the road so as not to overwhelm the animal. He patted Poseidon's flank, then unstrapped the leather bag and its contents from the saddle.

"Good boy," he said. "Forgive me for treating you like a beast of burden, but you're carrying a very special item."

He opened the bag to check inside, caught sight of the golden cherub, then smiled at the prospect of returning it, at last, to its real owner.

Finally, justice is done.

He knocked on the door and waited. Moments later, it opened, to reveal the familiar plump, gray-haired woman. But her usual sunny demeanor had gone. Her eyes were red and swollen, as if she'd been crying.

"Mrs. Bates, is anything amiss?"

"Oh, Lord Marlow!" she cried. Then she glanced over her shoulder and back again. "Wh-what are you doing here?"

He took a step forward, but rather than move aside to grant him entrance, she stood her ground.

"Aren't you going to let me in?" he asked.

"I-I don't know. The master isn't up to visitors. And he'd never admit *you*."

"Nonsense!" Peregrine said. He held up the bag. "I've something to lift his spirits—and Miss de Grande's, of course. Is she at home?"

Mrs. Bates drew in a sharp breath. "Y-you've not heard?"

"Heard what?"

"That we have suffered the fruits of your labors, Lord Marlow."

The skin on the back of his neck tightened. What the devil was going on?

"Please be so good as to admit me, Mrs. Bates," he said. "I'm come to see Miss de Grande and her father."

"You're not welcome, sir," she said. "Not after what you've done. I don't know how you can show your face here!"

"What the devil am I supposed to have done?"

"Let him in, Mrs. Bates!" a voice croaked from inside. "If only to answer for his actions."

The woman stepped aside.

"He's in the parlor," she said. "But if you say or do anything to harm him further, I swear to God, I'll—"

"That's enough, Mrs. Bates," the voice said. "*I'll* deal with him. You fetch your husband."

The woman sniffed, then ushered Peregrine into the parlor.

De Grande lay reclined in a chair, his legs propped up on a footstool, covered in a blanket. His body seemed to have shrunk—his hands, clasped together on his lap, were thin and claw-like. Deep lines were etched into his features—paper-thin skin that seemed to stretch over his cheekbones. He could almost have been mistaken for a cadaver, except for his deep-set eyes. Clear and bright, they focused on Peregrine with an expression of such hatred that he could swear he could almost taste it.

Footsteps approached from behind.

"What you be wanting, your lordship... Oh!" Mr. Bates stopped short as he caught sight of Peregrine. Then he took hold of his arm. "Shall I see him out, sir?"

"No, Bates, I..." De Grande broke off with a volley of coughs, then he drew in a wheezing breath. "I want him to explain himself, then you may remove him."

"I'm come to return the clock," Peregrine said, holding up the bag. "See?"

"The clock!" de Grande spat. "Is *that* all you care about? What about my daughter, you bastard?"

"I...don't understand..."

"I've lost her!" de Grande cried, then his body shook with his coughing.

Mrs. Bates shouldered past Peregrine and rushed to the old man. "Don't distress yourself, sir," she said, caressing the old man's head. Then she turned to Peregrine, her eyes hard. "Joe, get rid of him!"

Bates tightened his grip, but Peregrine wrenched his arm free. "I'm going nowhere until somebody explains what the bloody hell is going on!"

"My daughter's been arrested," de Grande said. "They took her yesterday."

Peregrine caught his breath as a shard of pain speared his chest.

"Lavinia..."

"It's *Miss de Grande* to you," the old man said. "Thanks to you, I'll never see her again!"

"Surely you can't think I had anything to do with it?" Peregrine replied. "I pledged to protect her!"

"Yes, you did, sir," de Grande said, "then you hid like a coward while your friend took her."

"My...friend?"

"Mr. Houseman," de Grande said. "He threatened me with a pistol, then his thugs dragged her out of the house like a common criminal."

Peregrine curled his hands into fists. "Houseman—you bastard!"

"And now he's got my daughter, my precious child..." De Grande bent his head. "I've let her down so badly. First after my darling Lily passed—then now…" He shook his head. "I'll never see her again!"

The weight of Peregrine's own despair threatened to crush him. But, seeing the broken old man, a core of iron formed deep within him, forged from the fires of his despair—turning into the impenetrable steel of determination.

Nobody, especially not that weasel Houseman, would defeat him. Lavinia was in danger, and he had to be strong for her, and for her father.

For that was the definition of love—the ability to set aside his own fears and fight for another.

And he *would* fight. To his last breath.

He wrenched himself free from Bates's grasp and crossed the parlor to kneel before the old man who looked so utterly lost.

"Lord de Grande," he said. "I give you my word that I'll do everything in my power to bring your daughter home."

De Grande shook his head. "There's nothing to be done. I have no one."

Peregrine reached forward and curled his hand around de Grande's ice-cold, bony fingers. "Sir," he said. "I accept that you have no reason to trust me. You may believe that you have no one. But you're wrong. *I* will fight for you. Not just because I owe you a debt of honor to atone for my father's sins against you, but because I love your daughter—and I will continue loving her until I draw my last breath."

"Why should I trust you?" de Grande croaked. Faith in a man's promises has only ever led me to ruination and despair."

Peregrine reached inside the bag and pulled out the clock. "Because of this."

De Grande's eyes widened, and Peregrine placed the clock on the old man's lap. For a moment, de Grande simply stared at it. Then he ran his hands along the body, as if he were caressing a lover. He sighed as his fingertips traced every curve, every feature of the ornate carving, dancing over the winged cherub at the top, until they came to rest at the base. Then he turned the clock around and flipped open the back.

"'To my darling Richard, with love, always, on the birth of our beloved daughter, Lavinia.'"

Tears glistened in his eyes, then spilled onto his cheeks.

"Lily…" he whispered. "My darling Lily."

Then his expression hardened, and he held the clock out to Peregrine.

"Take it."

"It's yours," Peregrine said. "I brought it here for you."

De Grande shook his head, and another tear rolled down his cheek. "I don't want it," he said. "It's just an object—a *thing*—and it's caused enough misery. It won't bring back my beloved Lily, nor will it bring back my child. My Lavinia will hang—and for what? For this? No!"

The old man threw the clock onto the floor. The cherub snapped off, rolled across the floor, and stopped face up, sightless eyes staring into the heavens.

"I care nothing about material objects, Lord Marlow," he said. "What matters most is my daughter."

"Then I shall ride to London forthwith," Peregrine said, "and I'll do everything I can to return her to you."

"Do what you will, sir, but do not set foot in my house again."

Finding himself dismissed, Peregrine retreated, and Bates ushered him outside, where Poseidon stood waiting.

"Sorry, boy," he said, approaching the horse. "I'm afraid I've further need of you."

He mounted Poseidon then steered onto the lane. With luck, he'd reach London before nightfall. But what would he find when he arrived?

In all likelihood, Lavinia would hang.

CHAPTER THIRTY-NINE

*D*RIP DRIP-DRIP DRIP—DRIP, *drip-drip drip…*
You're going to hang. You're going to hang…
Was there no respite?

Not even in the blackness of sleep could she escape the sneering voice of the jailer, the gap-toothed man who stank of sweat and death, who'd licked his lips with relish as she was pushed into her cell.

"Leave me be!"

Lavinia opened her eyes and sat up, raising her arms to fend off the foul-smelling man and his overly attentive hands.

But she was alone. Her only companion was a small, dark form that scuttled to and fro in the far corner. With a squeak, it turned and disappeared into a small hole between the bricks, and she caught sight of a hairless tail in the small beam of sunlight that filtered through the bars from the tiny window above.

She glanced about the cell. They had brought her here only two days ago, but in that span, her life had changed. Hope had sparked inside her when she'd been placed before Earl Stiles, the magistrate. But though he seemed a fair and just man, unlike that bastard Houseman, Stiles had explained that no matter what the justification—and no matter that she was a young woman—there was no escape from fact that highway robbery was a capital crime, and he had no option but to have her detained.

The image of a gibbet entered her mind, and she placed her

hands about her throat.

Would it hurt?

Though she recalled little of her childhood—fragmented images and memories merging with her imagination, until she couldn't distinguish truth from fiction—the memory of her beloved mama remained true. Mama's face on the pillow, surrounded by a halo of golden hair, eyes bright with pain, but clear with acceptance, as she slipped into the world beyond…

Would her own entry into the afterlife be as dignified? Or would she scream and jerk on the end of the rope—as the jailer had described with such relish—before securing her place in hell?

I'm going to hang…

I'm going to hell…

Drip drip-drip drip—drip, drip-drip drip…

Water glistened thickly on the cell walls, filling the atmosphere with dank and decay. She drew in a lungful of air, and almost choked. A bone-rattling cough echoed in the distance, followed by a long, low groan.

One of her fellow inmates.

There were worse ways to die than on the hangman's noose.

Perhaps, if she pleaded her case to Stiles, he might permit her to send for a swordsman to slice off her head to quicken her exit. Wasn't that what Anne Boleyn had requested when she was tried for crimes she'd been innocent of?

But you're not innocent.

Drip drip-drip drip…

She squeezed her eyes shut, willing her mind to slip away from the never-ending dripping. But it only grew louder, echoing around the cell, moving back and forth, until she could swear it was outside.

Then her heart jolted in fear as she recognized the jailer's footsteps. Had he come to torment her again?

Her skin crawled at the memory of the lust in his eyes. The law of decency had no place here, and there was no one to come to her defense.

Peregrine...

No!

To think about *him* would only lead to despair. Peregrine had betrayed her. He'd abandoned her with promises of protection, and then, unwilling to sully his own hands with the deed, instructed that vile Houseman to seize her.

But she wouldn't go without a fight. She was not Lavinia de Grande, debutante and simpering miss. She was the Phoenix—the daring thief who'd been the talk of Society.

She rose and curled her hands into fists.

A face appeared at the barred window in the door, and her stomach clenched as she recognized the pale eyes of the jailer. Then the key turned in the lock, and the door swung inside.

Her would-be tormentor stood in the doorway.

But the lustful arrogance had gone—replaced by a scowl.

Then another form appeared—a thick-set man in a footman's livery. He shoved the jailer aside.

"She's here, your ladyship," he said, "and she appears unharmed."

A female form appeared, silhouetted against the light of the torch in the passageway. "*I'll* be the judge of that, William," she said in a familiar, beloved voice.

"Lady Betty!"

The woman rushed into the cell and pulled Lavinia into an embrace. Lavinia closed her eyes, relishing the familiar, delicate aroma of rose cologne.

"Oh, my poor darling!" Lady Betty cried. "I can't imagine what you must have suffered in this vile place. But your nightmare is over, my love—I'm come to take you home."

"I-I don't understand," Lavinia said.

"Lord Stiles issued an order for your release earlier this morning. All charges against you have been dropped. You're free to go."

"B-but...how?" Lavinia shook her head. "H-he said that there was no circumstance under which he'd be able to order my release."

"No circumstance except one," Lady Betty said. "But let us not discuss it here"—she threw the jailer a look of contempt—"not when unsavory ears are listening. Come with me now." She nodded to the footman. "William—would you be so good as to help Miss de Grande to my carriage?"

"With pleasure, your ladyship." The footman held up a cloak with a cowl.

"What's that?" Lavinia asked.

"It's chilly outside, miss," he said. "We wouldn't want you to catch cold. And we wouldn't want no prying eyes on you, neither."

Without waiting for a response, he placed the cloak around Lavinia's shoulders. Then he took her arm and, together with Lady Betty, escorted her outside.

The onslaught of sunlight blinded her eyes, but the footman's arm was firm and reassuring as he steered her into a waiting carriage.

"Where are we going?"

"To my townhouse, darling," Lady Betty said, climbing in beside her, "where your father awaits you."

"Papa? He's in London?"

"Yes, he traveled here yesterday. He's..." Lady Betty's voice cracked.

Lavinia's stomach clenched with fear. She leaned forward and took Lady Betty's hand.

"Something's wrong, isn't it?" she said. "Is that why I've been freed?"

Lady Betty nodded. "Forgive me, darling. I am, of course, delighted that you're free, but it came at a cost, and your father has paid the price."

"How?" Lavinia asked.

"Your father has confessed to the robberies. He's due before the magistrate tomorrow, and then..."

There was no need to say what came next.

And then...Papa would face trial and execution.

Her father had exchanged his life for hers.

CHAPTER FORTY

PEREGRINE DRAINED HIS glass, then caught his breath as the liquor burned his throat.

Bloody Stiles—damn him!

Why did the man have to be such a stickler for the law? Not content with refusing to change his ruling, the man had also refused Peregrine permission to see Lavinia until he could secure a lawyer to act in her defense.

But he didn't know any lawyers—at least, none who were skilled in defending a young woman on trial for her life.

"More tea, sir?"

He pushed his breakfast plate aside. The untouched eggs had congealed into a sickly yellow mass.

"Fetch me another brandy."

The footman arched an eyebrow, then plucked the glass out of Peregrine's hand.

"No—wait," Peregrine said. "Bring the decanter."

"Sir, I hardly think it's the time of day to—"

"Damn it, man! You're paid to take orders, not to think!"

"Sir, I—"

Peregrine swept his plate aside, and it flew across the table, landing on the floor with a splinter of crockery.

"Devil take you!" he roared. "Do as you're fucking well told, or you'll be out on the street!"

The footman scuttled off, and Peregrine slumped back into

his seat.

His anger could do nothing to help her, but at least he could so something to numb the pain, even if it meant drinking himself to oblivion and smashing the breakfast table to pieces.

He curled his hand into a fist and winced. His knuckles were bruised, the skin broken, from when he'd finally caught up with Houseman at White's. At least he'd managed to satisfy his longing to smash the smug grin off that vile little man's face. And, like all cowards, Houseman had sniveled out an apology then fled, his tail between his legs.

Not a single man in the clubroom had turned a hair, save for Hythe, who helped Peregrine into his carriage and sent him home, where he'd drunk himself to sleep, then woke that morning with a headache that threatened to cleave his head in two.

His gut twisted with nausea. If that bloody footman didn't return with the decanter soon, he'd expel his breakfast. The odor from those damned eggs was already enough to make a man vomit.

He reached forward for a glass of water and knocked his teacup aside. The hot liquid scalded his flesh.

"Shit!"

He picked up the teacup and grimaced at the spike of pain. A shard of porcelain had sliced through his thumb, and a droplet of blood swelled on his skin.

"Fuck." He rose to his feet. "Fuck, fuck, *fuck!*" He threw the cup at the far wall, where it shattered on impact, just as the door opened to reveal the footman, a resigned expression on his face.

"You have a visitor, sir."

"Tell him to go to hell."

"Is that where *you're* residing, Marlow?" a familiar voice said.

Lord Hythe stood in the doorway.

"What the devil are you doing here?" Peregrine asked.

Hythe glanced at the remnants of crockery beside the door, and the egg on the carpet. Then he addressed the footman. "My good fellow—would you be so kind as to fetch a pot of strong, sweet tea and bring it to the morning room? There's no need to show me the way."

The footman glanced at Peregrine, apprehension in his eyes.

"Be assured," Hythe continued, "that if your master dismisses you, I'll not only kick his arse, but I'll find you a position in a more congenial household."

"Very good, Lord Hythe."

The traitorous footman scuttled off.

Peregrine opened his mouth to speak, but Hythe raised his hand. "Come along, young man," he said in the manner of a schoolmaster. "You'll achieve nothing imbibing brandy."

"It's my bloody brandy."

Hythe let out a sigh. "Whatever you pay that footman, it's not enough," he said.

"Why are you come to disturb my breakfast?"

"I have some news, which should be to your advantage."

"There's nothing you can say that would possibly be to my advantage."

"Not even the release without charge of a certain young lady?"

Hope flared, mingled with disbelief.

"The…what?"

Hythe nodded. "I have it on good authority that Miss de Grande is now a free woman."

"Whose authority?"

"Stiles," Hythe said. "Miss de Grande is currently residing with Lady Betty Grey, and recovering from her ordeal."

Peregrine suppressed a cry as a ripple of relief washed through his body. He pitched forward as the world slipped out of focus. Two thin arms caught him, and for a moment, he clung to his guest, weak with relief. Then he straightened himself and brushed his sleeves.

"Forgive me for making such an unseemly outburst, Hythe."

The older man laughed. "I'd have thought much less of you

had you weathered the information with dispassion. I always believed you'd grow up to be a better man than your father. I'm happy to be proved right."

He took Peregrine's arm and marched him to the parlor, where a maid was setting down a tea tray. She bobbed a curtsey.

"Thank you," Peregrine said. "Please tell…" He made a random gesture in the air. What was that footman's name?

"Simon?" the maid prompted.

"Yes, please tell Simon that his position here is secure—that is, if he still wants it after my behavior."

The maid's eyes widened, then she bobbed another curtsey and fled.

Hythe pushed Peregrine into a chair, then poured a cup of tea, tipped four spoonsful of sugar into it, and handed it to him.

"I'm trusting you, Marlow," he said.

"In what manner?"

Hythe nodded to the teacup. "Don't let Lady Hythe—or, indeed, *anyone* of our acquaintance—know that I'm capable of pouring a cup of tea. I'll never live it down. But needs must when you encounter an inebriated lord with the temper of a minotaur. Having entered his labyrinth, I trust I shall emerge unscathed."

"Why *are* you here?" Peregrine asked.

"I told you," Hythe said. "To tell you that Stiles has freed Miss de Grande."

"Why should you care?"

Hythe poured himself a cup and took a seat, an expression of guilt in his eyes.

"I suppose I consider myself partly responsible for what happened," he said. "After all, I was party to your father's scheme, even though I hadn't realized the true extent of it until a few years afterward—at which point I thought it too late to do anything, and decided that the matter was best left buried. De Grande was slowly restoring his fortunes with the rent from Fosterley Hall, and he never did set much store by Society parties."

"My father's scheme?" Peregrine asked. "You mean the bid rigging?"

"Told you that, did he?"

"After I confronted him about it," Peregrine said. "And you went along with it?"

Hythe shrugged. "I thought little of it at the time. Your father said it was a jape to get back at the man for stealing something that belonged to him."

"Which was?"

Hythe colored. "It matters not. What matters is that I gave Stiles a written testimony explaining the matter in detail. I doubt Griffin & Sons would take kindly to bid rigging on their premises, even if it was almost fifteen years ago. They value their reputation highly, and Mr. Griffin Jr. is not above suing the aristocracy for wrongful doing. And let's be honest—even the *threat* of a lawsuit would be enough to make the guilty party confess if he's a gentleman, for we gentlemen set such store on honor and reputation."

"Often to our detriment," Peregrine said. "I take it the item in question was something that money cannot buy. Such as a woman?"

Hythe's blush deepened. "Forgive me. I meant no disrespect."

"I've known for some time that Father wanted Lily de Grande for his own," Peregrine said. "My mother never said anything, of course, but she knew he didn't love her. And why should she expect it? After all, men like us don't marry for love, do we?"

Hythe gave a soft smile. "Some of us do," he said. "Those of us who care nothing for dowries or titles—we choose for love. It was plain, to even those of the meanest intelligence, that Lord and Lady de Grande loved each other—and your father resented it. He never loved Lady de Grande. He coveted her, like a possession he wanted to lock away. And when he couldn't get her, he took the next best thing."

"The clock?"

Hythe nodded. "De Grande never stopped talking about that clock. His wife had it engraved shortly before her confinement, saying that were she to depart the world, it would be a piece of her to remain here, on earth, so that he might not be lonely. After she died, that clock never left his side. Even during dinner parties, he had his footman carry the clock into the dining room during supper—then again into the drawing room. I always thought it pitiful, but your father…" He broke off. "No matter."

"I can hazard a guess," Peregrine said. "My father thought it an object of ridicule, and plotted to take it. But he took more than the clock. He ruined de Grande. He persuaded de Grande to enter into a partnership agreement with him—some form of investment in the South Seas, I believe."

Hythe nodded. "Yes, that was it. But as it turned out, the companies didn't exist, and de Grande, who'd signed to act as guarantor, found himself without a penny, his fortune tied up halfway across the world, with no means to retrieve it. Of course, at the time, your father persuaded us to believe that de Grande had attempted to defraud *him*, and got caught out in the process."

"And none of you challenged him?"

"De Grande was a difficult blighter at the best of times," Hythe said. "It was all too easy to believe your father's version of events. But I have since learned that the *appearance* of goodness often conceals a rotten core. Of course, over the years, that rotten core eats away at the person until it is revealed. I now realize that's why your father exiled himself in Italy these past fourteen years."

"Which was?"

Hythe smiled. "To conceal his rotten core from his friends. Francis and Houghton died with no knowledge that they'd been duped. Caldicott—well, he's a different animal and would sell his mother if it turned a profit. As for myself, I can only apologize for not speaking up before. It might have saved a whole lot of trouble for de Grande. But I always believed that the gentlemanly thing was *not* to tell on a friend. I've since grown to understand that the honorable thing is to stand up to one's friends when they're in the wrong. And your father was in the wrong. I only hope that one day you'll find it in your heart to forgive me."

"There's nothing to forgive," Peregrine said. "You were fooled, as were many others. The one at fault, the one man I cannot forgive, is the bastard who sired me."

Hythe drained his teacup, then stood. "I must be going," he said. "But in the absence of your father, would you take some advice from a man who has no son to bestow what little wisdom he has upon?"

"Of course."

"Forgive him," Hythe said. "Not for his sake, but for yours. Your father was, and most likely still is, driven by obsession, and a misguided lust for retribution. If you wish to stride out into the world a better man, then I urge you to seek not retribution, but redemption. Miss de Grande is a free woman. Therefore, you can look to your future."

"How did you know—"

"That you love her?" Hythe smiled. True love is such a rarity in our Society that it's easy to spot among the false niceties and declarations of affection. I saw it in your eyes when you danced with her at Hythe Manor." He smiled, his eyes twinkling with mirth. "Saucy miss, she was, leading us all on a merry dance over that painting."

"But you were so determined to see the Phoenix brought to justice," Peregrine said.

"Perhaps at first," Hythe replied. "I didn't take kindly to someone entering my home and stealing from under my very nose. But then, when I understood what had happened—what had *really* happened—I recognized it as retribution for the wrongs I'd done. There are worse misfortunes to befall a man than the loss of one insignificant painting that cost a shilling or two. I began to see that it was only right that particular painting was taken, and I saw the Phoenix as an avenging angel—righting the wrongs that had been perpetrated against Lord de Grande.

Though I had no idea that the angel was his daughter until I heard of her arrest."

"You told Stiles all this?" Peregrine asked. "Is that why she's free?"

"No," Hythe said. "It helped her case, but the deciding factor was the confession."

"What confession?"

Hythe let out a sigh. "Poor bastard. But perhaps he felt it was the only thing in his power to do."

"Of whom are you speaking?"

"Of de Grande. What's a man to do when he has nothing left but his life to give? He's confessed to the Phoenix's crimes. Traveled all the way to London—and in *his* state of health! I hear he was near to collapse when he arrived, but he insisted on going straight to the magistrate." He shook his head. "It's a sorry state of affairs, given that his choice was either to see his daughter hang, or to hang himself. But then—what wouldn't we sacrifice for those we love?"

What indeed?

Oh, Lavinia!

Never before had Peregrine felt so impotent. He, a respected member of Society—wealthy, educated, and supposedly intelligent—had failed her. But a frail, disgraced old man had done more for her than he ever could.

How could he even begin to face them—to atone for what she had lost, and what she was about to lose? He wasn't worth the ground that either of them walked on. Lavinia and her father didn't need him—they needed each other, and yet that was the one thing that would be denied them.

Unless…

An idea formed in his mind—a wicked idea, which risked his own head.

…unless he was prepared to blackmail the Crown.

But he'd be a sorry creature if he wasn't prepared to risk his head for the woman he loved.

CHAPTER FORTY-ONE

LAVINIA PUSHED THE bedchamber door open and stepped inside.

At this time in the morning, the east-facing window caught the full might of the sun. But the curtains were closed, and only a thin sliver of light stretched across the carpet toward the fireplace, where flames flickered with a soft orange glow.

At the far end of the chamber, a figure stirred on the bed.

"Good morning, Papa," Lavinia said. "I've brought you some tea."

The figure rolled to one side to reveal a pale face. Then he struggled to sit. His body jerked forward, beset by a volley of coughing, and droplets of spittle misted in the air.

Lavinia rushed toward the bed, set the teacup on a nearby table, and helped her father to sit, plumping pillows to support his back. Then she eased him back until he lay, propped up, straining for breath.

"Oh, Papa!" she cried. "Why did you do it?"

He reached toward her, and she took his hand.

"Y-you know why, daughter," he said, his breath coming in shallow pants. "I-I couldn't have you suffer for my folly."

"But the journey," she said. "You must have known it would be too much for you."

"What would you have me do, Lavinia?" he asked. "Languish in a cottage in the middle of nowhere, while my precious child swings from a gibbet? I…" He broke off with another fit of coughs.

She reached for the phial on the table and shook it. "Dr. McIver said you're lucky to be alive."

She bit her lip to stem the pain in her heart.

Lucky to be alive—but not for much longer.

Papa had barely weathered the journey to London. And now, despite the doctor's efforts, he would die. Whether from his illness, or by the hangman's noose, her beloved Papa would be dead before the month was out.

He must have known he was journeying to his death, and yet still he came.

Footsteps approached, and Lady Betty entered the bedchamber.

"Ah, Dickie darling!" she cried. "You've missed breakfast, but perhaps some sweet tea is the best thing for your constitution."

She spoke animatedly, in the voice she used to amuse and entertain at parties. But Lavinia saw through the façade—the moisture in her eyes as she smiled at them both, the slight trembling of her hands as she crossed the floor to draw the curtains, flooding the room with light.

"Betty!" Papa croaked. "Did you have to?"

"I most certainly did," came the reply. "I don't approve of my guests languishing in the dark, Dickie."

"It's hurting my eyes."

"Don't be such a child! It's the smoke from the fire that's hurting your eyes. I have just the remedy." She lifted the window sash.

"Dear God, woman—you're not going to open a window?" Papa cried. "It's September, for pity's sake!"

"You need fresh air, Dickie. Moping about in the dark will prolong your illness, and I want you up and about."

"What the bloody hell's the use in my being *up and about*, when—" Papa began.

"No, darling Dickie, we shan't speak of it." She took his hand

and lifted it to her lips. "Do you recall that beautiful, heady summer, when we were caught in a whirlwind of love, light, and laughter?"

A soft smile curled Papa's lips, and he closed his eyes and sighed. "How long was it?" he asked. "Eight weeks? Twelve?"

Lady Betty gave a gentle laugh, though tears glistened in her eyes. "It was only three, darling," she said. "And at the end of those beautiful, blissful three weeks, do you recall what you told me?"

"No, Betty, I'm afraid my memory is not what it was."

"You said that you'd found the woman you intended to marry—the one person in the world to complete your soul. You lay in my arms after we made love for the last time, and told me that while you would always love your dearest Betty, your heart and soul now belonged irrevocably to another, and that you would remain faithful to her for as long as you both lived."

A tear spilled onto Papa's cheek. "Oh, Betty, I never meant to break your heart. But Lily—my beloved Lily…"

"I know, darling." Lady Betty patted his hand. "Lily was an exceptional woman, and the two of you were destined to be together. I always knew our time together would be short-lived—I value my freedom too much to submit to the marriage state again—but we lived it to the full, did we not?"

"Aye, we did." A twinkle of mischief shone in Papa's eyes, and Lavinia caught a glimpse of the virile man her father must once have been.

"Then let us live our time now to the full," Betty said. "For none of us know how long we have, do we?"

Papa glanced at Lavinia, and the love in his eyes shredded her heart. Then he nodded.

"Yes, Betty," he said. "Why not? In fact, I believe I could manage a stroll in the park. I'd like to see if the swans that Lily and I once fed are still there. Then maybe we could take tea. Do you remember that delightful little tearoom we visited near Sussex Gardens?"

"Oh, yes," Lady Betty said. "And I could invite a few friends for supper tomorrow night."

"And a ball," Papa said. "I was a devil on the dance floor in my heyday, if you recall."

"Yes, I do," Lady Betty said. "The debutantes were so desperate to see your name on their dance cards. But there was only one who claimed the privilege of having your name on her card *twice*. From that moment, I knew the honorable Lily Bonneville ranked above all the other young ladies in quality, temperament, and character."

She approached the fireplace and rang the bell. Shortly after, two footmen trooped into the chamber carrying a number of items, which Lady Betty dotted about the room in positions that Papa could admire from his vantage point. Lavinia let out a low cry as she recognized them—a small snowscape in a delicate gilt frame, a thick steel sword with an ornate hilt, a necklace adorned with rubies and emeralds, a small ginger jar…

And, finally, a clock. The clock for which he would most likely hang.

But today was not a day for bitter truths. It was a day for dreams, and both Lady Betty and Papa were relying on her to play her part.

"On the table, please, William," Lady Betty said crisply. The footman placed the clock where she directed. "I'm afraid it's not working," she said. "But I have a dear friend who's a clockmaker, who, I'm sure, will repair it for me as a favor."

A twinkle shone in Papa's expression. "I forget how many *dear friends* you have, Betty."

She wagged her finger at him. "Now, now, Dickie," she chided. "I can have as many friends as I want. A well-behaved gentleman must learn to share, if he is to get his reward."

Papa let out a chuckle. "I doubt I'd survive one of *your* rewards, Betty. You'd be the death of me…"

Betty let out a gasp. The façade slipped and Papa's voice trailed away.

Any moment, perhaps even today, the authorities were to come for Papa and detain him to await trial. The only reason he hadn't been detained sooner was because the magistrate had advocated for compassion on grounds of Papa's health, arguing that an attempt to flee would bring about his demise quicker than any trial.

Betty's smile resumed, and she patted Papa's cheek. "Dear Dickie—you do amuse! And now, I must see about the menu for supper. I had my housekeeper order a side of beef—I know it's your favorite."

Hoofbeats echoed outside, and shortly after they heard a knock on the front door. Lavinia's stomach somersaulted, and she caught Papa's hand.

Betty glided to the door, maintaining her composure, through her voice held a note of tremor.

"Good heavens!" she cried. "Who can it be at this hour? It's most unsociable, when I could still be having breakfast. Have no fear, Dickie—I'll tell them that you're resting, and are in no state to entertain."

She swept out of the chamber.

"Papa…" Lavinia began, but her father shook his head.

"No, darling girl," he said. "If my time has come, then I'll accept it with dignity."

His stoicism in the face of what he was about to endure was too much, and she let out a sob. A thin, bony hand caught hers.

"Hush, daughter," he whispered. "I'm ready. Let this be my parting gift to you. Aren't parents supposed to give life to their children? To give them wings so they may fly unfettered and free? And think…" He gave a soft smile. "I'll be reunited with your dear mother. She would want this for you—as do I."

"Oh, Papa!" Tears blurred her vision, and she surrendered to her grief.

Then she startled as footsteps approached—Lady Betty's light footsteps, accompanied by a heavier, more determined tread. The magistrate had come to claim her father for the crimes that she had committed.

The door opened, and a man stepped inside.

But it wasn't Stiles.

It was Peregrine.

"How dare you!" she cried, rising to her feet. "You betrayed me, and now my father's life is forfeit! How could you do that to us? Were you so unsatisfied with how your father ruined us the first time that you plotted to finish the deed yourself?"

"Daughter!" Papa said.

Paying no heed, she strode toward Peregrine and pummeled his chest with her fists.

"You bastard!"

He made no attempt to defend himself.

"Lavinia—stop!" Lady Betty cried.

"No," Peregrine said quietly. "Let her continue. I deserve it for the part I played."

She struck him again, but, other than issue a low grunt, he did nothing. She rendered blow after blow until her arms ached.

"Fight me back, you swine!"

"I have no wish to."

She grasped his wrists, then drew in a sharp breath. The skin around his knuckles had been torn. Scabs had begun to form, and dark bruises adorned the flesh.

She ran a fingertip along one knuckle, and he winced.

Curse him! How was it that she felt his pain, when she should hate him… No, she *did* hate him.

Then she dropped his hand and stepped back, rubbing her own knuckles.

"Lady Betty, please escort this man out," she said.

"No, daughter," Papa said. "Lord Marlow didn't betray you."

"Papa, you don't know what you're saying," she replied. "Your wits have been addled."

"Lavinia Augusta Lily!" Papa roared, and she froze at the authority in his voice. "My wits are perfectly sound, thank you *very* much. If we didn't have company, I'd turn you over my knee and give you a thrashing! Lord Marlow had nothing to do with your arrest."

"Then why did he leave me to be taken by Houseman?"

Peregrine blushed and offered his hands in a gesture of conciliation. "I had no idea Houseman had worked out it was you—or rather, that my father had told him. Forgive me, Lavinia. I'd intended to return the next day and take you away, but I'd already ridden my horse too hard, and I feared I would lame him. I thought a day or two would make no difference. As it was, it made all the difference in the world."

He dropped to his knees, hands outstretched.

"Can you ever forgive me, my love?"

For a moment, she recalled what he'd said about Lancelot—the pony that his father had forced him to shoot. Tears of sorrow and regret had shone in his eyes at the notion of having brought someone he loved to destruction.

"You're within your rights to hate me," he said. "I hate myself for not acting sooner. But believe me when I say that I shall love you until my dying day. If you send me away today, still I would love you. To me, no woman can compare to your purity of soul, your passion for justice, and the kindness that runs so deep, I swear your very bones have been fashioned from it."

He reached for her hand, and she let him take it. He lifted it to his lips.

At that moment, another knock came on the front door.

"What is this—a luncheon party?" Lady Betty said. "William, go and see who it is, then send them on their way."

"Very good, miss." The footman bowed and disappeared.

Peregrine glanced about the room, and his gaze settled on the clock.

"Yes, Lord Marlow, it's taken pride of place," Papa said.

"*You* brought it?" Lavinia asked.

Peregrine nodded. Then, still on his knees, he drew closer and placed his head on her stomach, circling her with his arms.

"Yes, my darling," he said. "I promised I'd restore it to its rightful owner, and I did. I'm only sorry that I was too late." He raised his head and addressed Papa. "Sir, I do not deserve your regard, or forgiveness, but I pledge to you, here and now, that your daughter will want for nothing. And in the time that you have left, however long that is, I shall do my utmost to show you the sincerity of my love for her."

He rose to his feet and drew her close. The adoration in his eyes melted her anger, and she tilted her face toward him, offering her lips for a kiss. Caring not that Papa and Lady Betty bore witness to their love, she drew in a deep breath, relishing the woodsy, masculine scent of him.

His warm breath caressed her cheek, and she parted her lips in invitation.

Footsteps clattered outside the bedchamber.

Lady Betty let out a huff. "I *told* William not to bring anyone up! What the devil was he thinking…"

Her voice trailed away as the tall, lean figure of the magistrate appeared in the doorway.

"L-Lord Stiles…"

Lavinia glanced toward Papa. His face paled, and his eyes widened in recognition, as if the Grim Reaper himself stood before him. Then he nodded in resignation.

"Is it my time, Stiles?" he asked. "I'll come quietly, though I'd appreciate a little privacy while I dress."

Stiles shook his head. "No," he said, his deep voice sending a shiver of dread through Lavinia's bones.

"At least allow my father the dignity of leaving this house fully clothed!" she cried. "I care not whether you represent the Crown. There's a higher authority to which you should yield."

The magistrate curled his lip in the flicker of a smile. "And what is that, Miss de Grande?"

"Decency," she said, "and the basic difference between right and wrong. But I doubt you set much store by that if you're a puppet for the corrupt buffoon who calls himself regent."

Lady Betty drew in a sharp breath. But the only reaction from

Stiles was a slight tic in the jaw.

"Buffoon, eh?" Then he smiled and addressed Peregrine. "What say you, Marlow? Perhaps after your dealings with the regent this week, he might take more kindly to the words of this young lady here."

"Sweet heaven!" Peregrine said. "You don't mean to say it worked? Or are you come to drag me through the streets to Newgate in chains?"

"Your liberty is intact, Marlow," Stiles said. Then he turned to Lavinia's father. "As is yours, sir."

Hope illuminated Papa's expression. "The charges against me have been dropped?"

Stiles shook his head. "I'm afraid that was impossible, but you're a free man."

"I don't understand," Papa said.

"It seems, Lord de Grande, that you have a number of friends willing to plead your case. I was able to secure dispensation to restore your liberty."

"But aren't you supposed to act within the law?" Lavinia couldn't help asking, a sneer in her voice. "At least, that's what you said before you had *me* dragged into a cell."

Stiles raised a hand. "I know, Miss de Grande, and you have no notion of how deeply I regret what I was compelled to do. But when your father's case was placed before me, I found certain circumstances in mitigation that I was able to take into consideration."

"Circumstances?"

"Lord Hythe came to see me yesterday," Stiles said. "He's given a full and frank account, written and signed, of certain events that took place fourteen years ago in relation to a prospect in the South Seas, and of an auction at Griffin & Sons. It has given me enough justification for commissioning a full inquiry into the arrangement of the London and South Seas Securities and Investment Company."

Papa let out a low cry. "The..." He drew in a sharp breath,

then shook his head. "Th-the company collapsed," he said, "and took with it everything I owned."

"It seems that's not the case," Stiles said. "The assets were transferred to another holding company. There may be some residual funds to which you're entitled. It'll take some weeks to settle, and it may not be much, but I have my man working on it. I'm confident that a portion, at least, of your fortune can be restored."

"Why are you doing this?" Papa asked.

"Because you were wronged, Lord de Grande."

"And…the charge against me?"

"I've secured a dispensation from the regent with respect to your sentence."

"Which is?"

"That you live out your days confined to whichever home, or estate, in which you choose to reside."

Silence filled the room. At length, Papa spoke. "Is that it? Not that I am protesting, of course, but I fail to see why the regent should show compassion toward a man he's met only briefly at St. James's, and barely spoken more than two words to."

Stiles glanced toward Peregrine and winked—he actually *winked*!

What had Peregrine been up to?

"Let's just say that a little blackmail, sanctioned by the magistrate, in relation to a set of allegedly stolen apostle spoons that mysteriously reappeared in a pawnshop in… Where was it, Marlow?"

"Hatton Garden," Peregrine said.

Lavinia stared at him. "Did *you* have something to do with this?"

He smiled. "Can I not indulge in a little adventure in the name of justice, my love?"

"B-but isn't blackmail a"—she lowered her voice—"a *crime*?"

Stiles placed his hands over his ears in an exaggerated gesture. "I didn't quite catch what you said, Miss de Grande, but please, do *not* repeat it." He turned to Lady Betty. "Good lady, I'll trespass on your hospitality no further." He glanced toward Lavinia, then to Peregrine, and back. "May I be the first to wish you joy? While I consider myself the luckiest man in all England to be blessed with my own wife, I'll wager that you, Lord Marlow, will be able to rival me in your good fortune."

"Lord Stiles, isn't that a little presumptuous?" Lady Betty asked.

Stiles let out a laugh. "I flatter myself in that I can read a man as easily as if he were an open book. When Marlow here came pleading to me, offering to incriminate himself in a scheme to blackmail the regent, I asked myself why such a man, who prides himself in the application of the law, would wish to endanger his reputation and his life. And the answer was simple. It was for the woman he loves."

He bowed to Lavinia. "My dear, I am only too glad to see you, and your father, at liberty. It only remains for me to ask you to accept my best wishes for your future happiness as Lady Marlow. And now, I shall leave you in peace—if your man would be so good as to show me out, Lady Betty?"

Lady Betty nodded, then ushered Stiles out, leaving Lavinia with Peregrine and Papa.

Papa held out his hands. "Daughter—Lord Marlow—come here."

Peregrine's eyes widened, and for a moment, Lavinia thought she saw moisture there. Then he wiped them and steered Lavinia toward the bed, his hand placed possessively against the small of her back.

"Son," Papa said, and Peregrine gave a low gasp. "I wish to give you my blessing to marry my daughter."

"Sir, you have already done so," Peregrine said. "I—"

"I know, I know," Papa said irritably, "but the last time I delivered it as a warning that if you let her down, I would hunt you and finish you off with my bare hands." He took Lavinia's hand, then Peregrine's, and placed it over hers. "This time," he said, his voice barely a whisper, "I give you my full consent and blessing—without condition or warning, but in the knowledge that you love her above all others, and will cherish her as much as I cherished my beloved Lily."

"I do love her," Peregrine said.

"Then, in my eyes, you are already man and wife," Papa said. "I'm unlikely to see the day that the two of you marry, but I am content with that, for I shall be with my beloved Lily."

Lavinia blinked back a tear. "Papa…"

"Hush, darling child. My health is failing, such that, sentence or no, I'm unlikely to see the month end. But I've no wish for you to arrange a hasty marriage just to suit your foolish old papa. You must have the banns read properly, and declare your pledge to each other to the world. Will you promise me that?"

Lavinia nodded, and a tear splashed onto her hand.

"We'll have none of that," Papa said firmly. "Today is a day of joy." He nodded to Peregrine. "Son, fetch the item on that table, would you?"

Peregrine rose to his feet and approached the table. Then he smiled and returned, the necklace in his hands.

"That was your mother's," Papa said. "And I now give it to you, on the occasion of your marriage, to honor the love you bear for each other—and to honor the Phoenix, the angel of justice, who risked life and limb for those she loved." He gestured toward Peregrine. "You know what to do."

Peregrine approached Lavinia. Her skin tightened with want as he caressed the back of her neck. He placed the necklace around her, and she sighed at the weight of it—the delicious coolness of the gold against her skin. He secured the clasp and dipped his head to place a soft kiss on her shoulder.

"I pledge myself to you, now and for always," he whispered, his voice sending a thrill of desire through her.

"And I you." She tipped her head back, and his lips met hers in a soft, chaste kiss. But the hunger in his eyes spoke of raw need—a primal desire that begged to be satisfied.

They had the rest of their lives to satisfy each other's needs and desires. But here, now, in a small bedchamber, hidden from Society, the intimate little ceremony cleaved their souls together before her beloved papa, so that he could witness their union before he departed the world.

EPILOGUE

Springfield Cottage, one month later

"I NOW PRONOUNCE you husband and wife."

The vicar closed the Bible with a snap. A breeze drifted across the air, carrying the scent of blossom, and a tendril of hair worked loose from Lavinia's headdress to caress her cheek.

Before she could brush it aside, a warm pair of hands cupped her face and tipped it upward, and she looked into a pair of eyes—rich, warm brown eyes with flecks of green and gold. A spark of desire glowed within their depths, and her body gave a little pulse of pleasure at the prospect of the night to come.

Without waiting for instruction from the vicar, Peregrine brushed his lips against her mouth. She parted her own lips in invitation, and he slipped his tongue inside, caressing the inside of her mouth as if savoring a delicious sweetmeat—an appetizer before he devoured her.

And, *sweet heaven*, how she longed to be devoured!

Over the past month, the two of them had indulged in a glorious banquet of the flesh. Standing before the staid vicar, now surrounded by a small congregation of trusted friends, Lavinia felt the heat rise in her cheeks at the memory of the night when Peregrine had taught her the exquisiteness of being feasted upon—her body open and ready for him while he ran his tongue along her flesh, savoring every part of her, his growls of pleasure vibrating through her body while she threw back her head and cried his name.

And—*oh my*—when he'd taught her how to pay him the same loving attentions, savoring that part of him that elicited such pleasure…

She blushed again. Did their friends know the extent of the wicked premarital pleasures they'd already indulged in?

He deepened the kiss, and Lavinia could swear she heard a low cough from the vicar. But she was beyond caring—not when the pleasure to be had was too great. He tasted earthy and spicy, a taste that she knew intensified when they made love.

He lowered his hands to her shoulders and caressed the skin of her throat; his fingertips danced across her skin. His mouth curled against hers in a smile, as her nipples beaded against the fabric of her gown. Then he slipped a hand beneath her neckline, seeking a little peak. When he reached his quarry, her nipple hardened further. He gave it a little flick, then swallowed her cry, holding her close to conceal the wanton act they'd just committed—an act with the promise of more to come.

Then he broke the kiss and casually tucked the stray tendril of hair behind her ear.

She squeezed her thighs to ease the ache throbbing in her center, and his warm breath caressed her neck.

"Good girl," he said, his voice deep and low. "I long for the wedding breakfast—when I can feast on you again."

He took her hand, and they turned to face the witnesses—who, by the absence of blushes, were clearly ignorant of the wanton act that had just taken place.

Or were they?

A wicked smile shone in Lady Betty's eyes.

The vicar was more liberal than most, given that he'd agreed to conduct the ceremony in the gardens at Springfield Cottage on receiving dispensation from his bishop. But he would, no doubt, have suffered a fit of apoplexy had he known half of the activities in which they'd indulged, in all manner of locations, inside and outside.

Peregrine extended his hand to the vicar. "I'm much obliged to you, Reverend Elliot."

"The Almighty looks upon us wherever we may be," the vicar replied. "A pledge of faith to one another, taken before Him, is just as sacred conducted in a cottage garden as it is in a church." He leaned closer and lowered his voice into a conspiratorial whisper. "In fact, I rather believe He looks more favorably upon a quiet, unassuming ceremony than the ostentation of a Society wedding undertaken in front of a full congregation who have come to church merely to further the appearance of virtue."

Yes—the vicar was more liberal than most of his kind.

"I trust both you and Mrs. Elliot will stay for tea," Lavinia said. "Mrs. Bates has baked her cherry fruitcake, which I hear is a favorite among your household."

The vicar's eyes illuminated with the expression of an over-excited child. "We'd be delighted, Lady Marlow."

Lady Marlow…

Lavinia shivered. She was now Lady Marlow. And, when Peregrine inherited his father's title, she'd be Countess Walton.

As if he read her mind, Peregrine dropped a kiss on her ear. "No matter what your title, you'll always be my little Guinevere." Then he took her hand, and they joined the small group of guests.

"Reverend Elliot's right, my love," Peregrine said, glancing about the garden. "An intimate ceremony with one's best friends is always preferable to a Society affair where we've been obliged to invite people we cannot stand—who cannot stand us in return, yet have to express the delight they do not feel."

"Not all of my friends are here," Lavinia said. "I wish Henrietta and Beatrice could have come."

"Lady Thorpe's still recovering from her confinement, my love," Peregrine said. "Thorpe would never allow her to curtail her rest cure. And Beatrice is unwilling to leave her side. I doubt the poor child would thrive at a wedding, given her husband's recent abandonment."

Lavinia shook her head. "I find myself disappointed in Lord Hardwick. He had all the appearance of a kind man, yet he's broken Beatrice's heart. He has no right to inflict such pain on that sweet girl!"

"Is my avenging angel coming to the fore?" Peregrine teased. "I forget, I've not married Lavinia de Grande. I've married the infamous Phoenix—righter of wrongs, purveyor of fiendish deception. A ruffian if ever there was one, who must be taken by a firm hand…"

"That's enough, Peregrine!" She laughed, though his words sent a wicked thrill through her at the notion of being *taken by a firm hand.*

"Hardwick will come to his senses," Peregrine said, "and if not, then it's his loss. Beatrice is surrounded by people who love her. Because of that, she'll thrive."

Lavinia glanced about the garden, where the guests were now milling about, and caught sight of a young woman in a plain white muslin gown. Her hair was already coming undone, with messy tendrils forming a halo about her face in the sunlight. She stood apart from the party, beside a rosebush, running her fingertips around the outline of the leaves, a peaceful smile on her lips.

"There's Eleanor," Lavinia said. "We must speak to her."

"She's not the best conversationalist," Peregrine said.

"I'll not hear a word against her," Lavinia said. "She's merely discerning—and a little shy. She sees the world differently to others, that's all, but I simply adore her, and I want you to love her as much as I do." She raised her arm and waved. "Eleanor!"

The young woman jerked her head up, then glanced about the rest of the party, her eyes wide with apprehension. Blushing, she fixed her gaze on Lavinia for a moment, before her focus slipped sideways.

"I'm so glad you could come," Lavinia said, rushing to take her friend's hands. "We both are, aren't we, Peregrine?"

"Of course," he said. "You must come to visit once we're

settled. Lavinia speaks of you so favorably."

Eleanor's blush deepened, and she lowered her gaze.

"I hear you're an accomplished artist, Miss Howard," he added. "Portraits are, I believe, your specialty—particularly portraits from memory, in the style of, for example, Peter Lely?"

Eleanor glanced up. "Oh!" she cried. "I-I…"

Lavinia slipped an arm through her friend's. "Peregrine is only teasing you, dearest Ellie," she said. "Rest assured, I'll admonish him later. It's not acceptable to tease one of the few friends I have who could attend today."

"I n-noticed Henrietta and Beatrice aren't here," Eleanor said. "It's a shame, for I was looking forward to seeing them." Then she lowered her gaze yet again, as if overwhelmed by her little speech.

"None of *my* friends were able to attend, Miss Howard," Peregrine said. "Therefore, you are to be commended."

"I-I don't know…" Eleanor mumbled.

"Well, I do," he replied. "Not even Monty turned up."

Eleanor stiffened. "M-Monty?"

"The Duke of Whitcombe," Peregrine said. "Surely you've heard of him? All young women in England clamor to secure his attention"—he patted Lavinia's hand—"save you, of course, my love." He resumed his attention on Eleanor. "Perhaps you're fortunate Monty's not here, Miss Howard. He leaves a trail of broken hearts wherever he goes. Best to keep your distance. I say—are you all right, Miss Howard?"

The color had drained from Eleanor's cheeks.

Montague, Duke of Whitcombe…

Lavinia recalled the subject of all the portraits in Eleanor's sketchbook.

Eleanor looked around, a wild expression in her eyes, as if she feared Whitcombe's arrival at any moment.

"Come along, Eleanor darling," Lavinia said. "Shall I return you to Mrs. Elliot? She's chaperoning you today, after all."

Eleanor nodded. "Y-yes please."

"Miss Howard," Peregrine said, "forgive me if I gave offense. I—"

"You haven't," Lavinia interrupted, glaring at him. Then she steered a grateful Eleanor toward the vicar and his wife.

"I didn't mean to distress your friend," Peregrine said when she returned. "Is Miss Howard a little soft in the head?"

"No," Lavinia said sharply. "She's quick-witted, intelligent, and caring—and the best friend anyone could have. She just doesn't like company, and is misunderstood by those who favor the superficial."

"I find myself chastised," Peregrine said. "I would be delighted to know her better, perhaps on a less formal occasion when she feels more at ease." He dipped his head and placed a kiss on her lips. "Forgive me?"

"Perhaps."

"Is there anything I can do to atone for my sin?" His eyes twinkled with mischief.

"Why, sir, I believe there is," she replied. "I shall collect my payment as soon as we're alone."

"Then I await my punishment with eager anticipation."

Her belly curled at the low growl in his voice.

"In fact," he continued, "I believe it's almost time to leave if we're to reach the inn before nightfall—but we mustn't depart before speaking to the guest of honor."

He gestured across the path toward a man in a bath chair, a thick blanket over his knees, Mrs. Bates standing at his side. His half-closed eyes opened as they approached, and his face cracked into a broad grin.

"Dearest Papa!" Lavinia cried. "I trust the breeze isn't too much for you?"

"No, daughter, the fresh air has done wonders for my health these past weeks—and Mrs. Bates's cooking, of course."

"Oh, you're a charmer, sir!" The housekeeper laughed. Then she bobbed a curtsey. "I'll leave you to take care of him, Miss Lavinia"—she blushed—"beg pardon, Lady Marlow it is, now. I must see to the tea."

Lavinia crouched beside her father and took his hands. "Dear Papa," she said. "I'll miss you—but we promise to visit as often as we can."

He shook his head. "You must life your *own* life, Lavinia," he said. "Today was the proudest moment of my life, of *any* father's life—to be able to give my beloved daughter away at her wedding to a fine man who'll love her"—he gestured to the bath chair—"even if you did have to wheel me in this thing. After years of caring for your foolish old papa, you now have another to take care of."

Lavinia glanced at Peregrine. He nodded, his eyes shining with love, and mouthed, *Tell him.*

"Papa," she said, "I have some news for you, though I fear you may be somewhat shocked to hear it. I'll soon have *another* to take care of."

"What do you mean?"

Slowly, she lowered her hand and placed it over her belly. Her father frowned, then he lowered his gaze to her hand, and understanding dawned in his eyes. He blinked, and a tear rolled down his face.

"Oh, Papa!" she cried. "I didn't mean to distress you. Forgive me."

Peregrine kneeled beside her. "Lord de Grande—sir—you must forgive *me*," he said. "I love your daughter—with every fiber of my being. But it was wrong of me to compromise her before our marriage."

Papa looked up at him. Then he glanced toward Lavinia, and her cheeks warmed with shame under his scrutiny.

Then his mouth curled into a smile.

"Well—if that isn't wonderful news!"

"You don't disapprove?" Peregrine asked.

"I'm delighted!" Papa said. "I must confess that I weakened with my beloved Lily on the eve of our wedding. But when you're in love with the best of women, where's the sense in waiting?"

He placed his hand over Lavinia's and caressed her skin with his thumb. "Dear child," he said. "I promise I'll do my damnedest to delay my appointment with the Almighty so I can welcome my first grandchild into the world."

Another breeze rippled through the air, and Lady Betty approached.

"Dickie, it's time we took you inside. It's getting cold, and Dr. McIver wouldn't thank me if I let you catch cold."

"Stop your fussing, Betty!" Papa muttered, though he shivered.

Ignoring him, Lady Betty continued. "We should let Lavinia and Lord Marlow be on their way. They've a long journey ahead of them."

"Then take me inside after we've waved them off," Papa said. "Must you order me about as if I were a child?"

"I'll order you about as much as I like if it's for your benefit, Dickie darling," Lady Betty said. She grasped the back of the bath chair and wheeled him toward the guests. "Darlings!" she cried. "The bride and groom are leaving."

Peregrine took Lavinia's hand and led her to the carriage at the front of the cottage, and the guests followed. Lavinia kissed each guest in turn, then paused when she reached Papa and Lady Betty at the end of the line.

"Be happy, darlings," Lady Betty said. "And don't worry about Dickie. I'll make sure he takes care of himself."

Lavinia gave her father one last hug, then climbed into the carriage. Her new husband followed, then he closed the door and they set off.

As soon as the cottage was out of sight, Peregrine reached for her and claimed her lips. Her body responded, and she devoured him in turn, thrusting her tongue into his mouth. Her desire, which had simmered throughout the wedding ceremony, now swelled thickly inside her, magnified by the rocking sensation of the carriage, and she shifted against him to seek the release she craved.

He fumbled with the fastenings of his breeches, then lifted her skirts and placed his hand on her knee. Need fizzed through her, and she parted her thighs in offering.

"Oh, my sweet wife," he growled. "Are we to enjoy our wedding feast in the carriage?"

"Break my fast, husband, for I am starving," she panted.

As he slipped inside her, she let out a mewl of pleasure and wrapped her legs around him to pull him deeper inside. He withdrew a little, then plunged inside her once more, and her body burst with ecstasy. Together, they rode the ripples of pleasure until their climax subsided and they clung to each other, him still inside her, as their breathing eased, their hearts beating in unison.

"Oh, husband," she whispered. "We have acted most inappropriately, debauching ourselves in a carriage moments after exchanging our vows."

He shifted inside her and let out a low chuckle as she sighed with pleasure.

"My darling," he murmured, "when you're in love with the best of women, where's the sense in waiting?"

Acknowledgements

Thank you to Family Royal, as usual, for all your support, and to the Scottish Chapter of the Romantic Novelists' Association for all those writing days that helped me get the words down. To my Beta Buddies, your support and encouragement always spurs me on and a particular nod to Liz Taylorson for your kind and considerate feedback on a very rough first draft!

And finally, to Violetta Rand, who entered Valhalla earlier this year, thank you for showing faith in me and this series. Godspeed, I owe so much to you.

About the Author

Emily Royal grew up in Sussex, England, and has devoured romantic novels for as long as she can remember. A mathematician at heart, Emily has worked in financial services for over twenty years. She indulged in her love of writing after she moved to Scotland, where she lives with her husband, teenage daughters, and menagerie of rescue pets—including Twinkle, an attention-seeking boa constrictor.

She has a passion for both reading and writing romance with a weakness for Regency rakes, Highland heroes, and Medieval knights. *Persuasion* is one of her all-time favorite novels, which she reads several times each year, and she is fortunate enough to live within sight of a Medieval palace.

When not writing, Emily enjoys playing the piano, baking, and painting landscapes, particularly of the Highlands. One of her ambitions is to paint, as well as climb, every mountain in Scotland.

Follow Emily Royal
Newsletter Signup: subscribepage.io/RKBvRE
Facebook: facebook.com/eroyalauthor
Bookbub: bookbub.com/authors/emily-royal
Instagram: instagram.com/eroyalauthor
Amazon: amazon.com/stores/Emily-
Royal/author/B07NCBKJZ4
Website: www.emroyal.com
Goodreads:
goodreads.com/author/show/14834886.Emily_Royal
Twitter: @eroyalauthor